When
Truth Is
Gangsta

ALSO BY TECORI SHELDON
(WRITING AS THOMAS SLATER)
Show Stoppah
No More Time-Outs

STREBOR ON THE Streetz

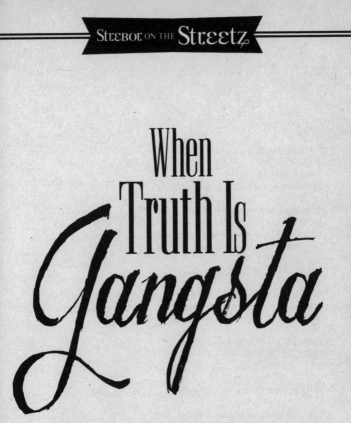

When Truth Is Gangsta

Tecori Sheldon

SBI

STREBOR BOOKS

NEW YORK LONDON TORONTO SYDNEY

SBI

Strebor Books
P.O. Box 6505
Largo, MD 20792
http://www.streborbooks.com

ISBN 978-1-59309-398-3
ISBN 978-1-4516-4564-4 (e-book)
LCCN 2011938325

First Strebor Books trade paperback edition May 2012

Cover design: www.mariondesigns.com
Cover photograph: © Keith Saunders Photos

10 9 8 7 6 5 4 3 2 1

Manufactured in the United States of America

For information regarding special discounts for bulk purchases, please contact Simon & Schuster Special Sales at 1-866-506-1949 or business@simonandschuster.com

The Simon & Schuster Speakers Bureau can bring authors to your live event. For more information or to book an event, contact the Simon & Schuster Speakers Bureau at 1-866-248-3049 or visit our website at www.simonspeakers.com.

In Loving Memory of my Nephew:
Jermaine Slater, Jr.

As a writer, my nephew, Jermaine Slater, Jr., was my biggest supporter. In those dark days when the doors that held access to the literary world were welded shut, Jermaine was there as a constant source of inspiration when I was ready to pull the plug. Cheering me on intensely, he would often say: "Unc, you're crazy to give up your dreams when you're so close—you feel me?" Of course, I couldn't do anything but laugh. He was right. I had come too far. The doors and windows had been opened wide enough for me to live how I dreamed.

Unfortunately, I could not physically share this wondrous testimony of faith with Jermaine Slater, Jr.

My nephew tragically departed this life April 15, 2011, leaving nothing behind but the devastation of heartache and emotional pain. After his untimely death I didn't care much about anything, least of all, my dreams for literary greatness. Unfamiliar with the new air I was breathing, my nephew was my familiar oxygen; one that I could count on for a positive word whenever I emerged from a creative solitude. I could remember taking deep breaths, but couldn't feel my lungs expanding.

Slipping into a sullen, somber sadness, weeks passed as I felt myself descending into the darkness of depression and pitching a tent in the name of "permanent residency." But before I could get comfortable, God reminded me that my nephew wasn't dead—and neither was my dream. The Lord let me know that anything He loved never died. And, Lil Maine, as long as I have oxygen in my lungs and blood coursing through my veins, I will honor your memory. Not by simply existing inside of the dream, but living it in the form of high-octane fiction that will become my staple for years to come.

Jermaine, with every word I write and every meditation I type, you will live.

So, from here on out, my writing career is dedicated to you, my loving nephew. Between you and me, one book at a time, we're gonna stake our literary claim inside the minds of readers—all with God leading the way, of course.

The boy with the charming, mega-watt smile, slick swagger, accompanied by crazy, cool charisma will always occupy a special place in my heart! I love you, Lil Maine!

—Your uncle

Acknowledgments

God is my light! In Him I shall find my way home!

To my brother, Jermaine Slater Sr., I pray God's continual healing.

Folks, before you get to judging a brother, I want you guys to know that I'm perfectly sane. There's a serial killer running rampant through the pages of this novel. You can blame one man for "Him's" inspiration: my cousin, James Melvin Clayborne. You can call it throwing a family member under the bus if you want, but I'm distancing myself from you, Melbox, and, your twisted imagination. Oh, don't act like you forgot, buddy. You remember that hysterical, soul-cleansing conversation about exes? Knaw, just joking, but my cousin's the bomb! Thanks for having a brother's back! Love you, man!

Y'all can partially blame my warped sense of humor on my Uncle Bubba—LT Posey.

To Pops—I always enjoy our conversations.

Roger Jones, man, I have to thank you based on who you are alone. God definitely has you in reaching distance.

Zane, I always have to thank you. When the others said "no," you said "yes."

Special shout-out to OOSA Book Club, ReaditAll BookReviews, Reader's Paradise, EyeCU Reading & Social Network.

To all the readers, I would just like to say: Thank you all for putting up with the insane, message-driven entertainment that I like to call "high-octane fiction."

Prologue

Somewhere in rural Pennsylvania…

The three men were dressed in black and blended in with the darkness of the early morning hour. Armed with night vision glasses, Colt AR-15 Carbine 9mm rifles slung over shoulder, and automatic handguns holstered at the side, they softly moved on to an enormous deck.

On their bellies, the shadows slid over to an enormous sliding-glass patio door with the natural creepy, cleverness of snakes in predation mode. As promised, the butler had done his job. The door was unlocked. To maintain a healthy level of uninterrupted anonymity, the silent, stealthy stalkers communicated through hand signs and directional gestures. Although the men easily blended into the element by dress, they were clearly distinguishable by height and size. The taller one seemed to function as the brains of the group.

One wave in the air, the men stood to their feet. One quick, simulated eye gouge dispersed them in different directions, all playing a very vital part at this thing going down smoothly. Other issues had to be neutralized before they could take out the intended targets, like slitting the throat of the heavyset black guard inside the guardshack in front of the property.

The door to the shack wasn't stubborn with noise, so it slid back without any resistance. A dark shadow surged up inside the night's blackness, brandishing a huge stainless steel Rambo blade. One swipe across the throat was enough to bleed the guard out—straight ear-to-ear job.

The short, stocky, armed security guard standing on the front porch, bumping his gums on a cell phone, didn't fare too well, either. From the background of darkness, an anorexic-thin razor wire was smoothly slipped over his throat. The dark figure pulled it tightly and hung on for a few moments until the struggling guard fell limp. The guard's lifeless body was then tossed over the banister and into a gathering of bushes.

The supervisor guard nearest the north end of the property must've smelled the stench of death in the air; felt a heavy, troublesome disturbance in the atmosphere. With his two-way radio, he tried to get a handle on his officers. He hadn't seen them since the briefing that had taken place three hours ago. Standing at an imposing six-eight and tipping the scales at nearly 300 pounds, the guard easily moved through the orchards with the cocky swagger of one who'd been battled-tested and survived the worst that the hood had to offer. Simply put: he feared no man. And he wasn't even startled when he stumbled upon what appeared to be a huge man dressed in black. It didn't take the guard long to figure out that this fool wasn't there to perform random sprinkler system inspection. The assault rifle slung over the man in black's shoulder was no instrument to gauge water pressure. The owner of the estate was rumored to be heavy in the game, so the guard automatically knew the intruder's intentions. When the guard had taken on the job, he knew the risk of running security for the estate's owner. But the rather generous paycheck he'd receive at the end of the week more than relaxed the consequences.

The ski-mask worn by this intruder didn't leak one bit of identity. The two men knew that a battle to the death was imminent. The best man left standing. The officer didn't know if that combatant would be him, and if he was victorious, would that be a good thing? Because poverty had taught him an honest lesson: a warning that where there was one roach— by lifting a dirty dish in the sink almost-always sent more scurrying. There were more shadows around here. He could feelthem. They were probably watching for the outcome of this battle. Like some initiation. And as soon as he won, they would take him out without breaking a sweat.

They faced each other like two Shogun Warriors, mutually laying down weapons and preparing for a man-style brawl. The shadow cast his assault rifle and sidearm to the grass. The six-inch Rambo knife was tossed also, the guard following suit, reluctantly unsnapping the waist holster and chucking his piece. He wanted to use it to blow the shadow out of his boots, but he knew before the body dropped, his bullet-riddled corpse wouldn't be too far behind.

This was it, the inception of a struggle for life and death; a winner, and a dead loser. The shadow slightly nodded his head, indicating the ringing of the bell.

The two combatants slowly stalked each other, circling like two powerful lions, searching for potential weaknesses. The noise *from the crickets stood as the only life-form to witness this potential bloody war for supremacy. Both men silently sized each other as if hoping to mount a deadly campaign for bringing about the quick demise of the opposition.*

The shadow's body language was unreadable; so damn relaxed that the guard never saw the first punch, but felt the blow as it violently snapped his head to the left. The officer stumbled, legs buckling but he managed to stay on his feet. The blood he spat to the ground looked darker than usual under the blackness of the early morning skies. His front tooth was loose and the pain radiating from a split bottom lip launched the guard into survival-mode. He exploded from his stance with a head-crushing right-hook-of-a haymaker, but was stopped in his tracks by the shadow's defensive counter. It was a short power-kick to the inner right thigh of the guard's lead leg, completely impeding forward progress and turning him sideways, leaving him open. The shadow's reflexes were swift and capitalized on the guard's vulnerability while capturing his neck inside of an inescapable headlock.

The guard's eyes protruded from the sockets like he'd been surprised by the Grim Reaper. The shadow stayed poised and calm, holding on to the headlock as if playing with the victim, allowing him to fight, struggle, scratch and buck like a fisherman giving the prized catch on the end of his reel enough line to grow weak. And when the guard began to grow powerless and limp, choking, slobbering and laboring for oxygen, the shadow wrenched his victim's neck in one mighty motion, taking pleasure in hearing the sounds of crunching bones and snapping muscle. The shadow released the dead man, letting his body drop to the dew-saturated grass; his eyes captured in a stiff, lifeless gaze.

Savoring his victory, he stooped down to retrieve his weapons. He was in phenomenal condition; hadn't once thought about breathing heavy or breaking a sweat. When he was done strapping his weapons back into holsters, a smaller shadow ascended from the darkness. The smaller one let his gaze drop to the dead man, and then back up to his superior as if to ask: Why bother with the struggle when you could've just as easily laid the guard down with a simple shot to the head with the silencer-equipped sidearm? But anybody familiar with his superior's taste for hand-to-hand combat with a worthy adversary knew not to ask those kinds of questions. He knew his boss had sized up the big guard to be a gladiator; and gladiators were made to go out like warriors.

The superior nodded his head at the body as if implying that the guard was good but not good enough. Fun and games were over. Their real test slumbered behind the walls of the mansion, an assignment in which the contractor warned before the mission that failure could end in the assassin's heads being stuffed and mounted on his wall. There was simply no room on the bandwagon for incompetence. They'd been hand-picked from a pool of excellence and given detailed orders to carry out to the latter.

Through the deck's sliding screen patio door, the men glided effortlessly over the dark floors with their 9mm AR-15 Carbines out in front. In a one-by-one cover formation, the team crept through, exploring every dark corner with laser sightings. The piercing red dots danced around the walls of darkness like playful fireflies chasing, playing a deadly game of Freeze Tag.

The place was huge and eloquently boasted of exquisite furnishings, priceless period paintings, and magnificent sculptures in antiquity. Expensive chandeliers hung from high vaulted ceilings like diamond- studded disco balls. Standing in the foyer on marble floors, the men stood unfazed by the owner's expensive taste. With their left hand underneath the barrel, stock snuggly fitting in the small of the right shoulder, eyes staring down the cross-hairs, trigger fingers ready for destruction, they crouch-walked cautiously up the spiral staircase, taking one step at a time.

The live-in nanny's room was just to the left of the staircase. The mark's room was at the opposite end of the hallway. The door belonging to the eight-year-old son was inches in front. The scary-ass butler had outlined the whole layout of the house.

Another simulated eye-gouge, followed by one finger being shoved in the air, quietly dispatched one man to each room. Almost on cue, the shadows slowly slung their rifles across their shoulders, removing sidearms and screwing on silencers. Kids were not generally part of the package when they rolled through on some death and destruction shit, but this one was different. They'd been given specific instructions to terminate the little bastard. The reason was overemphasized in the briefing: Sometimes little bastards grow up to be big bastards with powerful appetites for vengeance. The client who'd purchased the contract stated that he wanted all T's crossed and all I's dotted. Nothing was to live that could potentially come back and bite him in the ass.

The head shadow stopped short of the man named Walker Story's bedchamber door, giving the signal for the others to proceed with caution. He stayed put while the other two went on to carry out the order of termination. He was going to need all guns on deck when he tangled with the main mark. They'd been meticulously briefed on Mister Walker Story. The man wasn't just your average, run-of-the-mill drug lord, but a butcher who lived for war. He was a full load and cautioned not to be taken lightly. Those flashlight-wielding, rent-a-cops they'd executed were mere child's play compared to a man who prided himself on the numerous bodies of arrogant kingpins that had fallen to his trigger. The team's superior recognized that one fatal slip of concentration around Walker Story, and they could wind up as dollars, lining the inside of some mortician's wallet. They needed to be extremely careful. In all of his years working the business, he'd never lost one man to a mission and didn't intend to start now.

The nanny was sleeping when the first shadow infiltrated; an elderly Latino woman slumbering in a head scarf resembling the colors of the Mexican flag. The red dot from his sidearm rested on the center of her forehead. She didn't move after the shadow pumped two silent hot ones behind the red dot. Shadow number two shone the dot of death around inside of the bedroom belonging to young Walker Story. To his surprise, the child wasn't sleeping in his bed, or anywhere inside the bedroom. He walked back out signaling that the boy was gone.

They stood puzzled for the moment, but time restraints pushed them to abandon the search. The senior was their primary focus.

The lead shadow now had his hand on the doorknob, housing the man responsible for the total distribution of drugs circulating around the city and surrounding suburbs. Legend had it that Walker Story was grossly sadistic. Pittsburgh's underworld showered him with respect. Nobody opposed him. Rival crews were run out of town and those who stayed, paid a tax to deal on his streets. Walker Story was reported as being the worst of the worst, a Teflon Don who couldn't be touched by local law enforcement or government task force agencies.

Something creepy and totally unexpected happened as the shadows cautiously opened the door. The bedroom lights popped on, flooding the room as if they'd been wired to do so at the opening of the door. Walker's eyes popped opened like they had also been synchronized with the lights. The shadows had to move. No longer working with the element of surprise, the men rushed through the door like storm troopers, anticipating to be mowed over by gunfire. The room was enormous, almost doubling the size of a small apartment. They had some ground to cover because Walker Story and his wife lay in a huge California King bed at the very far end of the room.

The kingpin was lying on his back with both hands under the cover when he fired the first shot, sounding like a cannon going off, ripping through the comforter, blowing feathers in the air. The team scrambled behind furniture, breaking formation and quickly returning fire.

The blast startled the wife. She jumped up, frantically screaming, catching a bullet to the side of the head and one between her bare breasts. Walker Story let out an inhuman cry as he watched bullets rip through his wife's flesh. With a crazed look in his eyes, he jumped up on the mattress and whipped out a weapon that resembled a small hand cannon, blazing and dementedly shouting obscenities over the noise of the gun battle. Walker surgically worked with the .44 Auto Magnum, spitting round after round until the numbers game caught up with him. A shot tore through his left shoulder, forcefully slamming him into the headboard of the California King. He recovered. And that's when he tripped over his wife's body, receiving another blast, but this one tore through the flesh of his stomach.

In the blanket of gunfire, a small head popped out from underneath the bed. It was Walker Story, Jr. Surprise registered on the faces behind the masks. Like, what in the hell was the kid doing underneath the damn bed? Shock from the discovery of the kid lasted for about as long as it took for one of the men to get a bead on the youngster, lining the red dot right between his eyes. Without concern for his own well-being, Walker Senior dove to cover his son, relentlessly blasting away, fire belching from the muzzle of his weapon. Walker's efforts finally hit pay dirt as one of the shadows caught some lead. The man yelled out in agonizing pain. It was the superior of the team who had fallen victim to a high thigh shot.

The child screamed as his father's weight barreled on top of him. Walker tried to shove his son back underneath the bed with one hand, while firing the pistol with the other. He was able to get the boy's torso under the bed when he was hit in the back. His breath halted as his body shook in spasms, the .44 falling to the carpet. The child cried out as he watched one of the shadows step up and level a weapon on his defenseless father. He popped off two quick rounds, both violently entering Walker Senior's forehead and blowing out the rear.

Feathers still floated around in the air. The acrid aroma of gunpowder saturated the air and gun smoke gave away to poor visibility. The superior shadow wanted to scream out in pain as the slug inside his leg started to heat up. And while the other two stepped from the trenches, the superior tended to his wound by removing his belt and strapping it around his injured thigh, a few inches above, as a makeshift tourniquet. He pulled hard on the belt to stop the flow of blood and almost passed out. The pain was immense and caused him to clench his teeth tightly to suppress a scream. He took a deep breath and got to his feet, using the barrel of his AR-15 Carbine as a cane to stand. The other two took the time to reload their weapons.

The boy was weeping loudly over his father's body. Killing the child would be the last order of business. Little Walker Story looked to be no more than eight years of age. They all stood around the boy as he screamed, begging his father to wake up. The men didn't fully know how well the boy understood these kinds of things, but it wasn't their job to educate him. They were there to eliminate any future threat.

The superior surveyed the human carnage that could only

be caused by the violence of greed: men who had everything but still wanted more. It sickened him to waste the skills he'd learned while fighting for his country overseas, on cowards who didn't know the first thing about honor. All they knew was to pay somebody like him to do their dirty work. He looked at Walker's wife. His training forbade him to show any type of emotion, but the woman didn't deserve this. Blood smeared the wall behind the bed, but his most disturbing task lay in icing the child.

Before he could even begin to give in to human compassion, the leader smoothly shoved the barrel of the AR-15 inches from the boy's head, when the butler barged in, startling them and almost getting his ass blown off in the process. His hands were out in front in a pleading manner, begging to spare the child's life.

The nuts on the butler were the size of Florida oranges, thought the leader. He'd been warned to stay away from the house, in exchange for his life. But here he was, as bold as shit, begging like some third-class citizen for the child's safety. The old man all but tap danced in, trying to negotiate the release, until the smaller of the shadows aimed the red dot of death inside the butler's right eye. This action only intensified the butler's pleading urgency for the child's release.

And just when the shadow was about to pull the trigger, a loud boom pierced the atmosphere, sending everybody in the room for cover—everybody with the exception of the smaller member of the team, who was jerked off his feet and hurled violently into the wall by the impact. The old man was the first one to look out of hiding, only to observe little *Walker Story*, holding his father's gun, the barrel smoking. Because of the weapon's powerful kick, the butler couldn't understand how the small boy held on to the .44 Auto Magnum. But that was the least of their worries. With no room for more thought, the old man grabbed the boy and whisked him from the room, before the other two spooks could make light of how one of their best killers could've fallen at the hands of an eight-year-old.

Down the stairs as fast as his elderly body could respond, the butler and the boy were at the base of the staircase when the bullets started flying, zinging, and exploding anything made of glass. To maximize speed and provide the young child with a human shield, the butler pushed the boy to the front as bullets sprayed around them while they made their escape. The glass dinette table burst as they ran by, sending flying jagged glass chunks through the air. The butler could feel penetration of some kind to his back, but he wasn't about to stop to find out. Adrenaline caused him to push the boy to his limits. It was the only thing he could do after selling out his former employer.

Outside, sitting on the other side of the house, was a brand-new Corvette, clean and glistening under the stars. They ran right by it. There was no time to try and get away using wheels. The tunnels would be their best bet for survival. Trying desperately to fend off the fog inside his head, the sixty-year-old managed to make it to the orchards. The two avoided the body of the security guard supervisor that lay twisted in the grass. The little boy was crying loudly, begging for his father and mother. The butler tried his best to silence the kid. The yard was enormous and the hit team could be anywhere.

Straining to lift the manhole cover, the old man almost blacked out. There was a ladder leading down inside the hole. At the bottom sat a system of elaborately constructed tunnels. Walker Story, Sr. had secretly commissioned a private contractor to erect underground tunnels for emergency purposes. Lights were secured and firmly affixed to the ceiling, snaking down the concrete corridors. Halfway down, the bullets started again. The shadows were right behind them now. The old dude caught a hot one in the shoulder as he pushed the boy to run for dear life. The butler was growing weaker by the moment. He wanted to drop from extreme exhaustion, but he couldn't let his boss down again. He was going to deliver this kid to the planned safe house, even if it killed him.

The two arrived at a bend in the tunnel; the butler removing a nondescript white card the size of a driver's license and swiping across the scanner of a digital-faced unit embedded inside a wall. The action was immediate; a slab of concrete rose like something out of a 007 movie. They stepped through just in time as a hail of bullets slammed into the wall, kicking up concrete chips and dust. The concrete door dropped down behind the butler after he escaped.

Darkness was trying to pull down the butler's eyelids as they arrived fifteen minutes later at the door of a small wood-framed house in the woods, where he fell through moments after it opened. Another elderly gentleman stood over the butler as he informed the stranger of the tragic events that had gone down a few miles away. What the butler thought to be jagged glass from the dinette table was, in fact, two bullets he'd received in the back. Only the sheer will to accomplish the mission kept him on his feet. He died shortly after giving specific instruction to the stranger for smuggling the child to a safe house in Detroit.

Ante Up

Nine Years Later...

Known by staff and five-o as Walker Story, Jr., the hard banger walked the hallways of Northwestern High School, instilling fear inside the student body under the street-handle Ruffneck. He was seventeen and a complete beast. Ruffneck had spent almost four years with his finger on the pulse of the school's underworld, and spilled blood in its hallways in an effort to be established as the apex predator. It was a task that had cost him any chance of graduating on time with his class, but he didn't give a damn. Money was his only real reason why he hadn't dropped out earlier. The school was full of it.

It was the beginning of September; the second week into a brand-new school year. Ruffneck sat in his desk at the back of the classroom, totally unimpressed by geometry. He sat in the presence of what he called square-ass niggas. Displeasure tattooed his face while watching his classmates jump around like trained monkeys to answer one of the teacher's tired-ass questions.

Suckas, Walker thought. He understood the true net worth of lames. A sucka was only good for licking, and not the type of licking that appeased the taste buds. Ruffneck's definition was the one in which pimped out the pockets. And as his classmates jumped over each other like affection-starved dogs, he smiled, knowing that all of them at one time had supported his solid campaign to reign supreme in his quest to rule the school under one powerful lord. All had to pay for his protection. The weak had to be gobbled up inside the makings of the ultimate strength needed by a young, thug leader.

The same way the students were crawling over each other to answer the teacher, they lined up in dark places with money or other valuable possessions in exchange to be left alone to pursue a pain-free education. Anybody who opposed Ruffneck's will was usually laid out over the turf, the victim of a merciless beating, and left a bloody example for the rest of the student body.

Three months before summer vacation, the example had come in the form of James Nasmith, a senior classman. He was a popular boy with a brilliant football future in front of him. Paparazzi flashbulbs were the only things that could keep up with the All-American running back on the football field. The opposition was powerless against his phenomenal speed. Literally, the boy couldn't be touched—and along with his schoolyard celebrity, came the bravado that spelled out defiance. He was the only one that rejected Ruffneck's proposal for protection, boasting loudly in the school hallways about being untouchable.

Nasmith bragged in mock advertisement about his family being heavy in the game and his cousins notorious for their lack of patience when it came down to somebody fucking with family. But all that noise had been silenced two days before the Memorial Day holiday. James Nasmith had been beaten within an inch of his life. Ruffneck had caught the boy out in front of the building after school and beaten him bloody with an axe handle that had been wrapped in black electrical tape. There was never an arrest made because the students who'd witnessed the *Walking Tall*-style beat down were too terrified to identify Ruffneck. The brutal beating he'd laid out gained him the title of undisputed heavyweight, and crowned him as the grimiest cat to have ever walked the hallways of Northwestern High School.

"Who can tell me what is a hexagon?" the geometry teacher, Ms. Princess Alan, asked. Kids literally jumped up and down in the attempt to exhibit academic intelligence.

Ruffneck tuned out the classroom. He didn't give a damn about angles. The only angle keeping his attention right now was sexual fantasies of hiking Ms. Alan's dress up, bending her big ass over the desk at an angle, and sexing her until she fell under his spell. She was a second-year teacher, young, black and gorgeous, who possessed shoulder-length hair and bewitching ebony curves.

The more Ruffneck thought about it, the more the whole concept didn't figure into the grand scheme of life—angles, equations, and theories. Did they even apply to people like him? Or was it just another promise of a materialistic fantasy that the white man force-fed an anorexic, financially strapped black community. Ruffneck had been to McDonald's hundreds of times, and never had he witnessed an employee using an equation in dropping some fucking fries. A busboy would look pretty stupid trying to clear tables applying complicated formulas used in solving calculus problems.

Walker was not into buying the whole dream-selling notion. The shit wasn't flying. He'd seen the raw ass of the darker side of reality. It didn't resemble anything like *Happy Days*. He lived in the ghetto—a place where underprivileged niggas ravaged each other trying to grab the coveted spot that would grant them the riches needed to live lavish like niggas in the rap videos.

One glance around the classroom only heightened his will to be hood rich. The shabby and dingy clothes worn by his classmates incensed him. Yeah, they paid him a small piece of the pie for safety, but he was in no way responsible for so much damn poverty in one room. White America could keep their dream that bred slums. Ruffneck wanted his chips right now—with dip, if he could. And why not? He was fucking royalty, born from the loins of an African-American kingpin. He couldn't remember his father's face, but Ruffneck possessed enough memory to know that he'd lived like a prince.

Life was large—that was until those shadows had come calling and took it all away. The brutal murder of both his parents. Shot down like they were mangy, humping stray dogs in a filthy alley. Ruffneck remembered the murders all too well.

Life wasn't fair, and as far as he was concerned, life was on trial. He would preside over shit. Everything that had been done to him would be done double-time to the world. The world was personally responsible for the substandard living conditions that left him living in the ghetto, just like his classmates.

Ruffneck understood that his protection scam was peanuts, but it was a start. It had been putting food on the table for almost four years now. All the real money belonged to the old heads in the dope game: old niggas stuck in their ways with the game on lock and no room for new blood. Niggas whose time on earth was set to expire by the timer set on his rise to power.

Ruffneck lustfully stared at Ms. Alan's exotic, voluptuous ass as she erased the blackboard, making room to write more problems. It seductively jiggled inside a form-fitting skirt with every brush of the eraser, leaving him a stiff piece of wood that was harder than his desktop. Ms. Alan had always been a fantasy; one that he'd seen many times with her standing by his side as he took his place at the top of the game.

Ruffneck sat at his desk, with his pants around the ankles of his fantasy and him doggy-humping the hell out of his beautiful teacher, when the bell rang. It was a good thing his muscular, stocky frame was rocking one of those long white Sean John T-shirts. His hard dick had the opportunity to stay incognito.

He composed himself and walked out with the other students, glancing backward at Ms. Alan. Truly, he wanted nothing more than to *hit* that; beat it until she was pregnant with triplets. She had him by a couple years, but even age differences could be overcome with him making mad loot and giving her any fucking thing she wanted.

Scarface had that shit right, Ruffneck thought as he eased out into the sunshine. Money was the power in getting niggas whatever the heart desired, even Ms. Alan if he grinded hard enough for her. But he had the feeling that hollering at her wouldn't be too hard to accomplish. Ruffneck had noticed Ms. Alan's probing glances. They were subtle, but he was aware. He was seventeen but well-schooled in the art of reading women.

Ruffneck's apprenticeship had been completed seven years ago under the expert tutelage and guidance of a musty-pussy hooker who'd lived five doors up the street from his grandma. Lover Lips had been her name and she'd taught Ruffneck everything he needed in knowing about the art of satisfying a woman.

Lover Lips had also been his first piece of sexual experience. Twenty dollars had been the agreed-upon price. Ruffneck hadn't hesitated once, while stealing the loot out of his grandma's purse. He had been an enormously endowed ten-year-old, hung like a porn star. Within one week, Ruffneck was fucking Lover Lips with the natural ability of an experienced man. And over time, she'd also laid out to him the game needed in capturing a woman's mind. He sucked it all up, absorbing the knowledge like a sponge. Ruffneck had learned that game was strong enough to get from a woman, but thuggin' was made for a man.

The last bit of knowledge the prostitute had laid on him was that all women possessed thug-cravings. Lover Lips had told him that inside the naughty bedroom chambers of every female soul, lurked an insatiable hunger to be fucked down by a thug with a criminal record longer than hard dick.

Ruffneck knew Ms. Alan secretly dreamed of the cut of his jeans. One day, he would have the opportunity, but right now, he had to get his paper tight.

As he walked through the staff parking lot, students damn near broke their necks pushing each other out of his way. The damn school belonged to him. Everybody not bowing the fuck down was forced to the dirt by a grimy crew of hard pipe-hitting niggas he had under his thumb. His crew was soldiers who came highly skilled in the genre of ghetto guerilla warfare. And even though his street team was comprised of dropouts, Ruffneck didn't need them to run the school. He had his own back in a scrap, but if it caused for it, he had troops. Nobody in their right mind would step to him; but just in case some loser grew nuts, Ruffneck kept his army on speed dial. When they rolled through, it usually meant curtains for the opposition.

Walker pimped through the crowd of students with

the sun shining on his smooth brown skin. He wasn't a giant by any stretch of the imagination—5'8"—but he carried weight like a Mack truck. His high cheekbones, brush-wavy hair and thick lips gave him the Tyson Beckford profile.

Students stood around in cluttered, congregated bunches, covering every square inch of ground, but opened up as Walker advanced, giving him an undeterred pathway to the sidewalk of West Grand Boulevard, known as the Death March. The March was a long stretch of road that connected to Grand River Avenue. It was also dominated by fleabag motels, halfway houses, and violent thugs hanging out on every corner.

Beat-downs, robberies, drive-by shootings and sometimes murder, occurred on this hostile quarter-mile trek to the main street of Grand River. If they could, some students took alternate routes. But not Ruffneck; he was strapped for any and every possible situation, and jackers were hip to it. They knew he was never one to shy away from busting caps at a nigga. Plus, this was his domain. Anybody putting in work on the Death March without his verbal authorization would have to severely answer to him.

Ruffneck seldomly walked to the crib from school, but there were those days where he passed on a ride from his homeboys in favor of enjoying the sights and sounds of the ghetto. Those were also the days where his head ran heavy with the brutal demons of his past. They were painful memories of losing both parents to cowards who were punked out behind masks. The memories were lacerating for him. And it usually took walks through the hood to clear his head.

The other thing he could remember from that night was taking aim at one of the bastards and blowing the heart out his chest. They had taken the best things in his life. There was nothing he could've done to bring them back. Knowing he'd taken one of those niggas to the dirt was a small measure of retribution. Ruffneck knew, for some good reason, that the rest responsible were still out there, and one day he would have an opportunity at killing them all.

He figured the lady of karma was always deadly when you made love to the bitch without a rubber. She always came back mean, hateful and pregnant, and carrying the fucking seeds of revenge.

Now heading west on Grand River, Ruffneck thought about the best way to grab onto the horns of his dream. His protection racket wasn't gonna cut it. Shaking down broke niggas at school was barely keeping change inside his pockets.

Ruffneck knew that his old man was some kind of a beast—judging by the way he'd gone out. He idly wondered if his father had started out from the gutter. And if he did, what steps had he instituted to grab his place in life. Success had to hinge on proper planning. Ruffneck knew that he just couldn't step right in and start muscling the game. His plan had to be sweet on finesse, a plot, and strategy: The casual approach at gaining ground inch by inch. Starting out small and slowly building, while managing to fly under the radar of those holding power, would be the best way to attack and conquer.

Ruffneck wasn't much for reading that school-issued shit that domesticated young black males like him. When he did read, it was always for personal enhancement. Books like: *Art of War* by Sun Tzu; powerful information that he could use in the here-and-now for the vital growth and education of establishing an empire. He learned that kingdoms were erected brick by brick. In his language: one street corner at a time. Let those cats in control of vast territory stay drunk with the security of knowing that nobody would challenge. Tzu taught him that false security had been the downfall of many kingdoms.

But for now, he would settle on hollering at shit that would grow into dividends for amassing the loot needed to finance a war on his competitors, starting with jacking the punk that sat in a brand-new funny, custom-colored Chevy Tahoe. The twenty-four-inch aftermarkets dog was rolling on, were sweet as hell to Ruffneck. The fool would never see the jack coming. The sweet piece of candy chilling in the passenger seat in the form of a long-haired gold digger was stroking his ego, relieving him of his guard. The truck was parked one block ahead, on the corner of a side street off the main.

At two-thirty in the afternoon, many of the residents were at work or getting ready to go, but that shit didn't matter to Ruffneck. He needed this lick right now. The rims would fetch a pretty penny on the open market, and he bet the lame had sounds in the ride, too. All ballers did.

Two feet from the back of the truck, the Glock .40 seemed to appear inside Ruffneck's right hand as if he were a master illusionist. He didn't know anything about making women levitate, but he damn sure was about to make this nigga's truck disappear with just one wave of the weapon inside his hand.

"Get yo' bitch ass out the car, nigga!" Ruffneck insanely ordered, sticking the pistol through the open window and right behind the driver's left ear.

The woman screamed loud enough to make eardrums bleed.

"Shut up, bitch!" Ruffneck screamed at the girl as he held the cat stiffly in check by bringing the barrel down to the nigga's jaw.

"A'ight, nigga, chill—" the man made an attempt to say.

But without thought, Ruffneck roughly grabbed the man by the back of his long braids and slammed his face down so hard against the steering wheel, the horn blew. The woman screamed as blood poured from the man's broken nose. She managed to fumble open the door, falling out; her apple bottom hitting the pavement hard as she rolled over on all fours to make a mad dash for cover.

Ruffneck laughed harshly at the dude.

"Can't trust a bitch with yo' back, hunh, homeboy?" Ruffneck joked as he snatched opened the driver's door. "Get yo' ass out!" He pulled the guy out of the truck and stomped on his head for good measure.

Ruffneck hopped in the truck and peeled out, leaving nothing but skid marks on the victim's manhood. He tried to drive the speed limit but found it impossible. The dude was probably on his cell reporting the lick to five-o. Ruffneck couldn't and wouldn't be caught riding dirty in a hot truck with heat at his waist. It wouldn't be beneficial to his future kingdom. A leader was only as good as his ability to stay composed and focused in the teeth of pressure. He didn't think of himself as a thief. To him, thieves were the lowest forms of life that needed to be squashed like roaches crawling around on the floor. Ruffneck was a businessman and the streets were his office.

As he created distance between him and the jacking, Ruffneck allowed himself to come down from the adrenaline flowing inside his body. He could've killed the cat. Ruffneck was glad that it hadn't come down to it, but he could've wasted the fool. After all, his cherry had been popped when he'd put the work in on one of the team members who'd been responsible in taking out his parents. So killing wasn't a thing. Besides, Ruffneck knew leaving bodies lying around wouldn't be good for business. He wouldn't permit himself the room for sloppiness.

Ruffneck turned off the main street, trying to relax

and appreciate the butter-soft leather. He removed a CD from the visor's clip-on holder. It was music from some up-and-coming studio gangsta named 187. Even though the punk was a wannabe, the beat and lyrics were off the hook. The single "Ante Up" was da bomb. He cranked the volume allowing the base from the cabinet in the back to shake and rattle the windows.

He had been right. He knew the sucka had sounds. Ruffneck hopped the freeway as the smooth baseline thumped over the rapper's slick lyrical delivery. 187 rapped about coming up in the game and taking his place at the head of the table, becoming one of the industry titans. Ruffneck could relate. He wasn't trying to become a music industry *nothing*. His shit was for real. He was an authentic gangsta with major plans of redesigning the city's kingpin-hierarchy, a very lucrative vision that would leave him sitting pretty in a phat mansion. This feat would come with death. Ruffneck didn't have a problem with dirt-napping cats as long as it was going to provide the empire of his choosing. If he had to bury niggas to live out his dream, then the funeral homes were gonna be overcrowded by his product.

As Ruffneck bumped and rocked to the sounds of prophecy, he laughed at the major playas that were ignorant to his existence. But they would soon get a glimpse of the little nigga born from a bigger gangsta. Ruffneck was gonna bring it like it had never been brought before. His mental Glock was loaded as he visualized victims falling to the turf, holes in their bodies and pockets flipped inside out like they had been run.

Detroit was his home. And since he could vaguely remember the sweet memories of his old life, this would be the perfect opportunity at building a new one. Regardless, if his foundation would be constructed over the deteriorating bodies of his competitors, his goal was heaven on earth.

A war was brewing.

While he drove his way down I-96 freeway, Ruffneck had three words of advice to submit to his rivals: Ante up, niggas!

Let's Get It Poppin'

Ruffneck blew the Chevy's horn. Around the third honk, a motorized, rusty gate groaned to life with a squeaky chorus of disapproval as it retracted. Ruffneck drove right into the open gate of a junkyard the size of a major shopping mall. With the window down, the sweet fragrance from tree air fresheners hanging around the gearshift in the Tahoe, was losing the fight against the oily stench of rusted-out wrecks, piles of sludge-oozing car parts, and heavy machinery that belched blue smoke.

Ruffneck carefully drove the maze as directed by men wearing oil-covered overalls and crude-sludge-stained boots. He came across one of these cats at every twist and bend of the oil-slick, blanketed dirt road. He reached down around his waist, moving the Glock .40 in a position of readiness—just in case the nigga he was here to see wasn't who he claimed to be. The more he drove, the grimier the men grew until he reached the back; niggas started to look like oil monsters staring out of crackhead eyes.

He stopped on the side of a rickety old office building

the size of an outhouse. The Glock underneath his white T-shirt, Ruffneck exited the SUV, careful to step over a nasty-looking puddle of water that looked to have a hefty mixture of everything disgusting floating on top. Ruffneck felt that even brushing against the air inside the yard would leave indestructible dirt stains in the fabric of his crispy white Sean John.

"You Menace's boy, hunh?" asked something that looked like a man, but Ruffneck wasn't sure. The cat was greasy with long, dirty-looking dreads.

"Ain't that what Menace told you?" Ruffneck snapped with sauce. He was standing with his hands down at his side.

"Min' your tongue, boy." He looked toward the shack. "Ay, Greasy, you got one of these smart-ass lil niggas out here."

There was absolutely no mistaking the mountain with legs that wedged out of the narrow office door. The man named Greasy wore a black patch on his right eye like he was a damn junkyard pirate. Greasy was responsible for a hefty portion of cocaine dealt on the streets of Detroit. The yard was just a front for his operation. Ruffneck also knew the slob was into insurance jobs, contract hits, and prostitution.

"We don't usually deal with people we don't know. But since you Menace's boy, we're gonna make a one-time exception," Greasy explained in a voice plagued by nasal problems; his chubby cheeks looked to be swollen with tobacco.

Ruffneck stood silent, trying to get a read on Greasy. But the man was horrible to stare at. Even though Greasy was naturally dark-skinned, his junkyard profession looked to have compromised his pigmentation—mutating, adding a darker alien-shade to his spooky ebony demeanor.

Greasy rubbed his dirty hands along the SUV's highly polished finish, leaving an oily smear behind.

"Real slick, but unfortunately, young blood, we don't have a market to move vehicles with custom paint jobs. Most of our shit is local. We don't have an out-of-town market."

"So, what that mean?" Ruffneck asked calmly.

Everybody knew that half of the stolen cars in the city ended up leaving from the junkyard. Ruffneck already knew that the shit was personal for some reason. The SUV he'd jacked was butter, and would've been loot at any other chop shop. This nigga was on some other shit. Ruffneck's right hand eased down toward his shirttail in case he had to get to his heat and lay a few fools down.

"That means, young blood," Greasy said, "hop inside this niggered-out chariot and push out of here."

"Menace said that you were on the level. Said you was about business," Ruffneck said, bracing for shit to pop off.

Greasy disrespectfully spat out a nasty brown glob which landed close to Ruffneck's sneakers. The older man smiled at his boy as he continued to chew his tobacco and stare at Ruffneck like he was weak.

The volcano blast of rage went off behind Ruffneck's fiery blood shots. His forehead wrinkled into anger lines.

He slowly tugged at his shirttail with his right hand. Death was a few inches away. This nigga didn't know who he was dealing with, and Ruffneck was about to put some holes in his fat ass.

"It's like that?" was all Ruffneck could manage while trying like hell to keep his composure. He knew about Greasy. The blob might've been fat, sloppy and disgusting, but the nigga made his bones by making cats disappear. Ruffneck wasn't gonna take this fool lightly.

The sound of a slide being pulled back on an automatic weapon was eerily unmistakable. A round had been chambered. War was about to be waged.

Ruffneck slowly turned in the direction of the noise. It was the slim monster that he'd exchanged first-words with before he'd talked to Greasy. The chump was clutching a Beretta 9mm in his chubby right hand.

"Young nigga, first and foremost," said the fool, holding the Beretta, "you came up in here with the wrong attitude. Like we 'sposed to hook yo' young ass up. Nigga, do you know where you at? We can crush yo' young ass"—he paused to watch a huge car-crushing machine chew up a late-model Ford—"up in that machine, and nobody would be able to find yo' punk ass."

Four more dirtballs walked up holding heat.

Greasy sarcastically smiled again before spitting more tobacco juice and wiping away brown lines of slob from his chin.

"We seen yo' type of nigga befo'—wannabe gangsta-ass thug. That schoolyard shit might work in the schoolhouse," Greasy said, staring at the cats brandishing the hardware with his chest poked out, "but you see, we some grown-ass men up in here, dog. Ain't got time for young nigga games."

"Now jump back in that hot mothafucka and bounce yo' hot ass up out of here," ordered the pudgy dude pointing the 9mm.

It didn't take Ruffneck too long to choose options. These niggas were ready to open up on him. He might've been insane when it came down to his respect, but he wasn't stupid. Ruffneck studied each face carefully; almost like he was taking and storing mental Kodaks for future termination. He wasn't going to let this shit slide. The lines of anger eased inside Ruffneck's forehead.

He raised his arms in the air.

"All right…it's your world. I'm just leaving," he said as he stepped over a puddle and opened the door to the SUV. "But I'll see you niggas later."

"Get yo' bitch ass out of here, before I let these niggas get to dumping on yo' young ass," Greasy threatened.

Incensed, Ruffneck drove out of the gate. He'd been embarrassed. Humiliated. Greasy had wiped his ass with his respect. The Reaper was reflecting brightly inside the mirrors of Ruffneck's pupils. Greasy wasn't long for this world. Ruffneck would make sure of it. But right now, his first priority was to unload the hot SUV. The police were probably on to him by now. He couldn't run the risk of getting popped.

Ruffneck's cell joint went off.

"'Sup, Granny Sinclair?" Ruffneck answered, trying to chase away the leftover anger in his voice while gripping the wheel with one hand.

"Boy, where you at?" asked the old woman. "Told you to come right home after the schoolhouse let you out."

Ruffneck took a moment to answer. He'd violated his first rule by letting Greasy's fat ass get to him. And he didn't want the remaining anger he harbored to spill over into this conversation. The respect he had for the old woman ranked right up there with that of his father. Ruffneck had to admit: he hadn't been the easiest child in the city to rear, and in doing so, he'd more than maxed out the old woman's limits with all the bullshit he'd put her through. By right, most would've shown his little ass how hard the ground was after throwing him out of their front door, but not her. Granny was a trooper, and for that, he owed her his life.

"If'n you can get your head out of your ass, gangsta, I'm runnin' a little low on my heart medication and need a refill A-S-A-P."

"Granny Sinclair, I gotta few moves to make and I'll be there in a hot minute."

"What's so hot about it?" Granny Sinclair ripped off, with a throaty cough that sounded like she was about to hack up a lung. "How many times I gotta tell you that I'm not one of those hip-hop bitches?"

Ruffneck laughed. His relationship with the old lady had been erected on trust and humor. Even though she was in her late sixties, Granny Sinclair's mind was razor-sharp with superb wit.

"Listen, ol' lady, you need anything else besides the ticker medicine?"

"Some cigarettes, boy."

"I'm not gonna help you punch your ticket on the Heavenly Express. I'll get your meds, but William can cop the coffin nails."

Granny Sinclair barked out a set of coughs that sounded like they were sponsored by the Grim Reaper. William was her crackhead-ass biological, walking apocalyptic offerings to the world. He'd managed to spread unholy terror to the senior citizens in the neighborhood. Any old person that he'd catch coming out of a check cashing joint or a corner liquor store on the first of the month, was immediately checked in. William was a hardcore smoke-head who shared one single impulsive philosophy: rob, shoot, and run—but sometimes not all in that order. And even though he never pulled the trigger on the elderly, everybody else was fair game.

Ruffneck hated William and used to bump heads with the nigga when he was a little cat. That was, until Ruffneck had come into his own gangsta, sprouted a few inches, and started laying out bodies on his campaign for respect.

"You know I don't see that son-of-bitch 'til the first of the month," Granny Sinclair responded.

Ruffneck drove slowly, periodically checking his rearview mirror for the police. He had to get the old lady off of the phone to concentrate. The jacking had gone down, maybe a few hours ago, and One-Time would be looking for him and the truck. He had to get off of the streets; find a chop shop who would buy the SUV. Ruffneck had no choice. He knew just who to holla at. So he bent a few corners and headed in that direction.

"I hope his ass O.D.," Ruffneck said under his breath.

"What was that, boy?"

"Nothing, Triple Ol' G."

"You gonna need the money."

"I got the loot."

"Where you get 'the loot' from?"

"Granny Sinclair, I'm losing connection"—he blew into the receiver—"Granny Sinclair…"

"Boy, you need to stop playin'—"

"Can't…"—he blew into the phone—"You're breaking up."

Ruffneck ended the call laughing. Granny Sinclair could talk all day, but the sun was going down and he needed to unload the truck. And with that thought, he pulled up to the corner of Northfield and Tireman on a group of thugs sipping forty-ounces. A few of the cats were crouched down in the doorway of an old, burned-out storefront shooting dice. A dude rocking Timbs, jeans sagging off his ass and wearing a black hoodie, was the first to get to his feet at the sight of the Tahoe rolling on them. The young boy subtly removed a pistol from his waistband, ready to put in work, if need be.

Once the window rolled down on the SUV, the rest stood, shoving winnings into pockets, and prepared for fight or flight.

Ruffneck brushed off the menacing glares.

"Larceny," he called to a smooth, brown-skinned cat sporting shoulder-length cornrows. "Got some business I want to holla at you about, kinfolk."

Larceny jumped in without hesitation or explanation. The rest of the cats returned to the dice game except the dude wearing the hoodie. He stood with his pistol in plain sight, as if guarding the backs of his homeboys.

"Serious, cuz, don't know why you holding court with these grocery store-jacking bandits?" Ruffneck asked Larceny.

Larceny smiled like he had already been expecting the question. "I'm gonna tell you like I tell everybody 'round here: I'ma a bidness man, baby, and money ain't got no enemies, cowboy."

"Just remember to take a shower after dealing with them grimy-ass niggas."

Larceny looked out of the back window; the crew he'd just left was growing smaller as the SUV created distance. "No doubt, but what you need, cowboy?"

"Need to cash in this hot boy we riding in. Who you got turning jacks into cash?"

Larceny rubbed his hands together.

"Say no mo', mi nig. You stepped to the right cat. You know how I gits down." He whipped out his cell and made a quick call. A few minutes later, they were pulling into a small white garage with greasy, black handprints staining the rising overhead door of the garage on Livernois and Warren. Some fool named Sounds led them in, using directional hand gestures.

Sounds was an older, heavyset man with skin darker than oil slicks smeared across a dark county road. His circus freak-like overbite was making short work of the Big Mac clutched in his right hand.

"Give me 'bout two days," Sounds explained with a mouth filled with food. Big Mac drippings spilled as he chewed. "I'll make a couple calls to make this bitch disappear. How's 70/30 sound?"

"Like you been smoking crack and shooting heroin," Ruffneck retorted.

"Listen here, deuce, I'm taking all the risk and the heat." He took another plug out of the sandwich, sauce disgustedly caking the corners of his mouth. "This shit is custom. I can't sell it nowhere in the city, but I gotta partna in the A-T-L who got the market. Gonna cost me a grip to ship. Seventy/thirty or you can take yo' chances somewhere else."

Ruffneck studied the dirt and grime that covered the shelves of oily, assorted car parts and junk, he didn't recognize. He stared over at Larceny—who'd managed to stay out of negotiations to this point—as if questioning Sounds' mathematical abilities. Larceny wasn't hard to read. His smiling expression explained that he had done his part in supplying the fence. And other than the small fee for providing his services, Ruffneck was on his own.

Ruffneck played with the figures for a few before making his decision. Hell, it wasn't like he'd broken a sweat in ripping the wheels. Plus, he couldn't run the risk of letting the pharmacy close while trying to play "Let's Make a Deal." Granny Sinclair would bleed his eardrums raggedy by complaining.

"Listen, guy: get at me the moment you sling the whip." Ruffneck kicked the cat down with his digits and bounced.

"Larceny, this cat better not come with the game a couple days from now," Ruffneck warned after the overhead door fell at their backs.

"Sounds ain't 'bout the game, cowboy. He's been in bidness for a long time. Can't have that type of time tryna get over on fools. You ain't gotta worry, nig. If he gave you figures, it's a done deal—plus my modest fee, of course."

The two boys started off down the street.

"You don't miss a beat, do you?"

"Like I told you when you picked me up—"

"I know," Ruffneck said, breaking in, "You a 'bidness man.' Well, all right, *bidness man*, you'll get yo' cut the moment that fool get at me."

"But yo, peep game: what dup with Monique's party?" Larceny asked.

Ruffneck watched the police cruiser turn the corner. Even with the heat at his waist, his ability to remain calm was remarkable for a young man of his age. He wasn't gonna run. That was the rule. Never panic. Especially when walking around dirty. As far as he was concerned, the pigs were searching for a suspect driving a Chevy Tahoe with fresh-ass rims. Not a cat pushing the pavement. The police slowed down as if trying to place his face. But after no registration, they moved on down the street.

"You know I don't get down like that. Ain't no money in partying. And I ain't tryna to open myself up for some getback by some fool's people we put the work on, in the past," Ruffneck said, glancing in the direction of the fleeting police cruiser.

"Yo' ass forever paranoid," Larceny joked.

"Not 'noid at all. Just careful. My dream is to own these streets and I can't make that happen at no basement party, ya dig?"

"I can dig it, but that leaves mo' broads fo' me."

"Do the damn thing, playboy. I'll holla at you later." Ruffneck dapped Larceny and stepped away.

Although the two boys never hung out together, a mutual respect painted them associates. Each calling upon the other, pooling resources when there were ample opportunities to put some cheese in their pockets. Larceny was all about his ends. Any nigga with a dollar and a mind to deal had his full and undivided attention. Nothing got in the way of that. Not even the retaliation Ruffneck had carried out against Larceny's two brothers about four years back. One Saturday, Larceny's two brothers, Pig and Box, had decided that they wanted to make a quick come-up. So, they'd run out the crib, while

Ruffneck was going door-to-door, delivering *The Detroit News* and collecting his money. They jumped him. It'd been the first time in his young life that Ruffneck had ever listened to Granny Sinclair about taking some responsibility and getting a job, only to end up stomped to the brink of unconsciousness by the two neighborhood bullies.

The beatings and Saturday morning shakedowns continued on a regular until Ruffneck went nuts and started packing a screwdriver. The next confrontation, Pig ended up stabbed twice in the abdomen and Box caught cold steel in the left jaw.

Street justice.

No police involvement.

Ruffneck never suffered any more stickup attempts from Pig, Box, or anybody else for that matter. Larceny never held Ruffneck in contempt with the revenge game that he'd put down on his people. He understood the wild code of the streets and what it took to earn respect. And as far as he was concerned, his brothers were bums and had gotten what they deserved.

Ruffneck walked off in the direction of the pharmacy. He might've done tons of dirt in the 'hood, but he always found time to take care of his grandma. Besides, the ol' girl was holding family secrets. One day, Granny Sinclair would give up the information in order for him to piece together his true self. Until then, he would be about putting bricks together to create the perfect empire that would soon be erected off the dead and dying.

Holdin' Out

"Granny Sinclair!" Ruffneck shouted as he walked through the front door.

"Up here, boy," came a deep and husky voice.

Ruffneck followed the voice upstairs and appeared at the old lady's bedroom door. He clutched a small bag from the local pharmacy.

For somebody that was in her sixties, Granny Sinclair's mocha skin was flawless, almost absent of Father Time's spell. She was thick-framed with sagging breasts. Her hair was cottony white, and her bifocal lenses were thick enough to make her eyes appear abnormally small. And even though she was slightly stooped over, relying on a cane to get around, Granny Sinclair's smile was her most prized possession.

Although her skin revealed no signs of advanced aging, her health was the stuff of constant doctor visits and sporadic hospital stays. Taking on an orphaned boy had come with its share of stress-induced illnesses: migraine, ulcer and heart problems.

"You get 'hold of William on that cigarette tip?" Ruffneck asked with a smile filled with amusing mischief. He got a rise out of knowing that the old woman craved nicotine like the stuff was tobacco-crack, but her doctor had prohibited her from smoking.

She tried not to look too frustrated by taking a seat at the edge of the bed, leaning forward, using the handle of her cane as a prop for her weight.

"See you done cut them ugly-tail braids out your hair, lookin' like Iverson Alan."

"That's Alan Iverson. Can't you pick somebody in today's generation of basketball stars to compare me to? Iverson's a relic."

"Whatever. I'm sho nuff glad you did. Didn't know if'n I had a grandson or a granddaughter."

"Old lady, that's about all the jokes I'ma take from you. You need me to get you a glass of water so you can pop one of these pills?" He held up the small bag.

"Yeah. And I just wanna know where you getting money from to buy all those nice clothes that be hanging off yo' ass?"

"Here we go…" Ruffneck breathed hard from his mouth.

"'Here we go,' my ass! You heard what that judge man told you: if'n you come befo' him one more time, he was gonna put yo' ass underneath the jailhouse."

"Granny, I can take care of me."

"You can't take care of a wet dream. You better cut all that stealing out, takin' them chil'ren's clothes up at that schoolhouse. Get a damn job, if you wanna—what them stupid rappers' word for it?—yeah, if'n you wanna bling-bling."

"Don't nobody use 'bling-bling' no more but the white people. Are we about done?" Ruffneck said, his smile replaced by frustration.

"You make me sick; all that fuckin' attitude of yours. Get yo' ass out from in front of my door—mannish-ass little boy."

"Temper, temper. Old women ain't supposed to talk gangsta"— he playfully rubbed his fingertips around his nipples, slowly gyrating his pelvis—"Talk some more, you making me hot."

Granny pointed the tip of her cane at him.

"This cane is gonna heat yo' ass up, if'n you don't stop playin' and get me a glass of water."

This was their routine. They went after each other, good-naturedly, of course, trading insults the way that Fred Sanford and Esther Anderson used to on *Sanford and Son*. The old woman enjoyed playing the dozens, but she knew it went much deeper than jokes, punchlines, and laughter. It was a way to defuse those uneasy and awkward periods of silence. The silence only known to secrets and mysteries—mysteries that the boy wanted desperately to know about. Frankly, he wanted answers about his past—his father, mother. They were answers that she'd taken an oath not to reveal until he was mentally mature.

Granny Sinclair popped her lips. She took out her false teeth and dropped them inside of a glass fizzing with colored water that sat on her nightstand.

"Ruffneck," she said. Her mouth was sunken and she worked her gums as if chewing on tough steak. "You hear me, boy. I called you by ya hoodlum name."

"Here we go again," Ruffneck said, handing the glass of water over to his grandmother.

"I don't know what you talking about. You can just call me what you've always called me: Walker."

Nothing got underneath his skin more than his grandmother calling him by his jungle handle. The name belonged to the streets. It had been designed to simply have the same foreboding effect on the community: much like standing in front of the mirror and chanting the name "Candy Man" three times would have in the movie. The ghetto wasn't Hollywood, or special effects and blood made from corn syrup. Coming inside his neighborhood and speaking his name the wrong way would leave a nigga twisted in his tracks. But the name coming from his grandmother's mouth left him feeling like dressing up in a green uniform and traveling door-to-door to sell Girl Scout cookies.

"*Ruffneck*, hunh?" She took the water and swallowed the pill. "Sounds like you auditioning for some jailhouse time, boy."

"You judgin' me?" he asked in a firmer voice.

"I don't even know who you are anymore, Mr. Ruffneck."

The old woman knew when the statement came out of her mouth, she had placed herself directly inside the firing range for his line of questioning.

"You're right. Who am I?" he asked. "I can't tell you because I don't know who the hell I am." The confusion going on inside his eyes was intense with body language bordering on hurt, pain, and frustration. "The only memory I do have of my folks wakes me up in cold sweats at night—the bullet-riddled bodies of both my parents." He pointed to his chest. "Tell me who the hell I am."

"You watch your damn mouth in my house! You may be Ruffneck out on the street, but in here, you Walker, and Walker respects his elders."

"But keep it real, old woman. How do you connect into this picture?" He looked around the hallway in which he stood. "In my old life, I remember a big house, nice things. If I can't remember anything else, I remember the house."

"That's that posttraumatic stress, got you where you can't 'member," Granny tried to joke her way out of it. "If'n you'd had taken those pills like the doctor man prescribed, you would have yo' memory back."

"Got jokes, hunh. I'm real with this. You don't know what it feels like to carry your mother's scream around inside your head, the jacked-up pictures of your dead parents. Sometimes I can still smell the gunpowder."

Granny Sinclair sat speechless. They'd gone down this road plenty of times, and almost every time, they would arrive at this frustrating destination. She was anything but dumb and knew that ignorance was the boy's guardian angel.

Ruffneck's wounds were deep and infected with the revenge game that only the dead bodies of his parents' killers could heal. But he knew he was beating a dead horse. Ruffneck knew the only way that he would get info from the old woman would be to turn her ass upside down by the ankles and shake the shit out of her.

"Remember one thing," Granny Sinclair warned, "Some doors are best left closed."

"Whatever. I figured you'd end with the 'some doors are best left closed' blast." Ruffneck's blood pressure was up and his heart was cold, thumping out icy beats of retribution. He started down the stairs, pissed.

"'Member what I tell you, boy," Granny Sinclair yelled.

He loved the old lady more than life itself, but sometimes she really got underneath his skin with her shit. There were times he wanted to shake her—but never that. Principles didn't permit harm to befall women and children; a luxury that hadn't been extended to his mother. She'd been shot down like some mangy dog. The trigger-niggas responsible were gonna have their day inside his court; the barrel of whatever tool he'd be rockin' acting as judge, jury and executioner. The come-up had to happen before that little piece of business. He had to get his army up to challenge.

He said it before and he'd say the shit again: Niggas

were gonna die behind the building of his empire. Some said the road to hell was paved with good intentions. If that was so, then his intentions were blood-thirsty, and his kingdom would be constructed with the headstones of the competition.

Ruffneck lived down in the basement. It was a tiny enclosure with a full-size bed; crunchy, compressed wood entertainment center, and a moody, sometimey 27-inch, old-school color television. But all that didn't matter. He had to keep his shit under lock and key. His uncle didn't discriminate when it came down to anything he could hit a lick on. Once William rolled through, whatever wasn't nailed down walked out to crack spots and pawn- shops. But Granny Sinclair's son was her pride and joy. Ruffneck wanted nothing more than to put his heater in William's foul breath-smelling mouth, but he didn't. He didn't want to bring the old lady any more heartache.

Inside his room, Ruffneck eased into his closet. It was a long, narrow area with racks belonging to a few throw-backs, hanging True Religion jeans, button-downs, and plain white tees on one side. A shelf on the left was home to a couple pair of Airman sneakers, ranging by number, a pair of Timbs, and assorted colors of Air Force Ones.

Ruffneck threw on a slick button-down and True Religion jeans. His entire fucking family had been anni- hilated—taken out—and no doubt ordered by some coward living in the shadow. A real warrior handled his business with his own hands. He didn't have to hire assassins that were probably hand-selected from some underworld Yellow Pages.

Ruffneck slid into a pair of sneakers. He walked from the closet and modeled them in view of a full-length mirror. Somebody had to pay—both parents, dead. Somewhere in the country dwelled the beast that had sanctioned the hit. And if he breathed air, put on his pants one leg at a time, and maintained enough rhythm to perform the hustle, the nigga could and would be got.

Ruffneck looked inside the mirror. Questions stared back at him. He didn't even know who the fuck he was. Yeah, he could remember the night the shadows had come to his world and snatched away everything, but for the life of him, he couldn't remember the faces of his folks. Posttraumatic stress—it was the diagnosis from one doctor. The psychiatrist had seemed to think that Ruffneck's inability to recall the faces of his parents might've been triggered by the gruesome event in which they'd been murdered. The doctor had gone on to further explain that the absence of memory was merely an avoidance symptom, and he prescribed high dosages of antidepressants to treat Ruffneck's condition. Granny Sinclair had taken the prescription, but never got it filled. She'd tried to make him take the meds, but Ruffneck wasn't buying it. The old woman stopped after finding the pills she'd been giving him in a collection underneath his bed.

"Did my fam even get a proper burial?" Ruffneck grilled the man inside the mirror, expecting answers. All he received was torment. It pissed him the fuck off. Somebody was gonna pay. Bodies would drop until he was satisfied that he'd gotten either the cat that had green-lit the murders, or the actual crew who'd put in the work.

A few strokes with the brush started the ocean of waves inside of hair flowing with endless consistency. He grabbed his cell, trying to get a leash around the neck of personal demons. Ruffneck was known for amazing control at his age. He didn't understand why, but just accepted it as a tool needed for future emperors. Maybe his father had had it. Wherever *it'd* come from, he needed it. Fucking around inside of Detroit's harsh jungles without it could get a nigga's ticket punched the hard way.

The shrink had also expressed to Ruffneck that failure in opening up to people would prolong the condition. But Ruffneck wasn't buying that shit. Apparently, the doctor had never lived in the ghetto, where the less people knew about your personal business, the better off you were. To Ruffneck, mystery was the rawest street rep that one could possess. It kept other dudes off-balance, second-guessing about bringing drama to a nigga's manhood. Knowledge meant power to some, and Ruffneck wasn't about to give it up. Over the years, he'd learned to hide the pain from his past deep down inside the pockets of his soul. The less a nigga knew about you in the streets, the higher the survival rate.

He kept his crew ignorant of his demons. The city morgue was filled with fools who'd revealed weaknesses to the dogs they trusted, only to end up served up by the coroner and waiting for process time on slabs.

The streets were watching; they always did. Ruffneck retrieved his pistol from the hiding spot, tucked it under his shirt and bounced.

The Body Bag

The playground known as the "Body Bag" was legend-ary in the hood. It was nothing more than one full court, tall chain-linked fences, decades of decaying blacktop, faded white lines, litter, graffiti-painted bleachers, weather-beaten backboards, and tattered blue nets hang-ing from rusty rims.

Even though athletes ran everything inbounds, the underworld dominated the sidelines. Thugs, gamblers, and dope boys owned the shadows. It was nothing to see a dice game turned deadly or a dope deal ending in auto-matic gunfire. The Body Bag, once named "The Run," had lost its innocence, beauty, and rich history. The park had quickly turned to ruins after a deadly shootout between two crews beefed out over total control, a gun battle which had ended with three fatally wounded. One of the victims had been a six-year-old boy.

Aside from its dark history, the park acted as a well-oiled manufacturing line for basketball talent. It released top-notch players to local high schools and universities across the country, with more than a handful making it to play on an NBA level. The park was Detroit's version of New York's legendary Rucker Park. Competition was ferocious, and those looking to make a name stood in a long line to play against some of the hottest talent in the country.

Ruffneck and his crew were posted on one-half of the two sets of elongated aluminum bleachers that ran along courtside. Ten hard-bodied, sweaty cats hustled up and down the court as if they were auditioning for NBA scouts. They pushed, grunted, shoved and cursed in eighty-degree heat. Money was on the line and tempers were flaring.

Ruffneck sat with his soldiers—Menace, Fly, Lil Shorty, and a hard-ass chick named Poison. Menace was the physical enforcer, a prized bull that knocked niggas the fuck out without breaking a sweat. At nineteen, he was the oldest boy in the crew. He stood at a silent six-seven with solid muscle. Menace was a chocolate complexion and probably tipped the scales at a cool two-fifty. The full beard he rocked gave him the look of somebody well into their twenties. Ruffneck knew what time it was when it came down to assembling a street squad. Balance was essential. All his dogs were ruthless when it came down to rockin' cradles, but he needed his posse to be equal at the head-crushing task of going toe-to-toe. Menace was perfect and had inherited everything from his old man, who'd been killed in a shootout with the police in southwest Detroit.

"What's your thought on Michael Jackson, dying and

shit, mi nigga?" Lil Shorty asked, taking a swig from his forty-ounce.

"I can't believe the nigga dead," Fly said.

Fly was seventeen with a twelve-month-old baby girl, and a baby momma who was milkin' him for his hustle. He was a chestnut complexion, average height and build, but the young cat had mad heart. Fly never looked for trouble; it always found him. And when it did, he usually left one or two lying on the pavement, bleeding from multiple gunshot wounds.

"Niggas is dropping, yo," Lil Shorty interjected. "Gerald Levert, Bernie Mac, Heavy D—all our peeps have left this piece, mi nig."

Lil Shorty was brown-skinned with an apple-shaped head. Where Menace stood a titan, Lil Shorty stood five-seven and weighed a measly buck and a quarter, soaking wet. He was a fourteen-year-old runaway with a Napoleon complex and a sizzling willingness to put a few hot ones into anybody who stared at him cross-eyed.

"True dat. All the icons have kicked: Isaac Hayes, Ray Charles—" Menace tried to say before he was interrupted.

"Isaac Hayes and Ray Charles—fool, what the hell do you know about Ray Charles and Isaac Hayes?" Fly joked, smirking. He sat close to Ruffneck.

Fly tapped Ruffneck when a crew of cats walked in through the fence opening like they owned the whole damn world, all rocking True Religion jeans, Airmans, Timbs, button-downs, and huge gold chains.

"If it wasn't for Jamie Foxx playing the nigga in the

movie, wouldn't none of you fools know a damn thing about Ray Charles," Ruffneck butted in.

"Ruffneck, you right, homeboy," Lil Shorty said and slapped him five.

The action on the court heated up:

"Nigga, you foul me like that again!" a young, lanky boy named Ups shouted, hopping up off the blacktop inches away from where the faded white lines intersected to make the key of the *visitor's* basket. He was about to go into the chest of a shirtless dude with a huge beer gut, stopping the action on the court. They were center stage and everybody in earshot of the drama paused to peep. Ruffneck never let his eyes drift away from the crew that were now checking out the smoke on the court, pointing and laughing.

"It was a pick, little nigga," the cat with the beer gut shouted back. "This here's a man's game, punk! It's a contact sport, and if yo' faggot ass can't take it, go play Double-Dutch with yo' sister or some shit." The boy laughed so hard the rolls of fat around his sides shook like jelly.

"Ya'll either take that shit off the court and handle it, or play ball," one of the older heads yelled from the sideline.

Ruffneck studied the leader of the crew; a man who went by the street name of Billy the Kid. He'd been named after the actual movie character because of his lightning speed and accuracy at pulling his pistol on a fool. And much like the movie depiction, Billy's pistol was rumored to have been involved in over two-dozen murders.

Menace was looking in the same direction as Ruffneck. Billy was the shit and had Detroit's underworld on lock. He ran a mega-crew of niggas who called themselves the Ghetto Mob.

Fly knew what Ruffneck was thinking.

"That nigga Billy think he's that *guy*—Mister Fucking Untouchable," Fly whispered softly. He hated Billy, but his disdain didn't dismantle the respect the man commanded.

"Ghetto Mob," Ruffneck said. He'd never lost focus on the ten niggas that stood by Billy. Around town, Billy and his crew were treated like fucking celebrities. They pushed in the best that money could afford—from high-end European joints to anything that could roll a twenty-four-inch rim. Bread-loaf-sized bankrolls earned Ghetto Mob the red carpet treatment. They popped bottles—VIP style—in all the tightest nightclubs around town, and banged all the finest gold diggers money could attract. They were simply the golden boys of the game. And everybody from hustlers, players, to crackheads, bent over to kiss ass-crack wherever they posted.

When play on the court resumed, Ruffneck wasn't interested. Billy had broken away from his boys to holla at a plainclothes officer known around the hood as Roscoe. Ruffneck watched as Billy lifted his head to scan the area, making sure nobody was looking at the exchange. He went into his pocket and came out with a knot of cash. The white detective took the loot by covering the transaction with an innocent handshake. A greasy smile cut across the cop's smug mug. Roscoe looked around like everything breathing was filthy and disgusting. He jumped back inside his unmarked and drove away without a glance backward.

"You see that shit, dog?" Fly whispered to Ruffneck. "Roscoe's dirty cop-ass don't miss a beat."

"Yup," Ruffneck said, never taking his eyes from Billy. The chain Billy wore hung low with a huge lion-head medallion dangling down to his nuts. The sun's rays brilliantly picked up the reflection of the high-quality stones inside the lion's mane. His wrist was frosty as well. The diamonds around the bezel of his Audemars glittered like fireworks lighting up darkened skies.

"Greasing Roscoe in broad daylight," Menace said. "They getting sloppy, man."

"Just look at how niggas be falling all over them fools," Ruffneck added, almost in admiration.

"You want that power, don't you?" Fly asked Ruffneck. "I can see that junk in your eyes, God. Just wait, kid, it'll be yours one day. Them cats getting relaxed, cuz—paying off the hook in broad daylight." Fly was digging their style—name-brand clothes, jewels, cars. "Those fools definitely got taste."

"To hell with the clothes and jewelry, fam," Ruffneck

stated with conviction. "It's about these fools bowing down to royalty. And we are royalty."

"Fuck that," Lil Shorty said, maybe a little too loudly. "I don't know why we gotta wait. We should be making noise, letting fools know we coming."

"Man," Menace started, "you think you could possibly say that shit a little louder? You're a little dummy…you do know that, right?"

"Whatever, Frankenstein," Lil Shorty spit. He walked to the other end of the bleachers.

"Frankenstein these nuts, punk," Menace shot back.

Poison sat quietly watching the game from behind Chanel sunglasses. She never said much, but danger lived inside her five-five frame. She was a mysterious, light-skinned dime with long flowing braids that fell around her shoulders. Poison's body was banging. Her titties were well-proportioned and complementary of her small frame. The magnificent curve of her backside was wrapped in loose-fitting jeans. MAC lip gloss captured the thickness of her lips as lady Timberlands completed the look. But her most sinister feature was the .380 that silently rested in the small of her back.

She'd caught Ruffneck's attention after putting out the eye of a wino in front of the House of Liquor with a Popsicle stick. The nigga had slapped her ass. The stick had been the only thing she could find on the ground for defense. In a blur, the Popsicle stick was protruding from the wino's bloody eye-socket. And while the nigga was rolling on the ground, screaming and holding his bloody injury, his boy tried to creep on Poison with a steel pipe. She hadn't seen him, but Ruffneck did and beat the brakes off his ass. Poison owed Ruffneck her life. In that one moment, Ruffneck became her family. Brought together by a mutual respect for power, their arrangement went without words. Poison was sweet to look at, but Ruffneck never saw anything but her viciousness. She would make the perfect weapon. Poison could get next to the mark without gaining suspicion. And before they knew what hit 'em, her pistol was out and somebody's mother was left with the task of selecting a black dress.

Everybody in the immediate vicinity erupted with excitement. Ups had stolen the ball and run in the direction of his basket. With one defender guarding, he took off a foot inside of the free-throw line, glided gracefully past the defender's outstretched hands, and brutalized the rusty rim with a monster slam dunk. He hung from the rim and taunted the beer-belly dude.

"Game, nigga!" Ups yelled. "This is a man's game. Now get yo' fat ass off the court—next game!" he shouted at the players on the sideline.

Ruffneck sat unmoved by the action. His eyes never left Billy. He wanted that nigga's spot so badly he could taste it. Billy could keep the spotlight, though. He'd seen so-called drug czars go down for bringing attention. They either met their demise at the hands of the Feds, or set up by jealous cats looking to make a come-up.

Billy the Kid went into the other pocket, pulling out another knot of cash and called to Ups.

Ruffneck could hear the exchange between Billy and Ups:

"What dup, B?" Billy asked, smiling and shaking Ups' hand. "Nigga, you still doing yo' thing out there on the court? You got two more years 'til you go and play for the Tar Heels—Michael Jordan's country, hunh? All I ask is that you remember the cat that's feeding you, B." He shoved the money into Ups' hand. "And don't worry about that fat-stomach muthafucka over there; my soldiers gonna have a word with 'im as soon as he walk his stanky ass home later. Don't nobody disrespect you, B."

"Thank you, Billy," Ups said. He stuffed the wad of cash into the pockets of his shorts.

Lil Shorty walked back over to his crew and had a seat next to Poison. He'd caught the money exchange between Billy and Ups. "Look at that fake nigga."

"There your lil ass goes with the loud mouth again," Menace chastised. "Damn, nigga, why don't you look up *discreet* in the dictionary?"

"What, yo' bitch ass must be scared?" Lil Shorty cracked back, letting his scowl speak volumes of disapproval.

"It ain't about being scared," Ruffneck finally broke his silence, "it's about being smart. At least make it seem like you fear and respect those who hold power—at least until our time to rule swings around."

"'Neck's right," Fly interrupted, "keep y'all voices down. The last thing we need is a war."

"We ain't exactly in a position to match muscle with Billy's Ghetto Mob," Ruffneck expressed.

Poison never broke silence. She just sat there, popping her gum.

"I got an idea," Lil Shorty said. "Since she never says shit anyway, ask Poison what she thinks about them niggas over there."

Poison looked Lil Shorty off like he wasn't shit and never stopped popping her gum.

"That's what yo' punk ass get," Menace said.

"I'll tell you one thing: Ups better not let his coach catch 'im taking cheese from Billy," Fly enlightened.

"I'm hip. All it takes is one phone call to North Carolina to report his stupid ass. That fool's scholarship would get snatched," Menace explained as he scratched his chin.

"Y'all tripping, because that little nigga better be worried about his old man finding out he's taking money from Billy," Ruffneck explained. "Detective Webb don't play when it comes to his son."

Another game broke out with Ups throwing down an alley-oop right out the gate.

"Menace," Ruffneck called out.

"What dup, mi nig?"

Ruffneck waited a minute as if weighing out the words.

"That car connect—that old head named Greasy. I thought he was on the level."

"He is," Menace assured. "I sent a lot of bidness to that funky-ass junkyard—why, what happened?"

"I took the jack to 'im and the old buster had his oily-ass henchmen stick heat in my grill."

"Damn, dog, he ain't never did that before. What'd you do?"

Danger rippled through Ruffneck's eyes.

"Nothin'. I just jumped back in the whip and dipped." Ruffneck sat studying a dice game over in the corner of the park by a dumpster. "Is he your fam?"

"Nope, G; don't really know 'im like that."

"You want him smoked?" Poison asked.

"Naw, we got other shit to do," Ruffneck answered. "Let's go."

Big Thangs Poppin'

"I don't see why we gotta be waitin' on them trick-ass old fools to get older," Lil Shorty pipped, putting his lips around a blunt. "Why can't we get rid of 'em now?" He took a drag, holding and blowing.

Ruffneck sat at the head of the table. Fly, Menace, Lil Shorty, and Poison gathered around the old rusty card table like they were the Knights of the Round Table. Usually after the Body Bag, everybody crashed at Menace's joint. It was a rundown apartment high-rise hosting Third World living conditions. The air smelled of mildew; the carpets were old and the walls were peeling dingy, battleship gray paint. But, at two hundred-fifty-bucks-a-month rent, Menace wasn't tripping. Compared to some of the roach-infested dives he'd stayed in before, to him, his apartment was ready to be unveiled on *MTV Cribs*.

Smoke filled the air, blunts were passed, forties were guzzled, and Jay-Z bumped from a brand-new stereo that sat atop a milk crate in the corner.

"Listen, Shorty," Ruffneck started, "these streets ain't no joke. Look around you. We have about—what, five soldiers? Not enough to try and take nothin' from nobody."

Menace laughed; a cloud of smoke rushed from his mouth. "Four and a half—that lil nigga ain't really a whole."

The room cranked with drug and alcohol-induced laughter.

"Fuck you, Frankenstein," Lil Shorty cut back. He blazed from his chair; anger being the ambassador of his emotions.

"Sit your little ass down," Ruffneck ordered. His voice was low, cold and deliberate.

The room grew quiet. Lil Shorty could be disrespectful when it came down to the speed of Ruffneck's plans to restructure the city's underworld hierarchy. The little cat had plans of his own and they didn't include Ruffneck being the head of a damn thing. And even though he never mumbled a word of his ambition, everybody in the room knew that Lil Shorty would ice Ruffneck in a heartbeat, if he thought he could get away with it.

Ruffneck understood all these things, but he liked the little cat anyway. A few years back, one of Lil Shorty's people had broken Ruffneck off with a favor—a life-or-death heads-up. Some fool named Easy-Down had leaked to the streets that he was looking to gun Ruffneck down. Lil Shorty's oldest cousin had sent Ruffneck a text to warn him. Two weeks later, Easy-Down's body ended up in a dumpster with his brains hanging out. So, in some weird kind of way, Ruffneck felt like he was paying off a debt by looking after Shorty's little stupid ass.

Poison silently sipped from her plastic cup of malt liquor.

Fly stood from his chair.

"If anybody got any more jokes, complaints or anything else stupid to add, speak the hell up." He waited for responses. "Nothing. Well, listen to what the fuck 'Neck has to say." He nodded to Ruffneck.

"Like I was saying: I ain't got no problem with putting one in Billy's head. But we gotta be smart. That nigga's connected to some powerful people."

"Niggas that lurk in the shadows," Fly elaborated. "Nobody exactly knows who it is he gets his shit from, but word on the street is that you don't wanna fuck with him."

"Yup," Ruffneck stepped back in, "with that kind of power, I think we all know that we can't bully our way into the front door of the game." He stood from his chair. "But the back door is wide open to be bum-rushed. Nobody will be expecting us. They won't be able to deny our fucking invitation. I have a plan, but I'll tell you all about it later."

"In the words of the immortal Tupac Shakur: 'Don't try to go to war if yo' money ain't right,'" Fly added.

Ruffneck said, "Right now, we might not be able to match muscle with Billy or none of that action, but I promise you that we will live like royalty, once it's all said and done."

"Yeah, fam, I'm with you," Menace cosigned, jumping up.

And even though his jaws were tight, Lil Shorty was on board. "Yeah, I'm with that. Twisting wigs and splitting nigga's heads to the white meat is what I've been waiting for."

Poison offered no response; she merely nodded her head and tipped her cup.

"Let's make these niggas feel it," Ruffneck said. "We gonna step on some toes. Our first stop on the train to getting bread is that fat muthafucka, Cadillac. The lame got a few lottery houses on the west side. Knocking over one or two of those would set us straight with seed money." He let the weight of his words settle in. "Cadillac might be soft, but he's definitely not stupid. Nobody has tried the old head yet because he's in bed with that nigga Bundy McGurk—"

"Bundy McGurk?" Menace repeated.

"Is there a problem, Menace?" Fly asked.

"The Bundy McGurk that smokes niggas just for looking at him sideways, Bundy McGurk?"

"What's your problem?" Fly asked again.

Lil Shorty stepped in. "That nigga scared—is his only problem."

"Bundy McGurk works for Billy."

"Nobody knows that for sure," Fly said.

"It doesn't matter," Ruffneck interrupted. "If this thing is done right, nobody will ever know shit."

"I'm with it," Fly added, picking up his plastic cup and filling it. "Soldiers, raise y'all cups to toast in the start of this new family. We ride to die."

Everybody followed, tipping their drinks.

"Remember…" Ruffneck said, tipping his cup filled with water. Ruffneck didn't drink. In his business, he couldn't afford habits. He was their leader and they depended on him. "If we roll as a family, nobody will be able to do shit with us."

Lil Shorty sat at the table. Burning, his jaws were tight and his temper made his body temperature soar past meltdown. He wanted shit his way and right-the-hell now. Waiting was for cowards and suckas who only did most of their dreaming about the good life in their sleep. It was easy for these fools to be okay with starting shit from the bottom. They weren't fucking hungry like him.

The way he saw things, the top was way better than the bottom. Knocking off Cadillac's fat ass was tight, but the real loot was waiting out in the street.

Drinks were being passed, but Lil Shorty wasn't with it. He wanted loot, and he wanted it like yesterday. At the moment, so-called ballers were out bouncing high-profile whips, rolling twenty-whatevers, had grips of cash at their disposal, and were surrounded by tramps giving up the head at the sight of a hustler's bankroll. And here he was listening to some bullshit plan that would probably leave him collecting social security before he would get a taste of the life Ruffneck was speaking about.

He was destined to stand amongst the top of the food chain; some Boss Dog shit.

The nigga Ruffneck had better watch his ass, Lil Shorty thought, smiling like he was in total agreement with the slow-to-get-big-money scheme. Yeah, he would sing, skin and grin, and dance to Ruffneck's beat, but homeboy had better watch his ass. If Ruffneck was caught slipping, Lil Shorty would be standing over his dead body with a smoking heater.

Crack Attack

With Ruffneck's big-money scheme in place, somehow, putting the mash on his fellow students for cash had lost its appeal. After all, he was regal, and royalty didn't engage in the practice of running the pockets of peasants. Shaking down cats who shared the same poverty plague as he, wasn't gonna place power inside his hand. He'd stepped up his game. From now on, no more putting in one-hundred-dollar work and getting change. It was degrading. The blueprint exposing his kingdom had been drawn; the ground-breaking ceremony in place with Cadillac, the neighborhood lottery man as the first brick of his empire.

"Listen, Timmy," Ruffneck explained as he stood in the school lavatory on the fourth floor, "as of today, y'all ain't gotta pony up the pennies for a nigga no more. I'm done."

Timmy was a nerd. He wore the typical black-framed glasses and button-down shirt that was buttoned all the way up and choking cider from his Adam's apple. The boy had a massive overbite, and feet covered by loafers.

"Ruffneck, dude, I don't mind giving you money for my protection. Unlike other extortionists—no disrespect."

Ruffneck had to smile. "None taken."

Timmy continued, "You actually keep other bullies off my ass. God only knows how much I appreciate your services. So that little bit of money I give you is well worth it. But if you quit, that dude Rebel gonna take your spot.

"And that fool is worse than Satan himself. Nobody will be safe. Just last week, Rebel was hanging out in my neighborhood. He robbed a preacher and duct-taped the old man inside his own home. Rebel forced the poor man to watch as he violated the preacher's fourteen-year-old daughter. You're leaving us in the hands of a fucking lunatic."

"I understand your problem. But, homeboy, I'm done. I got shit to do."

The door of the lavatory opened, interrupting the conversation. Timmy froze like an Alaskan freeze had ripped through his drawers; his eyes huge and guilty of backstabbing.

"Partna," Ruffneck addressed Rebel with his fist balled and tone deadly. "This shitter is out of order right now, playboy. Why don't you take your ass somewhere else and drop ya' load?"

Rebel walked by, almost ignoring Ruffneck like he was invisible. He was a light-skinned pretty nigga with short, wavy hair. Said to be half Latino with nitroglycerin for a temper; and rumors had him carrying a butterfly knife.

Rebel stepped right in front of Ruffneck, surprising and exciting him at the same time.

Timmy, wide-eyed with fear, took two steps backward.

Rebel's eyes were cold and disrespectful, defiant. Cocky. Young. Hungry and challenging.

Ruffneck, on the other hand, was cool. But his temper was explosive. He possessed the venomous reputation for...

Ruffneck backhanded the dog-shit out of Rebel and the boy fell backward to the floor. Ruffneck smoothly went underneath his Sean John shirt and pulled his pistol.

Rebel had made it to his knees when Ruffneck stuck the barrel of the Glock to the side of the nigga's head.

"Listen, bitch," Ruffneck said, speaking slowly, but menacingly, "don't ever forget who got the biggest nuts in this school." Ruffneck turned the pistol around and brought the butt of the weapon down hard across the back of Rebel's skull. The force of the blow sent Rebel back to the nasty floor.

It took a minute for Rebel to shake off the cobwebs. He picked himself off of the floor and stood to his feet. His eyes might've held contempt, but Rebel lowered his head as a sign of submission. The boy walked to the door, holding the lump on the back of his head.

"It takes a real man to know when a bigger man is swinging a bigger dick," Ruffneck said. He laughed while tucking the gun back into his waistband.

Timmy thawed enough from his frigid grip of fear to say: "See what I mean. Now that fool is gonna take that shit out on us."

Upstairs in geometry class, Ruffneck sat in his usual spot, not even fazed about Rebel stepping to him on the revenge tip. Right about now, the boy should've been somewhere getting stitched up.

With five minutes to go before the bell rang, Ruffneck was watching Ms. Alan's apple-ass shake as she erased the blackboard. His mind should've been on his exam, but nothing about shapes and angles were gonna do him any good in the real world. To him, that shit only had a place inside the bedroom. He fantasized about running up in his young geometry teacher at an angle that would produce award-winning porn. Her hips, along with the sensual intoxication of her thick lips and the sexy sway of her ass, were exotic concoctions. And they were all playing out behind Ruffneck's zipper.

He wondered if his father ever cheated on his mother. The thought seemed to come out of nowhere. But looking at Ms. Alan, Ruffneck came to the conclusion that he could never cheat on a woman like her. He would rob, steal, and kill for a woman like Ms. Alan.

"Put your pencils down," Ms. Alan sweetly announced to the class.

Ruffneck's exam was blank. He hadn't touched it. The entire hour was spent with him wondering how the teacher's body would look in lingerie and stilettos.

The bell rang. Ruffneck was usually the first student out of the door. With this being his last day in class, he couldn't go out like a sucka. Ms. Alan was digging him and he knew it. During the exam, she hadn't seemed to mind him staring openly at her ass. He could've sworn he'd seen her wink at him when she'd caught him staring.

"Can I have a word with you?" Ms. Alan asked Ruffneck.

Ruffneck had purposely lagged behind, hoping he could get a crack at her fine ass. He smiled, trying not to show his excitement like a cat without game.

"Can you close the door, please?" she asked.

Ruffneck closed the door. He turned on his heels and sheepishly grinned like his teacher had a surprise for him.

Ms. Alan was seated at her desk.

"Yes. How can I help you, My-Favorite-Teacher in the whole world?"

"Oh, I'm your favorite teacher today?" Ms. Alan asked, the corners of her lips holding back a smile. "I would like to speak with you about you not turning in assignments. You're not going to pass my class, if you continue to behave in such fashion."

Ruffneck was right next to her desk now, and he had to say that ol' girl's body was off-the-hook. This close, he could actually smell the strength of the fragrance that had been responsible in past classes for leaving his dick hard enough to poke through cement walls.

"Keeping it real, Ms. Alan, I don't see where this crap— I mean geometry—can benefit me in the real world of numbers and figures." Ruffneck drew closer. "It is *Ms. Alan*, ain't it?"

"That's *'isn't it'*—and yes, it's Ms. Alan. Let's not get off the subject. How do you figure that this class is irrelevant in the *real world?*"

"We ain't gotta really go there. I'm about to shake this school business anyway."

"Why?" she asked. Ms. Alan stood from her chair and folded her arms.

"It's just my time. For what I'm majoring in, y'all don't have any classes around here to prepare me for transition."

"Oh…" Ms. Alan raised her left eyebrow like Dwayne "The Rock" Johnson. "And what is this so-called chosen field of endeavor that this institution cannot prepare you for?"

"Ms. Alan, I hope I'm not stepping on some teacher/student rule, but since I'm no longer a student, I think you are the most sexist woman alive."

"I think your little seventeen-year-old hormones are doing the talking for you."

"I'm eighteen, thank you."

Ms. Alan turned her back to walk over to the window. But it was too late; Ruffneck had already peeped the confusion in her face by her reflection in the window. *He was in like Flynn*, he thought. If she had been offended, Ms. Alan would've reacted accordingly. But that wasn't happening here. It was his green light to press forward.

"I think you know how I feel about you," Ruffneck confessed as he cautiously walked behind her, pushing boundaries.

"I think you should go," Ms. Alan protested. She turned

on her heels, not realizing how close he was behind her. She almost fell into his arms. "Walker, get out of here."

He had her. "Do you really mean that? Do you really want me to go?"

Ms. Alan nervously eyed the door. "You don't need to quit school…"

"You won't be able to see me, hunh?"

"No"—Before she could even get that weak bullshit out, Ruffneck threw his tongue down her throat.

Ms. Alan quickly broke contact. She smoothed the wrinkles from her skirt and wrapped one arm around herself. She glanced out of the window of the classroom door, praying that nobody had seen the exchange.

She turned on Ruffneck. "Get the fuck out of my classroom before I call for security—now!"

"Here"—he picked up an envelope from her desk and scribbled down his cell number—"Call me, Ms. Alan. Well, you already know how I feel about you. Don't let this institution tell you what's age-appropriate."

"Get the fuck out, now!" she said, raising her voice.

Ruffneck's cell went off.

"Calm down," he spoke into the phone. Lines formed inside his forehead and his nostrils flared like the hood of an agitated cobra. "He did what?" Ruffneck listened for a few ticks. "Hold tight, I'll be right there."

He glanced at his teacher. This time his eyes were hellish. Ruffneck tossed the envelope on the desk, not even remembering opening the door and almost taking the stairs by the flight.

"So your son, William, just walked up in this piece and macked the television. Is that what you're tryna to tell me?" Ruffneck asked. He stood in the living room of Granny Sinclair's crib, staring at the hole inside the entertainment center where a 32-inch, flat-screen television once sat.

"As sure as I'm sitting here," Granny Sinclair explained. "I was watching *Sanford and Son* when that bitch brought his narrow ass up in here and started unplugging shit. Didn't even look back at me when he was taking it out of here, either."

Granny Sinclair was dressed in a floral-printed house duster. You couldn't tell it, but the old woman was pissed. She didn't want to rile up Ruffneck any more than he already was. William was her only son and she knew Ruffneck hated the ground he walked on. Granny Sinclair didn't want William hurt, but she wanted the television back.

She watched as Ruffneck removed the padlock and chain from the basement door and disappeared down the staircase. Menace was standing at the front door talking on the cell.

"This shit can't keep on happening," Ruffneck said as he stormed back through the door.

"Please don't hurt that boy, Walker," Granny Sinclair pleaded. She knew damn well, once Ruffneck got going, it would take the police to pull him off of her son.

"Menace, you ready?" Ruffneck asked. He'd switched into black jeans and a Carhartt sweatshirt. "Did your people track that fool?"

Menace carefully glanced at Granny Sinclair. His look was that of sympathy. He knew William only had a few minutes of pain-free oxygen left on this planet. So he simply nodded "yes" to Ruffneck.

"Ruffneck, please don't," Granny Sinclair begged. She stood from her recliner and followed Ruffneck to the door. "That damn television can be replaced, boy."

Ruffneck answered back over his shoulder, "But you can't."

Her pleading fell on deaf ears. Ruffneck and Menace bounced out the front door, both with severe plans for crippling a crackhead.

William wasn't where Menace's homeboy had said he would be—at a smoke spot ten blocks away from Granny Sinclair's.

Outside was dark and gloomy with scattered showers. It was prime condition for teaching a crackhead the painful lesson about getting his money the good old-fashioned way: by caving in the head of somebody else's family member to support a junkie's habit.

A light sprinkle began falling over both boys as they moved through the hood, shaking down spots and putting the word out about not buying a television from

William's crackhead ass. Ruffneck made it a point to tell niggas in each house to warn William that he was a dead man walking. The same threat applied to whoever did business with him.

Ruffneck was hot. The raindrops did little to cool his ass off. Drops seemed to evaporate into a wisp of smoke upon contact with his skin. Nobody disrespected his granny and lived a healthy life. If he didn't body their asses, they would sure as hell be left lying fucked up and on the borderline of death.

"Yo, 'Neck," Menace said. He wiped rainwater from his brow.

"'Sup, fam?"

"You really gonna drop the boom on this nigga?"

They were walking on a street that housed more crack spots than the Mall of America had stores.

"The old woman is all I got, guy."

"Enough said," Menace replied.

The two boys stopped and stood in front of a corner store. Menace was dressed in black Dickies, puffing on a peach-flavored Black and Mild cigar with his heater tucked in his waist. His eyes roamed to a light-complexioned cat with super-keen facial features. The guy stepped out of an older-model Lexus. Menace made eye contact with him as he passed the two of them to walk into the store. The nigga cracked a cheesy-ass grin at Menace and spoke.

It didn't get by Ruffneck. At this point, he didn't feel like addressing the shit.

"Say, let me get at you with something personal," Menace asked.

"Go to it," Ruffneck said.

"You know damn near my life story, cuz. How come you don't talk about your family?"

From the moment Menace spit out the words, he wished he could've sucked them shits back in. The grim flicker of danger that filled Ruffneck's cold, dark eyes was unmistakable. The smile he wore looked like it was endorsed by Satan.

"You sure you wanna know, fam?" he asked.

Menace choked, gulping on smoke from the cigar.

"Naw, dog, I'm straight, playboy."

Ruffneck stood stone-faced. There was no question that Menace was a complete beast with an impressive résumé of putting in work on fools. But he wasn't tough enough to have gone through the pain that Ruffneck had endured. Again, this was the perfect opportunity to tell one of his homies about his past. He just couldn't do it. Maybe there was some truth behind the shrink's diagnosis—that shit about avoidance symptoms. There could've been, but Ruffneck still was riding with holding back info from his niggas. Knowledge was power and nobody would have shit on him. So he swallowed down the thought of telling Menace about what had happened at his family home years ago.

"Let's get at my people," Ruffneck said to Menace. "Hootie should know where we can find William's punk ass."

Menace puffed on the Black and Mild. "It's yo' game, 'Neck."

A few minutes later, they walked in front of a decent colonial redbrick. Hootie opened the front door to his girlfriend's crib after three rings of the doorbell.

"What's poppin'?" Ruffneck asked his cousin. Hootie pulled Ruffneck in to that too-cool-for-a-full-embrace man-hug.

"You got it, baby boy," Hootie responded. He was wearing a red do-rag over freshly done cornrows and rocking a Polo sweat suit with crispy white Air Force Ones on his feet. "Ruffneck, I need to be asking you that question, since you only show up on my doorstep when you need guns or information."

"William, man," Ruffneck began, "you seen 'im?"

"What he do this time?" The smile disappeared on Hootie's face.

"That clown ran up in Granny's crib and got down on her for her television."

"Ruffneck, partna, I ain't in it"—Hootie threw his hands in the air like somebody had a pistol at his back.

"Man, William's your father. You mean you're telling me that you don't know where his crackhead ass is?"

Hootie nervously ran a hand over his do-rag. He knew Ruffneck was going to lay into his old man on sight. Even though he and his father weren't going to win any potato sack races at the father/son picnic anytime soon, Hootie didn't want to see his sperm-donor's face decorating the cover of some black-and-white obituary.

"Look, man, have I ever lied to you before? So you gotta believe me when I say: I don't know."

The boy wasn't lying. Ruffneck was aware of it. He knew the look that cats wore on their faces when he rolled through playing Twenty Questions. Pure terror would be in their eyes as they shook underneath his dissecting gaze.

To hell with that drama series Lie To Me, Ruffneck thought as he stared into his cousin's bloodshot eyes. And much like the television show, he didn't possess some fancy college degree to peer into a man's soul and pull out the truth. His rep for mashing liars had become legendary and niggas around him knew to just come with the truth.

"All right, cuz, I'm out," Ruffneck said as he was about to bounce.

"'Neck, lemme holla at you for a few ticks," Hootie said.

"Before we get into that, man, why don't you go and see the old lady anymore?"

The question totally caught Hootie off-guard.

"Man, Granny Sinclair don't like me. I think she looks at me and sees the failure in my father, William. She treats me like shit, Ruffneck."

"Dog, she treats me like shit, too, but that's her way. She doesn't mean anything behind it."

"You're right, man. I should go see Granny Sinclair."

Ruffneck looked out at Menace holding down the sidewalk, talking to somebody on his cell.

"Anyway, what you have to holla at me about?" Ruffneck asked.

Hootie looked back at the door and windows to make sure his nosy-ass girlfriend wasn't ear-hustling.

"Listen, man, I need yo' advice."

"Go 'head."

"That cat Billy the Kid hit me up last night to cop a load of choppers. What do you think?"

Ruffneck scratched his head.

"Why ask me? You the one wholesaling heaters. I don't care what that fool buys."

"I asked you 'cause you want the nigga's crown. I didn't wanna sell that fool no AK-47s if you were planning to take 'im to war."

"Look, dude, you can sell that punk AK-47s by the caseload—money is money. Because when I roll through on 'im, his ass can have a tank if he wants; his reign is a done-dada." He looked straight into Hootie's eyes. "You feel me, homeboy?"

"No doubt, cuz," Hootie replied.

Ruffneck gave his cousin some dap and walked out to join Menace.

Menace's sources had come through. The phone call he'd gotten a few minutes ago proved to be solid. William had traded the television for ten rocks and was smoking his lights out in a spot four blocks away from Hootie's.

Ruffneck and Menace walked up on the porch. The flimsy front door of the crackhouse splintered underneath the thick sole of Menace's right Timberland boot. Before the workers inside had a chance to shake off the shock, Menace had everybody, face against the wall and hands raised high in the air, with a big Desert Eagle 9mm at their backs.

Ruffneck saw William break up the staircase and gave chase. He caught the nigga up in the first bedroom off the stairs, trying to escape out of a window. The smoke head had one foot out when Ruffneck ran behind him.

"Where the fuck you going, bitch-ass nigga?" Ruffneck yelled, grabbing at the foot that hadn't quite cleared the window.

"Please, nephew, don't hurt me!" William screamed, trying desperately to shake Ruffneck off.

"Coward, you wanna bully a woman. Come at a man with that noise."

Ruffneck tried to pull William back into the house with all his might, but William was strong for a crackhead. He held on to the outside frame of the window like it was the last crack rock on the planet. William's body was halfway out and flailing around, hollering for the police to rescue him. But Ruffneck was determined to bring the fool back into the house and beat the brakes off his rusty ass.

"Nephew, I'll make it right," William screamed. The palms of his hands slapped against the shingles of the roof as he tried frantically to hold on for traction.

"Fuck naw," Ruffneck shot back. He was straining so hard to haul William back inside that an anaconda-sized vein popped up on the left side of his neck. "It's gonna take more than the promise of making shit right to make shit right. It's gonna take blood, mutafucka."

He had hold of the crackhead's left foot, pulling— William pushing. It went on like that for a few seconds longer before one final push–pull, and William's dirty, crusty Adidas came off, with Ruffneck falling backward with the shoe and onto a piss-stained mattress. With the shoe in his hands, Ruffneck had the pleasure of listening to his uncle's blood-curdling cry as the man bounced off the roof a couple times and landed with a grotesque smack on the walkway, cutting short his screams.

Ruffneck didn't even look out of the window. He couldn't care less if the chump was dead. But one thing was painfully certain: if the nigga wasn't dead when he hit the ground, he was about to be stomped to hell. Ruffneck had made it out of the house and was slowly walking off of the porch. He looked back inside the crib to check on his boy, but Menace looked to be enjoying himself by running the pockets of everybody in front of his .50 cal.

"Didn't think I was gonna catch yo' half-slick ass," Ruffneck yelled; the smile on his face was insatiable pleasure. His eyes were small and filled with all the rage of a mighty predator toying with his prey. He slowly Jason Voorhees-stalked after William, noticing what looked like Tic Tacs sprinkled around his uncle's body. But what Ruffneck thought to be Tic Tacs were actually bloody, jagged bits of teeth that William had spit up the moment the ground had sucka-punched him in the mouth.

William had painfully made it to his stomach and was dragging his two lifeless, broken legs along the pavement, using his hands to pull his body. He had compound fractures in both legs—meaning broken bones had penetrated the skin and protruded from the sides of both calves. He left blood trails behind. As neighbors stepped to their front porches to witness the disturbance, William begged and pleaded for their help.

Ruffneck's eyes held dark deeds. He looked around the porches before him.

"This coward robbed his mother and he deserves the mashin' I'm about to put on his ass," Ruffneck explained to the neighbors as crowds started to form. "The punishment is just for this muthafucka, but if anybody calls the police for help, I will come back and you'll end up in this position." Without thinking about shit, Ruffneck powerfully kicked William in the left temple so hard that his uncle flipped over onto his back.

Menace's big ass emerged from the house, his 50. cal dangling down by his side. He was just in time to watch, as Ruffneck tried to monkey-stomp William's punk ass through the fucking concrete.

Come Up In Progress

The first week of October found Ruffneck setting up surveillance on Cadillac's lottery joints. He attentively studied the *comings* and *goings* like a NFL quarterback would dissect and go over game film, making last-minute adjustments the night before a marquee matchup on NFL Sunday. And just like a quarterback, Ruffneck needed to know the positioning of every man on the field. Cadillac was soft, a real cock-sucker, but he had cops on the payroll, trained killers with badges who hunted niggas like Ruffneck and his crew for blood sport. The fool was also in bed with Bundy McGurk. In the past, niggas who'd run afoul of McGurk always ended up in funeral homes.

But Ruffneck wasn't sweating that shit. Their identities would be concealed when they broke it off in the fat man's ass. So the lick had to go down sweet. They couldn't afford casualties. If one of them was made, the shit would get thick. Ruffneck and his soldiers were too few for a large-scale battle. Cadillac's fat ass had that kind of cheese to have mothers emotionally tripping while trying to identify charred remains. So Ruffneck took his time setting the lick.

He sat in a vintage GMC Suburban surrounded by 2 a.m. darkness, five houses up the block from one of Cadillac's lottery joints. For some strange reason, the theme from the movie *Halloween* started up inside his head, and he soon started to whistle the haunting tune.

"Yo, 'Neck, man," Menace said from behind the wheel, peering through binoculars. "'Sup with the spooky shit, guy?"

"Halloween, fam," Ruffneck replied.

"I'm up on *Halloween*; Michael Myers was—"

"Not talkin 'bout the movie. Halloween night is when we roll on Cadillac's lame ass."

"Why Halloween?"

"It's perfect. Peep: shorties'll be out rocking masks, collecting candy, and trick-or-treatin'."

"I'm not following."

"The only time of the year when niggas can throw masks on and not attract attention. Nobody will know we're coming. When we kick that fat bastard in the nuts, all the men in his family gonna go limp, cuz."

"I got you, guy." Menace peered through the glasses again. There was activity at the house. Cadillac, surrounded by three big bruisers, escorted him from the porch to a brand-new Cadillac truck parked in the driveway.

Menace passed the glasses to Ruffneck. "Check this shit out, 'Neck."

Ruffneck didn't miss the briefcase one of the bruisers lugged as he spied. Cadillac was known to carry large sums of money inside black briefcases.

"Trick-o-treat, muthafucka," Ruffneck said sinisterly, whistling the *Halloween* theme again. He gazed as the truck backed out and sped away with taillights glowing.

"This dancer named Berry-Flavor said the workers out of this spot be up in Simply Naked throwing stacks around like they major-getters," Menace informed. He took out his smartphone and started checking his messages on Facebook.

"That's what fake cats do. Always wanna be the loudest niggas in the room. Just tell Berry-Flavor and the rest of them broads up at Simply's to keep stroking their egos. Get as much info outta of them clowns as possible. We need to know how many, and where they're posted inside that crib."

"Ruffneck, man, you sure this hit gonna be easy?"

Ruffneck removed the glasses and examined his partner's eyes. The traces of doubt were highly visible. Where there was solid loyalty, trust, and faith without conditions, fear was clear as a naked bum taking a piss on the sidewalk of a busy street in broad daylight. Ruffneck knew the kind of shit he was asking of his crew. He was aware that there was a possibility the shit could go sideways and lives could be lost. But kingdoms were erected from risks and gambles.

"Listen, Menace, we can do this. I wouldn't ask you to

kill if I couldn't dispose. Yeah, I'ma square it with you, cuz: getting at this clown's loot is dangerous, but we can do this. We go in that fool's place looking out for each other. We'll be tight, guy. Besides, we're royalty, baby."

Menace continued to thumb away on his smartphone.

"This shit is our seed money, baby. It's the key to the front door of the game. For all the old heads, it's over. It's a new day, brah. Believe dat! When cats like us roll through, we gonna be shutting shit down." Ruffneck gestured toward the windshield with the glasses. "Ain't no blimp floating above our heads with 'the world is ours' *Scarface* shit running across the screen, announcing our come-up. If we want it, we gotta go get it!"

"Let's go get it, homie."

The two shared some dap.

"What 'bout that lil fool Shorty, though?" Menace asked. "That lil nigga needs a leash. You think you got that clown under control, man?"

"Don't worry about youngin'. He'll be tight."

"All right," Menace said. He wasn't totally convinced. The kid was a fucking ticking time bomb looking for someplace to explode.

Ruffneck's cell went off. A Young Jeezy ringtone let him know that Fly was trying to grab some ear time.

"Go to it," Ruffneck answered. What he received was static mixed in with women screaming, and what sounded like an AK-47 going off in the background. The sound was very discernable. It was a weapon that had become a violent-staple in the drug war- struggle for "urban landscape" supremacy.

"Ruffneck"—Fly's voice came hard but choppy—"niggas rush the crib with…" The cell phone transmission fell, and so did the cemetery-like silence inside the car.

Ruffneck and Menace stared at each other. What little transmission that got across was loud enough for Menace to get the picture. Their nigga was in trouble.

"Stab out, dog!" Ruffneck ordered.

No questions needed asking, Menace cut the wheel hard to the right…and *gunned it.*

The streets were bare; naked of traffic and pedestrians. Menace kept his foot on the gas of a stolen '82 Cadillac Eldorado hooptie—they'd grabbed the hot car when gathering the troops. And even though the fate of one of their own hung in the balance, Ruffneck had Menace stick to the side streets. The main streets would surely bring the attention of five-o to four-deep pushing a stolen El-dog rag. Besides, they were strapped, almost all packing automatic weapons: an AK-47 rested on Lil Shorty's anxious lap in the backseat; Poison next to him, dark shades, gripping a Glock .40 cal; an AR-15 lay on the floorboard underneath Menace's huge legs.

Try as he might, Ruffneck was having a real difficult time trying to keep it together. Fly was his dog and he couldn't picture building his empire without him. But a leader had to stay composed at all times. He knew his troops fed off his energy. So he concentrated his nervousness by intensely squeezing the rubber grip he held belonging to a pistol-grip pump.

The cell had dropped the call, leaving them without a clue as to where the hell Fly was posted. It didn't matter, though. Fly almost-always rested his head over his baby-momma spot. They were six blocks away from her crib when they heard what sounded like a full-scale battle being waged. They piled out of the car two blocks away, ready for war.

Ruffneck headed his soldiers, thinking: bodies would be left leaking, and lifeless eyes would stare up at the sky as if begging God to rewind time. He never asked God for anything and wasn't about to start now. The fact that bullets were still being exchanged let him know there was a chance Fly might still be alive.

This was the point of no return; each one of his crew had been given specific instruction to lay down anything with a weapon. This shit was personal. A message had to be sent. Nobody was about to stop the getback. And if the police got in the way, they could get it, too. A block away, the gunfire lit up the darkness looking like Fourth of July Freedom Festival fireworks popping off on the riverfront of downtown Detroit.

Baby-momma was two houses off of the corner. Ruffneck instructed Menace and Lil Shorty to work their way around the action to the back of the shooters. He and

Poison took the opposite route, staying low, sticking to the shadows until they had the best view in the house. Four pricks dressed in ski-masks, all working from the street with AK-47s, reducing Fly's baby-momma's crib to Swiss cheese. Jagged glass projectiles from house windows and car glass sailed through the early morning air; the streetlights giving them the look of wet diamonds falling to the ground. The front of the house was splintered. Smoking holes completely covered the face.

From the look of the bullet-riddled crib, nobody inside could've possibly survived the barrage.

A simple text message let Ruffneck know that Menace and Lil Shorty had moved into position, awaiting the order to start blazing their way into relevancy. The shit was all about respect, reestablishing a pecking order. At present, Ruffneck and his goons were the lowly mutts, begging for scraps to fall their way from the table of those who were holding *Big Dog* status.

The gunmen looked to be having a blast. Nothing was left of the house, but yet they still pumped in round after round. Spent shell casings were ejected, all in unison, hitting the ground with a metallic *clink*, dancing, reflecting the awesome flames belching from Russian-made assault rifles.

Ruffneck's rage grew hotter than the heat radiating from the weapons. Then just like he predicted: they reloaded. The two on the left side of the street dropped magazines to reload. It was the perfect opportunity, Ruffneck signaled his crew into action. Menace and Lil

Shorty sprang from the shadows, blazing, totally shocking the gunmen. Menace sliced through the first creep on the far end like a chainsaw through skin with his AR-15. And before the victim could drop to the ground, his partner joined him, courtesy of Lil Shorty's AK-47. The kid got a little too cocky on the trigger as he broke ranks, running up to the wounded man, and wildly spraying him bloody. Lil Shorty was so into his work, he didn't see one of the goons' AK-47s aimed right at his dome. But Poison did. She shoved the barrel of the Glock behind the third gunman's right ear and squeezed the trigger. The .40 cal jerked as the dark lens of her sunglasses caught the fiery reflection of the bloody explosion.

The lone gunman lost his nerve at the sight of the gory carnage that used to be his nigga. The coward dropped his heat and got in the wind. He didn't get too far. Ruffneck stepped from the shadow and pulled the trigger. The powerful blast from the pump took the man off his feet and knocked his ass backward, violently slamming him against a parked SUV.

Ruffneck walked up to his victim with the weapon hanging down by his side, stalking the wounded man. The hot lead had caught the creep in the guts, but he held on to life like a child holding on to his favorite teddy bear.

Ruffneck was about to give the dying man the business, as the flimsy door of Fly's baby-momma's crib burst open. Fly bounded out the door.

"You all right, baby boy?" Ruffneck asked, examining his dude's head. Fly had bloody cuts all across his face, probably from flying glass, but he looked to be tight.

His eyes rested on the last gunman, who had finally stood to his feet and was slowly limping away. Lil Shorty took aim…

"That's not your body, youngsta," Ruffneck yelled at Shorty. "Put it down, fam, that's Fly's work."

Poison handed Fly the stinger. The wounded man was up on his feet. Fly circled him, ending in front and stopping the man in his tracks. Before he raised the heat, Fly reached out and removed the mask. He knew who the bitch was right off: a nigga named Go-Hard. They'd bumped heads in a nightclub about a month ago, ending with Fly whupping Go-Hard's ass.

Go-Hard stood there like a real G, not even flinching when Fly raised the gat to his head. He was holding pressure to his stomach. Blood seeped between his fingers.

Go-Hard laughed; long, bloody strands of saliva hanging from his mouth.

"I'm 'posed to be scared?" he asked in taunting fashion, smirking. "Nigga, take that"—he took a deep breath—"lying bitch on the *Maury* show…and all you gonna hear is: you are not the—"

Fly smoked Go-Hard before he could finish Maury's world-famous line of elation or embarrassment. The body dropped like cement hitting cement.

The glass-shattering shriek came from the porch of

the baby's-mama. She stood there with her hands up to her face screaming like the baby had been hurt. Brenda was her name. She was fair-skinned with long, wavy hair. The broad was gorgeous and filled out in all the right places. The chick was crying so tough over the body, Ruffneck couldn't do anything but shake his head. He already knew what time it was. And even when Brenda's mama walked out on the porch with the baby in her arms, perfectly fine, Fly's baby-mama still wailed like somebody important had passed away.

Police sirens whined in the distance. They had to get in the wind, and fast.

"Let's bounce," Ruffneck ordered. He looked at Fly like his homeboy was stupid. He didn't know when the boy was gonna wake up. Brenda was a hoe. And everybody knew it.

Menace had to pull Fly by the arm. He just stood over the victim, the barrel of the pistol still smoking, with a glazed-over look of hurt and pain in his eyes. He looked from Go-Hard's dead body to the uncontrollably sobbing Brenda like he was watching a damn tennis match. One last look and Fly took off in the direction of the others. They made it back to the hooptie and burned rubber, escaping into the darkness.

As Menace gunned the car down side streets, Ruffneck mentally toasted his arrival into the game. The bodies they'd left behind would serve as the first shovelful of dirt at the ground-breaking ceremony in building his empire. Most kingdoms were erected one brick at a time, but Ruffneck's would be established on the bullet-riddled corpses of the competition.

"Y'all know Fly smoked the baby-daddy, right?" said Lil Shorty as he popped the top on a forty-ounce. "You see that shit, mi nigga. It was like that hotel scene in *Scarface* after they sawed ol' boy into pieces with the chainsaw. But once Tony got away, he chased one of the jackers into the street, circled 'im until he was in position, blowing his shit all across his shoes. That's how Fly looked tonight. That shit was beautiful."

"That's enough, youngsta," Ruffneck warned, sitting in his favorite chair in front of the TV. "That's Fly's business. Sit your ass down somewhere."

"Shorty," Menace chimed in, shaking his head. "You need some ack-right."

Menace lit a Cherry Blend cigar. Granny Sinclair had laid the law down, making it clear that her house was a marijuana-free zone. Menace wanted to blaze to calm his nerves, but thought better of it ever since Granny Sinclair had threatened to put a *hot one* in his big ass for disrespecting her crib. So he opted for the cigar.

They were holed up in Ruffneck's room. Early morning news was playing on the television. The gory scene of destruction Ruffneck and his goons had left behind was now playing out in the form of a *Fast-Action* news break on every local channel.

He didn't let it show, but the power Ruffneck felt coursing through his veins was like nitroglycerin. The way he'd rushed Go-Hard and his dogs to the dirt was brilliant; a born military mind. He didn't give a fuck about it either. Pulling triggers on fools was the ghetto inside his DNA. His old man had to have been a general who ruled his own empire. To rule, one had to be able to acknowledge the fact that he could be *got* at any given moment. Ruffneck was okay with it. Death couldn't shake him; it was life without loot that horrified him the most. The kind of empire he had in mind was sure to raise the death toll every time a fucking wing was constructed.

"Look at that shit," Lil Shorty yelled, pointing at the news broadcast. His adrenaline had him bugging. "We made the news, mi nigga! We gonna be front-page action tomorrow! Our trigger-game put them clowns on their backs! We gotta let these fools know we comin' for their crowns!" Lil Shorty sipped from the bottle. "I was a nigga-Rambo tonight, mi nigga. You see me body that fool. My trigger-game is a straight beast. I could've taken all those fools out by my-damn-self."

"Youngsta, don't make me tell you again," Ruffneck calmly repeated himself.

Menace puffed on the cigar. His hatred for the little punk was thick as the sweet, grayish smoke bellowing from his mouth.

Menace said, "You almost got your lil ass smoked running up on Go-Hard's crew like that."

Lil Shorty shook off the comment. He took another

swallow of beer, then he said, "Aw, com'on, y'all know that nigga Go-Hard is the baby-daddy"—he laughed into the top of the beer bottle—"Whoops, my bad, I mean *was* the baby-daddy." He was damn near on the floor with laughter.

"Lil Shorty, your ass gonna get hemmed up and shit," Menace butted in. He flicked his ash into the cap of Lil Shorty's forty as he sat on an old couch Ruffneck had in his bedroom. "Keep poppin' that crap about Fly, and homeboy gonna split your shit to the white meat."

Lil Shorty took a swig from the bottle.

"Fly better be worried 'bout paying child support on a baby who ain't gush up from his nuts." He belched, looking in Ruffneck's direction. *"Boss,"* he said sarcastically. "Why you send a bitch and a whipped nigga to get rid of the heaters?"

"That *bitch* saved your ass, lil nigga," Menace jumped in. "And don't let Poison hear you call her a bitch. You know what happened to the nigga Easy-Down, don't you?"

"I ain't the nigga Easy-Down."

Menace said, "You need to learn some damn respect."

"You gonna teach me *some*, Frankenstein?" Lil Shorty whipped out a blade so fast his last name could've been Copperfield.

Menace stood from the couch, towering and laughing over Lil Shorty flexing the blade.

"You get one stick, lil bitch, and then your peeps gonna cry over the body at your funeral."

Ruffneck finally removed his eyes from the television.

They were cold and reprimanding. He simply nodded his head at Menace to take a seat. Once Menace returned to the couch, Ruffneck suddenly rose from his seat and cold-cocked the shit out of Lil Shorty. The blade went one way, the bottle fell to the carpet, and Lil Shorty stumbled into the weight bench. To keep from meeting the same fate as his forty-ounce, Lil Shorty desperately snagged the straight bar resting on its perch, supporting two enormous forty-five-pound plates of equal distribution. But his falling body-mass was too much to support, tipping and dragging the bar from the perch on his way to the floor. The weights, along with the bar, went along for the ride; the forty-five-pound plates *clanking* together as they came to rest. The little cat was buried under a ton of workout equipment.

"What the fuck is y'all doing in my damn basement, you sumbitches?!" Granny Sinclair yelled from somewhere upstairs.

"Y'all better stop tripping down here. Granny ain't no joke." Menace busted his gut laughing. But the truth be told, none of them wanted the old lady to come downstairs. Her flavor could be vicious, especially if she came down with that damn Louisville Slugger and started trying to batter up fools.

Lil Shorty had been auditioning for an ass whupping for quite some time. And now the little rat lay twisted underneath a home gym. The shit was extremely funny with Menace eating it up. Lil Shorty wasn't moving.

"That's what your dumb ass gets." Menace got to his feet. "Told your stupid ass you needed some ack-right. Aye, 'Neck, you ready for a laugh? You know this lil fool calls himself the 'Bambino of Terror' in the hood now?"

"I heard it," Ruffneck said nonchalantly as he calmly sat back down in front of the news. The white news reporter had long, black hair blowing into her face as the wind picked up. She was interviewing an elderly man with a plumped, Easter egg-sized bald-spot, surrounded by a tropical rain forest of kinky salt-and-pepper hair. The camera zoomed in for a much tighter shot.

"We're live from the 1500 block of Mandelin, from the city's West Side. The site where a savage shooting has taken place, leaving four dead…and an entire neighborhood shaken."

The reporter turned to the older man and asked him about the neighborhood before the shootings.

"This neighborhood used to be safe until the gangsters moved in," Receding Hairline spoke into the microphone in a very low and distinguished voice. *"Now it's nothing but a maze of crackhouses, abandoned properties"*— he looked around the street, then pointed at the taped-off crime scene—*"and now this."* The senior slowly shook his head like this latest act of violence was unspeakable, adding the headstone to a once-prominent, middle-class neighborhood, now dead and buried under a scourge of gangs, violence, drugs, murder, and a bad economy.

Brenda was holding the baby in the shot. Homegirl was still boo-hooing. Her mother and family stood off to the side, all behind the yellow crime scene tape. The scene was textbook: bright lights from sirens and news cameras; detectives working the crowd of rubberneckers, trying to establish leads.

"Look at this bitch," Ruffneck whispered as the camera zoomed in on Fly's baby-momma and the people nearest her. The broad still was cutting loose with tears. To Ruffneck, Brenda looked like she wanted to jump in front of the camera and start diming on niggas. But she knew better. The consequences were stretched out in front of her in the form of four covered bodies. *Snitches gets Stitches* was more than an expression in the hood. Cats really got twisted for turning informant.

Menace was still tripping on Lil Shorty's tag. "Bambino? The lil nigga probably can't spell 'Bambino.' And he went there in Italian, too."

"Bambino is Italian for infant," Ruffneck explained, not taking his eyes from the television.

"Ruffneck, this lil fool ain't moving."

"He's tough. After all, Bambino was talking that tough shit, right?" Ruffneck stood from his chair. The beer had completely drained from the bottle and settled into the light-colored carpeting in the shape of a camel.

Lil Shorty wasn't moving; hadn't said a word since Ruffneck had pieced 'im up a few short ticks ago.

"Menace, help me pick this bench up off 'im."

Menace hopped off of the couch.

"'Neck, I got this idea, when things really get pumping

for us. What do you think of a brotha owning a hip-hop clothing boutique, man?"

Ruffneck grabbed one end of the straight bar.

"I think that's cool. Go for it. You've wanted a business for a while. I think it's cool. Hook a nigga up with a discount."

Menace laughed.

Lil Shorty still didn't move.

"You sure this lil fool ain't dead?" Menace asked, showing a little concern, grabbing the opposite end of the bar.

Together they hoisted the bar and straightened the bench back vertical. The straight bar was set back on its perch; the plates loudly *clanking* together.

"Naw, Menace, this fool all right. Look, he's still breathing."

Menace stood erect, rubbing his hands together.

Ruffneck stood over Lil Shorty's motionless body.

"Hey, youngsta"—he slapped him softly—"you in there?"

Menace watched with his heart inside his shoes. He really couldn't stomach the punk, but kept his fingers crossed that Ruffneck hadn't bagged the little busta.

"Hunh...w-w-h-a-a-t...h-h-happened?" Lil Shorty answered groggily, stirring a bit.

Menace leaned in and hit Lil Shorty with his best Chris Tucker impersonation: "You got knocked the fuck out is what happened."

They helped Lil Shorty to the couch. His bottom lip was split and he rocked a huge Fred Flintstone-sized knot on the back of the noggin.

"Bet you keep your mouth closed the next time," Menace suggested.

Ruffneck disappeared up the basement stairs. The side door opened. Fly and Poison made their way down into Ruffneck's bedroom.

"Dup, Fly?" Menace greeted, dapping his dog. "You all right, playboy?"

"Yeah, I'm tight. Good thing y'all got there when you did. Cats had me penned."

"No doubt, fam, we always got your back." Menace pulled Fly in for the brah-man hug. "Remember: we scrap for ours," he whispered into Fly's ear.

Poison walked through quietly, still rocking her Chanel designer shades, braids pulled back into a ponytail and wearing a black Dickies outfit. She plopped down in front of the television.

Lil Shorty was still holding his mouth when Ruffneck reappeared, holding a rag in an ice bag.

"Here, put this on your mouth to keep down the swelling, youngsta."

Fly pointed, asking, "What happened to him?"

Menace smirked venomously. "Too much *him*, not enough *us*."

Fly simply shook his head. This wasn't the first time Ruffneck had beaten the brakes off the little fool for bumping his gums.

"Y'all take care of that?" Ruffneck asked.

"Done dizzy, baby," Fly answered, still looking a little

shaken up. "They at the bottom of the river. What's the next move, man? I mean: do we lay low for a few ticks or step on Cadillac?"

Menace took a seat next to Lil Shorty.

"They make a pickup from that house around seven in the evening. Next month is Halloween, and we gonna get at him then," Ruffneck explained.

"What's with Halloween, dog?" Fly asked.

Ruffneck looked at Menace, as if to give him permission to answer.

Menace stood. "Halloween is the perfect time, homie. That's the only time when a nigga can rock a mask and won't get sweated by five-o, fam."

"We go in, get the lick, and get the fuck back out," Ruffneck instructed, "No cowboy shit up in that piece." All eyes rested on Lil Shorty. He sat there licking his wounds, his temper on boil. He didn't like being fronted on by anybody.

"I see no problem with it," Poison commented.

"Menace, them dancers holla back at you yet with that info on how many workers in the crib, and where the guards are posted?" Ruffneck wanted to know.

"I called Berry-Flavor a few minutes ago. She didn't answer and I left her a message. I'll have it for you before sunrise."

Fly's cell started vibrating, almost sounding like a swarm of angry bees. His grill twisted when he peeked at the caller ID.

Ruffneck automatically knew his boy's head wasn't in the game. That bitch had his nigga's nose open, wide. Ruffneck needed his troops to be on the same page. If one was caught slippin', the whole damn thing could start smelling—quickly. Ruffneck was responsible for his people. Five were going into Cadillac's joint and five were expected to come out.

From here on out, Ruffneck would monitor Fly's state of mind. If he couldn't get his shit together, the lick would have to be postponed. Fly's bitch was seriously eating into Ruffneck's pockets now. She was seriously pissing on the first leg of his plans to build the kind of empire that would warrant the attention of the ghetto *Guinness Book of World Records* for the largest drug cartel in the world.

"Listen—" Ruffneck was about to start when his cell went off. The number wasn't familiar so he let voicemail handle it. "Everybody straight on what we 'sposed to do next week?"

"Yeah, we up on it." Menace was the first to respond. "And I'ma make sure I get at Berry-Flavor first thing and get back with you on that info."

"Fly, you still on for our method of transportation?" Ruffneck asked. His cell was buzzing inside his hand. Whoever it was had left him a message. Cats only left messages on his phone if it was extremely urgent.

"In keeping with the Halloween theme, it's only right that we represent, homie. I'll hit this crackhead alley mechanic off with a few of them thangs in exchange for an old church bus he tagged a couple weeks ago.

"I have this idea that we can dress up like priests and nuns for the occasion—masks, outfits—the whole sha-bang. Cadillac's corndog-munching ass won't know what hit 'im."

Menace thought it was funny.

"Fly, you going to hell wearing a gasoline rubber, nigga," Menace joked.

"Ya mama, nigga," Fly shot back.

Ruffneck was still examining the strange number on his cell. "Bring it in."

His crew formed a loose circle around him like they were in a huddle before the next play on a football field. Lil Shorty was slow about joining in. He was still salty at the humiliation served. Regardless of the volume of venom coursing through his cold, black heart, he kept the ice on his mouth and his comments to himself.

"All right, it's set then," Ruffneck said. "Halloween, we take our first steps to claim what's ours. It's our time."

Her Thug Of Choice

Ruffneck's curiosity was at a fever pitch. The phone call he'd gotten a few moments ago was seriously unexpected, but one tainted by eventuality. He was headed west on the I-96 freeway. His destination: the suburbs.

Ruffneck kept his cool. He wasn't even sweating the anticipation of a face-to-face with the caller. He'd had her ass by the first charming sentence that had dripped from his mouth, flavored with the mystery only a true thug nigga could deliver. Thugs ruled the game and always hustled the dames. Only lames popped off about not landing the good girl. There was definitely no love lost in the age-old battle for thug-supremacy over the lame-ass office, suit-and-tie wearing squares for that most coveted prized-piece of ass. It was all about the thug. Ruffneck had been schooled by the best that money could buy when it came down to spitting game at a woman. Only a lame could get his jimmy slobbed down by Lover Lips, who was one of the best gamers on planet-whore, and not learn a thing or two about manipulation.

Ruffneck was gripping a clean old-school Buick Regal. He'd borrowed the whip from his cousin, Hootie. The Regal was hot. Hootie had thrown down big loot for a tagged whip and dressed it up in high-priced aftermarket parts.

The origins of the strange phone call had ties out in Farmington Hills.

It was still dark out. The morning hadn't advanced but a few hours, since Ruffneck and crew had shown Go-Hard and his boys that it was immensely hard to breathe when lungs were left filled with blood and slugs. Go-Hard and his goons would be the first ground-under victims—but definitely not the last—on Ruffneck's blue-print in building his ice-palace from platinum riches. Homicides weren't a thing for him. The dark art had come early in his life—while barely able to pee straight— Ruffneck had made his first kill. He'd given one of the shooters who'd snuffed out his family a point-blank-range, lead makeover. But the short-lived victory was nothing compared to what those masked shooters had taken from him. Ruffneck wished that he'd laid the murder game down on them all, and left them lying where the bastards had left his mother and father. The feeling in his gut was one of reckoning. The shit they'd done to his family was far from over. If it took the last ounce of oxygen he had inside his body, street-justice would be served on the cat that'd green-lit his parents' demise.

Now that Ruffneck had gotten a little older, he couldn't

understand why his father didn't have more security inside the crib. His old man had to have been some kind of warrior for them to have gotten at him in such fashion. The old dude had been caught slipping, one thing Ruffneck vowed he'd never do. And that's why Poison was at his back, driving behind him in a passable bucket of a late-model Ford Taurus. There was nobody he'd rather have watching his back than his girl. She was cold, calculating, and lived on a very short leash of violence and mayhem.

Ruffneck peered into his rearview, catching glimpses of his braking taillights reflecting in Poison's Chanel lenses. Even though the call had been legitimate, there wasn't much room in Ruffneck's heart for trust. Poison was there simply for backup. His thinking was critical, all about survival inside a game dominated by sharks that played and preyed on guppies. The normal-world rulebook had been burned when it came to the streets. When they wanted your head, sometimes the messenger of death was wrapped up in the sweet and seductive package of the deliciously built light-skinned lady inside Ruffneck's rearview mirror. The way Poison was skilled with the trigger, she was the perfect bogeyman for the hood. But even she wasn't scary enough to frighten the police force of the city that they were now carefully riding through.

The city of Farmington Hills played by a no-nonsense set of rules of its own. The police were iron-fisted and did whatever they had to do to keep the peace. Their streets were a completely different beast at night, one with the munchies for feeding on young, black motorists. Five-o especially feasted on young, black knuckleheads mashing out in their district in whips with expired plates and suspended licenses. And even though the plates on Hootie's ride were legit, Ruffneck was bouncing with a dirty license. So he stayed low and in the shadows by rolling the speed limit on back roads.

Ruffneck found himself on a long stretch of dark road that seemed to supply streetlight every mile or two. The headlights of the Taurus beamed brightly inside his rear-view mirror. Poison tried not to play Ruffneck's bumper so snugly. She didn't want to give the impression that the two cars could be linked. The backseat of her hooptie held a small cache of firearms, carrying enough charges to land her in jail until people were supplied ice water in hell.

Ruffneck couldn't afford to see one of his get popped on a humble. He'd come too far to see his game shitted out in the toilet and flushed down the drain of "what could've been." The plan that he had for restructuring Detroit's brutal underworld would be epic. Ruffneck's hood exorcism would make those kingpin-governmental bodies holding power shake, cry, curse, and spew up money-green until, eventually, the streets would yield those forces and power over to him. He would go down in history as the only single Don-mega-Messiah to unite Detroit and her surrounding cities under the youngest regime to ever have done it. Cadillac's fat ass didn't know it, but his generous contribution was about to fund Ruffneck's military campaign war-chest with the means to bring about the apocalypse to competitors. Rising from the ashes would be a new world order; a new breed of shot callers that would lock up the game tighter than a head cold.

Ruffneck signaled left; two streets up was a condominium community. He sinisterly laughed as he thought about all those swaggered-out niggas like Billy the Kid and his Ghetto Mob, and those others that popped off at the lip about their reps and how they were untouchable. Well, he was about to put his hands all over 'em.

Ruffneck turned into the well-lit property with Poison shadowing his every move. He activated the dome light and slowly rolled while reaching over to the passenger seat and retrieving the envelope of an old cell phone bill that he'd scribbled the caller's address on. The shit was difficult in the dark. Every street he rolled up looked damn-near the same. All the units were identical—same tired-ass white paint, no distinguishing flavor, and addresses prominently featured two inches above every doorbell.

It was a good thing he'd had something to write with laying near him, because she'd quickly prattled out her address and immediately hung the phone up afterward. Anything beyond that would've been his ass, because she hadn't issued a return number. The game had been on from there. She wasn't trying to make it easy for him. To

Ruffneck, it almost appeared like she didn't want to be found. And even though the call had been short, Ruffneck could hear indecisiveness in her voice. She'd also blocked her number on the caller ID. The lady was leaving their encounter up to fate.

The sweat on his hands let him know his nervousness recognized that she was beyond the stratosphere of all the little rats he might've thrown cheese at and popped in the past. It didn't put her out of his league, though. Ruffneck's age might've left him unable to legally pop bottles in the clubs, but he was old enough to understand two things about women: the first one being that a freak was the reflection staring back at every woman from her vanity mirror, and two—her freaky ass worshipped the orgasmic-rush the element of danger produced. This was his playground. The thug nigga was regarded as Mister-Long-and-Strong, and harbored no problems with scratching the itch of those women who yearned to be fucked down by danger wearing Timberland boots.

The last condominium on the corner matched up with the address on the envelope.

On the left, underneath two gigantic pine trees, Ruffneck whipped the Regal into the parking lot for visitors. The headlights of the Taurus swept over his body as he stepped from the Buick. He glanced around, examining the darkness for cats looking to catch him slipping. Ruffneck knew the caller wasn't cut like that. It didn't matter to him. His imperial endeavors would revolutionize the hustle and he couldn't afford to let his guard down.

The window of the Taurus rolled down and pulled up right alongside Ruffneck like he was valet.

Poison asked, "You straight?"

"Baby girl"—he reexamined his surroundings again— "I'm tight. You can bounce. But do me a favor, though. Be careful heading back to the city. Stick to the back roads. You gotta be there when we go to the fat man's pockets next week."

Poison smiled.

It would've meant the ass of anybody else who caught the ghoulishly sexy smirk Poison offered him. Ruffneck had witnessed the girl go to the head of a few dudes while wearing that fatal smile. It was her trademark of terror. She was harder than any other nigga on his team. He was proud of his selection. He watched Poison reach to the floor of the backseat and retrieve a .40-caliber Sig Sauer. She gently pulled back the slide, readying the weapon. To cover up the exchange, Ruffneck leaned into the window and removed the gat from her hands. The Sig was stored in his waistband underneath his pullover with one motion.

Ruffneck was halfway up the walkway to the condo when he turned to watch Poison slow-roll from the visitor's parking lot and creep off down the dark streets. Every now and then, her brake lights would pop on. He already knew what that was about. He just smiled. No man could have a better woman watching his back than one that showed her love by the willingness to leave it all on the field of battle for him.

More from comfort than fear, Ruffneck brushed his hand across the side where the Sig rested. He couldn't understand why Poison's fleeting taillights triggered thoughts of the kid. Lil Shorty was a hot head with the single, simple ambition of getting himself bodied before his eighteenth birthday. The little muthafucka had already dubbed himself the Bambino of Terror. The shit was pretty funny to Ruffneck. He knew imitation was the highest form of flattery, and the little chump was trying to walk inside a pair of shoes that was two sizes too big for him.

"Bambino of Terror." Ruffneck laughed as he stepped to the door.

Ruffneck had even gotten reports that the little nigga had spray-painted the tag all over the walls of the ghetto in red. That kind of ambition would only set the stage in a future challenge for the crown. Cutting off the head of mutiny would be the logical solution for a young nigga with his chest poked out. The only thing stopping the mash was Ruffneck being cool with Lil Shorty's peeps. That alone was the only reason the lil nigga still had life inside his body. Word on the street had Lil Shorty going behind Ruffneck's back and chin-checking every little nigga in the hood. He was trying to build a rep for himself outside the crew. Demanding that the baby gangstas pay him protection to sell their licks on the corners without having him roll through and punch tickets for delinquent payment. If it's one thing that pissed-off Ruffneck more than a thief, it was somebody jonesing to take his kindness for weakness. Lil Shorty was pushing his luck. Ruffneck didn't know how much longer he could stomach the little roach before he stepped on his ass.

He pressed the doorbell and stood facing the street. The truth behind Farmington Hills being one of the safest cities in America rested solely in the strength of its police force, using everything within its power to keep the riffraff out of the city. Ruffneck recognized the achievement as total bullshit, a political sleeping pill that was supposed to issue the citizens a piece of mind, which promoted a good night's sleep. The shit was a false sense of security. It left their communities vulnerable to the grimy, nomadic predators roaming from the mean jungles of Detroit for an easy meal in the form of carjacking, home invasions, bank robberies, and petty street stickups. Ruffneck wasn't about to get his shit pushed back, relying on Farmington Hills' finest. If it did get funky, he was about doing a fool dirty and getting low. The game plan didn't call for loitering around until five-o rolled. Oakland County was notorious for its high-percentage-prosecute-a-nigga fetish.

The opening of the door framed Ruffneck's back with soft, yellowish light that grew brighter as the door opened wider.

"I didn't figure you for the rude type," the woman stated.

"My neighborhood is safe. You don't have to worry about anybody sneaking up behind you and clubbing you into headline news out here."

She laughed a little, but Ruffneck had the scoop from the opening tip. She was nervous and he could see it, smell it, like most sharks using their heightened senses to pick up the scent of blood in the water. The mental note was made.

"I see you got jokes?" He downplayed the moment with a charismatic smile.

"That's grammatically incorrect. It's *have* jokes," she corrected.

"You always working, hunh, Ma?" he teased.

The lady did some little thing with her mouth that women often do when hearing something agitating, but can't offer an immediate response because of politeness.

"Let's move this conversation off the front porch and inside, shall we?" She opened the door wide to let Ruffneck enter, but her intoxicating fragrance rushed out before he could step in. He prided himself as a youngster with die-hard dick control, but whatever perfume she was wearing left him hard as a rock and tip-pulsating as he passed through, purposefully brushing against her body.

Damn, she was more beautiful than he could remember. Even in the darkened areas of her house, she rocked a certain kind of sex appeal. But once she stepped into the light, baby girl's body was banging. Her dark chocolate skin looked soft and moist, like she had just stepped out of the shower. Where she'd worn her hair in a bun before, it was now loose, silky, and flowing gorgeously around the shoulders of her royal blue, silk kimono robe. Her girls were sitting pretty, too. The robe was tastefully opened just enough to display the perfect model-cleavage Victoria's Secret must've considered, when first producing its line of bras.

Ruffneck's shit kept getting harder and harder as his eyes left her chest and flowed with the symmetry of her body. Her measurements tapered into a thin waistline and then expanded into a nice voluptuous ass with the silk material clinging to every curve of her body.

"Are you just going to stand there and stare?" she asked with attitude, putting her hands on her hips. "Or are you going to come and hug me?"

Ruffneck studied her for a brief moment, not wanting her to get it twisted. He was in control of this show. Raw confidence was in every step of his swagger. He slowly walked over and took her into his big, strong arms, rocking with her from side to side. The sensual fragrance heightened with every pulse of her heart and pulled him deeper into the quicksand of X-rated intentions, as he took small whiff-samples from her neck. There was no question about what he wanted to do, so he did it. He smoothly, but tenderly, grabbed her ass with both hands and pulled her closer to him. She tried not to let the surprise register in her eyes when their pelvises bumped in her discovery that her little pupil wasn't so little after all.

But Ruffneck did catch the question in her eyes: "No, that's definitely not my ruler, Ms. Alan," he informed, wearing a devilish smile.

She pulled away from him.

"Princess," Ms. Alan said, "My first name is Princess."

"What's your deal?" Ruffneck asked, feeling the tension.

"I wasn't aware that I had a deal."

She was so transparent. The problem was apparent. Ruffneck could sense her apprehension and he understood. Their meeting would've been frowned upon by her professional peers and parents alike. It was a sexy-ass taboo; the type of shit that could cause scandals and rip apart families, careers. She had a lot to lose if the secret ever became public.

"Baby, don't worry about nothing. I'll never tell a soul," Ruffneck promised with a straight face.

"Who said I was worried about some—"

Before she could finish, Ruffneck kissed her. The tenseness of her body revealed hesitation. He kissed her deeply and could feel her rebellion ease up and melt away into affection as he firmly, but gingerly, held her in place while gently sucking her tongue as if her warm saliva was flavored by a unique blend of passion fruits.

She was completely relaxed inside his arms when he scooped her up like a baby, breaking their connection just for a moment. She whispered the directions of her bedroom into his ear.

Princess felt good in his arms as he carried her from

the living room, where an earth-tone color scheme was energetically alive and showed up in every piece of leather furniture, with the most influence resting inside the unique tapestry of a beautiful area rug. Beige, brown, and bone-colored candles lined her mantle, sitting in fly candleholders with a few inches between them and a magnificent piece of artwork in the form of an abstract painting hanging on the wall a few inches up, inside of a 20-by-24 frame.

Ruffneck found it difficult to stay focused with Princess nibbling on his neck. Her body was so warm inside his arms. It was like carrying the sun that had shape-shifted into the magnificent body of a woman.

"I want you inside me right now," Princess professed in a naughty voice that had Ruffneck so hard, the skin on his manhood seemed to be stretching beyond crotch capability. He stumbled with her on his way up the stairs.

"Please don't drop me," she moaned as she went back to licking, sucking, and feeding him the directions to her bedroom.

Ruffneck jammed on the brakes and held it tight as he leaned against the wood banister for leverage. Princess wasn't heavy. The awkward angle required a little extra muscle to keep his balance and avoid them both from spilling backward. That type of strength was all day long for him, as he pulled from his nuts to keep it moving.

By the time Ruffneck arrived at the top of the stairs, his erection was on some ol' swollen "Ford-Tough" mission statement: 'built to last!' Princess' room was the first door on the left. Scented candles were known to be a baby-making aphrodisiac. Aromatherapy greeted him as he paused at the threshold and allowed the arousing fragrance to seduce him into believing that he was going to spill so much nut inside her, she would be the black octomom in nine months.

Like newlyweds, he carried her over the threshold. Princess' lips were sucking everywhere there was skin, like he was some chocolate-covered, ice cream thug bar.

The peace Ruffneck experienced as he toted his armload of teenaged fantasies across the room and to the foot of her king-sized poster bed was different. Candles varying from size to color lined the tops of her dresser and chest. They brightly burned and separated the room into a soft, flickering amber glow, intricately woven by dominating pockets of darkness.

"Not the bed yet, baby," she purred, stopping him short and giving him the body language that she wanted to be put down.

Gently, Ruffneck lowered her onto the plush carpeting. With only a couple of inches difference in height, Princess stood on her perfectly polished toes to sling her arms around his neck and slip her hot tongue into his mouth at the same time. The sloshing was loud and intense as their tongues tussled back and forth in a molten-hot saliva exchange. It was on and popping from there. Princess went underneath Ruffneck's hoodie and undid his belt buckle, not missing a beat.

She dropped to her knees and finished unzipping his pants. Her next move was reaching inside and allowing her hand free-reign to explore the tubular bulge straining against the material of his boxers. The butterflies inside of her stomach danced excitedly as the heat that radiated from Ruffneck's meat rushed out in waves, catching her breath. The searing heat from Princess' hand stroking his wood rushed through his body. He fancied himself as the hunter, but right now, he was the prey, and she wielded absolute power. At this point, he couldn't care less about who was on top. He wanted her in the worst possible way.

Ruffneck stood there, looking up at the ceiling. He had completely given it up to her as he thrust his pelvis forward while arching backward with his mouth open, panting as Princess pulled his snake all the way out the fly. She wasn't really surprised by the length, but the girth of his monster was enough to find her covering the head with steamy, hot kisses, while still feverishly working his shaft. Ruffneck's eyes almost rolled to the back of his head when he felt the warmness of her mouth closing in around the head of his member, allowing inch by inch, deep-entry, and setting off her gag reflexes.

Princess had adorable bedroom eyes and every now and again, Ruffneck would find them on him. She was handling her business, sucking like his dick was a yummy new Popsicle flavor. She clamped both of her hands around Ruffneck's ass and slowly began to help him find his rhythm. She pulled him into her, in and out, swallowing his offering inch by inch. Princess was serving up porn-star status head. He had never seen or felt anything like what he was experiencing now. He was hooked. No other woman had ever delivered up mouth-action to him like this. Ruffneck figured, if this had been a contest where Princess and his old head-coach, Lover Lips, were going head up, sucking dick side-by-side, Lover Lips would've stopped sucking to watch Princess while pulling out an ink pen to jot down some notes on how to properly polish a knob.

Ruffneck had gotten used to her taking him a certain distance, relaxing his guard. And that's when she flipped the script. Princess stuffed so much of Ruffneck's shaft into her mouth, she violently gagged. But Ruffneck was feeling too good to be concerned about if she'd lost her mind in trying to swallow his sword. He was about to come.

Not like this, though.

Princess was turning out to be a worthy bedroom adversary. He wanted to really test-drive her ass to see if she could hold up under freak-a-leek conditions.

Ruffneck shed his clothes until he was butt-ass naked and careful at keeping the pistol out of sight. He pulled Princess up, wrapped his hands around the thin waist of her robe, and in one fluid motion, he hoisted her small frame so that she was eye level, her legs constricting around his torso. He carried her around the room looking for a place to work. The marble counter of the master bathroom looked promising enough. He gently placed her on the flat vanity between the his-and-her sinks. Princess savagely cleared the area with one swipe of her forearm, sending toiletries flying. Her heart was racing, and her skin, boiling for the anticipation of a hot return.

Ruffneck was in control of his shit. He pushed her back into the mirror and at the same time, the move acted as a spring-loaded mechanism in popping her legs open. Hot pheromones invaded his senses instantaneously. As his little head pulsated and his pole grew quicker than a line for free iPads, Ruffneck's bigger head grew dizzy from the suspense of running up inside her. Princess was a dime and Ruffneck couldn't afford to blow an opportunity in making her his queen on some "young nigga" selfish bullshit.

Ruffneck gently placed her heels on the edge of the counter, giving her legs that McDonald's golden arches look. Kneeling as if to be knighted by the moment of submission, Ruffneck slid her thong to the side and eased his index finger into her wetness. Princess jumped, and then relaxed as he withdrew to taste her juices.

Sweet!

Like nothing he'd ever tasted. Ruffneck parted her pussy lips and tongue-teased her clit. He watched Princess' forehead crinkle with intense lines of desire as her head slowly slid across the mirror. Princess' tongue rolled over her beautiful full lips as they puckered into an "O"; the sound of her moans barely audible. Softly, he pursed her clit between his lips, loving the effect he had on Princess. She pulled both breasts from under her bra and started tracing her fingers lightly around her nipples.

No motion was wasted. Ruffneck applied his special trade until Princess was yelling his name—screaming that she was coming and begging for him to put it in. He understood power. It often took the shape of patience and self-control. He was the possessor of those traits. They were universal in winning wars on the battlefield as well as establishing bedroom dominance. And right now, he was a bedroom general in full command of a naughty-style that was taking Princess to a victory where burdens were non-existent and orgasms came easy as breathing. While Ruffneck stroked himself, he denied her of what she pleaded for and kept up the suspense.

Ruffneck resisted his ego-trip in staring up inside of a face that was contorted with millions of fuck-me-hard frowns, produced, designed, and copyrighted by the freak-ass twin sisters named pleasure and pain. Princess' skin was sizzling to the touch and sweaty, sticky-good. Ruffneck stood to line up entry and slowly worked it in. She cringed at his penetration. The nigga almost passed out. Her gushy was warm and extremely wet. He wasn't even tripping at the fact that he'd left the Magnum XLs in the pocket of his hoodie, in a pile of clothes on the bedroom floor. Ruffneck had been surprised at her acceptance of a missing rubber. But who was he to remind her? As far as he was concerned, he'd worked too hard to stir the juices. He reasoned that sampling her hot honey while riding through bareback country was his reward. So he stroked with the power and gracefulness of the USA Olympic rowing team.

Candle flames flickered as Ruffneck, going deeper and deeper at Princess' request, caught a glimpse of his image in the mirror. The soft candlelight was enough to separate his reflection from the darkness inside the background—much like spotlights would in singling out actors in a play where the stage was completely covered by darkness. He could no longer see the thin film from her juices inside of his moustache, but the scent left behind made him feel like two-for-one. He rolled his tongue over the hair on his lip as if he was still eating her pussy, while his dick feverishly worked inside of her wetness.

Ruffneck continued giving it up in a steady rhythm, holding his gaze until he had completely tuned out every sound around. Even though Princess was underneath and urging him to stick harder, her voice was lost as he locked like a pit bull on his expression. The fire from the candle reflected brightly, dancing around inside his pupils. He could feel the power inside his soul. It surged through his blood.

His plans for underworld restructure were as hard as the dick he was running his queen with. Some niggas referred to it as "lovemaking." But right now, there was no love being made. He was straight-up fucking his former twelfth-grade geometry teacher on her bathroom sink, without a condom. The city was in for the same deal. He would take the rubber off of his brand of war and give it raw to any nigga who held an ounce of power. Ruffneck had his army, a plan, and now he had the queen. Ruffneck broke contact with his image just as Princess was hollering about coming again, but this time he pumped his way into releasing his load and collapsed on top of Princess.

Darkness encompassed Ruffneck; like he'd been pushed in, and locked away inside of a small utility closet at night, with walls that had been covered in black paint. But this was no closet. Even though he couldn't see his hand passed before his face, the place in which he stood was much larger; a warehouse of some sort. The echo of him striking his foot against the hard surface resonated throughout the enclosure, giving up the confirmation.

The place felt cold and damp and smelled of mildew. The teeth-chattering draft was enough for him to pat himself down to see if he was wearing clothes. His touch revealed a fleece hoodie and jeans. Ruffneck ran over his pockets with the hopes of finding his smartphone. He'd gone hard on Twitter, blasting out a tweet on how stupid the flashlight application was, but would sell his left testicle to Sprint right now for the light. The bright beam would've been perfect in finding out the condition of the flooring. Ruffneck cautiously took two steps forward, but really couldn't tell if the third would send him freefalling to his death. The last thing he needed right now was to wind up lying at the bottom of some hole with a busted leg or even worse: incapacitated by a serious neck injury.

He wanted out, to keep it moving, try and tip through the darkness of his murky confinement. The answers surrounding his mysterious location rested out there somewhere inside the sea of gloom. And from the sound of heavy breathing, so did something else. Ruffneck couldn't tell if the labored breathing belonged to a human or an animal. He didn't dare move a muscle. Black folks didn't fare too well in situations like these. This was that horror-movie shit where gullible-ass white folks lasted longer than a nigga who'd exercise common sense in using the peephole before opening the door to some psycho axe-wielding sonofabitch.

The breathing sounded close at times, but for some reason seemed to keep a respectable distance. It slowly circled him, like it was stalking, testing his heart, waiting for the perfect opportunity to reveal itself. From left to right, it moved. Back. Side to side—the breathing came ragged.

As quick as it started, the thing withdrew. Whatever it was, would be back. He knew it wasn't finished with his ass by a damn sight. Ruffneck had spent far too much time in the jungles of his hood to know that a predator

stalking easy prey never relented. Nothing about Ruffneck was considered soft, or easy. The truth was butt-
naked, though. He *was* easy picking. Alone, unarmed,
and not being able to see the threat, made him feel
vulnerable. Sooner or later, it would come for him.
Ruffneck was a brawler with almost ten hardcore years
of checking punks and pushing in the grills of fools.
Running away had never been an option. And he wasn't
about to start that shit now. He had no other choice but
to stand and scrap.

The freaky breathing was back and had circled, ending
up behind him, but still giving respect to the distance.
Ruffneck stepped around in that direction with his
adrenaline on bump. His fists were cocked and loaded
and ready to swing out into the darkness.

He could feel his body tense, ready to meet the predator with deadly force, when the foul odor belonging to
shit and cold, harsh air assaulted the right side of his
face. It triggered him and he spun to his right, putting
his weight behind the punch and swinging blindly into
the night.

No dice!

He missed with a right-cross that would've folded the
normal nigga.

The thing was to his left now, as if toying with its
food. Ruffneck turned, tracking the sound, ready to drop
bombs. With nowhere to run, he braced for another
assault. The hood had never prepared him for this type

of an encounter. Ruffneck was on that old-school tip: you had to see a nigga in order to whup his ass. But this thing wasn't human. And it definitely wasn't a nigga, not with that breath. Nobody he'd ever come across had breath that smelled worse than human shit mixed in cow manure.

Seconds, more like hours, had passed without action. He didn't drop his guard because he knew the moment that he did—before he could finish the thought, Ruffneck was lifted off of his feet by a blow in the back that seemed to have a ton of pressure behind it. His stomach dropped as he took a ride through the darkness and felt the ground come up hard under his back. The colorful lights inside his head hadn't stopped flashing when the thing jumped on him. It straddled Ruffneck, sitting with massive weight on his chest and wrapping hands the size of cinder blocks around his throat. The thing was heavy and seemed to apply more pressure every time that Ruffneck exhaled.

It was extremely strong. Ruffneck tried to pry the powerful hands away from his throat. He trembled, straining to match the thing's strength and ferocity. He had to think fast. Ruffneck was choking and begging for oxygen.

Instinct caused him to run his left hand up the attacker's powerfully constructed forearm, abnormal-sized chest, but the fur on its neck had Ruffneck stumped, and a little worried. He'd never run into a foe with this much juice. Then again, Ruffneck had never witnessed anything in the ghetto that flexed with this much heat. The nose under his touch felt more like the snout of an animal; a cow, bull, but definitely not human. Shit like this wasn't supposed to happen to G's like him. If it was up to him how his ticket was punched, gunfire from the enemy's tool would be his vehicle. Anything beat being choked out by some shit fresh out of a sci-fi movie.

Ruffneck could feel himself fading, giving up the fight. This one would go down in the win-lose column as an "L". The beast in the dark was just too much to handle. One thing was on Ruffneck's mind as he slowly slipped into the darkness of his surroundings: How in the fuck did he arrive in a place where shit like this existed? Just when he was at the point of totally stepping into the light, brightness flooded the entire area. He didn't even blink when he finally faced his attacker. Seeing something with a human body rocking the head of a bull would've melted the heart of a lesser nigga. But Ruffneck didn't blink. He took it like a straight-up G. If he had to roll out this way, then it would be what is.

From somewhere came a whistle. The beast released its grip. Ruffneck coughed and grabbed his throat. He tried to suck up as much air as he could. The beast was now dragging him by an untied Timberland. The battle had zapped Ruffneck of his energy. He could do nothing but hold his head up to avoid it striking the lumps and bumps in the ground.

At this point, Ruffneck could give a fuck. He just wanted

out of this backward-ass sci-fi flick. He was barely conscious when they arrived inside of a small room. Activity was jumping off at the far end. He was released a few short feet away from what appeared to be a small stage—he couldn't really tell yet, still trying to shake off the cobwebs and focus. When his eyes finally adjusted to the bright lights, a man standing on the stage with his back to him, came into view. This shit just kept on getting weirder. The beast took its place beside the man who was dressed in what appeared to be a long, black cape with a hood draped over his head.

Ruffneck slowly got to his feet. The man in the cape turned to face him. He was a light-complexioned black man who looked to be in his mid-to-late forties. Once you got past the blood-seeping bullet hole that was lodged between his eyes, he was perfectly normal. Not like his beastman homeboy at all.

Without words, the man snapped his fingers and the monster disappeared behind the stage curtain. And for the length of time that it took for the beast to raise the curtain, Ruffneck and the man stood there staring down each other. Ruffneck's gaze was filled with familiarity; the man on the stage—his eyes lifeless. The man-beast was back, but this time he was clutching a machete. He obediently surrendered the weapon. Ruffneck was tripping so tough on the man and beast that the third person on stage had gotten past him. When the curtain had risen, the first thing he should've peeped was the person who was kneeling with their neck stretched across what appeared to be some type of wooden block. Their identity was concealed behind a drawstring burlap bag.

The man walked over to the wooden block like his entire body was in severe pain. He gestured for Ruffneck to follow and waited until he had a ringside seat. He stared once more in Ruffneck's direction before he placed the keen edge of the machete on the back of the victim's neck, as if trying to get an accurate measurement on the appropriate force needed for the job. Once he had the measurements, the man positioned himself, raising the blade as high as he could go. When the beast removed the bag, Ruffneck's face held that "what the fuck" look. The man in the cape was cheesing his ass off now. Ruffneck tried to break for the stage, but the soles of his Timberlands seemed to be nailed to the floor. He savagely ripped at the strings to come up out of them.

Nothing doing.

Princess was about to have her head chopped off and there wasn't shit Ruffneck could do about it. The blade fell, there was a scream…

"Fuck!" Ruffneck yelled, popping up from the sheets, his fist balled, ready to go to the head of the first mutha-fucka who was the closest. A thin layer of sweat covered his face and bare chest.

"Ruffneck," Princess said. "It was a dream—just a dream." Princess made sure that she stayed her ass a safe distance, because Ruffneck was a hard body who could do unspeakable amounts of damage. "You okay?" she asked.

That shit wasn't just a dream, but a major league fucking nightmare, he thought.

"Princess, I gotta bounce. I'll holla at you later."

"Wait," she said to him.

But Ruffneck was out of the bed and collecting his clothes with the quickness. It wasn't the foul-smelling breath of Man-Beast or his dude, Hole-in-the-Head, that had spooked him. Ruffneck knew that a warning came stamped on the ass of every nightmare. His coming here had put Princess in harm's way. The kingdom that merely existed in schematic form would come with its fair share of headhunters—niggas who would try and get at family members to make a point. His road to success would be paved by the bodies of his competitors, and to achieve imperial status, one couldn't afford to have visible weaknesses.

Ruffneck dressed as he walked down the stairs. He could give two-fucks for putting it to a nigga who stood in the pathway of him sitting on his throne, but Princess, Princess deserved better than him. He wouldn't be able to live with himself if she got her cradle rocked by some cat trying to make a statement. In his eyes, Princess symbolized the highest form of purity. The title of hustler's wife was beneath anything that she stood for.

Ruffneck put the keys into the ignition of the Regal. He turned over the engine, backed out of the driveway and then flipped it into *Drive*. He'd kill himself before he let the fate of his mother befall Princess. He gunned the car down the street, leaving distance between him and his visible weakness.

You Feel Me?

Ruffneck checked the calendar on the wall in Granny Sinclair's bedroom. The date was Friday, October 24, a week from Halloween. He and his crew had been going over the plans relentlessly. Cadillac was due to fall, so that he could rise from the ash of the ghetto and take his place inside the game. Princess had been calling and texting, but he kept blowing her off. That fucking weird-ass dream was all too real. He could've easily explained the nightmare away as one of the symptoms for posttraumatic stress disorder. But whatever the shit was, he couldn't risk Princess' life. Maybe it was a warning; either way, Ruffneck had to bury the idea of taking Princess as his queen.

He peeked in the bathroom.

"Hey, old lady, what you getting all spiffed up for?" Ruffneck joked. "It ain't Sunday; where you about to step to?"

Granny Sinclair was standing in front of the bathroom mirror applying the finishing touches on her makeup.

"You know that young bo' that got shot over his tennis shoes—Michael Steel?"

"Aww, snap, the cat that got his wig pushed back for his Airman sneakers, walking home from school."

The old woman stopped brushing on the foundation. She rolled her eyes.

"Must you be so fuckin' insensitive? Don't talk ill of the dead."

"Just stating the facts."

Granny Sinclair went back to attending to her face. "Just make sure you don't get yo' 'wig pushed back.'" Her arthritis was kicking ass, but she managed to place a string of pearls around her neck and pinned a sparkly butterfly brooch on the right breast of her black dress.

"Now you're talking crazy. Where they having his thing?"

"If'n you referring to his funeral—it's going to be held at that big church house on Woodward." Granny Sinclair dabbed on perfume and placed on a black church hat the size of a Grand Torino. The black veil obscured the left side of her face.

"That's jacked up. Heard the lil cat was a pretty gifted student, too."

"So young, he just a baby—fourteen years old. I swear I don't know what this wurld is coming to. He was just walking home when some other chil'ren shot him down like a dog in the street."

"Triple Ol' G, when did it happen?"

"Last week, 'bout the same time them other chil'ren got gunned down actin' a fool outside that woman's place on Madelin Street." She tugged on her hat.

Ruffneck knew just what *chil'ren* she was referring to.

It had been a done deal. There was nothing to speak on. Go-Hard and his boys were so yesterday, mere trophy heads hanging on the wall of a future game room belonging to his palace.

"So, Michael ain't the only one getting buried today. I swear I don't know what this wurld coming to. The Lord ain't too long from making his second appearance."

Shit, Ruffneck thought. Anytime the old woman started dropping the "End of the World" bombs, he knew that the rest of the King James wasn't too far off his ass. He normally dealt with her sermons by falling the hell back.

"Boy, you hears me?" Granny Sinclair asked.

"What you say? The last things I heard were 'Lord' and "second appearance.'"

"I knows that head doctor said you had PTSD, but I didn't know you had that ADHD, too, boy? Don't be funny. Gonna be needing my prescription—heart medicine." She took one last look in the mirror, grabbed her cane, and walked out of the bathroom smelling like freshly cut roses.

Ruffneck moved to the side of the door and allowed her exit. "I got cha... I saw Hootie the other day," Ruffneck mentioned. "He seems to have this idea that you don't like him much."

Granny Sinclair rolled her eyes at Ruffneck. "Boy, I ain't too fond of you neither. Don't mean that I don't care for you no less. Hootie is as worthless as his old man." She brushed it off. "Gonna be needing some cigarettes, too, boy."

Ruffneck shook his head. "Nope. Not going there with you. Told you, old lady, get your own squares. I'm not gonna be responsible for you coughing your way into the grave, Triple Ol' G."

Granny Sinclair made her way down the stairs. She picked up her clutch bag from the couch. The old woman turned on him with cold eyes. "William's been staying away ever since you almost stomped him into a coma. I don't have nobody to go get my cigarettes."

Ruffneck followed her to the front door. "William ain't never brought you nothing besides trouble."

She turned on him with fire in her eyes. "That's my boy! You didn't part yo' fucking legs to spit 'em out!"

"Kill all that noise, ol' woman. Ain't you about to go to church—using all that foul and filthy language. What is Jesus gonna say when he comes back at the 'end of this world' about you popping off like a rapper?"

"Get a job, hoodlum."

"You get a man, old broad."

"I got your stanking ass. Don't needs no mo' than that."

She kissed Ruffneck on her way out of the front door.

"You behave, ol' woman."

"Yo' upper lip, young fool."

"Whatever."

Ruffneck helped his granny down the steps.

"Granny Sinclair, how do you know this dude, Michael Steel, anyway?"

She rambled out to an older-model white Malibu that

was parked at the curb; one of her friends named Mattie sat behind the wheel. Never offering an answer, the car pulled out and took off down the street.

Ruffneck took out his cell and thumbed a text out to Menace. He needed for everybody to have their asses up at the Spot tonight. It was time for the kingdoms of those holding household names in the game, to be infected with the virus of poverty. And when niggas started sneezing, he would be there holding the heat to blow noses.

It was a rap for Cadillac's pudgy ass. He was stamped. The key to Ruffneck's come-up rested inside the pig's chubby palms. The lick would go down Halloween. Next Friday. On the night that little ghosts and goblins would be out collecting scores of treats, the trick would be on the fat man.

The blood-curdling theme music from the movie *Halloween* was back and playing inside his dome. Ruffneck walked back inside the crib, whistling along.

It was pretty chilly for an autumn night. Ruffneck and his crew were posted up in front of his cousin's Regal and enjoying the show of wannabe high-profile niggas. This place was called the Spot and everybody who was somebody chilled here. Sounds bumped, niggas flexed— custom rides of all kinds rolled around the Spot on expensive rims, while the women talked much shit and showed more skin than material. It was a rundown stretch of road that spanned six blocks with abandoned buildings, crumbling liquor stores, and a few decaying storefront churches sitting on either side of the street.

Since being here, Princess had called him three times and left three text messages. As much as he wanted to, Ruffneck didn't answer the phone. He deleted her texts without reading. He knew that his type of war would bring casualties to his yard and couldn't bear the thought of her left lying as collateral damage at his front door. And that's why he'd never shared with his crew. Much like his past, Princess had to remain in the shadows for her own safety. He couldn't trust any of his people with that information. Ruffneck knew his soldiers weren't weak, but under pressure, one never knew what information might be passed on to stop the torture. They were about to get knee-deep in the shit and it was prone to be a lot of angry cats left behind with scores to settle. Ruffneck just couldn't take that risk. Princess's survival depended on him keeping her secret.

The night was off the hook, jumping like it usually did around 10 p.m. Dope game royalty was in the house, all swagged out, and dressed in the finest 'fits that dirty money could afford. Niggas stepped around wearing so much alligator that it looked like an Animal Planet documentary on the explosive gator population inside Everglades National Park. Politics separated the crowd by classes. Ballers hollered and talked dick-measuring shit with those in the same weight class, while lower-level cats mixed in to discuss big-money schemes to get it like the elite. No watering hole was complete without the absence of the predator community that lurked and stalked the shadows, in search of easy opportunity; stick-up kids who fed themselves off carelessness.

Just two months ago, a stick-up goon named Scoundrel had caught a grotesquely overweight baller in an alley taking a piss. The dude, Fat Albert, had been a heavy-weight in the game, and was in the middle of a buzzed up, forty-ounce malt liquor piss when Scoundrel crept from behind with a baseball bat. He turned out Fat Albert's lights with a single, solid blow to the back of the head so hard that the handle cracked, sending wood splinters and the bat's barrel flying off into the darkness. Before the slob could hit the ground good, Scoundrel had managed to lift over $60,000 in cash and jewels off the body. The big fella's murder had sent shockwaves and outrage throughout the drug community. The under-world offered up a price for information. Fat Albert's piano box-sized casket hadn't spent two days inside of the earth when Scoundrel was caught and punished. Three days later, the police had found his badly mutilated corpse inside of a vacant house with the tongue cut out, and the dick stuffed down his throat. Scoundrel's death had served a powerful warning for those who looked at the Spot as an easy meal.

"Look at these fools," Lil Shorty said as he stared at

the crowd with much contempt, "Niggas walking around here like they can't be touched. We about to put our hands all over 'em. You think they know we on the come-up?"

"If your little stupid, loud-mouth ass don't blast us out first," Menace scolded.

Lil Shorty moved from the back of the Regal where he'd been leaning. "I'm not gonna tell you again, Frankenstein. You better watch your tongue before I cut it out."

Menace thought the shit was funny. He smirked and said, "Like you tried to do back in Granny Sinclair's basement, nigga? I'll knock you the fuck out like Ruffneck did you."

Lil Shorty reached underneath his Rocawear button-up like he was going for his heat.

"Youngsta—" Ruffneck spoke to Lil Shorty in a way that left no doubt of the horrible consequences that would follow his actions.

The little nigga heeded the warning and fell back, mumbling as he walked his way to the rear of the car.

Poison sat her pretty, high-yellow ass silently behind the wheel of the Regal, door open, left heel of some expensive chocolate boots touching the pavement, Glock resting on the floorboard. Her braids had been freshly done, lips covered with MAC red lipstick, and she stared out at an underworld high-end fashion show from behind her signature Chanels.

Poison didn't even blink when she heard the music powerfully knocking from inside of an O.J. Simpson-style white Ford Bronco that was rolling down the strip. Her shades clocked the fool as he whipped up inside of a vacant lot and parked. The driver and two of his passengers jumped out, and looked to give it the count of three before lifting the top away from the vehicle and placing it on the ground behind the SUV. The three then backed away from the truck slowly, like they had just been alerted to it being wired with explosives. The driver pointed a remote control at the truck and detonated, exploding a slick baseline boom from the powerful sound system. Anything made of glass within the immediate vicinity, violently shook and vibrated. The lyrics to Biggie Small's joint "Hypnotized" were crystal clear. Hands started waving to the beat, but all eyes feasted on two chicks that slid off the back of a couple of crotch rockets and started freaking each other. The two girls went after it like they were waging a war for strip club supremacy, jeans so tight and ass shaking so hard that dudes started making it rain.

"'Neck, let me go and talk to little nigga," Fly said to Ruffneck. "The plan to stick it in Cadillac calls for five soldiers. We need his little ass."

Ruffneck nodded at Fly, and then in the direction of a newer- model black DTS Cadillac. An older gentleman dressed in a tight-fitting, black linen two-piece suit and two younger hoodlums with hoods pulled over their heads emerged from the car.

"Speak of the devil and he appears," Menace said.

"That's Cadillac's fat ass, all right," Fly added.

Cadillac shook hands with some rock star named Bundy McGurk. He was a young hothead off the city's East Side. Somewhere down the chain of commands, he was employed by Billy the Kid. He dealt in some-of-this and some-of-that, but mainly trafficked heroin. His outward grimy appearance wasn't even on the same page as the paper he stacked. It was reported that his net worth was over a million dollars, but he dressed like a bum and was rumored to have a bad hygiene problem. Bundy had put in so much work that it wasn't the glamour of the game that turned him on anymore. Violence was his craving. Bundy was a ruthless power-lord with a terrible temper and quick to bust his gun.

"The chick Berry-Flavor come up with that info, yet, Menace?" Ruffneck asked.

"Yep. Cadillac runs his houses in shifts. Flavor said the change of shifts makes them vulnerable. The afternoon shift will have gotten off an hour after we take 'em. It's usually five cats in the house at that time. One dude in the kitchen, another one in the upstairs bedroom off the stairs, a guard posted in the garage out back, and a nigga on the side door."

"Damn, if that's what she calls vulnerable," Fly joked as he walked back up to the front. "I hate to see when those niggas are fully staffed."

"She knows her role?" Ruffneck asked Menace.

"She's fuckin' the cat that guards the side door. Homeboy's got her coming through for a kitten-call. She knows once she makes it in, to leave the front door as well as the side, unlocked."

Little Shorty rejoined them in front of the Regal.

"I thought we wasn't supposed to talk business out in the open?" he asked, trying to be cute.

Fly looked over in the direction at the owner of the white Bronco. "I doubt if anybody can hear our conversation with all the noise that ol' O.J. Simpson is making over there." It was a party popping off near the white SUV and everybody and their mamas were jigging to the music.

Lil Shorty peeked at Bundy for a few. "Cadillac and Bundy do business together, money laundering and shit."

"And…what's your point?" Ruffneck asked.

Lil Shorty carefully selected his words. "We knock Cadillac, and Bundy's money might be in the take."

"Do I smell a bitch?" Menace blazed.

The kid was about to jump bad when Fly said, "Got is *got*. We gonna be on the low with the masks and shit. We'll be in there and ghost before those chumps know what hit 'em."

"What about the bitch? What's to stop her from frontin' on us?" Lil Shorty inquired.

"Berry-Flavor is getting paid for the job. Besides, it's personal with her, because Cadillac's fat, funky ass raped her girl right there in front of her," Menace informed. "She hates his bitch ass."

"Listen," Ruffneck interjected, "since when have we given a fuck about niggas holdin' power? The last I checked, kingdoms were built from stepping on toes. So if Mister Bundy's toes have to be underneath our wheels, when we drive our way to the top, so be it. Everybody in the game gonna bleed when it's our time to shine."

Everybody took notice of a convoy of tight-ass, custom-painted whips riding down the street. A colorful parade of American-made craftsmanship floated by as GM, Ford, and Chrysler rode down the block in a show of solidarity. Nothing under sixty-grand rolled in the procession; the lead vehicle being a funny wine-colored Cadillac Escalade sitting on twenty-fours.

"Billy the Kid's in the house," Ruffneck heard some dick-sucking dude yell from three cars down.

"The ultimate prize," Ruffneck expressed to nobody in particular.

"We comin' for your crown, Kid," Fly said in a whisper to be heard by the ears of his people only.

O.J. turned down the sounds with the remote, as if to pay homage to Billy's Ghetto Mob crew as they rode through. His fleet of flashy custom joints looked to be endless as they slowly wheeled down the strip looking sweet; headlights cutting through the darkness and the streetlights catching the sparkle from the chromed-out wheels.

"The light is yours for right now, Big Dog," Menace commented.

The area grew quieter than a mouse pissing on cotton as Billy and crew cruised through like some high-end funeral procession. Billy the Kid was that hardcore deal and demanded mad respect from all in the game. He'd bagged the crown at the tender age of twenty-one. At an age where most were graduating college and pulling out plugs of hair to repay student loans, Billy was already living the American dream.

Ruffneck had to give it up. Billy was a prince; heir to the throne if his superiors were to ever meet with some tragic ending. But the way that Ruffneck saw it, the young nigga was sitting in his seat, keeping it warm. He was coming for that number one spot and would give lead makeovers to whoever stood in his way.

Ruffneck had stopped paying attention to Billy's crew. His new focus shifted to the cat bouncing on a 250cc silver scooter with thirteen-inch aluminum rims, windshield, and rear trunk compartment that followed the last car in Billy's entourage. Not wearing a helmet, Ruffneck recognized Nizzo's crusty behind right off.

"Ain't that Nizzo?" Fly asked. He already knew the answer. After doing what Nizzo did, Fly just couldn't understand why this fool would show his face in public, and riding the scooter.

Nizzo was swerving and bouncing up and down, just showing his ass for those watching. He rode the scooter on to the vacant lot and parked it about sixteen to seventeen feet away from the white Bronco. Ruffneck didn't give Nizzo a chance to get off of the bike when he was running full-tilt in that direction.

"Shit, here he go!" Fly said, taking off behind Ruffneck.

Ruffneck swiftly wove his way through the thick crowd toward Nizzo. His temper was boiling. As far as he was concerned, the world would profit dearly if every fool like Nizzo was marched out to huge, pre-dug holes in the desert; shot, buried and left unmarked. Ruffneck sprinted like he was in training to dethrone Usain Bolt in the 2012 Olympic Summer games. The closer Ruffneck drew to Nizzo, the thicker the crowd became until Ruffneck could no longer see his punk ass.

He slowed his pace until he was jogging. He removed his eyes from his direction and damn-near knocked some liquored-up brother out of his cheap three-piece suit and alligator shoes. Ruffneck didn't have the size but carried weight and was built like something that had been produced from the assembly lines of the Big Three. The impact jarred homeboy's teeth and knocked the red plastic cup from his hand. The drink flew up into the air and descended back to earth, giving all around a very unpleasant alcohol shower. Ruffneck didn't even stop for those who yelled threats of revenge and voiced their objection in profanity-laced tirades.

When Ruffneck finally got to Nizzo, the punk was still sitting on the bike. Nizzo was too busy styling in front of some chick with a booty the size of Detroit's famous landmark, Uniroyal Tire, to see Ruffneck barreling in on him. Ruffneck slammed into him with so much force that both boys spilled over the scooter. The woman quickly removed herself from the violent photo as Ruffneck was the first to recover from the fall. He viciously monkey-stomped Nizzo across the forehead. The blow was enough to daze Nizzo's stupid ass until Ruffneck could figure shit out. Not long after, he snagged Nizzo by the right leg of his pants. An alley was off to the left of where Nizzo had parked the bike. Much like a jaguar would pull his kill to a secluded location to enjoy the spoils alone, Ruffneck dragged Nizzo's carcass into the darkness of the alley.

Nizzo was starting to recover from the hangover caused by the blow. His vision was grainy at first, but focus eventually returned and the horror of seeing Ruffneck savagely rip a two-by-four off the back of a garage with his bare hands, fueled him to his hands and knees.

Nizzo immediately tried to plead his case.

"Look, man, I—"

Ruffneck brought the wood down hard across Nizzo's back. He had completely lost it. Sanity had left town for a vacation and hatred was now in the house.

Nizzo yelped out in pain. He fell flat on his belly and was attempting to crawl out of harm's way in true snake fashion, when he received a bone-crushing blow to the back left shoulder.

Ruffneck ignored Nizzo's chilling screams for mercy.

"Turn your punk ass over!" Ruffneck yelled. He kept

the wood pointed at Nizzo's back like he was holding a pistol on him.

Nizzo struggled but wouldn't turn over. "Man, we can work this thing—"

His plea was cut off by a hard blow to the right Achilles tendon. Nizzo rolled the fuck over and grabbed the back of his foot, screaming like he'd lost his damn mind. He made an attempt to get up.

Ruffneck circled and kicked Nizzo squarely between the eyes with force, sending his body backward. The boy's coconut bounced off the piss-smelling pavement with a grotesque thud. Nizzo seemed to be out and flat on his back. Nizzo's body was in perfect position for Ruffneck's next trick. He measured the nigga's right knee with the club and raised the thing high in the air. Ruffneck brought the force as the club crashed down across Nizzo's joint so hard the wood broke in half.

Nizzo woke the fuck up and was loudly screaming like the big, bad booty-daddies of D-Block were trying to bang him out in the shower. He lay curled up on his side, both hands clutching his damaged foot, shaking and shivering. The action was framed by the moonlight and Ruffneck could see Nizzo's tears mingling with the snot that ran from his nose.

He rocked and cried trying to catch his breath.

"No more...please...no more," he pathetically begged.

Ruffneck didn't feel shit for the nigga. He hocked and spat on the boy, throwing the remaining piece of wood in his hand next to Nizzo's writhing body.

Ruffneck's blood pressure wasn't given a chance to drop when some nigga yelled from the opening of the alley near the strip, "...fuck was all that about?"

There was a fenced-in church parking lot just to the immediate right of where everybody was standing. The four lampposts on the property lit up the lot and the surrounding area—the location in which the crowd stood being one of the beneficiaries of light.

Menace, Fly, Lil Shorty, and Poison stepped from the crowd. And so did the owner of the voice. Bundy McGurk waited patiently at the opening of the alley until Ruffneck emerged from the shadows. He stepped right to McGurk.

"Lil nigga, you must don't know the G code up in this piece. Niggas don't flex around these parts," Bundy pointed out.

Ruffneck weighed the situation. Bundy's violent game stopped at his trigger finger. The nigga was tall and slim. He lacked the necessary weight to go toe-to-toe with Ruffneck's bulk. The end result would be terrible for Bundy. Ruffneck would smash his ass out in less time that it would take to smoke Bundy's entire crew with an AK-47. But Ruffneck wasn't stupid. He didn't possess the crew-muscle than was now lining up behind Bundy, almost two dozen soldiers that were built like gorillas and dressed in designer urban gear.

Ruffneck's crew fell behind him as the crowd started inching backward, opening up space in anticipation of what could be a slaughter.

Ruffneck nodded in the direction of cries that sounded

more like a wounded animal's—"Nigga had it comin'."

"Do I have to repeat myself: There ain't no gangsta activity around this area, you dig?"

Little Shorty got involved. "How you gonna tell another nigga his bidness?"

Ruffneck let his stern stare put Lil Shorty back in his place.

"Look, man," Ruffneck begin, "that bitch beat a woman. Then he shot and jacked her fourteen-year-old son for his scooter."

Bundy's laughter incited the rest of his goons to join in.

"That's some touching shit, but your little show could bring the heat around here. This place was discovered for the true ballers, lil nigga, and ain't nobody gonna fuck it up, you dig?"

Menace glared at the soldiers behind Bundy. They were all his size, or bigger. He kept his hand down around his waist. His strap rested underneath his Polo shirt. There was no chance of his crew winning in a scrap, but if it came to it, he was ready to blast.

"Well, I did what I had to do, homie," Ruffneck said, trying to keep his growing anger in check. "If you don't like it, then you make a move."

"McGurk, fuck that lil broke muthafucka," said an enormous, black fool with pink lips, dripping in jewels. "Lemme turn my strap loose on his punk ass."

Poison let her actions do her talking. She pulled her pistol.

The crowd dispersed, running wildly in every direction.

Bundy stood his dudes down with the wave of a hand, amused. "Y'all fools, hold off. Look at this shit here. This light-skinned, pretty bitch got some balls."

"Bundy!" Pink Lips piped again. "McGurk, fuck that bitch! Let's dead 'em, right here!"

"Fuckin' her is what I have in mind," another one of his gorillas shouted.

"Y'all chill the fuck out," Bundy said with lust in his eyes for Poison. He said to Ruffneck, "You better put a muzzle on this pretty bitch, you dig?" He rubbed the stubble on his chin, staring at Poison like he was trying to eye-fuck her. "I would hate to smoke such a fine piece of pussy."

Bundy's goons broke into laughter again.

"You lil muthafuckas are lucky tonight," Bundy McGurk expressed. "I'm gonna give you a pass, this time. One-time just opened this place back up two months ago"—Bundy blew a kiss at Poison—"stay the fuck away from here. Next time, I let my crew get after yo' niggas with that thang. All except her ass, though. Cutie, you'll be going home with me, you dig?"

Ruffneck and his crew carefully backed away from Bundy's bunch. Bundy's boys were wildin', blowing kisses at Poison and grabbing their dicks while telling her how she could suck 'em.

Ruffneck handed the keys to the car over to Fly.

"I'ma ride this scooter back to the crib, dog. Tail me in the Regal." Fly ran toward the car. The rest stood by Ruffneck, just in case Bundy tried to get cute.

Ruffneck jumped on the scooter and started it as Fly whipped the Regal around behind. The rest piled into the Buick. Ruffneck gunned the bike and stabbed out down the street. He was pissed at himself for letting his anger get the better of him. He'd let his emotions control him. Shit could've gotten real ugly. General Custer came to mind. Ruffneck knew that a true general always maintained composure. Never broke under pressure. His soldiers fed from his energy. It was the stuff that erected empires. Ruff-neck had to get a better grip on his temper. The fate of his future kingdom depended on it.

Years ago, Granny Sinclair had wood paneling installed along the basement walls that completely covered up the windows. Without the house lights, Ruffneck's bedroom was always dark. So when he when woke up coughing, Ruffneck couldn't tell if it was night or day. Smoke was strong inside his bedroom. Throat irritation sent Ruffneck into a coughing frenzy. Waking up suddenly had him disoriented and wiping his eyes.

In his boxers, Ruffneck rolled out of the bed, thinking that the old bag had finally gone and done it. Her old, absent-minded ass had fallen asleep with a burning cigarette resting between the wrinkled slots of her fingers. And if it was true, then the whole upstairs was probably ablaze right now—which meant that he had two possible avenues for escape. The absence of the key to the side door security gate all but eliminated that possibility. So the only route was through the basement door leading to the kitchen.

Not knowing if Granny Sinclair had gotten her old ass out safely lit a fire under his ass. He grabbed clothes and shoes and was ready to go through the fire to save his people when her voice floated from a dark corner of the room.

"Yo' breath stink, hoodlum," Granny Sinclair joked as she sat smoking in an armchair, silhouetted by darkness.

"You think you funny?" Ruffneck asked. He put a hand to his mouth and coughed a few more times. Afterward, he took in a deep breath to calm his heart rate. He yawned and dropped his clothes and shoes to the floor. Ruffneck sat on the edge of his bed, dropping his head inside his hands. "You need to go smoke those cancer sticks upstairs. Don't come down here trying to puff me to hell with you."

She pulled on the cigarette, the glow from the fire penetrating the shadows. "If'n I recalls correctly, the name on that deed reads: Stephanie Morgan Sinclair. So with that shit said, I can smoke anywhere I very well please."

"What time is it, ol' woman?"

Ruffneck wasn't able to see her face all that well. So in the gloom, it looked like the orange glowing ash was moving up and down by some type of invisible force.

Granny Sinclair blew smoke from her mouth. "Time fo' you to get yo' unemployed ass up and go get you a job."

He took another deep breath. "Serious, what time is it?"

"What you need the time fo'? It ain't like you got nowhere to be off to."

"You got jokes. Well, I got a joke for you: who am I?"

The old lady took a pull from the cigarette. "You Ruff-neck. The one that them chil'ren in the streets are 'fraid of."

"Well, since you can't come correct with the answer to my question, then I got another simple one for you: who are you?"

She let the question marinate for a minute, as if to roll the answer around inside her head. She took a long drag from the cigarette, inhaling the fire deeply inside her lungs, the orange glow from the burning butt turning a crimson red.

Her answer was simple: "I'm the one that needs you to go do something 'bout that funky breath and go get mi pressure pills."

Ruffneck was feeling the weight of the world on his shoulders and she wasn't doing anything right now but adding to the strain. The frustration of not knowing who the fuck he was crept into his soul. He felt trapped by time and mystery. Ruffneck's brain only held fragmented memories from his deleted past. Not enough to remember the faces of his folks. Sometimes he felt like he'd just dropped the fuck out of the sky and crash-landed on

Granny Sinclair's front porch. Anything was far better than the memories that he was carrying around now. The truth was that somewhere sat a heartless bastard that had ordered the murders of his family. The old woman sitting in front of him was on lock with the information. But he was going to make shit right. Wherever the murdering muthafucka laid his head, Ruffneck was intent on finding his ass and laying down the revenge game.

"I see we ain't never gonna get anywhere, Granny. You ain't got nothing but games for a nigga."

"I gots me some chores for 'a nigga'. You got some errands to run for yo' old helpless grandma."

"I'll tell you what: when you're ready to get at me with my history, then I'll get back on the stroll. But until then, I'm on strike, ol' woman." Ruffneck lay back down on his bed.

"We'll see how far you get, Mister Gangsta, without the food from my kitchen."

"Man, please"—Ruffneck sarcastically made a blowing sound with his mouth—"I have plenty of spots waiting to feed me. The last thing I'm stressed about is a meal."

If Ruffneck could see the cloud of cigarette smoke in the dark, it meant that the old lady was smoking up some shit.

"Where the heck you cop the cigarettes from anyway?"

"Boy, the last time I checked, I had a few miscarriages, a dead husband, a grown-ass kid and a gallbladder the size of the tires out there on that motor scooter parked in the backyard. Now if'n that don't declare me legal age to do what the fuck I want, without answering to lil unemployed shits like you, I don't know what does."

"Did you really have to go there? And I can explain the scooter."

"No need. I believes you got that scooter back from that stick-up kid whence shot Jamaal. And if'n I knows you, that nigga laying in the hospital with nothing but pain up to his eyebrows. Spare me the details. It was good for whatever you did to his ass."

"Yeah. He broke Mrs. Johnston up pretty bad and blasted little Jamaal in the shoulder."

She flicked a lighter, producing a flame, and touched the tobacco. Granny Sinclair took a puff from a fresh cigarette.

"When you gonna take Jamaal his bike?"

"Soon as I get up."

"What time would that be? I told you I needs my pressure pills."

"As soon as I get the answer to the riddle about my history." With that said, Ruffneck rolled over and closed his eyes.

A couple hours later, Ruffneck was up and moving about. Ol' Lady Johnston's crib sat three blocks away, on the opposite end of his street. He didn't feel that it would be appropriate to ride the scooter to return it. He'd decided to push it instead.

Upon doing so, he had time to reflect on all the bullshit

that had taken place last night. Ruffneck hadn't exactly shown Bundy up, but he didn't give him ground in front of a crowd when the nigga was trying to dog-check him. It was written all on the big dog's face that he wasn't used to such defiance. Ruffneck recognized weakness. Bundy was one of those insecure assholes who used violence and intimidation as a means to demand respect. And now Ruffneck's resistance had threatened Bundy's hold. The big money asshole hadn't come out and said it, but bad intentions had oozed from his lips in the form of jokes and insults. He'd mentioned that they were lucky and would be given a pass, but it was total crap. Controlling types like him never believed in letting shit slide. The streets were watching. There was almost-always a consequence when stepping on somebody's corns in the game. Bundy had wanted to give his cats the order to start popping last night. He could've missed Ruffneck with the sorry bullshit about him having enough respect not to leave bodies at the Spot. Ruffneck was up on how he got down. McGurk needed to be heard. His thing was publicly murdering cats in broad daylight to make his point.

Ruffneck knew last night that Bundy had put a price on his head. It would serve as a warning that his type of G wasn't to be fucked with. Ruffneck wouldn't have a problem with it, though. He knew that Bundy would come calling for his respect one day. The only thing that had Ruffneck worried was the nigga attacking him before he could get shit up and running; have enough soldiers to match Bundy's muscle.

It was then determined that Bundy's bitch ass had to go bye-bye. Even Ruffneck knew that the best laid plan wasn't worth a damn if it had no chance of getting off the ground. This shit was personal. Bundy had made it that way when he'd threatened Ruffneck with his eyes.

Ruffneck was two to three houses down from his destination when he began toying with the idea of killing Bundy. It wasn't gonna be hard to find out about the fool's comings and goings. Ruffneck was definitely gonna do this dirt by his lonely. He would do Bundy on the solo-tip—creep into his world and turn out the nigga's lights by his muthafuckin' self. There would be no cause to involve his crew. The plate was already full with the first leg of their come-up. His soldiers didn't need the minor distraction that Bundy's hit would present. On the Cadillac job, he needed for his crew to be sharp and focused. To bounce up in the spot, grab the lick, and jet without any of his peeps getting bodied.

Ruffneck stepped on, guiding the kickstand to the ground and pulled back on the bike to park it in the walkway of Mrs. Johnston's colonial. Since there was a piece of cardboard taped over the doorbell, Ruffneck knocked hard, allowing for a few seconds between. After a series of tumbling clicks, the door opened and an older, heavyset, light-complexioned lady with a short hairstyle and a huge neckbrace, stepped out. She saw the bike down on the walkway behind Ruffneck and immediately started screaming her son's name, while holding on to the brace.

Jamaal was slow walking to the door, but once he got there to see what was behind the ruckus, he joined in. The gunshot wound didn't stop the kid from celebrating the return of his bike. He held on to the black frames of his glasses with the extra-thick lenses, and jumped for joy. He continued walking to the outside. Although his left arm was in a sling, Jamaal climbed his fat, pudgy frame on and started to feel the instruments like he'd expected the bike to vanish inside of some dream.

Mrs. Johnston thanked Ruffneck over and over for the recovery. She begged him to take her money, but Ruffneck would have none of it; said that it was his pleasure and apologized for all the hurt that they'd suffered at the hands of their assailant. She knew Ruffneck's reputation and stayed away from the "hows" and "whys." The less she knew, the better.

Jamaal gave up dap as Ruffneck made ready to bounce from the spot. He assured Jamaal and his mother that nothing like this would ever happen again. But he purposely omitted the part where the nigga responsible was now laid up in the hospital, recuperating from a multitude of surgeries. Ruffneck had learned about Nizzo's condition the moment he'd gotten to the crib this morning. He had made damn sure that Nizzo's bitch ass would feel him for the rest of his worthless life. Ruffneck might've been a stickup kid, but women and children were always spared. Anybody feeding on them wasn't fit to breathe the same air as everybody else. The news had already gotten around to the scumbag community that Ruffneck's block was off-limits. The vicious trashing of one of their own would stand as a stern reminder of what would happen if they tried to eat off people from his street again. And if niggas weren't convinced, the proof was in the multiple surgeries it took to reattach Nizzo's Achilles tendon, reconstruct his knee, and repair his badly broken shoulder.

Mrs. Johnston hugged Ruffneck and told him to kiss his grandma for her. He wanted to kiss her all right. The old bag was frustrating him by withholding the information needed for him to reconnect with his history. There were things about him that needed understanding. He had gone HAM on Nizzo because the punk had committed an offense that was punishable by what he got. But the intensity in which he'd taken it to Nizzo was nasty, downright vicious. It felt like something inside of him had snapped. There had been a desire for torture and maiming. Was he insane? Or did his old man possess the traits of a killer?

He needed answers about his fam, and the old woman was sitting on her lips.

Those worries would be put on the backburner for right now. An immediate threat needed to be extinguished. Bundy McGurk had sealed his own fate. Bundy didn't know it, but Ruffneck was about to bring the fight right to his front door. The nigga had had the last laugh. Now Ruffneck was bent on sending his black ass to Hell's version of *Showtime at the Apollo* where there, he would be able to perform his stand-up for all eternity.

Sweet Mutiny Is Her Name

I t was Tuesday night. Four days before the hit on Cadillac's joint. Lil Shorty sat inside of a car bumping his gums on a cell.

"Ruffneck is a done deal," Lil Shorty said. "The nigga is reckless; talking that shit about making waves and he's the main one putting fools in the hospital with a two-by-four."

The heavy voice on the other end of the phone belonged to a small-time crack dealer named Sin. "The nigga think he's the Rock on some *Walking Tall* shit or sumptin'?"

"I'm the Bambino of Terror," Lil Shorty claimed. "I'm supposed to be the head of this muthafuckin' crew, dude, not Ruffneck's ass. This slow creep-on-the-competition shit is beneath a cat like myself, you dig? I'm from that part of town where we take shit while making as much noise as possible. Gotta let these clowns know who the fuck runnin' things, you feel me?"

"Fo' sho', fam. That's why lions eat and every other predator wait they turn," said Sin.

"And now this nigga has gone and started some shit

with the nigga Bundy McGurk. And you know how that fool is cut."

"Nigga, what? McGurk carries major weight, man. That fool ain't got nothin' but bodies lying buried in shallow graves across the city, fam. But that nigga Ruffneck got nuts, though."

"Bambino," the young, cocoa-complexioned girl with the soft, doe eyes cooed from the front passenger seat of her 2001 Monte Carlo. "I'm tired of sitting here. Let's go to the club." The Chevy was parked on a dark side street on the city's East Side, right next to a weather-beaten, bed bug-infested, two-family flat where the girl and her auntie occupied the upstairs unit.

"Bitch, chill the fuck out. Can't you see I'm gettin' at my peeps right now? You know what you should be doing, anyway." Lil Shorty unzipped his pants and reached in. "Damn, Sin, now you're riding the nigga's dick?" he said to the party on the other end of the phone.

"Not riding shit, fam. Just saying the boy Ruffneck ain't no joke. Nobody stands up to McGurk, guy. Real recognizes real, is all I'm trying to say."

"Ruffneck ain't long for this world. His time is shorter than a fat man's thang."

"You sho' the rest of the crew gonna fall in line?"

Lil Shorty stopped fumbling around inside of his pants and whipped out nothing but hard dick.

"They gonna have to." He grabbed it and slowly began jerking.

"I think that bitch Poison is gonna be trouble. She ride and die for homeboy," Sin revealed.

"I hate to quote the nigga Beans from the movie *State Property* and shit: but that bitch can get down or she can lay down. The way I see it, my dude, they ain't got no other choice. I'm the little Bambino of Terror and I got some plans of my own that don't include Ruffneck. And once we juice Cadillac's old, musty ass, Ruffneck's reign is a done deal, baby. It's gonna be me and you then."

"You're talking some sweet mutiny, my nig. But I like that shit. I got the connect and all we need is the muscle. I believe it was destiny that we met up in juvie, fam. You and me, we share the same passions. To be larger than anybody who's done it in the game. We gonna get bloody behind this one, mi nig. But peep this, fam: how you plan on getting rid of Ruffneck, anyway?"

The girl took Shorty's hand away and began playing with his meat. A soft moan escaped Lil Shorty. With his eyes rolling around upstairs, mouth open and tongue slowly licking at his lips, the little chick leaned over and swallowed half of his pole.

"I...I got the chump's...num...number," Lil Shorty struggled to say as his breathing became labored. Her head bobbed up and down inside his lap, in a rush—like she had someplace to be and was trying to get him off so that she could get there.

Lil Shorty slapped the shit out the top of her head. "Bitch, slow that shit down," he barked. "Fuck you think this is, the dick-sucking version of the hundred-meter dash?"

"So you get your dick sucked while we talkin' business, right? What type of nigga does that?"

"A nigga that's about to get me and you paid, playboy. Don't worry about how I'm gonna handle that fool, Sin. You just be ready when the jack goes down." He pressed the *End* button, not really giving a fuck if the nigga was still holding the line. "Now, where were we?—oh yeah." He guided her head back into position with his left hand and with his right, he pulled a pistol from his waist, placing it to her temple.

She stiffened up.

"You better come correct with the head, or I'ma splatter yo' shit all across the interior of your car. You make a choice."

Hot tears slid down her face. She nodded her head in total submission and slowly gave it up sweetly, like her very life depended on it.

To Live And Die In The Dark

Ruffneck woke up exactly at 10:30 p.m. on a Tuesday night. His nightmares were getting worse. He was sweating, with his heart wildly beating like he had two kilos of pure cocaine hidden away inside the trunk of his car, and was now involved in a high-speed chase while trying to shake the police. Hole-in-the-Head and his foul-smelling-breath companion, Man-Beast, was back. This nightmare was worse than the first. Granny Sinclair had been the victim this time with Ruffneck waking up just before Hole-in-the-Head's machete had time to fall on the old woman's frail neckline.

The messages inside the night terrors were right in front of him, but Ruffneck couldn't put a finger on the pulse of the conundrum. It was eating away at his soul. This shit was getting completely out of control. He was starting to believe the hype from the psychiatrist. Ruffneck was prepared to pop antidepressants for his posttraumatic stress syndrome, if it would help. He just didn't know what to do.

He hadn't wanted to admit to himself that he could

feel something sinister growing inside of him after every nightmare. He'd made several efforts at putting a lid over the darkness in an attempt to contain the evil, but failed every time. It was powerful. Something that he'd never experienced before. It made Ruffneck feel a hundred times mightier than when he had lain the murder game down on one of the killers who'd been responsible in the deaths of his parents. The cruel intentions of a powerful cat had left Ruffneck an orphan at getting his dough the legal and moral way. He was now a ward of the state, and in Satan's sole custody, to go after the dollar without any remorse or compassion for twisting niggas out. For Ruffneck clearly understood that evil men showed no mercy on their blood-thirsty climb up the ladder, and onto the lavish rooftop of wealth and power.

Ruffneck checked the time on the clock. He squeegeed the perspiration from his forehead. Fucking nightmares. The dead nigga with the hole between his eyes, and the thing with the bull head, were becoming a major problem that Ruffneck just couldn't handle. He was sure that their presence was on some symbolism shit. He wasn't gonna lose it to coincidence that the pair showed up on the night belonging to McGurk's last breath, either. He didn't exactly know how Granny Sinclair had earned a spot on the dead nigga's chopping block.

Ruffneck jumped out of the bed, taking the shit for what it was: some type of dark entity that was trying to lead him to the Promised Land. He didn't see a problem with it—hell, as far as he was concerned, his old man had probably promised the devil his soul, and the soul of his firstborn, for a reigning seat on the throne. It was what it was.

He set his mind back on Bundy McGurk and the job at hand. Sources had the fool routinely frequenting a Tuesday night spot: some dance club downtown on Franklin, a couple of blocks away from East Jefferson Avenue. The building was purposely made to look like it was abandoned, not to attract too much attention. Some high-powered dope boy had come up with the idea to create a safe-haven for his fellow ballers. The guest list was exclusive with the only other way inside being an invitation. Ruffneck wasn't a VIP, nor was he waving an invite around. But what he did have was some bitch named Daphenie, who supervised the huge kitchen inside the joint. A little while ago, Ruffneck had come to the chick's rescue when her ex-boyfriend started stalking her. Ruffneck had caught the dude outside of her home and he and Menace put the smash on dude. The broad had been in his debt ever since.

Her favor to Ruffneck would be sneaking him in through the backdoor and giving him a pair of coveralls worn by custodians. She didn't want to know his business, but told him that they could never contact each other again after that night. And he didn't have to worry about her saying shit to the police, either. The near-death condition that they had left her ex in went for her, too, if she started running her trap to five-o.

So, he had to be at the back door by midnight. Without much time, he set to work. He slid one leg at a time into the blue coveralls, and pulled the top portion up to his waist, with the sleeves dangling. The Kevlar bulletproof jacket was a perfect fit. Horizontal, double-shoulder holsters wrapped around his torso, holding twin Glock nine-millimeters. The sound of somebody slowly walking down the basement steps made him stop admiring his *Commando* Arnold Schwarzenegger look in the full-length mirror of his bedroom, and pull the entire suit up over his body, hiding the weapons.

"Gangsta, what you doing down here?" Granny Sinclair asked as the steps continued to groan and moan underneath her weight. She stopped at the door of his bedroom before going into the laundry room. "I ain't gonna ask you what you wearin' them clothes for. You ain't got one hint of a job. So, where you getting off to, boy?"

Ruffneck laughed.

"Old woman, what you doing out of bed at this time of night? Ain't *Sanford and Son* on?"

Ruffneck couldn't see her, but the noise she was making loading up the washer made him ask before she could answer his first question: "What, you got a date being the reason behind you being down here, washing at this time of night?"

"See, right there, is that very same reason you young

folks are seeing y'all's Maker at an early age—always being up in grown folks' bidness."

Ruffneck moved away from the mirror and over to the closet. He had to wrap his mind around the details of the job. The nigga Bundy was gonna be amongst nothing but love, and one slip-up could leave Ruffneck going against an army of guns. The odds left him salivating. He didn't have an answer for the hot rush of anticipation that slithered through his blood. But he knew who did.

Ruffneck retrieved a few extra Glock magazines from an empty shoe box.

"Hey, old chick," he called out.

"Yes, young punk."

"Every once in a while I get these uncontrollable urges." Ruffneck tucked the clips into a pocket of his coveralls.

"What urges are them?" she asked out of concern.

The sound of the dryer door shut.

"Just urges. The thing is: I don't know where they come from."

The old lady showed up at his door after starting the dryer, holding a plastic clothes basket.

"Boy, I'm gonna ask you to forget about what you thinking 'bout. 'Cause I don't knows a damn thang about yo' momma and daddy—you hear me?!"

Ruffneck recognized the fear in the old woman's eyes. He'd never seen anything of that nature in them before. And that type of fear only drove his hot desire to know.

He assumed that she was protecting him from something dangerous.

"What are you afraid of?" he probed.

She tried to sound convincing: "I don't have nothing to be 'fraid of."

Granny Sinclair saw the look of determination on Ruffneck's face. She knew this wasn't the last time that he was going to come at her with questions about his past. It was etched in his eyes.

"Boy, you look like you 'bout to get into some misdeeds," Granny Sinclair pointed out.

"Well, the way I see it: you can tell me who and what my father was, or do I have to keep finding out about him through my 'misdeeds'?"

"I'll advise you to not. One thing about Satan is, he'll open up that do' to your curiosity, but once you cross over, he'll lock it shut and seal it with yo' blood behind you."

"Too late, Granny," Ruffneck said as he looked her straight in the eyes, while remembering the bloody massacre the assassins had left behind in his parents' bedroom. "You don't have to worry about Satan closing the door behind me…I was born in hell."

Ruffneck looked at the clock on his nightstand. He had to be at the back door before midnight, the darkest of the hour. Granny Sinclair didn't have to tell him shit about his pops. The pleasure of knowing that he could pull off a murder, and not feel shit behind it, was all he needed to know about his father. He had inherited his heartlessness from somebody. It definitely wasn't his mother. She'd received two bullets, but his father had been riddled by them. The heavy concentration of firepower on him alone led Ruffneck to believe that they were there to knock off the old dude. His mother had been collateral damage. The way his father had gone out only fueled his speculation that his pops was probably the muthafuckin' King Snake in Pennsylvania's underworld.

"Boy, 'members what I tell you: you don't want to open that do'," Granny Sinclair repeated.

But it fell on deaf ears because Ruffneck had made it up the stairs and out. Granny Sinclair tracked him by footsteps through the living room as the floorboards squeaked above her head. The screen door slammed shut moments after, with him bouncing down the weak wooden steps and off to his destination.

"Dang fool!" Granny Sinclair exclaimed. The boy was hardheaded and listened to no one. It wasn't his fault he was becoming something that the world could do without. He knew nothing else but violence. The same monster that was now growing inside him had consumed his father as well.

She grabbed and pulled on the banister with her one strong hand, and toted her clothing basket with the other. It terrified the old woman to know the shadows that had devoured the boy's parents still whispered in the dark. The boy was drawing attention to himself. It was making it harder for her to keep him hidden. Her grandson was building quite a reputation for himself in the street. If it reached high enough, those same shadows might decide to come down and take a look.

The boy was wearing her the hell down. He just didn't know how close the truth was to her tongue. She was getting on in years and far too old for this shit. Keeping a secret that she'd been sworn to, was coming with a nerve-wrecking, gray hair-producing price. He was at her about his folks every time she turned around. It was the same old junk. Night and day. He was unrelenting.

She knew the drill, though. The boy was trying to grill her into submission. She really didn't know how much more she could take. The look he had in his eyes worried her to no end. It was the same blood-thirsty look that she'd seen in his father's eyes many a time— death, the gaze of the Grim Reaper. Recalling some of the senior's exploits was enough to know that it would be just a matter of time before the boy turned into a monster much like his father.

Granny Sinclair trudged until she finally made it up to the third level, briefly stopping along the way to catch her breath. She moved to her bedroom closet. Shoe boxes lined both sides of the wall, neatly stacked three high. Her back had been bothering her for the first half of the day, but didn't give her any trouble when she stooped down to clear a row of boxes out. The corner of carpeting came out pretty easily as it slid from underneath the trimming, revealing a small electronic metal safe in the floor. The last four digits of the boy's social security number opened the box. The safe was stuffed with all kind of valuables. She pulled out a blue .38 revolver with a pearl handle, some important papers, a couple banded stacks of cash, and a large envelope.

Nobody knew about her safe. And as far as she was concerned, the thing was death to break into. Well, at least that was what she remembered the installer saying when he put the damn thing in the floor: that it was fire resistant, and burglar proof. To make sure she was alone, Granny Sinclair peeked out of the door into her bedroom. She hadn't heard the boy come back in, so she started out with the envelope.

She wiped away a single bead of sweat that had cascaded down the bridge of her nose and collected into a droplet at the tip. One more glance around before spilling out the contents. There were some old Polaroids; but what really moved her were the newspaper clippings. The fading, yellowish color gave away to a time that had spanned over several decades. After all this time, she still received goose bumps whenever she read them—which weren't often. The boy's father was evil, pure evil. The Jeffrey Dahmers, John Wayne Gacys, and Ted Bundys were just a handful of mere underachievers compared to the boy's old man. He had truly built a kingdom from the blood of his victims.

Granny Sinclair hustled the content back into the envelope, but not before brushing across a photo of the boy's father. The old dude and his son looked like they could've been identical twins. Looked like he'd spit the boy out—they were so close in physical similarities. It wasn't that fact which terrified her. The boy had a bona-fide mean streak in him, just like his old man. Chills seized her flesh as she gazed into the eyes of the devil, damn-near dropping the Polaroid.

She threw the picture back into the envelope and rushed it back into the safe. The unspeakable acts of insanity the senior had committed were enough to move her into trying harder to save the boy from the inevi-table. Not to mention that the killers of his parents were still at large. Sure, the murders had happened many moons ago, but the one responsible was still in a position of power. She couldn't risk the boy finding out anything. It would surely seal his fate as well. His very safety depended on a horrifying secret that the old woman was determined to take to her grave. Though she had led a much-checkered life herself, there was no way in hell the boy was gonna know shit about his father.

It was one helluva time for Ruffneck to pick to start thinking about Princess. He'd all but forced her out of his heart, mind, and spirit since her texts stopped. He'd had shit figured wrong. He'd been on some other stuff with the original plans of having a queen by his side, when the world would be at his feet. The formula didn't work so well for his old man. Ruffneck never wanted to admit it, but he held his dad personally responsible for not protecting his family. Walker Senior knew the nature of the business. A kingpin was never safe. At any given moment, somebody could spring from the shadows and punch his ticket. His father had to have most certainly known the rule. Therefore, he should've taken the appropriate measures in better securing his homefront.

Ruffneck wasn't gonna make that same mistake. He wasn't gonna do it because he wouldn't put anybody in that situation; understanding the reason as to why he had to let Princess go. No weakness. Princess most certainly would've provided one, like he and his mom had been to his old man. But unlike his father, Ruffneck would be ready to put holes in anybody sent his way on some creep shit. He wouldn't have any distraction that would keep him from sending the bastards back to the flames of hell.

It didn't matter, though, Princess was officially history. Right now, Bundy McGurk was the nigga who needed his immediate attention. At ten minutes to twelve, Ruffneck was pulling up three blocks away from the nondescript building in a stolen, black, late-model hooptie of a Honda Accord.

He was a true warrior who didn't mind putting the dirty in by his lonely. As he jumped out of the car, the rush he was feeling about the job left him hastening his steps to arrive at the backdoor on time. While he walked, Ruffneck had to kill the excitement that was surging through his body like water moving through a rapid, and powerfully pouring over the falls. There was something about taking a life that left Ruffneck feeling intoxicated with power. Before he could fetch his mind toward a potential answer, he took out his cell and hit Daphenie up with a text. He was still walking and his ETA would probably be two minutes.

The coveralls weren't the most comfortable gear he'd ever rocked, but they helped him connect with the whole janitor character. For a moment, he felt like one of those square cats who busted nuts behind punching a clock to put food on the table. Reality of his true intentions quickly set in when he felt one of the heaters strain against the material in the chest area of the coveralls. He doubted very seriously if janitors went to work wearing a bulletproof jacket, and Glocks shoved into twin shoulder holsters.

The thrill of the kill left his mind focused on nothing but the mark. In a matter of a few days, there was nothing that he didn't know about Bundy: favorite food, cell number—his overactive bladder problem. Bundy's weak-ass bladder would be his own undoing. The lame even had set times he visited the bathroom at the club that Ruffneck now stood at the backdoor of. McGurk and his fellas were notorious bottle poppers, who enjoyed sharing the wealth. Their VIP section was always live and the flow of booze and broads rocked around the clock. So it was nothing to see the nigga staggering off to the toilet. Almost everyone knew each other, which relaxed his need for bodyguards. Catching Bundy right where Ruffneck wanted him, wouldn't be a problem. The janitor's getup would be more than enough to put him in close range. With Ruffneck hiding behind janitor's garb, his all-black Detroit Tigers baseball cap with the white Old English "D" pulled down real low on his eyes, McGurk's one-thirty visit to the can would be his last.

Before Rufneck entered the building, he slid on a pair of black Isotoner gloves. He wasn't going to risk leaving prints on shit. The backdoor crept opened. Ruffneck wasn't to walk in right away. He had been instructed by text to wait a moment before entering. He wasn't a fool. The reason was bright and wearing sunglasses: the bitch didn't want to take a chance of being seen with what could eventually turn out to be a person of interest. Although there were no cameras in this part of the building, she wasn't taking any chances. The chick didn't know what Ruffneck's business was, nor was she stupid. Ruffneck had quite a reputation with dealing with fools and it moved her with urgency at covering her ass.

Once Ruffneck completed his task, he'd been instructed to exit the building the same way he'd entered, leaving the door open behind him. It would be staged to look like a random robbery. Ruffneck would leave the nigga's pockets turned inside out, to give the police that impression. The lick would be more than enough to convince five-o that it could've been anything but a hit. McGurk had been known for carrying large sums of money on his person. So the back door left open would give investigators the theory that some hungry, low-life opportunist had taken advantage. And after the detectives ruled out the guests and started working the staff-angle, the old careless-worker-out-to-have-a-cigarette-and-didn't-lock-up-afterward alibi would be the reason as to why the intruder had been able to gain entry. To give the scene the look of authenticity, Daphenie had even taken the liberty of scattering cigarette butts on the inside and outside of the door. Everything looked tight on paper.

At least that's how the plan was supposed to work. But Ruffneck knew that *underestimation* was a hardcore whore that fucked niggas spermless until death. He was firmly pregnant with the idea that this shit wasn't gonna be a cakewalk; that Bundy wasn't gonna be easy to deal with. He tried to stay away from the thought that shit could actually turn in McGurk's favor. If it happened like that, and Ruffneck fucked up and fell to his enemy's heater, then nobody in his crew or family would be safe from McGurk's get-back. The hit had to go down in his favor, because if it didn't, his peeps would be undertaker dollars by the end of the week.

Ruffneck took a deep breath before entering. Opening the door, he was met by strong bass from the music before taking in the long, narrow, dimly lit corridor. The cleaning cart was waiting on him halfway down the hallway, loaded down with all the essentials. Ruffneck pulled the brim of his hat down a little lower and grabbed the handle of the cart, wrestling to stay in character. Turnover in the janitor's position kept a fresh body in the building, so there was no arousing suspicion by the cooks, when he pushed the cart through the kitchen and out of the swinging doors.

Ruffneck pushed into what appeared to be a brightly lit foyer. The bass boomed so loud that the silencer Ruffneck had scored from his cousin, Hootie, probably wouldn't be necessary. On his way to the main area, he pushed past artificial shrubbery that was stationed in front of every brick-faced column. A few wrought-iron benches lined walls that hosted imitation works by great Renaissance painters.

He stood there at the enormous opening, behind his cart, wearing dress blues. His hat was pulled down low over his eyes and he peered right into the main ballroom. The place was a hollowed-out building with plenty of space. A simple but huge balcony for the DJ to spin records overlooked an open area, featuring plenty of real estate for dancing. There were a few couples on the dance floor going hard to an uptempo joint by Usher Raymond.

Niggas were all over the place and definitely dressed to impress. Ruffneck had never seen so much alligator,

Cartier glasses, gold, diamonds, and weaves inside one friggin' area before. His first impression of the spot was that the owner didn't travel to great lengths to appease his guests with luxuries. The VIP sections looked plain, but were determined by status. The cats flexin' with the most cheese played host to the biggest box. Those areas had recessed lighting. But you couldn't tell because ballers were shining all out in front, extra with it, talking mad shit and boasting about the loot they were holding. Women sold to the highest bidder. On occasion, over in the far corner, Ruffneck peeped at guys leading ladies through a door and up a dark stairwell to probably exchange money for pleasurable favor.

An elaborate elongated bar sat off to the side of the dance floor. Women sat on barstools, some drinking from the wallets of niggas who were trying their hardest in getting the digits. Ruffneck didn't want to appear out of place by just standing and people watching, so he pushed the cleaning cart over to a group of trash cans not too far away. He began dumping the cans as he scanned the joint for paid security. The bouncers in the house didn't disappoint. They wore black shirts with "Security" plastered across the back in huge white lettering. There wasn't one guard under six-five. The force was intimidating and ready to do work whenever a nigga got out of line.

Ruffneck hadn't seen his target yet. There was no sign of Bundy McGurk; not even inside the large VIP section that sat a few of his gorillas. Drinks were flowing and women right along with them. Ruffneck checked his watch: fifteen minutes to one. He had in his mind that he would go the fuck off on the informant, when McGurk and a few of his monkeys filed in through the front door. The cats following McGurk were the same dudes from the night he was popping that slick shit. Ruffneck guessed the cats had to conform to the club's dress code. They'd traded in the jeans and Timbs from that night for high-priced suits and shoes.

Bundy's clumsy nature gave Ruffneck the idea that the chump had probably started drinking way before arriving at the club. And if his informant was right, McGurk was due to go to the toilet in forty-five minutes. Ruffneck emptied a few more cans into the waste bag on the front of the cart, and pushed off toward the bathroom area. The lights were dim once he got inside. The place was pretty plain and spacious: urinals off to the left of the stalls, liquid soap dispensers sat inches above and between several sinks that were positioned underneath generously sized mirrors. The lock on the bathroom door was committed to memory. He didn't want anybody walking in when he was singing McGurk an eternal bedtime lullaby, especially not his goons.

Ruffneck searched under the sinks and found what he was looking for. One of the sinks had a ledge underneath, a place where one of his pistols would fit snuggly. He was on some old crazy shit. It didn't take any balls to pull a trigger, but only real men settled their differences by toe-to-toe combat. Bundy was still going to die, regardless. Ruffneck just wanted to beat the shit out of him before he sent him on his way. He unzipped his coveralls; went in and removed one of the Glocks from the holster. He placed it carefully underneath the sink. On his way out, he checked the door lock for accuracy. Everything seemed to be in working order.

With nothing else to do, Ruffneck went to work like he was actually a man with a passion for cleaning. He dusted, swept, mopped, and removed trash, while watching the fools in their clown suits make monkeys of themselves to impress the women who surrounded them like they were gods of the game. Shit would be different when he grabbed the spotlight. The cats before him seemed to be satisfied and content with just a slice of the city's lucrative drug trade, but not him. Once he was done, his empire would be comprised of every major city in the mitt of Michigan: Detroit, Flint, Kalamazoo, Battle Creek, Jackson, etc. He would be the first to have ever unified the underworld economies of one state's major cities.

The nigga stumbling to the bathroom by himself with a bottle of Patrón in his hand at one-thirty, wasn't exactly standing in the way of progress; he was just in the fucking way, period. Nobody threatened Ruffneck and got away with it. The taps from Bundy's multi-colored alligator shoes clicked against the hollowed floor, creating echoes. Ruffneck calmly stood with balls of steel by the bathroom door, behind his cart, watching Bundy stagger toward him from underneath the visor of his baseball cap. The drunk and stupid expression on McGurk's face told of somebody who thought that they were "made it, Ma" on top of the world.

"Hey, n-i-g-ga," Bundy stammered his words. He held up the empty bottle in a threatening gesture and swung downward, stopping abruptly at the wastebasket opening.

Ruffneck held his tongue.

"You see all this fly shit I got on"—he stepped back as if to model his two-thousand-dollar, funny-colored blue suit—"You need to step yo' game up, nigga. Get you a real job and you'll be able to afford slick shit like this." He pulled up his right sleeve to show off a watch with diamonds cluttering the bezel. He handed the bottle over to Ruffneck and laughed harshly in his face before walking into the bathroom.

Nitroglycerin-type adrenaline exploded throughout Ruffneck's body. His blood turned ice-cold as his heart rate increased. One last glance in both directions left the coast clear to deal with this fool on a more personal level. Ruffneck reached down and snatched up a free-standing, "Caution: Wet Floor" fold-up sign from a side pocket of the cart. He took one more glance up and down the corridor before propping the thing in front of the door and walking into the bathroom. Ruffneck eased into the door, gently locking it behind him.

The music was on bump. He could hear the voices of

drunken women chanting "Put a ring on it" as they tried to sing along to Beyoncé's vocals. With the seat of his trousers sagging, Bundy McGurk leaned in to the urinal with all his weight resting on his left hand, laying flat against the wall. Ruffneck stood behind him as McGurk farted while releasing his water.

"Nigga, this ain't no muthafuckin' peepshow, you dig! Get yo' struggling, nine-to-five-working-ass the fuck up out of here!" he growled, looking over his shoulder. "I piss alone, nigga!"

Ruffneck didn't say shit. He just silently, but menacingly, stood with his hat pulled low; his hands down by his side.

"You fuckin' deaf or sumptin'?!" Bundy yelled even louder.

Ruffneck kept up with the eerie silent routine. He slowly started to pull on the zipper of his coveralls and reach inside, with all the creepiness of a deranged serial killer.

His actions were causing Bundy to blow a fucking gasket: "Okay, muthafucka, when I put my dick back in my pants, nigga, you better be gone; you dig?"

Ruffneck didn't miss Bundy trying to pull some slick shit. McGurk almost had his heater out of his pants when Ruffneck drew his shit first.

"Whooooa, my nig," Bundy shouted at the sight of the Glock, "it's okay. Don't do that shit. Whatever it is, men like us can work it out."

"I don't think we can," Ruffneck responded, holding the nigga in check with the Glock. He slowly pushed up the visor.

"You lil muthafucka," Bundy hissed as he made the discovery. "I knew I should've took care of yo' little ass a few nights ago."

Bundy was still standing there with his pants unzipped.

"Take the gun out and slide the shit over here," Ruffneck instructed.

Bundy reluctantly complied. But he wasn't stupid. He slowly slid his tool across the floor.

"See, niggas like you," Ruffneck explained, "you fools are all about the trigger game. I know cats like you, Bundy. No scrapping skills."

"Won't you put the gun down and see, lil nigga."

Ruffneck allowed Bundy the time to put his dick back inside of his pants.

"I hoped for nothing better," Ruffneck said. As soon as he holstered his gat, Bundy rushed at him like a snarling bull. Ruffneck side-stepped his opponent and caught a handful of Bundy's suit coat. He slung him head-first into the middle sink. Blood spurted like a geyser from Bundy's forehead. Ruffneck held on to the back of Bundy's coat and swung his ass around once more. When Bundy's face struck the hard ceramic urinal, the sound was grotesque. Ruffneck was getting off from the pain and agony etched on McGurk's face as he tried to roll over onto his back. Bundy spat blood and jagged teeth on the floor. Ruffneck stomped him in the head. The punk cried out in pain.

"Like I said, nigga"—Ruffneck took a breath—"I know fools like you: Won't fight because you're too scared to take an ass whupping."

"Fuck you, nigga," was all Bundy could muster as he lay in a heap, bleeding from the head and mouth.

But the episode was far from over as Bundy exploded from the floor, knocking Ruffneck off-balance. Ruffneck fell to the floor by the sinks as Bundy scrambled for his pistol that lay right in front of the bathroom door. Ruffneck couldn't stop him, nor did he have time to reach into his coveralls and grab his stinger. Bundy desperately grabbed the weapon. At the same time, Ruffneck reached underneath the sink and came out with the Glock. Bundy was too slow with the iron. He turned and stared down the barrel of Ruffneck's heater. The bass from the music boomed. Ruffneck fired. The round traveled through Bundy's right eye and exploded through the back of his head. He slumped to the floor.

The nigga was dead all right. Ruffneck wasn't about to stay around and check for a pulse. Bundy's cold, lifeless eye stared up into nothing. Ruffneck had to remain calm. There was no telling who'd heard the gunfire. Just in case he'd encounter any resistance in trying to get the hell out of the building, he kept one of the pistols in his hand, ready for whatever. He dragged Bundy's corpse back out of the way and ran the pockets. He removed two huge knots of money wrapped in rubber bands.

Ruffneck stuck to his plan and left the nigga's pockets turned inside out. He pulled his hat down low over his eyes and unlocked the door. To his relief, there was nobody outside waiting to get in. He looked down toward the main ballroom. The music was still bumping and people were still in groove mode. There were a few cameras mounted on walls in this part of the building, but Ruffneck didn't have to worry. The visor of his baseball cap was too low to make out anything. The security feed would be useless. Nobody would be able to identify him.

As he grabbed the cart, he pushed slowly, not to rush, but trying to put this saga in his rearview mirror. With his heart pumping savagely against his chest, Ruffneck pushed the cart back through the kitchen. He walked out of the back door and out into the fresh early morning air. The nigga Bundy McGurk was in the history books. Cadillac's bitch ass was next on deck.

The rush Ruffneck was feeling, while driving back to the hood at a moderate speed, left the darkness inside of his soul wanting more blood sacrifices, in exchange for his future empire. Offing Bundy McGurk felt as good as busting a nut. He'd given the nigga a chance to prove his manhood by going toe-to-toe. At the end, Ruffneck found Bundy, and other punks like him, to be all trigger and no fight. Ruffneck had busted the fool up and it hadn't taken any overtime to get it done. The mental flashing frames of Bundy spitting up blood, along with teeth, amusingly entertained Ruffneck as he moved down the John C. Lodge Freeway, on his way to holla at Menace. His nigga stayed the closest of all his crew. If they had already found Bundy's bitch ass, Ruffneck knew the police would be out, trying to establish the identity of the killer. He wasn't gonna take chances with keeping the murder weapon on his person.

Ruffneck still couldn't figure out how Menace had done it. His boy used to live in a roach-infested dump of an apartment across town, and now he was staying in a decent neighborhood. It was a tight colonial, too. Ruffneck was thoroughly in tune with the financial situations of each one of his soldiers. Every last one of them was 'Craig and Day Day from the *Friday* sequels' broke. Menace had to have some kind of side hustle going to afford the rent at the spot. Ruffneck didn't meddle in the business of his peeps. Just as long as they were ready to get their money game right with him, he could give a fuck. Everybody had their fair share of secrets. He'd been hanging on to his shit without telling anybody for years.

At Menace's joint, he could stash the heater until a more permanent accommodation could be found. Police presence wasn't so powerful around Menace's way. For the most part, elderly homeowners still occupied their cribs on his street, leaving renters to account for a small percentage—not nearly enough to bring trouble to the peaceful block.

If Ruffneck had gambled against Bundy McGurk being this simple to handle, he would've been minus some loot. The whole idea of this so-called kingpin falling so easily to his trigger-game, proved that the industry was simply one huge pussy, just waiting for some long dick action to come along and fuck the shit out of it.

Ahead, on the shoulder of the freeway, the bright red and blue flashing lights of the State Boys cut through the darkness as they had some fool pulled over. Ruffneck checked his speed, driving right by the police. They had some dumb-looking cat stuffed in the back of their cruiser while they tore up his car, searching for whatever. The empty beer bottles sitting on the hood of the perp's rimmed-out Mustang with the custom paint, had given five-o the legal green light to be all up in ol' boy's shit.

The brush with the State Troopers was too close for comfort. All the pigs had to do was stop Ruffneck, take him to jail for the tainted burner, run ballistics and bam!—off to jail for life. With that thought free-grazing in the back of his mind, he pulled out his cell and hit Menace.

There was no answer.

Ruffneck checked his rearview, now putting distance between him and the police. He placed the call once more.

No answer.

He had to get rid of the piece; and he wasn't gonna ride all the way back to the hood to do it. Menace had to be at the crib, possibly getting his sleep on. Ruffneck then determined that it was worth the trip. If he couldn't raise Menace, then he would go behind the house and hide the gat in the backyard, until the crack of dawn the next morning. One more fruitless phone call sent Ruffneck heading in Menace's direction. When he got on the block, Ruffneck parked a couple houses down on the other side of the street. Menace's neighbors could be extra nosy at times, and he didn't want to bring his boy no grief.

Before Ruffneck got out of the car, he tried Menace once again.

Still, no answer.

He pushed the car door shut, careful not to slam it. He walked on the opposite side of Menace's street until he came upon the house and crossed the street. He moved on the porch and was about to knock, when he heard something that sounded like a bed rocking on rusty springs. Ruffneck peered over the railing, looking on the side of the house. There in the backyard, behind tall, private wooden gates, sat a late-model Conversion van, rocking side-to-side like the thing had hydraulics. He couldn't place it. Menace rolled with a few cats he knew about, but this van didn't belong to any of them.

Ruffneck went inside his coveralls and came out with his tools. He didn't know what the fuck was going on. As far as he was concerned, Menace could've had a broad in the van, banging her brains out, but he wasn't gonna take any chances. For all he knew, some cats on a gank move could've had his boy hemmed up inside, too. Menace was the physical enforcer of his crew. That meant the boy was a bad-ass bull when it came time to flex muscle. He'd saved Ruffneck's ass on more than one occasion. And that's exactly the reason why Ruffneck found himself creeping between houses. He softly opened the latch on the gate, ready to put in work on whatever posed the threat. He slithered through like a hungry anaconda in search of a meal. With his pistols out front, Ruffneck carefully took steps toward the van. The vehicle was dark, with the exception of a soft amber glow emanating from the windows. He slowed his racing heart to take a peek. Not knowing what the fuck he would find had him on edge.

There were no noises coming from inside, other than the squeak from the springs as the van rocked.

One more peek around, then Ruffneck walked up to the van and peered in. He couldn't make out much at first, staring through the heavy tint of the side windows, so he moved around to the windshield; and what he saw was enough to rock him to the core of his gangsta. Never in a million years would he think…his boy…his fucking raw dog, would be involved in the disturbing scene playing out in front of him. Ruffneck had been ready for everything else but what he was now witnessing. The shit didn't compute. Niggas feared Menace in the streets. And if this crap got out, his crew would be laughed off the block.

It was chilly out, but Ruffneck found himself wiping the perspiration from his mouth with the back of his hand. He didn't know how to fucking deal with what he was seeing. He backed away from the truck. Ruffneck was dazed and confused. Hurt. But he had to get a lock on his emotions. Bundy's murder put him back in the frame of mind for what he'd come to do. Ruffneck had to get the hell off the street. It was priority. He knew this was the type of shit that could pose as a distraction and get a nigga locked up for life.

So he collected himself and holstered one of the nines. He walked over to the the back steps and placed the weapon that he'd used on McGurk underneath, against the foundation. About an hour ago, he'd bodied one of the biggest names in the game, and now it didn't mean a damn thing. Nothing else would after this discovery. Ruffneck walked back to his ride. He jumped in and started it with one thing on his mind: his boy Menace was a fucking homo-thug. Ruffneck had gotten a good look at the nigga Menace was fucking. It was the dude that had passed glances with them while Ruffneck and Menace stood in front of the corner store, just hours before he'd beaten his cracked-out Uncle William senseless for stealing Granny Sinclair's TV.

Didn't matter, though, his dude was a fucking homo-thug.

Trick, You The Treat

It was Halloween, Friday afternoon. Ruffneck was still fucked up by what he'd seen. It freaked him out because Menace and his punk had been going at it in the back of the van like they were a heterosexual couple. Menace had his punk bent over, banging, kissing up the dude's back—damn, Ruffneck couldn't think about the shit anymore. He couldn't deal with this latest problem. The streets had taught him how to go for the brass ring. This was that reality TV drama. Junk he'd kicked back to while watching the *Jerry Springer* show. He'd never been equipped to handle problems like this one. So naturally, he'd stayed away from it. He'd put the issue out of his mind until he could properly digest it all. Besides, he had more pressing business. The hit on Cadillac's lottery joint was popping off tonight, and he had to force his mind around the job. Didn't wanna get caught slipping. His aim was to get in and ghost, before fools could form the nuts to play hero.

Bundy McGurk was officially history. "Kingpin Slain in Public Restroom"—was the headline story of his murder, with a picture of his face plastered across the front pages of the *Detroit News* and *Free Press* papers. All the news stations seemed to be running the same line. Microphones were shoved in the grills of club patrons hoping to shed light on such a brutal crime. At one point, Ruffneck watched the Chief of Police stand on a podium. The chief stared at cameras and made a sincere plea to the citizens for help, saying something about taking the city back from the gangstas.

Ruffneck could give a fuck, though. He turned the channel. McGurk had gotten what he had coming. Now Ruffneck was on to the next one.

Granny Sinclair had started in on him early that morning about those damn cigarettes and heart medication. So, after he finished his afternoon grub, Ruffneck made his way to the pharmacy.

The robbery was scheduled to go down tonight, right at shift change. He would meet his crew over at Fly's spot around seven. From there, they would go over the final details of the mission. Shit had to be executed perfectly. Ruffneck wasn't gonna tell his soldiers that he was the one who was personally responsible for rocking Bundy. He believed that every leader had to take one for the team at some point in leadership. He trusted his niggas; but the less that they knew, the better, especially after jacking Cadillac's main lottery house. It wouldn't take too long for cats to start playing Kojak and connecting the dots from Bundy's murder to Cadillac's misfortune. And if any of Ruffneck's crew were caught, they would not only be in the cross-hairs of Bundy's and Cadillac's people, but local law enforcement as well.

The move had to go down flawless. There was absolutely no room for error. Pull off the heist and everybody would be set. Fail, and his crew and their families would be ruthlessly slaughtered. It was a scene that Ruffneck was all too familiar with. He wasn't about to have a repeat of his parents. He was responsible for getting his troops there, and bringing them back out alive.

Ruffneck was walking down his block on his way back from the pharmacy, when his cousin pulled alongside in the Regal. He rolled down the driver's window.

"Cuz, let me holla at you for a few," Hootie asked in a voice fueled by anxiety. Ruffneck could see that the boy was stressed. Hootie's face held a wild and foolish look.

Ruffneck looked around before sliding into the passenger's seat.

"What it do, pimpin'?" Ruffneck asked as he paid close attention to his cousin's unsettling behavior. Something was up with him. First off, Hootie was a nocturnal creature; a vampire who beat the sunrise back into the crib and didn't come back out until night. Seeing him out at this time of day, cruising the block, didn't sit too well with Ruffneck. Trouble was in the air and he could feel it.

"You were right about that snake nigga," Hootie professed, peeping around nervously, exhaling.

Ruffneck covered his nose and screwed up his face.

"Damn, cuz, what the hell you been drinking?" It was only then that Ruffneck had located the source. He picked up the bottle. "Wild Turkey—fuck is you drinking Wild Turkey for?"

Hootie grabbed the bottle from his cousin, unscrewed the cap, and took a long swig. His hand trembled so badly that the liquid inside the bottle splashed around like it was in an electric blender.

Ruffneck pulled the bottle from his lips. "You all right? Now, chill the fuck out and tell me what's up."

Hootie's eyes were bloodshot. The nigga suspiciously peeked around a few more times before saying: "Remember me telling you that Billy wanted to buy some AK-47s?"

"Okay. That was a month ago. What's that got to do with now?"

"A month ago, the fool killed the deal, citing that he could cop them for a cheaper price. 'Bout a couple days ago, Billy had his boy Chris call me and set the deal up again. I told him the usual price, plus my fifteen percent.

"So me"—Hootie grabbed his pistol from underneath his seat when an SUV rolled by. Once he discovered that it was just a neighbor, he settled back into the story. "So, we get to the spot last night and me and mi nigga was unloading the heat, when cats started coming out from the woodwork. Billy walks up behind them talking shit about, if we move, our eulogies would be read by the end of the next week. I'm about to go for my gat when my homeboy Delo comes up with his, blasting."

"Billy set you up?"

Hootie took another hit of Wild Turkey, practically ignoring Ruffneck's questions. "Billy gives one of his goons the go-ahead to start letting off with an AK. They straight smoked Delo, dog. I barely made it out with my life, cuz."

Ruffneck took a long stare out of the passenger's window, thinking. He hated Billy's flashy ass, but he deeply respected what he'd done in the game. Bundy McGurk might've been a lower-level dealer of Billy's, but he was no Billy. Billy the Kid was that nigga you didn't cross swords with if you didn't have an army. The cat was the dude under the nigga, who was underneath the man that had a thumb on the pulse of Detroit's underworld. Ruffneck admitted to wanting Billy's shine, but wouldn't challenge him until he was able to match forces. Hootie was in serious trouble and Ruffneck knew it. His cousin had witnessed a murder and was the only living witness who could put Billy the Kid behind bars, for life.

"Hootie, listen to me," Ruffneck spoke slowly.

Hootie didn't like the look in his cousin's eyes. He tried to down the bottle.

"Give me that shit." Ruffneck snatched the bottle out of Hootie's hands. "It ain't gonna do nothing but make it worse. Listen, man, you need to get out of town. Billy's gonna kill you, dog. I love you too much for that to happen. Here's what we're gonna do: You go down South to Monroe, Louisiana. Go stay with Aunt Edda

Mae for a year. About the time you come back, Billy and everybody else in his crew will either be dead or rolling with me. That's my promise to you. But you have to get the fuck up out of here."

Hootie let disagreement settle into his inebriated, clown-like facial expression. He grabbed the bottle and turned it up.

Ruffneck lunged at it, but Hootie blocked his efforts, pulled back, and continued chugging until the bottle was finished. He belched hard.

"You sound scared, mi nigga," Hootie said to Ruffneck. "This ain't like you to be talkin' like a pussy, man! What's up with that?"

Hootie was definitely drunk and Ruffneck was aware. In a sober mind, Hootie knew that coming at his cousin in such a manner would've brought pain to his front door. Ruffneck gave the cat a pass. The kind of pressure that his cousin was under, mixed with the Wild Turkey, would give anybody the balls to speak from the heart— even if it was to the face of a stone-cold killer.

Ruffneck sized his cousin up. "I'm no pussy, man. I'm just looking at the bigger picture. Billy is gonna fall, whether you here to see it, or in hell, so that the nigga can come tell you about it. But that fool's gonna drop, cuz."

"You talking about a whole year, dude. I can't wait that long. My business, man—what about my business?" Hootie whined.

"Man, later for them guns, G. When you get back, I'll

would take out the guard in the garage and penetrate the side door, while everybody else stormed through the front. But the jack had to be in sync. Everybody had to be in place. Subduing the guard inside the garage would be critical. Menace would then advance on the guard in the basement. It would give them the time needed to get up to the third level and neutralize the workers. If the information he'd gotten was correct, the niggas would be up in the main bedroom goofing off, playing Madden NFL 12, around that time.

Ruffneck and Fly put on their rubber masks to complete their costumes. They were dressed in the hooded robes of medieval monks from the Middle Ages. The Red Monk masks were extra scary and quite disturbing to look at, but they would get the job done. Nobody would look out of place. It was Halloween, and everything bearing an ugly face had the right to prowl the night.

Ruffneck concealed the Glocks underneath the robe, shoved inside the horizontal shoulder holsters sitting on top of the Kevlar vest. Fly had his heat at his waist.

The masks were pretty hard to breathe and see through, but they got the hang of it as the two strolled right along with the cheery crowd of goody-bag brandishing gremlins. They were two houses from the joint when Lil Shorty and Poison stepped into view. Both were dressed as nuns; even had on the false faces of old white women.

Since there was no porch light on at Cadillac's, the rest of the trick-or-treaters kept on going by, while Ruffneck and crew walked onto the porch. He nodded his head and all came out from underneath their robes with fire-power, careful to keep the weaponry out of sight. His stomach was turning flips because he didn't know Menace's status. The big man was supposed to have both guards in gags and Zip Ties by now.

Ruffneck slowly turned the doorknob with his free hand and held one of the Glocks out in front with the other. His crew was behind him as the door opened, and he slowly stepped in, looking over the top of his raised weapon. The lights inside the living room were on, but nobody was in sight. The noise, only created by niggas thoroughly enjoying a video game, was coming from upstairs. Ruffneck was about to enter the dining room to see if Menace was tight, when he saw him sitting in one of the chairs at the dining room table.

He whispered, "Been waitin' on y'all."

"Funny," Ruffneck whispered. "I'm assuming you sitting here means the other two niggas are out the way."

"I did my part," Menace said. "Now let's get paid."

The sounds of Madden NFL 12 were on bump. The workers upstairs were shouting loud enough to be at a real stadium. Ruff-neck nodded in the direction of the stairs. He and Fly, followed closely by Poison, took the staircase in single file. Ruffneck had his stingers out in front, as he quietly rounded the banister and cleared the first set of steps. Although, he doubted that the bums could hear him with all the noise they were creating. The bedroom was right off the stairs. He could even see one of the cats with the PlayStation controller fixed in his hand, and a childlike smile on his stupid-looking mug.

Without thinking if the goons were all in the same bedroom, Ruffneck burst up the last few steps. The fools didn't know what to do with themselves. There was a scream, a gunshot, and then another scream. Afterward, Ruffneck gave the order.

"Don't fucking move!" he commanded. "Y'all know what time it is." His voice was muffled. The Red Monk mask looked like death in the form of a walking zombie.

"The other two rooms are clear," Fly informed.

"Clear on this end," Poison announced as she entered the room, wearing the latex face of an old, decrepit white woman. Zip Ties were in her right hand.

"Face first, against the wall," Ruffneck barked at the three men. They shook as Ruffneck held them in front of his weapon. The blood on the floor was coming from the biggest one. He'd been plugged in the right shoulder during the melee. It was supposed to be a simple warning shot, but the nigga panicked and ran in the same direction of the traveling bullet.

"I...need...a doctor," the big man struggled to say. He was leaning against the wall, breathing heavily.

Ruffneck hadn't counted on the shooting. The neighbors had to have heard the shot. The area they were in was slowly dying from crackhouses, Section-8, and good old-fashioned city neglect. So police were slow, if anything, in responding to 9-1-1 calls. But Ruffneck couldn't chance it. The police could be on his ass at any moment. He sized up the situation. There was one man injured and two more who were scared shitless—not to mention the condition of the two guards that Menace had left in the garage and basement.

He made his decision. Ruffneck gave the order for the two smaller cats to be tied and placed on their bellies on the floor. He left the big fool, leaning against the wall. The cat was crying and whining like a bitch.

"You," Ruffneck said, pointing to the big, black, smoke-colored nigga wearing braids with fat, discolored lips. He walked right up to the cat and placed his tool to Big Black's temple. "You got one minute minus fifty seconds to tell me where the loot is."

Before dude could spill the beans, Ruffneck heard Menace call out from downstairs. "Aye, man, we got company. Looks like that fool, Cadillac."

Ruffneck hadn't planned on Cadillac visiting at this time. The intel he'd gotten had been pinpoint accurate up to this point.

"Tie this big fool up," Ruffneck ordered Fly. "Fly, you babysit these niggas, and, Poison, you come with me downstairs." Gags went around mouths the second Ruffneck moved out of the room.

Downstairs, Ruffneck spied out of the peephole. Yep,

it was the fat bastard all right. One of his goons was with him, too. In one of Cadillac's pudgy little hands was the handle of a briefcase. If the rumors were true, the pig carried large amounts of cash around in those cases. Ruffneck couldn't help it, but his dick jumped hard. The cash register inside of his head started ringing like Las Vegas slot machines when paying off big.

He instructed Lil Shorty to go behind the long couch in the front room. Poison was directed to stand in the dining room behind an adjoining wall. Menace laid his big ass on the staircase, concealed by a wall. The Desert Eagle rested by his side.

Ruffneck hugged the wall behind the door, hoping, almost praying, that they didn't need to open it up all the way. Then he thought about Cadillac's big Krispy Kreme doughnut-munching ass, and became paranoid.

The element of surprise was on his side. The screen door opened, screeching on its hinges. There was muffled on-the-other-side-of-the-door small talk from Cadillac and his man, followed by keys jingling in the lock. And then the door opened.

Ruffneck let Cadillac and his henchman get all the way through the door before smashing the butt of his gun against the back of the bodyguard's melon. The cat with the long dreadlocks, square jaw, five-o'clock-shadow beard, and the high-powered gangsta swagger plummeted to the floor—lights out. Cadillac let out a little-girl-just-seeing-the-boogeyman-standing-over-her-bed-in-the-midnight-hour scream, when he saw the mask of the Red Monk. Lil Shorty rose up from his position like a dead nun coming back to life. Poison rolled into the room and Menace stood tall, wearing the mask made famous by the killer in the movie *Scream*. With so many guns on him, Cadillac didn't know what the fuck to do. His man was lying on the floor, knocked the hell out, blood caking his dreads.

Ruffneck held his burner to Cadillac's forehead, snatching the briefcase from his hand.

"I'll take that," Ruffneck said in a muffled tone. "Money in here?" Ruffneck shook the case.

Cadillac reluctantly nodded his head in submission.

Ruffneck said, "This ain't all. Where's the rest of the dough?"

Cadillac was going to try and play hard at first—that was until Poison shot his right knee from underneath him. He dropped beside Dreadlocks, holding his shit and crying like a baby.

Ruffneck leaned on his haunches.

"Where the loot, fat man?" he asked. He looked back at Poison. The .380 was still smoking from the barrel. "The nun ain't fucking around with you. Now, where is the bread, old nigga?"

Cadillac was crying real tears. Poison moved toward him to take another shot, but he bitched up before she could pull the trigger. The money was down in the basement, locked away in a safe inside the wall behind a laundry dryer. Menace snatched Cadillac up by the collar and marched him down to it.

In the basement, one of the guards had been Zip Tied and gagged. Berry-Flavor was too, for the playoff. The blood pouring from Cadillac's wound caused him to struggle with the combination at first. He eventually got the thing opened and filled two duffel bags up, before the safe was completely empty. Cadillac was then Zip Tied along with the guard, and the bitch in the basement. Ruffneck also bound Mister Dreadlocks' unconscious ass before they made ready to shake the spot.

Menace left the same way he'd come; slightly jogging back to the ride in the alley and peeling off. Ruffneck and the rest of the crew took to the dark street, making it back to the church van within minutes. Back at Cadillac's joint, Ruffneck had ditched the briefcase. He'd spilled its contents into one of the duffel bags that he was now carrying, with his chest stuck out by extreme pride. They'd hit pay-dirt. Ruffneck didn't know just how much loot they'd jacked, but if the zipper not fully closing on the bag was any indication, it would be more than enough to buy them a ticket into the game. Nobody had to die behind it, either. Sure, they'd left in their wake two gunshot victims and a nigga with a possible concussion, but no stiffs—absolutely no bodies.

On the way to the rendezvous spot, Ruffneck took out an untraceable minute-phone and dialed 9-1-1. It wasn't that he was going soft or no shit like that. Cadillac, nor any of his boys, deserved to die. They hadn't crossed Ruffneck like the others he'd rush to the dirt. Ruffneck reported the shootings at the address. He tossed the minute-phone out on the freeway as they sped along.

The first phase of his plan was complete. They'd gotten over the hump. But he wasn't gonna start popping bottles yet. Although he'd just laid the foundation of his kingdom, Ruffneck was keenly aware that building his empire would run the streets red with blood. And each stone in the erection of his castle would soon represent death.

Typical Niggas

It was the last week of November, almost four weeks after Cadillac had inadvertently supplied Ruffneck and his crew with a stake in a game dominated by selfishness, ruthlessness, and betrayal. But they were up for the task.

The cold weather was extreme and a light snowfall had dusted morning rush hour. Meteorologists had all Michiganders bracing for what could possibly be the coldest winter in decades. Ruffneck rarely found himself up early on chilly mornings, but the news that Fly had called with, made him jump from a warm bed, ready to smash shit. Ruffneck had immediately pulled on his clothes and rushed over to Fly's momma's bungalow-style home; and just in time for breakfast. Fly's old girl, Rhonda, brought out the dishes and set the dining room table before the two boys.

Rhonda was mid-forties, dark-skinned, with pretty white teeth, and her natural hair pulled into a ponytail. She was rocking a low-cut blouse, showing off almost perfect cleavage. She bent at the waist and kissed Ruffneck on the jaw; set the food down and got out of the way. Over pancakes, bacon, and cheesy scrambled eggs, Fly plugged Ruffneck into the gossip on the street.

"'Neck, dog, I don't know if you heard, guy, but word on the street is that Lil Shorty is out recklessly spending money like he was printing the shit inside his basement."

"I told y'all to lay out for a while before any change was spent," Ruffneck said, now with regret.

He'd gone against his better judgment in breaking his crew off the night of the lick. He'd regretted it the moment the take was revealed—one hundred-thousand dollars. Ruffneck had to admit that he'd gotten caught in the number-hype and split the shit five ways. Unlimited possibilities had blinded his judgment. He hadn't thought about the damage that could possibly be caused from a nigga wilding out with the loot, until they had all gone their separate ways. Ruffneck's high had quickly come down after he'd reached his crib. When the vision of Lil Shorty—or should he say, the Little Bambino of Terror—out popping bottles, buying up the malls, and on lavish jewelry shopping sprees sprinted through his mind. Betrayal had been hot in the little nigga's eyes once he'd received twenty Gs, too. Ruffneck didn't want to believe it, but he knew that the little punk was gonna go buck-wild with his share of the cheese.

"It hasn't been a month yet," Fly explained, "and your boy's out tricking away some change—Old School Monte Carlo with the candy paint, sounds, twenty-four-inch rims—man, this little nigga's out there."

Ruffneck hadn't touched his grub, but Fly was eating like there wasn't going to be a tomorrow. And with Lil Shorty out letting the streets know about his new-found wealth, Ruffneck knew it would be just a matter of time before niggas came to investigate.

"Where he at?" Ruffneck bluntly asked.

Fly swallowed some pancakes and chased it with OJ. "Don't know."

"Where the rest of us?"

"Don't know that, either. 'Member you told us to get low and not contact each other for a while. You the first one I've seen since we hit Cadillac's spot."

Ruffneck sat there gazing off into nothing. He knew what had to be done. Though he didn't like it, it still had to be. He kicked around the setup inside his mind. The little nigga had dug his own grave; but he damn sure wasn't about to drag the rest of them to hell with him. He had to be silenced. Ruffneck had come too close to grabbing that brass ring to have this pint-sized bitch spend it up on rims, Timbs, and hoes.

Fly forked down some eggs, chewed, swallowed and said, "The fucked-up part about it, man, is that everybody knows that McGurk and Cadillac did business together. Now, I don't know how much of that loot we took was McGurk's, dude, but his people, as well as the police, are saying the same person who killed him is probably the same one who ran Cadillac."

"Where you hear all this from, G?" Ruffneck asked.

"Man, it don't matter because the streets are talking,

fam. And being that the lil loudmouth rolls with our set, you know the conclusion cats are gonna draw."

Ruffneck blew out frustration.

Fly went on. "'Neck, I know you ain't stressing Cadillac's bitch ass, but McGurk's niggas want blood, dog. And those are the fools you don't wanna wake up, with them standing over your bed." Fly sipped a little OJ. "Cadillac ain't no slouch, either, though. He got that kind of cheese to bring in out-of-town hitters. You remember the nigga Moochie? That nigga fronted on Cadillac, and later on, those out-of-town fools cut his nuts off and mailed them in a box to his mother."

Ruffneck finally spoke up. "I ain't sweatin' them fools. But a nigga gotta do what a nigga gotta do."

Fly caught the drift. "I hear ya. Just say the word, cuz, and Shorty's ass is canceled."

Ruffneck could appreciate his homeboy's heart. He was down to bang—one hunnit, boots laced up, and ready to floss grimy.

"Naw, fam, that body belongs to my trigger. I brought his little ass in. I'm responsible for seeing him through to the next destination. I gave his ass plenty of chances, too. Looked out for him. But now, I gotta put the mack on him."

"I hear ya," Fly said. His cell rang. He looked at the caller ID and yelled, "Bitch! Stupid bitch!"

Ruffneck was aware who was hitting his boy on the cell. He stepped around Fly's baby-momma moment. "Anybody else been spending?"

"Not to my knowledge, man. As far as I know, we're all waiting on you to give us the go ahead so that we can put our pieces together and get some air under our wings."

"Yeah. That won't be too long. I hollered at Truck: the old head from the poolroom, for the connect. But now we gotta put shit on hold to deal with this small problem."

Fly's phone jumped off again. He called his baby-momma a few more bitches. Then he said, "Oh, yeah, I saw your boy Nizzo the other day. The fool had just got out the hospital. You broke that kid up pretty bad. When he saw me, the nigga boned the fuck out." Fly laughed like Kevin Hart was inside of his head performing standup.

"What about you, Fly, have you spent any loot?"

The question was direct. And the way Ruffneck sounded, he wanted a no-bullshit answer.

"I—you know, I bought my baby a couple pieces, man."

Ruffneck sat there, looking at his boy like he'd just caught him in a lie. And he had. He already knew Fly was full of shit. Lying through his teeth. Judging from the stupid look on his grill and his phone blowing up every other minute, it didn't take a detective to figure out who Fly had tricked his money with.

Ruffneck slammed his fist against the table, agitated. "Y'all niggas slipping. I thought every last fool in our family wanted riches. But I was fucking wrong—unbelievable. Little kids. I should've treated you fools like little kids and kept all the loot until we were ready to move forward."

Ruffneck pushed his chair back and stood from the table and pulled on his coat.

He looked at Fly with disappointment registering in his face. "I ain't tryna tell you how to handle your business, nigga, but you need to leave that bitch alone. Your skirt is showing, mi dude." Ruffneck walked to the door, consumed by dark deeds. He opened the front door. "But the most tripped-out part about it is that…you can't see it. Tell your momma I said bye."

He walked out of the crib with shit heavy on his mind. He hated the thought, but this was the first time since starting with his crew that he questioned their character—Menace was a homo, Fly was letting his baby-momma run freely up in him by using the baby-card as a stiff non-lubricated dildo, and Lil Shorty, well, the little nigga had some 'splaining to do. But unfortunately, it would be to Satan, because the hunt was on for his little ass. Nobody got in the way of Ruffneck's destiny. It saddened him to admit, but the only one who seemed to be solid was—next to himself—the deadliest one in the clique, and she was a bitch. Ruffneck was aware of Poison's value to his future organization. He would need the loyal, mysterious beauty whose silent, but deadly, demeanor would definitely come in handy in the form of kryptonite, in a world where niggas ruled with dick and Superman-sized egos.

Ruffneck went to take out his cell for cab service, but decided that a long walk in the cold climate would help him put shit into perspective. He wondered if his father had to put up with shit like this: a crew who seemed to be imploding in front of his very eyes. It seemed to him that he was the only one who wanted that Tony Montana-the-world-is-yours blimp to hover over his fifteen-acre estate as he watched the crowning moment from the balcony of his multimillion-dollar mansion, while smoking on a Cuban cigar dream.

Ruffneck had some thinking to do. He had massive plans for the underworld, but how could he achieve it, if he couldn't keep the structure stable in his own family? Issues—so many fucking issues to deal with.

As he started off down the street, Ruffneck looked around like he always did, and bunched the neck of his coat inside his fist. He would eventually get around to addressing all of his issues; Lil Shorty being the first one in need of his immediate attention. And as the hawk picked up, whistling, gusting down the street with so much frigid force, the chilly wind paled in comparison to the coldness of the still photo in Ruffneck's mind; Lil Shorty's face decorating the front of an obituary.

Time On Hand

Ruffneck drove Hootie's Buick down Grand River at eight in the evening. Ever since Fly had hollered at him about Lil Shorty's fuck-you-all spending spree, he'd been trying to get at the little nigga on the cell. For most of the day, Lil Shorty had rushed many of Ruffneck's calls straight to voicemail—until an hour ago. The chump picked up. Ruffneck told Lil Shorty that he wouldn't talk over the phone, but he would meet him somewhere to spit game at him for a few. He almost never discussed business over the cell, so he opted to meet Lil Shorty at one of their old dope spots from back in the day. The old house on Sorrento now belonged to a smoke head named Boogeyman, who rented it out to other crackheads to get high. It would be the perfect spot to leave the little fool lying in a pool of his own blood. Ruffneck felt on his chest. The Kevlar vest was there, but he was minus one of the Glocks. He could remember strapping on the twin holster and hurrying to the car to go meet Lil Shorty. He'd made the discovery halfway into the drive. Ruffneck blew it off. Seventeen shots would be more than enough to step on a rat.

Ruffneck had ignored the cockiness inside the kid's voice and went out to meet him anyway. At the rate that his punk ass was spreading loot around town, it wouldn't be too long before cats—and five-o—would come around asking questions. Much like he'd dealt with Bundy McGurk, Lil Shorty was now a threat to the health and welfare of his crew, and family.

As usual, Ruffneck moved around in the shadows by his lonely. He wouldn't need extra muscle to deal with the likes of Lil Shorty. One to the head would leave his ass at peace. The little nigga just so happened to try and wear shoes that were much too big for his feet. Time and time again he'd given the dude a pass. Ruffneck had never flexed on him, because he felt that he owed it to Lil Shorty's people. But it was his fault. First rule of thumb was not to play with the dog too long, because eventually, the little bitch would lick you right in the face.

Ruffneck was five minutes from Sorrento in Puritan when he felt his old friend, darkness, creep into his soul, beckoning for him to come back and play in a zone devoid of feelings and emotions. He was up to the moment. Tapping into that animal part of him that saw no wrong in standing over a man while emptying an entire magazine into his ass. It was pretty spooky how he could summon dark forces at will. Sometimes he swore that he could hear Hole-in-the-Head and his homeboy, Man-Beast, call out the plays for murder. This kill would be different. Lil Shorty was somebody he knew;

hung out with for years. The two had history together. They were supposed to make history together. Now, Ruffneck was about to make his bitch-ass history. For this job, Ruffneck would need to go deeper into the chaos that existed in his heart. He would travel back to the night inside his parents' bedroom; a time when his childhood innocence had been taken by those on a quest for murder.

Sorrento was mostly dark with two or three lampposts spread out over each long block. When he rolled up to the crib, something didn't feel right. Ruffneck couldn't quite put his finger on it. The little nigga's pimped-out Monte Carlo was nowhere to be found. He knew Lil Shorty didn't have the balls for double-cross, so Ruffneck parked the ride in front of the house. But just in case, he removed the pistol from its holster. Five minutes later, Ruffneck spotted a set of headlights coming from the opposite direction. The closer the car got, he could make out the custom, candy paint job. Lil Shorty pulled abreast of Ruffneck's driver's window and rolled down his. Ruffneck was in perfect control of his anger. Nothing, not even the kid's nonchalant attitude, or his shiny, new twenty-four-inch rims, could provoke him.

Ruffneck rolled down his window.

"What dup, B?" Lil Shorty asked with the same cockiness that Ruffneck had heard a half-hour ago.

Ruffneck's face held no expression as he gazed at a dead man.

He looked over Lil Shorty's tricked-out whip.

"Nice ride," Ruffneck complimented.

Lil Shorty smiled and looked over his ride like he was stroking his own ego. He stuck his pinky ring out so that Ruffneck could see the karats that he was working with.

"You dig it? It's one of a kind in the whole city, fam," he bragged.

"You got time to talk?" Ruffneck asked. "I seriously need to holla at you about getting this paper."

The pause Lil Shorty offered, as he looked around inside his car like he was signaling somebody, or going for his weapon, excited Ruffneck. Ruffneck smoothly readied his pistol; careful not to arouse the little fool's suspicion. Even if somebody was hiding in the backseat, Ruffneck would have the drop. But it was always the nigga you couldn't see that you had to be worried about—or in this case, the police. Because red and blue flashing lights seemed to come from every direction, sweeping over and lighting up the block.

Lil Shorty laughed, and said as he looked at the action, "You have to speak to them first, you bitch-ass nigga."

Police vehicles blocked Ruffneck's ride in tight. They shined the lights on his face, and yelled loudly for him to drop any weapons and get the fuck out of the car, slowly. Police were everywhere, standing behind their cars for cover, but all had service automatics trained on him.

"Nigga, it's a new day," Lil Shorty boasted and slowly drove out of sight.

Ruffneck couldn't feel shit. His mind was on how the little muthafucka had managed to set him up, and with the police of all people. Ruffneck simply didn't see this bullshit coming. He'd allowed himself to slip by dealing with other problems. He'd heard his Granny Sinclair mention that an idle mind was the devil's workshop, and if that was the truth, then what could be said about a nigga trying to rule the fucking world with a cloudy head. The answer to the latter was now playing out in front of him as he slowly put his weapon down on the passenger seat and stepped from the car.

Ruffneck was aware that felony firearms carried the maximum of two years. The only bright spot was that it wasn't the gun Bundy McGurk had fallen to. He'd had good presence of mind to throw that heater into the Detroit River one cold, dark night.

Through blinding lights from the police cruisers, Ruffneck could barely make out folks stepping out on porches to watch his ass get hauled away. He was repeatedly ordered to lie face-down on the cold ground. Before he could comply, two beefy uniformed officers rushed from behind the bright lights and took him by both shoulders, yanked his hands behind his back, and slammed him to the ground so hard that it knocked the wind from him.

Everything else was a blur. On the way down to the station, the only thing that Ruffneck could remember at the arrest spot, was five-o making jokes about finding history on the gun and him going to prison, only to wind up washing the drawers of the rapist he'd be punking to. Ruffneck hadn't even felt them slip the cold bracelets over his wrists—that were now threatening to cut off his circulation. He was hit. Even with a paid-for mouthpiece, he'd be looking at some years. He was more worried about the old woman, though. Ruffneck knew he could take care of himself in the joint, but Granny Sinclair would be all by her lonely. It was a thought that scared him more than him not accomplishing the job that he'd set out to do in amassing the ultimate empire.

He'd fucked up, royally. Unless the old woman was down for telling him who his folks were on visiting day, he would have a long time before he could seriously harass her ass in the privacy of her home. Ruffneck tried to laugh at the situation, but his ribs hurt like hell behind the cops punishing the ground with his body.

The only thing going through his mind, while the pigs fingerprinted and took pictures of his mug, was how in the hell did Lil Shorty get the drop on him?

Under New Management

A few hours after Lil Shorty had gift-wrapped and handed Ruffneck over to five-o, wearing a pretty pink bow, he went to blow off some steam at a local hangout.

It was always popping at Truck's poolroom; especially on a Saturday night. Everybody with the superstar ghetto-claim showed up dressed in the fruits from lucrative street-trappings. Despite the star-studded crowd, Truck Turner, the owner, had gone out of the way to make his place decent, and open to all who had a desire to come in and enjoy the friendly atmosphere.

Troublemakers were not welcome. Truck's spot might've sat in the heart of an area that the locals deemed Death after Dark, but the old hustler wasn't buying any shit from what the younger generation was terming as the "new ghetto." Those coming into his place half-cocked would experience what it was truly like back in his day, when cats used to get an ass-whupping by the now outdated art of hand-to-hand combat. The old player might've been a couple years over middle-aged, but he still stood a towering 6'6" and tipped the scales at a solid three hundred pounds. Truck was a serious Triple O.G. who'd made his bones in an era where heavy industrial chains, knives, and brute strength, were the only things needed to settle differences. For the most part, Truck was highly esteemed by his community for diligently working with juveniles who'd taken a wrong turn, and were now trying to glue the pieces of a crumbling life back together.

He couldn't, for the life of him, figure out the new school thinking of these young, stupid fools, or what he called, knuckle-headed crack babies. But, whatever their beefs were on the outside of Turner's pool hall, nobody brought trouble into 300 Tireman Avenue. He ruled with an iron-fist, a pool cue, beer bottle, or whatever he got his hands on, to show that he was not the one to be fucked with.

On the outside, Truck's image seemed to be squeaky-clean for the benefit of those who held him up as a community activist, leader, role model, and inspirational story to all looking for a shot at redemption. After hours was an entirely different stretch of road. Truck's spot doubled as a hub for a fraction of Detroit's cocaine distribution. He had been plugged into the main vein of the underworld ever since coming home from serving a fifteen-year prison sentence in the murder of his wife's brother, for trying to play him out of some product. Truck had everybody fooled, pretending to be fully reformed. He was just the opposite: anybody who crossed him found themselves in pieces and spread throughout the alleys of the city.

Truck's after-hours joint had taken tempting acts of debauchery off the streets and placed these services under one roof. The big man was working the back room when Lil Shorty had offered the secret knock on the steel door. Truck made him out through the tiny peephole. He didn't really know the kid personally, but had seen him come in with Ruffneck a time or two. And to be truthful, he didn't like the little nigga's look. Truck had been down and dirty for a long time, and he'd stared in the face of many snakes in his day, but there was something extra slithery about the young boy that rubbed him the wrong way.

Truck had tried to warn Ruffneck about the bad vibes the little fool was giving. But in true fashion, Ruffneck simply made excuses until Truck would drop the subject. So, when Truck saw Lil Shorty bop through the door like his shit didn't stink, without Ruffneck, red flags started waving around inside the older man's head.

The poolroom was in front, but everything else was located near the rear of the building. The back door opened up into a small room, no bigger than the space it took to hold a circle of fools on their knees throwing bones. There were additional rooms behind another steel door at the opposite end, off the back entrance. These were usually reserved for ballers with a different definition to the phrase "throwing bones." Truck had personally hand-selected the ladies who manned these rooms according to their specialty.

He watched with much interest as Lil Shorty strolled over to where a dice game had been going on for about thirty minutes. The young fool's style of dress had picked up, too. The lifeless rags he'd worn into the poolroom before, had now transformed into an expensive brand-name leather jacket, True Religion jeans, high-end leather boots, with the cherry on top of the sundae being the massive gold cable around his neck that almost hung down to his nuts with an iced-out charm in the likeness of a vicious pit bull. Truck knew he wasn't going crazy when he observed the boy go inside his jacket and pull out a huge roll the likes that Pillsbury couldn't duplicate. He kneeled down, blending in with seven other dudes and bought his way into the game, after which he immediately started talking king-sized shit.

Truck made sure that the door had been locked behind Lil Shorty. He shook his head at the little fool and disappeared behind the door that led into the poolroom.

"Okay, fellas, the G with the biggest nuts is now in the house," Lil Shorty yelled, shaking the dice. He rolled them and clocked seven. "Shit, mi nigs, somebody going home broke tonight." Shorty shook the dice again and rolled. "Damn, seven again, niggas! Y'all let the wrong guy in the game. I'm the Little Bambino of Terror. You fools, don't forget the name."

"For being such a little guy," some brother with charred dark skin said, rising up from the game, "you talk a lot of big shit. Nigga, you just got here. Won't you shut the fuck up and play the game."

Lil Shorty stared up from the game with a fist full of cash. "Nigga, you sound like you've been losing all night. Okay, I see what this is." Shorty peeled off a twenty spot and shoved it in old boy's direction. "Here, take this twenty and get yo' mad, broke ass back in the game."

Everybody else found the shit funny, but the cat with the charred flesh. He took exception. He mumbled something under his breath; turned his back on the game, only to go into his cheap-ass pleather jacket and pull a pistol.

He turned around and held it on the circle of fools who were surprised; a few of them losing balance and falling to the floor.

"Y'all don't think I'm Eddie-fuckin'-Murphy funny now, do you muthafuckas?" Charred Flesh asked with spit flying from his mouth.

Nobody said anything. The dude looked to be seriously unstable and the least little noise or movement could possibly set him off. This group held no heroes. Nobody wanted a hot one in the ass.

"Listen, you fools, strip!"—he waved the gun downward with his demand.

There was grumbling at first, until the cat dramatically yanked the slide back on his automatic weapon to indicate that he wasn't bullshitting. Niggas started dropping, shedding clothes like they were in a contest, where the winner who was the first to get naked, would win a cash prize. While dudes where stripping, Lil Shorty was still staring at Charred Flesh through the lenses of his Cartier glasses, like the fool had lost his fuckin' mind. There was no way he was giving up shit. He'd worked hard jacking Cadillac for his loot, and getting rid of Ruffneck. This dice game was supposed to be a celebration for him. He'd earned his newfound wealth and was hell-bent on enjoying every penny, even if it meant being popped out. He'd heard Tupac go hard on one of his tracks about it being better to live like a man than die like a coward. So, it was what it was for him.

Charred Flesh seemed to go into a fit when he looked up and saw everybody else standing naked as the day they were born, but not the little punk.

"Okay, Mister Loud Mouth, you wanna act like you in control"—spit bouncing off each word—"Take your shit off, now! You look like you got some loot—fresh cards and shit. I want everything. Run yo' pockets, little nigga."

Lil Shorty didn't miss the curtain move in the window of the door that Truck had disappeared through. He knew that the owner didn't take kindly to fools coming in and shaking down his patrons. He didn't know what the old man had up his sleeve, but Lil Shorty needed to find a way to stall without getting his ass blown off.

"Okay," Lil Shorty said, trying to make up shit as he

went along. He removed his glasses. "These here, Black, cost me three gee's. On the street you should be able to move them for a grand or so, playa." Lil Shorty went inside his jacket pocket, taking out a large roll of bills. "This is four G's in cash and together with the glasses, fam, makes this a pretty decent score."

While Lil Shorty kept the greedy fool busy, Truck had crept from behind the door with a pool cue, and put the fat end on Charred Flesh. He came across ol' boy's noodle with so much force that the stick snapped, blood spurted, his trigger finger clenched up, there was a shot, a scream, somebody got hit, but Charred Flesh ended up on the floor. He was out cold and bleeding from a large hole in his head, where a fat chunk of meat was on the floor beside his body.

Truck held the skinny end of the broken cue in his hand. He examined the fools standing around in their boxers and laughed. "Ain't y'all the most pathetic things that I've ever seen? I thought y'all were gangstas? How y'all let this nigga"—he pointed to the floor—"get the drop on y'all? You fools didn't see it coming?" He looked at the guy who'd taken the blast in the shoulder, some man named Cless. Cless had snatched his shirt off of the floor and was now holding pressure against the wound. The cat was the only one in the room sporting leopard print bikini drawers. Truck joked: "Leopardman, seriously, dude, you need to stop bleeding on my clean floor."

He looked at Lil Shorty who was putting his glasses

back on and money back into his pockets. He still didn't like the nigga—and the news that he'd heard while in front, made him highly suspicious of the boy. But he had to give the devil his due. It took a huge pair of cojones in standing up to an armed jacker like he'd demonstrated. "You mean to tell me that this was the only one of you who really had some balls?"

Nobody said anything.

Lil Shorty was caught off-guard when Truck took his right arm and raised it into the air. "This little nigga has heart. Son, I got to buy you a drink." He looked around at everybody else. "And as for the rest of you"—he pointed to Charred Flesh's unconscious body —"get his ass out of here. If the nigga ain't dead by the time y'all reach the dumpsite, make sure he is before y'all leave."

Truck glanced in Cless' direction. Dude had managed to get his pants and shoes back on and was now sitting on the floor with his bare back resting against the wall, still applying pressure to the wound with his bloodstained shirt. Huge beads of sweat bubbled from his brow and cascaded down his face.

Truck pointed to Cless. "Take his ass to the hospital after y'all dumped the body. I swear, this fool actin' like he gonna die from a flesh wound."

Truck and Lil Shorty disappeared behind the door leading to the poolroom.

A man accompanied by a bad-ass female was shooting pool, drinking and laughing around the huge orange-cloth table toward the front door. It was one of fifteen tables in his place. Six of them were occupied by dudes who were smoking cigarettes or cigars—Truck didn't allow any Kush blowing in his place—talking shit while hustling others out of their loot.

At the bar, Truck had a huge flat-screen mounted on a wall. More people sat around drinking and watching a Blu-ray of Chris Tucker acting a clown in *Money Talk*.

He led Lil Shorty to a seat near the corner. Regardless of the young boy's age, Truck had a sexy-ass bartender bring over a bottle of Patrón. The old man was known for letting a few minors into his after-hours. Every last one of them served him in some capacity or another. Plus, the police looked the other way because most of them received some type of policeman's discount for the many illegal services he offered.

Truck poured the little nigga a shot of Tequila and fixed himself one.

"You hear about your boy, Ruffneck?" Truck asked as he sipped from his drink. And then he sat back to watch the little cat's reaction.

Lil Shorty didn't disappoint, either. He nonchalantly downed his drink like the old dude hadn't said a damn thing.

"Naw, but I got a feeling you about to tell me, though." Lil Shorty gestured with his finger for Truck to hit him again.

Truck did just that.

"Cops rolled on him about an hour ago. He was found holding a pistol."

"I guess we gotta be more careful riding dirty." Lil Shorty slammed home another shot.

"Do the rest of the crew know yet?" Truck poured another for Shorty.

Lil Shorty rubbed his hands together as if trying to do something with nervous energy. Didn't nothing get past Truck. He knew the little fool had something to do with it. Truck could tell that by the dryness of his responses.

"I'm sure they know by now," Lil Shorty answered.

Truck was through with the little punk's attitude. He poured Shorty one more shot as he rose to his feet. The kid would have to go to that fat knot in his pocket to do the rest of his drinking.

"Well, I gotta be getting back to the job. But thank you for what you did back there. Things could've gotten a lot uglier, if you hadn't bossed up." Truck went to walk away.

Lil Shorty said, "Let me holla at you for something, Truck."

Truck sat back down, eager to hear what the fool had to say.

"Aye, man, I'm gonna come straight out. You and Ruffneck was about to strike up a deal. Now that that nigga's out of the picture, how about giving that same deal to me?"

Truck looked like he just wanted to grab the young

punk and do what he used to do with snake niggas back in his era. But the businessman in him wouldn't let his personal feelings get in the way of the almighty dollar— no matter how slippery the customer was.

"How much?" Truck asked.

"Don't know yet. I'm all set up to sell, but I'm scouting manpower talent."

Truck couldn't do anything but shake his head. He knew Ruffneck had put in the work to carve out some real estate to operate. Truck liked Ruffneck so much that he'd been thinking about fronting him some dope on consignment before the kid had come to him a few days ago with cash money asking to cut a deal. Now, this little bitch had the stones to walk into his place of business, asking for the same deal. In a way, Truck felt bad about entertaining business with this slimy little trader, but he wasn't gonna let feelings get in the way of paying bills.

Truck rubbed the gray whiskers on his chin. He was talking to the devil; but if Satan wanted some product, he'd come to the right place. He still couldn't believe the lack of loyalty that today's young punks had for one another. Although he had a soft spot in his heart for Ruffneck, he wasn't a guidance counselor. His money came before the problems of all. If the kid had some cheese to deal, then it was all about the quantity.

"Well, when you figure out what you need, come and holla at me."

Truck stood. Lil Shorty tried to shake his hand, but

Truck looked at the young boy's hand like it had shit on it. He offered Lil Shorty a very unfriendly look before moving on. Just because he was going to deal with a snake, didn't mean he had to take long, hot, friendly showers with it.

After Truck stepped off, Lil Shorty took out some loot and paid the bartender for the bottle. He scouted out a nice, cozy booth, away from everybody, to celebrate his rise to power. The booze had his little ass feeling like he couldn't be touched. Like God had formed and shaped the world to meet his purpose. He was king, and niggas would bow down or meet the wrath of the Little Bambino of Terror. Starting with his old crew. If they didn't want to play ball, he would get rid of them and start his own thing. Better yet, he didn't want Ruffneck's crew of has-been losers. He was about to turn the game on its ear, so he needed a family that could challenge the likes of Billy the Kid for that number-one spot. Real niggas that were heavy on the trigger and fast to stack cash.

Lil Shorty was halfway into the bottle when he saw his homeboy, Sin, walk from the back. He looked like he was walking over to start a game of pool, when Lil Shorty called out his name.

"Lil Shorty, what dup, guy?" Sin excitedly said, dapping.

"Sit down and grab a glass, my nig; and let's toast to me and you getting money and having power, fam."

Sin's skin was blacker than oil slicks floating around in space.

"All right, my nigga," Sin said. "What we toasting to?"

"Ruffneck is history. The police took him in a half hour ago."

"How you manage that?"

Lil Shorty whistled for a barmaid to bring over another glass. When she reached the table, she set down the glass and Lil Shorty gave her a fifty-dollar bill. He laughed as the two watched her float back to the bar.

Lil Shorty said, pouring Sin a shot, "The shit wasn't planned. A nigga had to play it by ear, you dig. Ruffneck had told Fly the little party he had planned for me and shit. But it just so happens that I'm fucking Fly's baby-momma and she told me what Fly had told her."

Sin guzzled the shot. "You fucking dude's girl?"

Lil Shorty looked at Sin like he was growing a titty out of his forehead. "Nigga, name me one fool in the hood with a dick that she ain't sat on?"

Sin shook his head. "Yeah. You right 'bout that. So what happened?"

Lil Shorty poured himself another shot, straight feeling the effects now.

"Ruffneck was supposed to lay the murder game down on me at a house on Sorrento. I knew that fool was riding with those two bad bitches of his, the Glock sisters. So I tipped the police off." Lil Shorty waited for the roar of laughter coming from the bar to subside. Chris Tucker and Charlie Sheen were getting their clown on in the telephone booth scene across from the club that they had under surveillance. "I rode up to him while he was sitting in the ride, said my piece, and rode off. The last I seen of ol' boy, One-Time had that fool hemmed up."

Sin's face became serious. "You ain't worried about get-back from the others?"

Lil Shorty made that fart sound with his mouth that folks make when they're not sweating shit. "Man, I'm the Little Bambino of Terror, fool. They come after me and I'm getting my body count up, you dig?"

Sin threw down another shot. He was feeling good.

"That's what's up," Sin replied with a drink in hand and foolish look on his face. He reached across the table and dapped Lil Shorty.

"You ready to become rich?" Lil Shorty asked. He went to pour Sin another one. But his aim was off and he missed Sin's glass and spilled the drink on the table.

Sin laughed. "Nigga, what you doing?"

"M-m-my bad," Lil Shorty stammered over his words. "Let's toast to two niggas on the verge of locking shit down."

Sin took the bottle from Lil Shorty and filled both glasses. "All right. Just let me pour. Patrón is too expensive to be sharing with the table, nigga."

Lil Shorty's arm shook a little as he held his glass up to Sin.

"Our time is now. Death to all who don't follow," Lil Shorty said.

The boys threw down the alcohol.

Sin sluggishly stood from the table. "My nig, I gotta roll. Hit me up tomorrow."

Lil Shorty glanced down at the floor, noticing Sin's new kicks.

"Damn, dude, when you cop the new Airman sneakers?"

"A month ago."

"Them boys fresh," Lil Shorty complimented. He looked at the shoes again. "I hope you're done stealing with them niggas, man. It's either you run with them lames and keep on jacking high school kids, or come get money with me. Your choice."

Sin didn't say shit. The two boys dapped again, and then Sin walked away.

Alone In The Dark

H im didn't consider himself as a psychotic predator. Him preferred to think of himself as a public servant for the masses, an extermination service for God and a garbage man who took out scum-and-evil-people trash.

Guided by a higher power, Him had been drawn to this hole of sin. Sometimes, Him could have a hard time remembering certain names of places or things, but Him believed this to be a pool hall. To Him, this was one more of those places that was merely used as a meeting house for evil souls: men who wanted nothing else but to keep selling their poison to little kids. Him hated it. And that's why Him was here. Him had followed one of the men that was on his list of men with dirty feet into the pool hall.

Him was mighty. Him had also come to find out that the doctor woman who worked with Him was a liar. Him could remember her saying that Him had Multi-Mul-ti-ple Person-al-ity Disorder. Yeah, that's right— Multiple Personality Disorder. She tried to say that Him was evil. She said that Him was just one more hard-boiled set of psychopathic urges underneath a bad haircut—those were the doctor woman's words. And then she laughed at Him. Him hated her then. So when Him escaped from the nervous-people hospital, Him caught the bitch walking to her car in the underground garage after leaving the office. Him waited until she had put the keys in the door before popping up from between the cars and ripping the bitch's throat out with Him's special tool.

Him loved the night. There was something magical about it. Plus, the darkness hid Him well. Him could move around in the shadows without people pointing and staring at what Him called God's little boo-boo. It had to be, because why was Him the only one who wasn't given a normal face at birth? Him's mommy said that Him's daddy was a bad man who ran off on Him. And because of it, Him was cursed with the face of a monster. If Him's father was still alive, Him would do to Bad Daddy what Him was about to do to the evil man who'd just stepped from the door of the pool hall.

Him had been watching the fella for some time. When Him was following the bad man, Him got close enough once to see that the man wore the Airman sneakers. Him remembered those sneakers because the Airman used to fly through the air and dunk the ball on the other team. Him even had a few of the Airman's posters on the bedroom wall. But now, Him no longer liked the sneakers because the dope-dealing scum wore them.

Him watched as the fella with the Airman sneakers staggered away from the pool hall. The fella wouldn't see Him's face and run because Him was wearing a hood. Other people weren't the only ones frightened by Him's appearance. Him was petrified, too.

Him didn't like mirrors. "No mirror! No-no mirrors!"

The evil man wearing the Airman sneakers was looking around as he walked. Yep, he was the one, all right. Him was sure of it. On Him's list of ten bad-evil men, the fella was number 10 at the bottom. Just like Him's favorite basketball player.

When Him was on the medicine, the voices would stop, and Him could get some sleep. But since Him broke away from the nervous hospital, Him couldn't get the medicine.

There were ten bad men total on Him's list. All were gonna die. Him would start from the bottom and work his way to the top.

Number 10 slowed down his steps and pulled out a cell phone. He lit a cigarette and started talking really loud, like he was yelling at the person on the other end. Him had been tracking 10 for some time. Him was familiar with 10's habits. So Him knew that the fella didn't have a car; 10 lived just around the block.

Him walked, staying to the shadows, stalking, waiting for a perfect opportunity to strike. It was like a game. Him liked to play kiddie games like Hide-and-Seek, Duck, Duck, Goose, or Him's favorite, Freeze Tag. Him was pretty good, too, until the evil-bitch doctor woman took Him's games away. Him got very angry—mad, very mad. Pain! Nothing but pain for Him.

But that was then. Him had a brand-new game now, called Your Feet are Dirty; Nasty Feet. Him loved to play the Nasty Feet game.

Ooops! Him almost lost the Nasty Feet game, because 10 looked around and almost spotted Him following. Him ducked around the side of a building. 10 turned back around and kept on smoking and talking. Maybe Him had better shut Him's thinking mouth up.

Him cut through an alley to beat 10 home. Him found the house and hid, ready for the game. Butterflies. Him had lots of butterflies. Him remembered this feeling. They always started flying around inside Him's belly right around Christmastime. Santa used to bring Him and baby brother lots of toys to play with. Him loved baby brother until evil men killed baby brother.

10 finally made it home. He came up talking loud on the phone and flicked the cigarette in the bushes. Him's timing had to be right; 10 walked onto the porch and took out the keys. Him was thinking about having a little fun with 10. Him would take off the hood and show 10 the ugly. Him tried not to laugh in the corner of the porch, while hiding behind an old refrigerator.

The keys jingled while the fella talked loud. It was time. Him came out from behind the refrigerator and scared 10.

"Who the fuck are you?" 10 yelled at Him.

The porch light showed just a bit, enough for Him to

take off the hood. When Him did, 10 screamed like a little girl. Him was laughing as the fella dropped his cell phone and tried to fight Him. But Him was too strong. Him overpowered 10 and started choking his throat like a mad dog. The fella started swinging and got lucky. Busted Him's lip. Him was angry now. Real angry. Him took the palm of his right hand and pushed 10's nose into his brain.

10 dropped to the floor. No more noise. It was quiet. Him had better work quickly. Police would probably come, because of noisy 10. Him took 10's keys and opened the door and dragged the fella in by his dirty Airman sneakers. Nobody should be home. Him had checked. 10 lived alone, much like Him. A special tool was inside of Him's hood pouch. Him stood over 10's lifeless body.

"You have nasty feet," Him said, laughing in a voice that sounded like Vincent Price at the end of the "Thriller" song. Him loved that song. Him missed Michael Jackson very much. With Vincent Price laughing inside Him's head, Him hacked and slashed until blood was everywhere. Dripping from Him's black gloves. Him had almost been caught once. Ever since then, Him wore gloves. No fingerprints.

Him went into the kitchen and removed black garbage bags from underneath the sink. Passing through the hallway, Him caught a reflection of his face in the mirror hanging on a wall. Him couldn't stand seeing the ugly. Him went berserk and smashed the mirror into pieces.

Him had hacked off 10's legs just underneath the knee.

Him put both of 10's feet in the garbage bag with the bloody Airman sneakers still on the feet.

"Now you have no more dirty feet," Him said to 10. Him slung the bag over his shoulder. Ooops, Him almost forgot to put the hood back on. Didn't want nobody off the list of bad men to see the ugly. Him was careful to avoid blood tracks on the way out of the door. "Now, you can be like Mike," Him said, toting the bag over his shoulder like Santa Claus coming down the chimney. Vincent Price laughter was chuckling inside Him's head when Him walked off and down the dark streets.

In The Air

Although it'd been almost twenty-four hours since her grandson had been arrested for possession of a pistol, Granny Sinclair was taking the shit pretty badly. The penalty for felony firearms in Michigan was a mandatory two-year imprisonment. There was no way in hell she had the money to retain an attorney. Ruffneck had called from the police station and told her not to worry about trying to raise cash. It wouldn't do any good. He was going to serve time, regardless.

She was missing him already. After all, he had been the centerpiece of her life for eleven years now. And those years had gone by quickly. It seemed like just yesterday she was picking up—well, she was still picking up—after him and cussing his tail out for his amazing powers of disappearing whenever there was a chore that needed doing. Hell, it wasn't until he was the trusting age of fourteen when she'd started training the boy to go and fetch her medicine from the pharmacy. She was even around for the little bastard when he first learned how to ride a bike without the assistance of training wheels. The boy was a quick study. As she could recall, it was his high IQ which had caused her to abandon her business.

In her heart, Granny Sinclair had felt sorry for the boy with him losing both parents to the violence of the game. The old woman had been the only chance of him getting a good start in life, and wanted to be around for him. She'd reckoned that every baby should have a decent start, with life being so damn hard already. So she sold off her merchandise, alerted the customers of her leaving the game, and placed an out-of-business sign on the door. She was going to raise the boy the way that God had intended.

Now, all of her work seemed to have been in vain. Him landing in jail for felony firearms made her feel like a failure at rearing him. She'd wanted so much for him, too. She was from the streets and vaguely familiar with the powerful lure; the pull it possessed over young men looking to live up to the materialistic expectations of those brand-name gangsters that had come before them. The boy's old man had been a stellar example— all the intelligence and know-how that he had been endowed with. Walker Story, Sr. merely used it to apply in the streets for the quick money. He'd built his kingdom off the blood of those who opposed him. The maniac didn't even have the natural fear of those men and women who bravely donned the blue uniform to protect and serve. And now he was reaching all the way from hell to infect his son's life with the evilness that had consumed him. But, it didn't matter how wicked his father had turned out to be, the boy still had a right to know who his parents were. She'd be the first to admit that she was wrong, for a good reason. His protection was all she had been concerned with. And if that protection meant lying to him, then, oh well. Her grandson going to jail had put things in perspective for her. She should've trusted him enough to handle his family history properly. He hadn't known about his father, and the boy still wound up in jail.

The old woman was growing tired. And it wasn't that kind of tired that one would get from a strenuous workout or long day at work, but the *tired* usually associated with the ending of a long, hard life. She could feel the season changing; the winds of death blowing in her direction, beckoning for her to lay it down.

She was tired.

The old woman sat in her recliner in front of the television. Her favorite show, *Sanford and Son*, was on, but today, it was playing for the companionship of sound. Granny Sinclair had gone into the safe and carried the envelope bearing the contents of the boy's history to her recliner. She could feel it in her bones that something was about to happen—didn't know what it was, but something. So she was preparing for it. If this was indeed the last time that she would smell the roses on this side, then she had to set the boy's soul right with the knowledge of his parents. With that, she needed a favor and knew who to call. Brenda Johnston was one of her trusted friends and the mother to Jamaal, the boy that Ruffneck had retrieved the stolen scooter for by trashing the nigga Nizzo.

Brenda picked up on the second ring and Granny Sinclair told her everything surrounding the case of her grandson. Brenda expressed her feelings and asked if Granny Sinclair needed anything. The old woman told her to send Jamaal down, because she had something that she wanted Brenda to keep until the boy got out of jail. No sooner than they got off of the phone, Jamaal was knocking at the door. Granny Sinclair sealed the envelope and handed it to the boy.

She was growing tired.

The old woman went to the kitchen to grab a snack. Prunes always calmed her. When she walked back to take her seat, the news interrupted her program with a gruesome discovery...

"We are live on location in the four-hundred block of Vine Street on the city's West Side, where a grisly discovery was made an hour ago inside the house behind me," the short black man with salt-and-pepper hair reported. *"Police have identified the body of a young, black male as Jackson 'Sin' Fuller. Witnesses say that around eleven o'clock this morning, the victim's girlfriend had become alarmed when she couldn't get him on his cell phone and came over to investigate. When there was no answer, she had a couple of neighbors break down*

the door, and what they discovered could best be described by witnesses..."

The camera zoomed in on the face of a muscular, older black man with a receding hairline and missing front teeth. He said, *"Both the boy's foots was completely gone. Cut off underneath the knee."*

The reporter removed the mic from the man's tooth-less grin as he stood there soaking up his two seconds. The camera rested on the reporter.

"But it doesn't stop there. A couple of blocks from here, they found the severed legs, still with the sneakers intact, tied by the shoestrings and dangling over a high-tension wire. The scene has law enforcement baffled. Right now, no one wants to speculate about the nature of the heinous crime, but this is one that has all the gritty substance of a CSI episode. We will keep you abreast of any new developments. Reporting live on location, I'm Gotter Bath."

Fred Sanford's face once again filled the screen as he insulted his son, Lamont, to the delight of the studio audience.

Granny Sinclair shook her head. Nothing in this miserable, little world surprised her anymore.

But she could feel it. It was coming in the air for her. And she knew it.

She was tired.

It's On

Lil Shorty drove his Monte Carlo down Greenfield, going toward North Land Mall. The New Year's Day sales were jumping off and Lil Shorty wasn't missing a beat.

He'd hooked up with Truck and was now challenging some of the lower-level dealers over territory. Even though the little nigga wasn't shy about putting in work on the competition by himself, he'd assembled a street team of hungry cats that didn't mind killing over prosperity. They didn't disappoint: the city's murder rate had picked up behind Lil Shorty's ambition to be a straight rider for sole possession of the spotlight. Although, still considered light in the ass and off the radar of the big dogs in the game, he was becoming a force to be reckoned with. The Little Bambino of Terror was quickly becoming a neighborhood brand in the lightweight division.

A January snowstorm was burying the city as Lil Shorty carefully worked his way toward the mall with his latest prospect riding in the passenger's seat. The twenty-four-inch rims had been replaced by the standard-size rims with heavy-duty rubber tread. As always, with his potentials, Lil Shorty's MO was to take them out and impress them with lavish shopping sprees, VIP at some of the exclusive titty bars around town, and crown the outing with a duplicate gold cable chain and a signature iced-out, pit bull face charm.

Hootie sat on the other side of Lil Shorty with the four-thousand-dollar piece of jewelry sparkling around his neck, like the thing was his version of an MVP trophy. And he was, too, because Lil Shorty needed guns. To make sure that he could get them at a reasonable price, the little, clever nigga put Hootie down on his team.

They were blowing Kush and still tripping over the fact that Lil Shorty's boy, Sin, had gotten his fucking feet chopped off by the Slasher.

"Man, I'd just seen the nigga Sin the night it happened," Lil Shorty explained.

"That's fucked up, G," Fly added. "Found the nigga's Airman sneakers dangling over a wire."

"I complimented the nigga on his kicks, too, just before he'd bounced."

"Here today and gone tomorrow," Hootie said.

Lil Shorty hit the blunt and passed it over.

He coughed deeply a few times before saying: "But anyway, how much time did ol' Ruffneck catch?"

Hootie took a long pull on the blunt, let the smoke settle, and coughed it out.

"His punk ass got twenty-four months, cuz. He up in Battle Creek some-muthafuckin' where."

"Only twenty-four months?" Lil Shorty said, sounding surprised.

Hootie explained: "Two years for a felony firearm charge."

"I thought Ruffneck always carried twin heat?"

"Yeah, he did, but when they jumped him, the nigga was carrying one. The judge gave his ass two years."

Lil Shorty was kind of heartbroken, but still feeling himself.

He'd set Ruffneck's ass up and was now poisoning Hootie to the point that if he saw his cousin, there would be beef. It didn't help matters none that when drinking one night, Hootie had regaled Lil Shorty about Billy's little stunt. Lil Shorty had sinisterly laughed at Ruffneck's usual timid diplomacy in handling threats.

It didn't matter to Lil Shorty when Ruffneck would be released. A price would immediately go out on the nigga's head the moment the punk's feet hit freedom-pavement. Lil Shorty would take the fight to Ruffneck, before the fool could get himself set up back in society.

"The shit don't matter, Hootie. When your cousin get out, we gonna have shit so sewed up that Billy and the cats he works for, gonna be begging us to cut them some space to operate, you dig?" Lil Shorty grabbed the blunt and inhaled.

"Let's get it poppin', playboy."

Lil Shorty stopped at a red light. "I ain't tryna dis your fam, man, but that Mr. Ambassador thought that if he didn't make any noise, he could sneak into the game."

He laughed like his funny bone was in jeopardy of cracking. "I kept telling the nigga that you gotta make noise when you take shit. Fuck that ol' quiet creep crap. I gotta tell you this…" The light turned green and Lil Shorty carefully touched the gas pedal. The car fish-tailed as the snow accumulated, making the road slick. "This cat thought he could get in the game by sticking up Cadillac. Man, all we got was some chump change. I blew through that shit in a week."

"Snap," Hootie exclaimed, putting the blunt out in the ashtray. "It was y'all who got Cadillac? You know the streets was saying that the person, or people involved, were probably the ones who put it on Bundy McGurk."

"I don't know shit about McGurk, dude. We hit Cadillac. Yo' cuz—"

"Let me school you for a minute, guy. That nigga ain't my cousin," Hootie proclaimed with venom. "Walker 'Ruffneck' Story, Jr. just showed up at my grandma's doorstep one night. She took his ass in and raised him."

"No, you didn't just put my man's gov'ment name on blast—serious, that's that fool's name…Walker Story, Jr? The shit sounds like something out of a fairy tale." Lil Shorty could barely maintain himself. At one point, he laughed so hard that he almost pissed his pants. "Ruffneck—I mean, Walker Story, Jr., a fucking orphan, just like me. What do you know about that?"

Lil Shorty was on Greenfield near the John C. Lodge Freeway when he met five-o. The squad car was hot on his shoes. But he was too slick to panic. Hootie was sweating the hook, though. The two boys were riding dirty. Lil Shorty had an AK-47 on the floor in the back of the ride, and Hootie's 9mm was stuck in his waistband.

The pigs looked to be running Lil Shorty's license plate.

Shorty looked over and noticed Hootie's blank stare. "Man, chill your nervous ass out. They're only running the plate. My junk is legit. Don't give them no reason to stop me, fool." The police trailed them until they turned into the mall parking lot. "Damn, they turned off. I'm sitting up tripping on your cuz—I mean, Walker Story, Jr.'s gun charge and I'm riding with an AK. Sumptin' that would get me sent underneath the jail."

Hootie let out a heavy sigh of relief.

Lil Shorty tried to ease the tension. "Nigga, you almost pissed on yourself."

He located a park and the two boys went inside the mall. The two balled until they had no more room to carry another bag. A quick bite at Tai po Asian Grill and they were back in the car, headed to one of Lil Shorty's spots. It was late evening and darkness had fallen across the city. Street traffic was still heavy because of the snowstorm.

"Okay, we gonna cut the shit," Lil Shorty said, reaching and popping on his headlights. The older classic didn't have the automatic lights like the newer models. "I need you to do sumptin' for me."

Hootie went to speak, but Lil Shorty cut him off.

"I've spent a lot of bank on you. Now, I need sumptin' done." He pulled out of the parking lot. "I want you to kill Billy."

The impact of the statement caused Hootie's stomach to drop. "Billy?"

"Billy."

"Billy the Kid, Billy?"

"Same muthafucka, Black," Lil Shorty said as he watched the impact of the deadly profession. "We gotta problem?"

Hootie let the stress show on his face. "When did you think this up? The last time you said shit about Billy—"

"Blah, blah, blah, blah, blah, nigga. You either with me, or you against me, fam. And you know what happens to cats who get on my wrong side."

"You serious?" The palms of Hootie's hands started sweating.

Lil Shorty whipped the car over to the side of the street, horns of motorists blowing in disapproval.

"If anybody got cause to off this fool, it should be you, cuz. This nigga took yo' choppers and smoked your homeboy in front of you. And tried to smoke you. You saw the nigga get down on your homeboy. Oh, that fool is coming for you, believe it. You need to get his ass before he gets you, you dig? In order to be the best, you gotta take out the best, you dig?"

Lil Shorty had sent one cousin away to jail and was now trying to mack the other into killing a crime boss. He was trying to push the underworld ecosystem into total anarchy. Billy the Kid was the bottom of the totem pole inside an organization that was rumored to have ties with the mayor of the city. One had to be considered insane to touch him without having the same muscle standing behind him as Billy possessed. But Lil Shorty's aim was to throw the game into complete chaos. Have everybody's attention on Billy's murder as he and his goons slowly gobbled up small-timers until his army was strong enough to move on the niggas who really had their weight up.

Hootie had determined his mistake. Momentary hatred for his cousin had blinded him. He was a gunrunner, plain and simple. His cousin had been right. Hootie did not possess the dark and cold heart that came as standard equipment for most killers. He might've been a merchant of death, but he was no murderer.

"Taking on Billy the Kid is suicide," Hootie explained with fear in his eyes.

"So, what are you trying to say, B?" Lil Shorty asked. Hootie was visibly shaken. Lil Shorty knew that with the right force applied, Hootie would snap like a twig.

Hootie looked Lil Shorty straight in the eyes. "You're out of your mind and I won't have any part in it."

Lil Shorty laughed wickedly. "So, is that your final fucking answer?"

Hootie went to reach for the handle of the door, when Lil Shorty reached over the seat and was quick with the AK-47. He stuck the barrel in Hootie's grill.

"Nigga, it don't look like you got much of a choice in this one, Playboy," Lil Shorty spat, digging the barrel into the side of Hootie's face.

Hootie flinched, letting go of the door handle.

"Homeboy, you better get your mind right. Because I'm about to tell you how it's gonna play out. Cousin, or no cousin, when Ruffneck finally comes to the crib, he won't be able to recognize you"—he pushed the weapon deeper into Hootie's face—"because you'll be the nigga wearing a casket and cemetery plot, you dig? Try me, if you think I'm bullshittin'. I'll blow those fucking corn-rows off yo' head!"

Hootie thought about going for the piece that rested at his waist, just inches from his hands. But he wasn't stupid. He'd sold tons of AK-47s inside the neighborhood. He, of all people, was familiar with the heater. The Russian assault rifle had been built for speed, accuracy, and stopping power. He wouldn't have a chance. Before he could go under his shirt and pull his heat, he'd have a magazine of bullets in his ass.

"You got it," came Hootie's meek submission.

"I didn't hear you. What you say?"

"It's your world, dog," Hootie said in a much firmer voice.

"That's what I thought," Lil Shorty said before laughing. "That's what I fucking thought." He slowly removed the weapon from Hootie's face; his laughter big on cockiness.

Hootie's heart was racing. He had fucked up in a major way. It was because of the anger he'd harbored for his cousin that he'd gotten into Satan's bed without protection. He watched out of the window as cars carefully inched along the street. Greenfield was a mess. The street was snow, slush, and water.

Lil Shorty put the weapon away. He looked out of the driver's side mirror before pulling the Monte Carlo away from the curb and working his way back into the flow of traffic.

The two rode along in silence. Hootie had to figure a way out of his situation. It was like a volatile time bomb, when lit with Billy's murder, would blow into a shit storm that would rain death down on everybody he knew. Everybody with his blood would be marked for death.

"The nigga Billy picks up two black duffel bags from a house on St. Mary's and Schoolcraft. I know a cat who works at that spot. The fool told me that each bag holds one-hundred grand; both bags total two-hunnit gee's."

"So, now you gonna rob Billy and kill him?" Hootie asked. "So what's so different from what Ruffneck did to Cadillac—aside from not killing him?"

"It's called makin' noise, son. Takin' shit from people who don't believe that they can be touched. Well, I'm gonna put our fingerprints all over him."

Hootie thought about his cousin and what he'd said about Auntie Edda Mae down in Louisiana. He'd give his left nut for a plane ticket right now. Ever since the murder of his homeboy, he'd been ducking, staying low, making sure that he wouldn't run into Billy. Now, here this fool was forcing him to put his head back into the lion's mouth.

"Well, man, drop me off at my crib, so I can grab some clothes," Hootie asked, trying to pull a quick one.

Lil Shorty saw right through the con. He knew that Hootie would break and run the first chance he got.

"Naw, Black. Think I'm fucking stupid or sumptin'? We just went and dropped a ton of paper on clothes. You ain't going nowhere."

"Man, all the little cats you know that would drop Billy's ass for a pack of Skittles, why me?"

Lil Shorty cracked a smile that would've made Satan jealous.

"Shorty, man, what is this really about?"

Lil Shorty's smile was an extension of the joy he was feeling for the diabolical plan that he had masterminded. He would stiff Hootie for the wallet he'd pulled out at Footlocker—which by the way, he couldn't believe homeboy still carried money in a wallet. Once they robbed and murked Billy, Lil Shorty planned to drop Hootie's wallet at the crime scene. The nigga would be hit either way. If five-o didn't scoop Hootie, Billy's soldiers would nail his ass to a wall somewhere. Sending Ruffneck's family to jail or hell—either way, would cause Ruffneck a world of pain. It would be a victorious win-win for Lil Shorty. He hated Ruffneck's bitch ass with all the hate in the world, and would stop at nothing until he was destroyed.

"It's about the chain you wearing, fam. The shit comes with responsibility to the team."

Hootie looked down at the chain hanging around his neck. The diamonds seemed to glitter as the car traveled underneath streetlights. "When is this supposed to go down?"

Lil Shorty foolishly looked at Hootie before saying: "Tomorrow night, fam. And that's the end of it." He turned on the Kenwood radio and blasted the volume, drowning out the begging that was going on in Hootie's soul. He didn't have a relationship with God, but old folks had told him: whenever one accepted the Lord, then all the bad done up until that point was forgiven. Hootie hoped so, for Christ's sake.

Who the fuck wakes up to the idea of bumping off a king-pin? Hootie thought as he and Lil Shorty waited in a cold, abandoned house next door to Billy's money spot. It was nine at night. The two had been posted in the freezing house for at least a couple hours. Both boys were strapped with AK-47s. The city's decaying housing market made it easy for the two of them to move unseen lugging the rifles. They'd passed through the yard of a vacant house on the next block to get into the one they were now sitting in. Hootie was fucking petrified. He'd attempted to turn back a couple times, but was dissuaded by the threat of Lil Shorty opening up on him with the rifle, and leaving his ass stanking in the alley behind.

They were in way over their heads. No plan. Lil Shorty was on some other shit and had dragged Hootie smack-dab into the middle of this *Get Rich or Die Tryin'* remake. A couple times, the urge had welled up in Hootie to just pull the trigger on the weapon and shut the little, deranged muthafucka down. But he couldn't do it. The heart of a killer didn't beat inside of his chest. To tell the truth, Hootie didn't know what good he would do, if the plan went south and they had to shoot their way out. Would he have it in him to murder?

Lil Shorty's plan was flawed with the urgency only brought on by the scheme to live high on the hog. Never once had Hootie heard the fool mention anything about the consequences of the plan backfiring and blowing up in their faces. Lil Shorty was so dead-set on money, clothes, and hoes; he hadn't stopped to consider shit.

The guy working inside the house had informed Lil Shorty that Billy rolled a black Yukon Denali with only one other nigga riding shotgun. Hootie was rubbing his hands together when he heard a vehicle pull up in front. He remembered the black Isotoners he'd packed before leaving the crib. It was quick thinking. He slid on the gloves and waited for Lil Shorty to confirm the vehicle out in front.

"Aye, nigga," Lil Shorty whispered from the window. "It's show- time. Put your mask on."

Hootie reluctantly obeyed orders. He picked up the weapon. The AK-47 felt like it had been stored in a freezer, it was so cold in the house.

"Follow my lead, nigga, and keep up." Before they left out, Lil Shorty warned Hootie once more. "Nigga, don't you bitch up on me out there, you dig?"

Hootie nodded his head.

Lil Shorty quietly walked out of the back door. The snow on the grass left by the storm made traveling a little difficult, but the boys were able to slip their way into position. The SUV was in the driveway, but they were stationed in the opposite direction, between Billy's spot and the abandoned crib. Hootie was a couple feet behind Lil Shorty; both crouched down and out of sight. Hootie's heart was beating like it was trying desperately to beat some courage into him to turn and run. The fatal vision of him being shot in the back killed that noise, quickly.

Hootie's mind was so focused on carnage that he'd completely forgotten about how freakin' cold it was out. To add a little extra chill in the air, the wind picked up and was whistling between the houses. Hootie thought about Ruffneck and wished that he'd taken his advice. Right about now, he would've been in a warm house with an out-cold country bitch, and dick-deep into some hot pussy.

Hootie's stomach turned a full cartwheel when the front door opened and both men walked out laughing and talking. He could remember the smile on Billy's face the day he'd given his soldiers the order to shoot. Gunfire that had left his boy dead and his pride wounded. But try as he might to cowboy the fuck up and take some get-back for his homeboy, he just couldn't see himself killing anybody. Hootie was so caught up in his thoughts that he hadn't heard or seen Lil Shorty creep off. When he looked up, Lil Shorty was holding the AK on Billy and his boy.

"Y'all know what it is," Lil Shorty said. "I come for the bags. Don't be no damn hero."

Billy spoke: "Just so we won't have any communication problems, my man. You do know who the fuck I am, don't you?"

"Blah, blah, blah, blah, blah, nigga. Save the damn dick recognition-warning speech and hand over the bags," Lil Shorty commanded, aiming the weapon at Billy's face.

Hootie trudged behind, holding his rifle down at the ground. He said nothing while he listened to the two go back and forth.

Billy dropped the bags to the ground. His man still hadn't said anything; almost like he was bracing for shit to pop off.

"Okay, nigga," Billy said with his hands in the air. "It's your world. Don't do nothing stupid. Keep your shirt on. Nobody has to die tonight."

The wind picked up and a heavy snowdrift blew flakes across Lil Shorty's face, temporarily blinding him for a fraction of a second. The distraction was enough for Billy to go for his weapon—his boy doing the same. Lil Shorty brushed away the snow before Billy could draw. Besides the biting cold winds, Hootie didn't know what ran his blood cold the most: the automatic pop of the AK-47, or the deranged, homicidal laughter that escaped Lil Shorty's mouth as he let his trigger fly, riddling Billy with hot rounds. The arrogant smile, now replaced by shock and panic, Billy tried to run, but his legs twisted and down he went. His homeboy was almost out with his heat, when Lil Shorty turned the chopper loose on him, and sprayed him bloody from head to toe.

"Nigga, get the muthafuckin' bags," Lil Shorty screamed at Hootie. The side door of the house exploded open and niggas stormed out like troopers—strapped, ready for war. Lil Shorty backed up popping; the fire from the AK muzzle lighting up the night as fools fell to the awesome force behind the lead.

Two houses down, on the same side of the street, cats started blasting at Lil Shorty. The night lit up once again like flashbulbs going off at an NBA game. Lil Shorty returned fire, noticing that Hootie was nowhere to be found, but one of the bags was missing. With bullets whizzing through the air, he didn't have time to figure shit out. Lil Shorty cut loose with a volley of shots in the direction of the shooters, and grabbed the bag. Bullets pinged and panged as car glass exploded around him. Lil Shorty ran like his feet were on fire, and the wind he generated was the only thing that would put them out.

Down the street and around the corner sat an older-model Ford Explorer. Lil Shorty fumbled with the door latch until he finally opened it. Hootie still was nowhere to be found, but with Billy's goons hot on Lil Shorty's ass, he wasn't gonna wait around. He tossed in the rifle and duffel bag. Behind the wheel of the stolen SUV, he started the truck and had pulled off when Hootie stunt-dived onto the hood. Hootie looked like he'd taken a round to the leg. With one hand holding on to the duffel, and the other one clanging to a windshield wiper for dear life, Hootie's face was pressed against the windshield in a cartoon-like horror.

He screamed like a bitch as Lil Shorty mashed out, creating distance. He had his foot on the gas; Hootie screaming on the hood. Through the rearview mirror, Lil Shorty could see the gunfire in the distance.

He had both bags and was feeling himself.

"I bust that ass, Billy! I bust that ass!" Lil Shorty yelled excitedly.

In all the hot action, Lil Shorty had failed to drop Hootie's wallet back at the scene. He hadn't expected things to get that far out of hand. But it didn't matter, though. He was two-hundred thousand dollars richer. Hootie wouldn't see a cent of the loot anyway. Lil Shorty had one more nigga to get rid of and he could do it while Hootie's ass was on the hood of the ride. All the noise generated by the gunfight would soon bring five-o. Lil Shorty wasn't gonna risk the two-hundred gee's, so he pulled over eight blocks away and let Hootie into the SUV. The two boys disappeared into the night.

Three The Hard Way

T he Avtomat Kalashnikova 1947 was also known as the AK-47 assault rifle that had been used in Eastern Bloc countries during the Cold War. It was primarily manufactured for stopping power, to mortally incapacitate the opposition.

Hootie was up on the history of his merchandise. In gruesome pictures he'd tracked on the Internet, Hootie had seen the gory devastation of a human body after being worked over by the weapon. But nothing he'd seen over the internet could've possibly prepared him for the real fuckin' deal. He couldn't get those mental still photos out of his head. Billy lying on the cold ground, blood-soaked snow, his lifeless body looking like human hamburger with eyeballs bucked wide, caught in a death-gaze.

It'd been a month since Billy's murder, and Hootie still couldn't shake the gory images from his head. The news wasn't gonna let him forget. For the first two weeks, top local and national headlines belonged to one of the bloodiest massacres that had ever taken place in the city of Detroit. Fifteen had been gunned down and so many more left wounded. And it had all taken place on St. Mary Street.

Hootie could vividly remember everything that had jumped off that night. After he'd grabbed the bag, he had taken a few steps before he found himself on the snow-covered ground; his left thigh burning like somebody had taken a lighter to it. It wasn't lost on him that he'd caught a slug in the leg. Hootie picked himself up and grabbed the bag, staggering off between houses. He'd been plastered across the hood of the Explorer when he'd remembered that he'd left the AK laying in the snow. Hootie had no worries, though. The quick thinking to bring the gloves along would spare him the headache of his prints being lifted from the chopper.

Lil Shorty had driven Hootie to a hospital way across town and let him out at the ER. Lil Shorty had promised Hootie that if he bitched up in any way, he would track him down and body his ass. That was the last time since he'd heard from the little maniac. Hootie didn't give a damn. As far as he was concerned, Lil Shorty could keep every dime of the money. He didn't want a cent of it.

He'd admitted himself under the alias of Tupelo Harrison. The injury was through and through, missing anything of major importance, but nicking a muscle. There would be some physical therapy in his future, but the doctor assured him that he'd make a speedy recovery. After the wound was cleaned, stitched, and dressed, Hootie had sneaked out of the ER and caught a cab to the crib. He hadn't felt like being questioned by the police, which was emergency room protocol in dealing with gunshot victims.

He'd been laying low at the crib ever since. Hootie had let the service on his Metro PCS cancel and wasn't accepting any visitors. Those who showed up on his doorstep were left knocking until they got the hint. He didn't trust a soul. Kept a burner in his hand. And when he did manage to go out for food, Hootie would move around at night, sticking to the alleys.

The paranoia he was suffering had him shaken and seriously on edge. The thought of Billy's goons creeping on him in his sleep had caused Hootie mad bouts of insomnia. As far as Hootie knew, he and Lil Shorty were the only two who knew about the murder. Somehow, that was little comfort to him. Even he knew that there wasn't such a thing as kept secrets in the hood.

Before the hit/murder, Lil Shorty had loot, but nothing to the tune of what he was holding now. It unnerved Hootie. The little nigga had two-hundred large, and that type of cheese was a cause for lavish spending sprees and popping bottles in celebration.

Everything was coming into focus for Hootie now. Shortly after Cadillac had been *got*, Lil Shorty copped the customized Monte Carlo. And if he'd gone baller after that lick, there weren't any limits to what he was gonna do with two-hundred Gs.

Hootie figured he'd better go out and hear the latest

gossip from some of his cats who had their ear to the streets. Because if anybody found out what he'd taken part in, all that he held dear would be in danger. He was a fool. Hootie had kicked the shit out of himself over and over again for not taking his cousin's advice. None of this would be going on, if he was down visiting Auntie Edda Mae.

The hole in his leg was slow in healing. The white chick he'd been fucking just so happened to be a RN. She would come over to the crib to periodically dress and change his wound. Therapy was out of the question. Hootie wasn't too gassed up about going outside. There was no telling who would pull up on him and start blasting. He'd let Lil Shorty fuck things up for him. He had to approach the entire situation like Billy's people knew about his involvement. And the first thing he'd done when he'd gotten out of the ER was try to find his old man. After an exhausting effort, he'd given up. Hootie concluded, if he couldn't find the nigga, then nobody could. Granny Sinclair was the one he was most worried about. Cats like Billy's people didn't discriminate when it came time for making examples. The old woman would be in the cross-hairs. He wasn't too worried about Ruffneck. Cuz could hold his own. But eventually, Hootie would make the trek up to visit him and tell about the madness.

His Buick Regal was history. The police had impounded the car shortly after arresting his cousin. He knew po-po had probably made the discovery that the car was hot.

Aside from the black-market accessories he'd invested on the whip, Hootie hadn't lost too much of his shirt. He'd bought the ride tagged, so he wasn't sweating it. Hell, if he had the car, he wouldn't drive it anyway. The thing was an original, and if Billy's people knew about his involvement, then they would be looking for the car. Hootie concluded that he would be better off on foot. Even though he was lame in one leg, he would take his chances walking.

Hootie slid on his pants, slipped into some Timbs, and threw on a hoodie and big jacket. The beginning of February, in his estimation, was the coldest month of the winter. Granny Sinclair's place was at least ten minutes away by foot. He grabbed a Glock from the nightstand next to his bed, and stuck the thing in one of the over-sized coat pockets. He would walk with his hands inside the pockets to give him better advantage, if some fool rode up and started tripping.

The clock on the cable receiver read 10:05 a.m. He would be somewhat at ease because he knew niggas in the hood weren't up at this time of morning. Hootie wouldn't let his guard down, though.

He started out. The freezing wind was whipping and blowing pretty hard. Within seconds, the mucus inside Hootie's nose began to freeze hairs together. Most of the sidewalks were now ice, making his travel difficult. Each foot placement met with crunching resistance, which jostled and jarred the injured muscle until pain slowed his pace. If it wasn't for the debilitating high produced by Oxycontin, Hootie would've swallowed one on the spot. He needed it, but he couldn't afford to get sloppy; had to stay on his toes. There was no telling when the get-back would be aimed in his direction.

Hootie wasn't three minutes from Granny Sinclair's when a huge crowd up ahead caught his attention. There was no smoke in the air, so it couldn't be a house fire that had the Negroes up so early in this part of town. The closer he drew, he could make out police vehicles and vans from local news crews, antennas raised high in the air. He was two blocks away when he discovered that the crowd was standing in front of the Body Bag. The ball-playing cats in the neighborhood he knew didn't get down with outside-winter hooping. This had to be serious.

Hootie brushed off the stares he was receiving, once he walked up to the gathering. People were looking at him like this whole thing was his fault. He dismissed it as his own paranoia and kept it moving.

The pain inside his leg was throbbing, but Hootie managed to jostle his way through the crowd. When he finally made his way up front to see what had everybody's attention, he wished he would've kept on walking by. His stomach dropped and fear ran his blood cold. The bile inside his mouth was struggling for release, but Hootie swallowed hard. In stunned silence, he stood shoulder to shoulder with everybody else. But unlike everybody else, Hootie knew what he was witnessing had been left as a warning; a grisly calling card with the promise of more violence to come.

As the fire and rescue retrieved a ladder from the truck, Hootie wanted to believe this to be the work of the maniac who'd butchered that kid Sin and left his Airmans hanging from a high-tension wire. But this body had the limbs intact. It was wishful thinking on his part.

Everybody stared at the badly beaten body of a young man that was naked from the waist down and hanging from one of the basketball rims, dangling, swaying in the cold breeze. His arms were over his head and duct-taped to the iron, as his body faced the crowd. The face had been caved in, but no matter how horrible the grill was, Hootie almost tossed his breakfast—and every other man in the crowd cringed—at the work that had been done below the dead man's belt. The focus had been concentrated on the crotch region. Surrounding flesh was unharmed. It was the penis that had been cooked extra crispy.

Hootie had seen enough. He had to get to Granny Sinclair's, and quickly. He moved back through the crowd with his hand clutching the handle of the gat. He wasn't gonna stay to see them take down Lil Shorty's body. Hootie was near the edge of the crowd when somebody touched his shoulder. He spun around, ready to whip out the weapon.

Some cat named Reno jumped back and said: "Damn, G, it's me."

"Man, what the fuck you doing? You could've got your

ass straight twisted, cowboy," Hootie said as he removed his hand from the pocket.

"Hootie, brah, let's take a walk."

The two boys walked to the far end of the playground, away from the scene and police officers working the crowd for information.

Reno was no taller than Spud Webb and light in the ass at a hundred twenty-five pounds. "Hootie, you got every right to be jumpy, cuz."

"The fuck you talkin', nigga?" Hootie asked.

Grief ripped loudly throughout the crowd the moment fire and rescue retrieved the body.

"You ain't heard?"

"Stall me out with all that Criss Angel shit, homie. Break me off."

"You got a contract on yo' head, guy."

It was no surprise to Hootie. He figured as much. Lil Shorty was an ass and he'd gotten what he'd deserved. Fuck 'im.

Reno nervously looked around as he went on to explain. "Look, man, Lil Shorty was going around buying up shit left and right. Niggas started raising eyebrows when he used this chick's company as a shell to cash out a Range Rover. Cats in the hood knew that little fool wasn't working with that much cheese, dude.

"Last night, Lil Shorty was a couple blocks away, iced out, talking shit as usual, when a black cargo van rode up, gorilla-looking niggas jumped out, and tossed his little ass and his bling inside. The niggas who jumped out—I'd never seen them a day in my life. This was the first time we"—he pointed in the other direction—"I'd seen him since last night."

Hootie was stepping off. He had to get to his grandmother's crib to check on her.

Reno looked around again. "It ain't your head that's wearing a contract alone, man. It's Ruffneck's entire crew, too. The streets are saying that you got pissed that Billy had played you for some choppers and smoked your boy. Your cousin's crew laid Billy down with the get-back and took his loot for payment."

"Damn, that's news to me, fam," Hootie responded. He was vaguely familiar with how the hood worked. You could hear twenty-million different stories before you got to the truth.

Reno rolled his shoulders as if to say, "oh well."

"On the real, Hootie man, on everything you love, guy. Pack up and get the fuck out of town before you be hanging like that little nigga over there."

Reno went to turn away.

Hootie asked, "What happened to the bitch that Shorty used to front the car for him?"

"They found her right before they found Lil Shorty. She was stripped butt naked, beaten, and left lying in an alley with her titties sliced off."

"All right, Reno, good-looking on the tip, though." Hootie bumped Reno's fist.

His leg was in serious pain, but he had to ignore it. Hootie hadn't gotten within three houses of Granny Sinclair's when a black cargo van whipped down the street and bounced upon the curve. Hootie tried to run but slipped on ice. The cargo door exploded open and a few big niggas popped out. They stomped Hootie within an inch of his life, picked his unconscious body up and threw him inside. The vehicle sped off as quickly as it came.

"Wakey, wakey, thief," a deep voice sounded from somewhere in the fog. "Time to pay for your sins."

Hootie's focus was blurry. The shapes and sizes moving around before him were dark and fuzzy. The pain in his leg wasn't shit compared to the volcano blast of pain shooting around inside his head.

"Thief," the man accused. Hootie could feel a thumping on his forehead. "You in there, thief? Come on now. It's time for your big send-off. And I know you don't want to miss it. I got your ticket right here, first-class accommodations all the way to your new afterlife destination."

Hootie tried to move, but severe pain stabbed through his body. From the position he was lying in, Hootie found it difficult to breathe.

And, although he couldn't make out a damn thing, Hootie could feel the presence of another, somebody who was gigantic.

"Ghoul," the deep voice called out. "Wake this thief up, so we can get this over."

Hootie was splashed with water. He gagged as if he was drowning, spewing the liquids back out of his mouth and nose. Hootie sluggishly started to stir.

"Hey, thief, you up?"

No answer.

"Ghoul," the voice said again.

The pain that Hootie felt across his back was intense, followed by what sounded like a stick snapping. He screamed. Hootie was fully conscious now and aware of his predicament. From the look of it, Hootie appeared to be in a basement. Wherever it was, there were no windows.

He panicked and thrashed around, trying to free himself from his restraints—but nothing doing. He was lying strapped, face-down, to a pool table, his legs spread-eagle with both tied to something on either side of the table. The draft he felt down below made him look to the immediate area. And much like Lil Shorty, he'd been stripped from the waist down.

"I wouldn't be concerned with trying to free myself, if I were you." For the first time, Hootie made the man that the deep voice belonged to. He was short, clean-cut, appeared to be in his early fifties, and wore what seemed to be a very expensive Italian suit. "My associate, Ghoul, is an expert at knot tying."

"Fuck," Hootie yelled as he squirmed, trying to get free. "Fuck is wrong with you, man?"

"Now, now, now," the man said, waving his index finger around. "I won't allow such words in my presence. You keep it up and I'm going to order my associate, Ghoul, to wash your mouth out."

"Fuck you!" Hootie yelled louder.

"Young brother—or should I call you by your birth name, Clarence Sinclair? It seems that we have a dilemma, Mr. Sinclair. You have a great sum of money that belongs to me."

"I ain't got shit," Hootie spat. The only thing he could move was his head, with which he tracked the man's movement.

"You ain't got 'shit'?" the man repeated with disgust at the language showing on his face. "Ghoul, teach our young ruffian here some manners."

It was the first time Hootie had seen the man named Ghoul. The bastard was an abnormal size. Long, sloping forehead with wide jaws and eyes that sunk into his head—Ghoul was a monster who stood almost seven feet. He moved to Hootie's right side and smashed him across the back with a pool cue; the stick snapping on impact.

Hootie screamed out in agony. The Ghoul stood there with half the stick in his large hands, making the thing look like a toothpick to him. When the pain subsided, Hootie figured a pool cue had to have been used in the first assault.

"Is this unfortunate pain doing anything to jar your memory, Mr. Sinclair?" the man in the suit asked. He had his arms folded. "I assure you, Mr. Sinclair, that I take no pleasure in this act of barbarity. It is a sad, unfortunate necessity that we have to apply these tactics to extract information." He examined his well-manicured fingernails. "I could be on a golf course in San Diego enjoying tee-time. So, please, dear boy, don't drag this out any longer than necessary. Where is the two-hundred thousand that you and Mr. Tyrone Wind—you may know him as Lil Shorty—collected off the dead body of one of my business associates?"

Hootie said nothing. He doubted if a confession would make a difference now. This man was going to kill him regardless.

"Here, boss," Ghoul spoke with a low eerie voice. "Nigga was carrying this." He handed the man in the suit Hootie's heater.

The man laughed condescendingly and held the pistol up to Hootie's face. "A Glock?—very ghetto, Mr. Sinclair. You gangstas slay me. I still can't believe you and Mr. Wind had the intestinal fortitude to bring harm to anybody in my family. But I'll have to admit that Spencer Hamilton—you may know him by Billy the Kid—was becoming rather sloppy at his business handlings. But that's why I was called in. Now, I have to make an example out of you, Mr. Sinclair. Just like I've done with your comrade, Mr. Wind. I do believe this to be what war experts call psychological warfare. Make it crystal clear that our organization is strictly off-limits."

"I don't know what you talking about. I don't have no money. Now, either let me the fuck go, or get the shit over with!" Hootie barked.

"Such a blatant disrespect for the King's English. Well, as you wish." The man nodded to the giant. "Ghoul."

On cue, Ghoul picked up a long, rigid funnel. The thing was black and seemed to be six inches long from head to tail.

The fear that was striking a pose in Hootie's eyes was open for the world to see. He tried not to say anything at first, but when Ghoul grabbed a tube of K-Y Jelly and started greasing the tail of the funnel, Hootie lost his composure. He screamed for help and wiggled, trying hard to free himself from bondage.

"I can assure you, Mr. Sinclair. You can do all the screaming you want. There's nobody around to help." The man in the suit slid on a pair of industrial-strength rubber gloves. "When I was torturing Mr. Wind, he told me lots of interesting things."

The man signaled for Ghoul to insert the funnel. Without any warning, the big man plunged the hard plastic into Hootie's rectal cavity. Hootie yelled like something was inside of him ripping his stomach apart. His eyes grew glossy and red, with tears trickling down his cheeks.

The man moved into position. "The interesting thing, Mr. Sinclair, is that this torture isn't just for you and your associate, Mr. Wind—no, I'm afraid we have to continue with your Granny Sinclair and one Mr. Walker Story, Jr. who's now, I believe, serving time to pay a debt to society in Battle Creek, Michigan. I can assure you that we have associates on staff at the prison. So, feel free to view this as an appropriate time to—as my young son would say— spill the beans."

"I told you I don't have your money and my family don't have a damn thing to do with it," Hootie struggled to say. He could feel warm blood ooze down his crack.

The man stuck out his hand. The Ghoul placed a glass beaker with clear liquid in it.

"Yes, you do. Mr. Wind took a lot of punishment before he broke. He admitted your involvement. The dear boy just didn't divulge the location of the money. Do you wish to have last words, Mr. Sinclair?"

Hootie thought about it for a few ticks. He looked up with hell in his eyes. "My cousin…my cousin gonna fuck you up real bad behind this, you bitch."

"Such a filthy mouth. Well, looks like we have no more to discuss. Next stop, Mrs. Stephanie Sinclair's house. We have men in place, as I speak. It's been fun. Ta-ta, Mr. Sinclair."

The man in the suit poured the clear liquid down the funnel.

Hootie instantly lapsed into unconsciousness from immense pain. A hot stench rose in the air, almost like the smell of meat cooking. A foamy blood mixture fizzled up out of his hole and onto the pool table.

Within minutes, Hootie was dead.

The Ghoul checked Hootie's pulse. He made that sweeping hand gesture across the throat. "Nigga dead, boss."

"Ghoul, what did you think the Liquid Drano would do?" The man in the suit put his lips to Hootie's ear. "The name is Bruno, not 'bitch.'" He turned to the Ghoul. "Clean up this mess and properly dispose of it. We have another victim."

Granny Sinclair sat in her recliner in front of the television. *Sanford and Son* was playing, but she wasn't paying any attention to Fred as he staggered across the screen, clutching his chest and having one of his signature "Elizabeth, I coming to join you, honey" moments. The old woman wasn't feeling her best lately. She wanted to believe that her pride had played a factor in her not reaching out to her friends for help. She'd been without her heart medication going on four days now. But nothing could be further from the truth.

She was ready.

Sweat poured from her face in large puddles. The pain inside her chest was crippling. Her breathing was erratic, but she calmly sat there as if at a bus stop, patiently awaiting the public eternal transportation that shuttled life in and out of this world.

She was tired.

Looking back over life, left the old woman with some reservations that her God would revoke her entry into heaven. She'd done a lot of dirt. Been involved in a lot of shady business dealings with what some would call the scum of the human race. The only thing which brought any comfort at the moment, was the fact that she had taken the boy into her home and done her best at raising him; a task at which she'd failed. The boy was in jail and not due out for years.

She was ready.

As the pain increased, the old lady clutched both arms of the recliner. Her breath was leaving her. The guilt she was feeling for leaving the boy behind was as large as the knowledge of harboring the information involving the identities of his parents. Much like Fred Sanford, Granny Sinclair clutched her chest, fighting for air.

She was ready.

She had gotten all of her affairs in order. No, she wouldn't be here to tell her grandson about his parents. The old woman was somewhat relieved that she wouldn't have to bear the burden of telling him about the monster who had fathered him, and all the sordid events that had led up to Senior's demise. A part of her was also relieved she wouldn't be around to see the monster that the boy was most certain to become. He was on his way. And, if he was anything like his old man, heads would roll. The call to be bigger than life was in his DNA. Unfortunately, it would probably be the same yearning for power that would bring the shadows who'd killed his parents to his doorstep for a little unfinished business.

Her one moment of humor had come in the form of remembering all those people on television, who'd given firsthand accounts of seeing a bright light before death, were liars. There was no fucking light, or maybe there was, but she couldn't see it. Darkness had descended on her time here. Her head slowly slumped to one side, and her hand lifelessly fell from her chest into her lap.

Granny Sinclair was dead.

She wasn't there when the front door of her home exploded off of the hinges, and armed men poured in like police through the front door of a suspected crack-house. All five were dressed in black, wearing ski-masks. The first man through held the old lady in check with his AR-15 assault rifle, as the others walked through the rest of the house. He couldn't believe what he was seeing. To confirm—keeping his weapon trained on her—he leaned in and checked for a pulse. There was nothing. She was gone.

"Believe this shit?" he said to the other four men as they gathered around. "The old bag checked out before we could assist her."

"Shit," one of the men spoke. "I could've been at the crib doing the girlfriend thing. Man, enough with these senior citizen hits, guy."

There was some laughter.

The first man ordered, "Pack it up before the police show up…gotta call the boss. He ain't gonna believe this shit."

The men backed out of the house and jumped into the black cargo van. They peeled off. They weren't gonna waste any time. There was much more to be done.

Adult Horror 'Tainment

Him was back. This time, Him was standing in front of a very wicked building around one in the morning; a place where Him's mamma described as Sodom and Gomorrah. Him didn't know what it meant, but it had to be a bad place, because every time Him used to pass one with Him's mommy, she would refer to it as wicked, and then use Sodom and Gomorrah behind it. It was an evil place where men sat around drinking, and disgusting women did the nasty-girl-dance on a pole for dollars.

The sign out front said FOOD AND SPIRITS. But when Him was younger, Him always mispronounced the word "spirits." Him used to think that the word was pronounced "sprite"—like the soda. Him blamed Him's mommy for not properly knowing how to pronounce certain words, because she kept Him from school. Him's mommy didn't want the other kids to see Him's ugly.

Him stood in the shadows across the street from the building, waiting on number 9 on Him's list of bad men to come out from shoving dollars down the naked-dance girl's underpants. Him had never really been in one of those places, but Him's mommy had put on the movie *The Players Club* to show the kind of sin and filth associated with strip clubs. Him was ashamed to admit that Him's thing-thingy had gotten hard from seeing Lisa Raye's big booty jiggle around on stage.

Him had done right to bundle up tonight. It was freezing, but Him had on gloves, a scarf, hat, and big coat. It was time for another game of Nasty Feet. Him had loads of fun in playing Nasty Feet with 10. In fact, Him had so much fun, Him was looking forward to playing with 9; probably show 9 the ugly. Ever since little brother had left, Him hadn't been able to have fun. But now, Nasty Feet had made little brother leaving all better. It was a list of very bad men who needed their feet disinfected.

Newspapers were saying that Him was sick for cutting off 10's feet. They just didn't know Him well enough. Him was working to restore balance back inside the city—to rid Detroit of all bad men who sold dope and killed little kids. The time on Him's digital watch read 1:30. Him couldn't tell time from a normal clock-face watch. Him's mommy had died before she could teach Him. Him's mommy was a nasty girl, but not like the ones who dance nasty for dollars. She was the type that let funky men—known as tricks—lie on top of her, while she made funny noises for money. One day, Him had come home and found Mommy on the floor with a needle sticking out of her arm. Him tore up the house, but before Him's mommy had gone to be with God, she had given Him a picture of Him's father and said that Him had a brother by Him's father's wife. Him's father used to be one of the funky men that bounced up and down on her for money.

Oooh—Him better shut Him's thinking mouth up because 9 walked out of the nasty-girl dancing building, staggering and talking to himself. Him was hiding in the shadows between Coney Island restaurant and a car-fixing place. Him could jump from the shadows, without his hood on and show 9 the ugly. But the evil place was set on a major street and Him would have to cross five lanes to get to the fella. 9 was so drunk on bad-man's juice that he didn't see Him start across the street.

It was so cold out. Him could see Him's frosty breath coming out in smoke. 9 surprised Him when the fella started around the corner. Him had planned to play Nasty Feet with 9 in the parking lot of the nasty-girl dancing-for-dollars club, but 9 wasn't playing fair, for some reason. Him didn't know why 9 was walking in the opposite direction of the parking lot. But Him was happy. Him had been following 9 for two Saturdays now, and Him had never seen a security guard man walking around in the parking lot. Him didn't want to play Nasty Feet with the security guard. The security guard wasn't on Him's list of very bad men.

Him was halfway across the street when Him's feet got cold. Him wasn't wearing any boots, so slush and snow were creating a problem. But Him was a trooper. 9 took the sidewalk around the building and to the alley behind, singing happy songs. The only times when Him used to see men that happy was when Mommy used to put her mouth on their special purpose area—Him was too embarrassed to admit it, but Him had peeked inside her bedroom a couple times. 9 was in the alley with tea-pot in hand, making water, still singing so happy. Him didn't know what song the 9 man was singing, because the "Thriller" song was playing inside of Him's head. Vincent Price was laughing wickedly in the "Thriller" song inside of Him's head.

9 was so busy making water that he didn't see Him just standing there. 9 wore braids and had on a pretty leather jacket, baggy pants…and the Airman sneakers. Him couldn't control Him's self; he was real angry at the Airman's sneakers.

"You have nasty feet," Him said in Him's best Vincent Price voice.

9 yelled at Him, still with thing-thingy in hand. "Yo, nigga. Get the fuck out of here; this ain't some type of peep show, pervert!"

Him wasn't a bird-brain; 9 carried a pistol. All the bad men on Him's list carried guns. Before 9 put his thing-thingy away and grabbed the gun, Him stripped off the hood—showed 9 the ugly.

"Awwww shit, Freddy Krueger!" 9 screamed like a frightened woman who was staring into the eyes of death.

Him was on 9 from behind, grabbing the fella around his neck with one arm and cradling his head with the other. Him had 9 in a death lock. 9 was trying to get to the gun, but Him continued the pressure until 9 stopped kicking and fighting. The sight of the Airman sneakers the fella had on enraged Him, made Him snap 9's neck like a twig. Him let 9 fall into pee-pee water. Special tools were on the side of Him's coat. Listening to "Thriller," Him hacked and cut until blood stained Him's gloves and turned the pretty snow red. Him took out a black garbage bag and tossed the dirty feet inside.

"Now you can go to heaven with clean feet," Him said, still trying to sound like Vincent Price. With the bag over Him's shoulder, Him walked into the darkness, whistling the "Thriller" song. Eight men were left on Him's list now—that was sixteen feet to disinfect. Him missed little brother, but Him had another brother to find; the son of the funky man who'd gotten Him's mommy pregnant. Him figured if the other brother came from a bad man, then the other brother was bad as well. Him had heard that other brother sold dope, too. He wasn't on Him's list of bad men, but Him was going to enjoy playing Nasty Feet with the other brother.

The alley behind the Bottom's Up adult entertainment bar was ablaze with the lights of police cruisers and EMT units. News crews reported live on location as police processed the crime scene for clues. The area had been roped off by yellow tape, keeping the large crowd of curious looky-loos from contaminating the crime scene.

"Did anybody see anything?" Detective J.C. Webb asked one of his uniformed officers. He was the senior detective on the scene who'd drawn lead on the case.

"The security guard said that before he heard the screaming, he saw somebody walking around the parking lot. He couldn't ID the person as man or woman, because they were wearing a hoodie," the uniformed explained.

"Question the old man again," J.C. Webb ordered. "Also, don't let anybody out of that bar until all the patrons have been thoroughly interviewed. We can't afford to miss anything."

Detective J.C. Webb was in love with wearing fedora hats. He had fifteen years on the force, with the last eight working in the Homicide Division. Webb stood just a shade over six feet with dark skin, a neatly trimmed goatee, and a tough resolve for getting his man. Highly decorated, the detective was the toast of his division and reported to be one of the very best to have ever worn the shield. He wore a black topcoat and a cashmere scarf. Webb stepped around a puddle of water with rubber Totes covering expensive Italian leather shoes.

"Y'all make sure you boys photograph that thing right," the detective said to one of the crime scene photographers. The elderly white man shook his head, but kept on snapping away at the mutilated body. With a flashlight leading the way, the detective walked behind the sphere of light as it highlighted freshly fallen snowflakes. He searched the grounds for anything out of the ordinary.

"J.C.," said a young, white, rookie detective from behind. "Find anything, yet?"

Webb knelt on his haunches to get closer to the ground. He'd heard the young detective, but seniority had played into the slow response. J.C. was not in love with the fact of training the rook. The boy knew his place, too. He'd been working with the black detective for a little while and was very familiar with his disdain for rookies.

"Detective," the rookie said, "you think that this may be related to the Jackson Fuller murder—that we may possibly have a serial killer on hand?"

"What do you think?" Webb sarcastically asked.

The young detective said, "Same MO: severed feet."

"As far as we know, it could be a copycat crime." Webb continued further down the alley with the young detective on his heels.

"The killer is smart. Both murders were clean, nothing left at the crime scene," the young detective insisted.

"There is always something left behind, detective," Webb explained. "But right now, we have to… We just have to find the man's feet."

J.C. Webb's cell went off. He answered it. "Okay" was all he said. He turned to the clean-shaven rookie. "Looks like they found the feet."

The two walked around the block from the strip club

to a side street. Police had roped off the area underneath one of the high-tension wires.

The young detective looked up at the blood dripping from the stumps that had been flung around and dangled on the wire. "I think it's safe to say that we have a serial killer," he proudly proclaimed.

Webb didn't even look at him. He picked up his cell and made a call. "Better get the fire department out here."

Bad News

Three weeks after the deaths of Hootie and Granny Sinclair, Fly had finally made his way up to Battle Creek Correctional Facility.

When Ruffneck heard that he had a visitor, he showered, threw on some fresh blues and damn-near ran over to the visitor's room. He'd been down for a few months now and none of his niggas had come to holla. He was a little pissed, but it wasn't gonna get in the way of his visit. He was just excited that somebody from the hood had finally put *self* behind to come see him.

After he'd been strip-searched and humiliated inside a private room by having to hold up his sack and spread his cheeks, he was allowed to get dressed and go in. His nigga Fly was sitting at one of the tables on the left side of the room by the vending machines. Ruffneck went to give his boy some dap, but was surprised when Fly bolted out of his seat and grabbed him inside a bear hug.

"'Neck," Fly said with excitement in his voice. "Dude, the streets are missing you, fam."

Ruffneck was happy to see Fly. They took their seats.

"Man, you want something out of the vending machine?" Fly asked, shaking a fistful of coins in his closed fist. Prison rules strictly prohibited cash inside of the visitor's room. Before entering, visitors had to turn cash into coins for the vending machine with the guard in the front lobby.

"Naw, man, I'm tight," Ruffneck said.

Ruffneck looked well-rested. His skin was clear, and for the first time since the two boys had met, Ruffneck looked to be free from burdens. But Fly knew that wasn't gonna last too long. Although he was here to see his dude, he had some very bad news to bring. Fly sat looking at all the love being expressed around the room by visitors and inmates in the form of hugs and kisses.

"How's my granny?" Ruffneck asked. "I know it's financially hard on the old lady so I stay off her phone. I've been writing her, though, for about three weeks now; she hasn't written a nigga back. That ain't like her, G."

Fly couldn't break the news to him just yet. He was gonna try to ease into it.

"Man, you heard about Lil Shorty?" Fly asked.

Ruffneck looked around as if to state the obvious. "Man, how could I? Nigga, I'm locked up. And I don't holla at any of these fools in here. The only thing I've been tripping on is the serial killer running around the D chopping off niggas' legs."

"Yeah, that fool is wild. He has Detroit on notice, that's for damn sure."

"Now, what's this about Lil Shorty?" asked Ruffneck.

"Oh yeah, the lil nigga finally went and did it."

"Did what?"

Fly waited, looking around at the security guards. "The nigga rubbed out Billy the Kid and jacked him for two-hunnit gee's."

Ruffneck simply shook his head. "That's on him, man. When Billy's people come looking for the get-back, y'all stay out the way."

"He already paid, fam. They left the little fool hanging from a rim at the Body Bag, butt naked, dick burned, and face bashed in."

"Damn. Sounds like they put the mack on his little ass," Ruffneck said. Before Fly had said anything, Lil Shorty had been at the top of Ruffneck's niggas-to-payback list whenever he was released. He could scratch his name off now. "Like I said: Ain't no get-back for that body. That little nigga was outside of our family the moment I got sent up here."

Fly wanted to ask Ruffneck what he meant by his statement, but thought against it. Ruffneck was always tight-lipped with information.

"It's too late for us staying out of the way, G," Fly explained. "We all got contracts on our heads—including you."

"Guilt by association, hunh," Ruffneck said, rubbing his chin. He wasn't gonna trip. There were certain rules to the game that he didn't like, but respected. "Well, y'all stay low until I get back to the crib. Then we'll pick shit up from there."

Some punk walked up to the vending machines and was

trying his very best to intimidate Ruffneck. He bull-dog-stared Ruffneck, all while making his purchase selections. Fly looked at dude like he could give two-fucks about the consequences behind beating the brakes off of an inmate.

"'Neck, who that nigga?" Fly asked in a regular tone. He wasn't hiding shit. He wanted the fool to hear.

Ruffneck didn't say shit. He was trying to compose himself. The judge's voice kept replaying inside his head about early release, if he kept his nose clean.

The inmate was light-complexioned; short but stocky, like he'd made the most of his prison sentences inside the weight room. The nigga didn't try to hide his taunting laughter while staring at both boys. Once he swooped in and retrieved his goods, he walked back to his table, periodically looking over his shoulder and laughing like Ruffneck and Fly were jokes.

"B, who's the nigga auditioning for an ass whupping?" Fly asked again. He watched the fool take his seat with what appeared to be a pregnant woman and two small children.

"Some Chicago nigga named Swoll—up in here frontin' like he's running things; a nobody. Those joker tattoos on his forearms are supposed to represent some Chi-Town gang."

"He's developed a yearning for your attention, I see."

"Anyway," Ruffneck dismissed the Chicago cat. "Back to my granny. I'm getting worried, man. I need you to go by her crib and check on her. I still have eighteen gee's from the lick. When you get back to the crib, I need you to go in the basement and grab it and give it to the old woman. It should tide her over until I can get back out on the street."

Ruffneck was starting to notice the look in his partner's eyes at the mention of Granny Sinclair. He became nervous.

"Fly, what dup, man? Ain't nothing wrong with Granny, is it?" Ruffneck tensed in his seat. Worry started to set into his face.

"This shit ain't easy to say, 'Neck."

"Well, give it to me straight and stop bullshittin'," Ruffneck said in a voice slowly crawling into aggression and anxiety.

Fly eyed the table. "Hootie," he mumbled.

"What about my cousin?" Ruffneck pushed.

"Lil Shorty forced Hootie into going along on the Billy hit."

"What the fuck are you trying to say, nigga?" Ruffneck asked a little louder, gaining the attention of a deputy that the inmates had come to know as Melonhead.

"They found Hootie…"

The stress in Ruffneck's face was rivaling the fury inside his heart. He said nothing, sat waiting for the bomb to drop.

"…found him in an alley with…with a funnel sticking out of his ass. Word on the street is that they used some type of acid."

Ruffneck sat there blown back. He couldn't say shit. He'd warned the boy to get low, but that was way past the point now. The people that Billy worked for had put their hands on his family. The veins in his eyes seemed to infectiously spread until the whites were completely red. Ruffneck's bottom lip had found its way between his teeth and he was biting the shit out of it, trying to stay calm. He trembled with anger, teetering on the brink of explosive rage.

Fly didn't like the look in his homeboy's eyes. A war was brewing behind them. Bodies would fall in the name of revenge. The streets would run red behind this one. Fly started to feel uncomfortable as Ruffneck's gaze rested on him, like his partner was about to erupt at any moment and kill the messenger.

Fly had one more bomb to drop, and this one was sure to send his homey over the edge of insanity. Suddenly, he didn't like the position that he'd found himself in, but as second in command, Fly had lost out to obligation.

Fly was afraid of the violence that would probably ensue behind the next death-disclosure. He took the time to choose his words carefully.

"Granny Sinclair is…she…she…dead, too."

Ruffneck looked like he was about to bite his bottom lip off. Tears fell from his eyes as he trembled from a gamut of emotions. But he forced himself to stay still because he knew there was more to come.

Fly looked around at the attention they were gaining,

including the guards. The tears on Ruffneck's face were visible for all to see. The Chicago cat was one of the ones paying close attention to the exchange at the table.

"Dog, they say that she had a heart attack, but the police said that her door had been kicked in. They found her in the recliner."

Ruffneck sat, head bowed, as if having a moment of silence. When he lifted his face from the table, rage was etched in his expression. Tears slid down his cheeks effortlessly, and his fist balled so tight that his knuckles popped loud enough to be heard throughout the room.

In a disturbing voice that sounded like Satan, Ruffneck said, "I'm gonna kill everybody involved, and anybody connected to them better move to the fuckin' moon."

Ruffneck hopped up from the table and walked off. Fly observed as his dude made an attempt to walk by the nigga Swoll's table. Swoll pulled some old first-grade tactic by sticking out his leg, so Ruffneck would have to stop and go around.

It turned out to be a bad move for the young cat from Chicago. He definitely was about to live up to his name, because Ruffneck threw a straight right that split Swoll's bottom lip. The nigga hadn't known what hit him as he fell backward from the bench. Ruffneck got after it. He followed up going straight at Swoll's ass. Chairs fell over, tables flipped, and people got the fuck out of the way as Ruffneck unleashed all of his hurt and pain. Swoll wasn't given an opportunity to recover because Ruffneck was stomping the shit out of the young boy. The pregnant woman screamed and shouted for Ruffneck to stop. The two small children were loudly crying behind her with hands over their eyes and ears.

Swoll's body violently shook with every kick and stomp. Blood spewed from his mouth and nose. Two deputies rushed over to grab Ruffneck. Fly watched as his homeboy was on the blink. Ruffneck turned his attention away from Swoll's unconscious body and attacked the two officers. He was giving the two all they could handle until backup came running. The last time Fly saw his boy, he was in a chokehold by one of the deputies. It took eight of them to drag Ruffneck's ass away.

Ruffneck spent the next two weeks in segregation. His cell was no more than a bare mattress with a thin covering. Logic and rational thinking had been replaced by fatal thoughts laced with primal, homicidal instincts of bodies falling to the turf behind his get-back. Everybody holding the blood of his family on their hands would be killed and tortured in the most diabolical way he could think of. He couldn't eat, didn't sleep—just kept thinking about Granny Sinclair.

Life had done it to him again: had crept up behind him and placed the barrel of tragedy to his temple and pulled the trigger, violently scrambling his world once more. Much like the night when he was a kid and those men had come calling. The streets had taken so many of his people that the shit started to look like an itemized grocery list of tragedy and pain. From here on out, nobody was safe. His trigger would be devoid of remorse, a cold-blooded killer with a hot fever for causing death to all those who opposed him.

It wasn't about a throne or an empire anymore; the shit would be strictly on the revenge tip. Now with nobody to stop him, he would find all responsible for the deaths of his parents as well. Even if he had to go back to Pennsylvania—on everything he loved, niggas were going to die. The Ruffneck that used to occupy the building had been evicted by hurt and pain. The new tenant was twisted and deranged without the tolerance for reasoning. His revenge game would be as personal as the results of an AIDS test.

Billy worked for some powerful franchise; one that didn't have a directory for its employees. It didn't matter, though. Ruffneck would work his way up, even if he had to start with the lower-level dealers. They were all gonna feel him, just as soon as his hour met the streets.

A Lead

Even though it had been quiet for two months now, J.C. Webb was still working hard to apprehend the maniac who had been responsible for two badly mutilated bodies. Local media was having a field day with the name they'd given the sadistic killer. The story of the "Sneaker Stalker Slasher" had slashed its way through to national news headlines. Once again, Detroit was receiving attention for all the wrong reasons. Photos of dangling, bloody stumps on high-tension wires were hot on the Internet, and the city was putting pressure on the mayor and police chief to bring this perpetrator to justice.

The one fact that had been ascertained was that both victims were drug-dealing scum who were killed while wearing the popular Airman sneakers. The case was still baffling, but Detective J.C. Webb was up to the task.

He was pulling into the parking lot of Northwestern High School for a meeting with the principal involving his only child. Anthony "Ups" Webb was a popular sophomore sensation who'd earned the nickname "Ups" for his amazing ability to jump and float through the air. He was the top scorer and team captain for Northwestern

High's basketball team. Lately, the team had been experiencing some trouble with closing out ball games. Webb and his son had an uneasy relationship. The boy blamed his father for splitting up the family, citing the detective's work schedule to be the reason behind a nasty divorce and a bitter custody battle. The two tried to resolve their differences in therapy, but the relationship seemed to be too far gone.

Detective Webb hated the fact that he had to be pulled from his job to deal with his son's behavioral issues. He parked his unmarked in the parking lot for visitors and walked through the school doors with the facts surrounding the case swirling inside his mind.

"Detective," said a young, hot, middle-aged black lady with her hand out and wearing a pretty dress, "I appreciate you being able to take the time in coming to see us."

He took off his fedora and shook her hand. "Ma'am."

She escorted the detective back to her office. It was nothing fancy: a few family photos on her desk, accomplishments hung from walls, and a few plants sat around. "Have a seat, detective."

He removed his topcoat, placed it in the second of the two chairs in front of her desk, and sat down, holding his hat in his lap. "Principal Ellen, is my son misbehaving?"

"Please, call me Ms. Ellen."

Webb smiled.

"I'm a little concerned about our All-Star forward," the principal informed.

J.C. never got caught up in his son's hype. He was a

hard-nosed guy who preached academics over athleticism; sometimes stepping on his son's hopes and dreams.

"Not only is his play slipping on the court, but he's been missing class and handing in incomplete assignments as well. His progress report states that he's failing, and if he keeps achieving below his apparent abilities, I'm afraid that he will eventually be ineligible to play his junior season."

"This has been going on for how long?" Webb asked.

The principal's brow went up. "Is everything all right at home?"

"I'm afraid no. See, my wife and I have been divorced for a few years now. I believe Anthony is still trying to adjust."

"I see, well"—she handed over the progress report— "Anthony's a really good student and I'm worried about him."

The detective received the paper and stood from his chair to slide on his coat. "I appreciate your concern. I will be having a talk with my son. He won't give you any more trouble."

Detective J.C. Webb shook her hand and was about to turn to walk away.

"Detective," the principal said.

Webb stopped and faced her again with a no-nonsense look on his face.

"I know that the police department has its hands full with this Sneaker Stalker Killer—or Slasher, whatever— but has anyone been brought into custody for the death of Michael Steel?"

Webb questioned with his eyes.

"Michael Steel was an academic-crowning jewel in our school. The young man had a real bright future. Someone killed him for his Airman sneakers. I just wanted to know if any arrests have been made."

"Ms. Ellen, would you happen to have an address on the young man, and a photo, if possible?"

"I sure do." The principal picked up the phone and dialed.

Moments later, the detective was pulling up to a house on Carter Street, near Linwood Avenue. On the drive over, he'd tabled his son's issues and set his mind back on the case. This was his first official lead and he needed to be sharp. But, seeing the abandoned house took all the wind out of his sails.

Huge snowflakes started to fall as the detective got out of his car and walked around the boarded-up colonial. He was around back when an elderly black lady walked out onto the back porch of the house to the left.

"Ma'am, how you doing?" the detective asked, slowly walking over to the lady. He flashed his credentials. "My name is Detective J.C. Webb and I'm looking for some information about the family who lived in this house."

The lady softened her stance and adjusted her bifocals. "I'll try my best to help, detective. What do you want to know?"

"Do you know this boy?" Webb asked, flashing the young man's photo.

The lady adjusted her glasses again and stretched her neck forward as if it would help her to better see.

"Michael Steel," she exclaimed.

"You sure?" the detective asked, pushing the picture a little closer.

"Quite sure. How can I ever forget such a darling boy? He stayed there with his mother and brother."

"Brother?" the detective inquired.

"Yeah—didn't see much of him. He would come out only at night; creeped me out, too. With the exception of Michael, they kept mostly to themselves."

"Do you know where I can find the mother?"

"I'm afraid you're a little too late for that, detective. She was found dead of a drug overdose after Michael was murdered."

"And her other son?" Webb pressed.

"Don't know."

The detective placed the picture back inside his coat pocket.

"Ms. ..." he went to ask her name.

"Lee—Gladys Lee."

Webb went into his wallet. "Ms. Lee, here's my card, if you should think of anything else. Call me on my cell."

He wondered if the Michael Steel murder had anything to do with the mutilations. Webb had a hunch, and he was aware that sometimes, detectives blew cases wide open by following their guts. It was a long shot, but one he had to investigate.

A Surprise Visit

The death toll steadily increased between the months of February and July. A total of eight dismembered bodies belonging to young drug dealers had fallen, as the Sneaker Stalker Slasher seemed to be carving up the underworld. Wide-spread panic had gripped the city with citizens barricading themselves in their homes at night, and parents refrained from buying their kids the popular Airman sneaker. The FBI had been called in on what they were calling a manhunt for one of the deadliest serial killers since Jeffrey Dahmer. The community was in complete panic as pictures of bloody stumps with the sneakers still affixed, hung dangling over high-tension wires, were popping up all over the place.

Thugs, drug dealers, and gangsters were arming themselves, determined not to be the next footless victim.

Ruffneck was going hard in the weight room when a deputy stepped up to inform him of a visitor. Butterflies fluttered in his stomach as he remembered the last time a visitor had come calling. He was still fucked up behind the deaths of his family members. Granny Sinclair had been the only unconditional love that he had known, and somebody was gonna pay for taking her life. Reluctantly, Ruffneck showered and threw on some fresh prison blues.

After they'd released him from segregation, Ruffneck had been ordered to undergo a psychiatric evaluation. It was a sacrifice that he had to make if he ever expected to see the outside again. Because the way he was going, without treatment, Ruffneck was sure to lose his patience from the bullshit offered by the other inmates, and kill one of them. He didn't need shit standing in the way of him getting back out to handle his fucking business. So he'd agreed to meet with the prison psychiatrist. And for the first time since the night of his parents' murders, he'd faced up to his demons. Ruffneck had never given the doctor the full story about the demise of his parents, but enough for the shrink to conclude he suffered from posttraumatic stress disorder. It had been the same diagnosis by the doctor Granny Sinclair had taken him to see. After the findings had been concluded, Ruffneck had been ordered to take antidepressants. He'd agreed.

The month of July had brought with it record-breaking temps. It was hot as hell out as he walked over. He'd damn-near forgotten about the day being his birthday. He'd turned twenty today, but hadn't felt much like celebrating. He went through strip-search and walked into the visitor's room. There were not too many people visiting, which made it easy for him to spot his visitor. He stayed calm as he walked over to the table. He hadn't seen this visitor in quite some time. The closer he drew, the very familiar fragrance took his mind back to a time where he thought that all he needed to strengthen his court was a queen.

"Why did you come here?" Ruffneck flatly asked Princess.

Princess was glowing. Her hair was pulled back into a ponytail and she was rocking a sundress and sandals. The girl was still breathtaking.

She brushed off his question.

"I have somebody I want you to meet," she said, smiling brightly. She went into the car seat on the table and gently removed a two-month-old baby boy. "It's your son, Walker Story III." She leaned over and kissed Ruffneck on the cheek, gingerly handing the baby over to him. "Oh, yeah, happy birthday, too."

The baby was another bomb dropped, but this one being a little more pleasant to handle. Ruffneck carefully took the baby into his arms. He couldn't process shit. The last visit had brought the messenger of death. This time the messenger was life. After seeing the little curly-haired baby with chubby cheeks and a pug nose, Ruffneck damn sure couldn't deny him. After all, he could remember that night in Princess's crib. He'd spilled so much nut inside of her, that he wasn't surprised there weren't twin car seats on the table.

"Princess, I thought I told you that this wasn't gonna work." Ruffneck couldn't take his eyes off the baby's face. He'd never seen himself as a baby.

Princess moved closer to Ruffneck and softly pinched the baby's cheek. "Don't think you had it like that, simply because you came over and laid it down. After you never responded to any of my messages, I moved on." She smiled down at the baby. "That was, until I found out I was pregnant. It changed everything, Walker." She looked deeply into his eyes. "Now what?"

"You mean you didn't come up here for closure?"

"And like I said: I'd already closed your ass out of my life until I found out about the baby."

"Granny Sinclair is dead," Ruffneck said without emotion.

"I know. And I'm sorry for your loss."

Ruffneck looked at her curiously.

"What can I say? Students talk," she explained.

"How'd you find me?"

"Like I said: students talk. I went on the Internet and looked you up under Otis—the State of Michigan's offender search. Once I located you on their database and found you here, I had my cousin hook up the paperwork for visits. She works in your warden's office."

Ruffneck let his eyes roam from the baby back to Princess. She was so fucking beautiful, and the baby, the baby was heaven-sent. He took it as God giving him the precious gift of life in exchange for all the death he'd experienced. He couldn't possibly say no to Princess, but the danger of keeping her around was too real.

"Listen," he started, "powerful men are responsible for killing my cousin and grandma. When I get out of here, I'm gonna murder everybody who had something to do with their deaths. Is that something you want to be a part of?"

She took his hand. "Baby, you have a family now. Let God take care of those people."

Ruffneck looked at her with no life left in his eyes. "I am the judge, jury, and the executioner. People are gonna die when I'm let out of here. I'm trying to be up front. Can you handle it?"

She took the baby from his arms and held him in front of Ruffneck. "Look at your baby. What the streets have taken, God has given."

"Princess, my baby is adorable and I love him more than self. But I have a price on my head and I can't take something happening to you or the baby. These men will stop at nothing until they kill everybody. They didn't have any fucking respect for an old lady. I can't risk you and the baby."

Ruffneck stood from the table.

"So, that's it?" Princess asked with water in her eyes. "Walker, the baby and I need you. Please don't walk out on us."

Life was pulling at Ruffneck; a second opportunity to get shit right. Start a new chapter. But he couldn't. Not until the old chapter was done. And he aimed to do it, once his hour met the streets. All the hell he'd gone through, not knowing who his parents were, got him to thinking. He couldn't put his baby out like that. He had to be there.

"Okay, listen," he said with a softer tone. "Once I finish with my business, if you can put up with my kind of man, then we can work on it."

Princess perked up. "Yes, baby. Just come back home safely."

Ruffneck smiled at her with the baby. "Listen, I need you to promise me something."

Princess didn't say anything. She just listened.

"I can't see you anymore until I finish my work out-side. It'll be too dangerous for you and the baby. And once I'm done, I'll come and be with my family." He leaned in and kissed Princess's lips. "I'm gonna also need you not to come back here again, please."

Princess reluctantly agreed. Ruffneck kissed her and the baby, and walked toward the exit.

Apparently, the meds were ineffective as Ruffneck woke up inside his cell, sweating from another nightmare. He'd dreamt about Hole-in-the-Head and his boy, Man-Beast. This time Ruffneck had been the one gripping the machete. And with Hole-in-the-Head coaching him, he'd cut clean through the neck of the man who was tied and on his knees, neck stretched out across the block. The shit felt powerful, like Ruffneck had found the answer. Hole-in-the-Head had shown him a new way. What Hole-in-the-Head had presented him in the dream, would be what he needed to send the message that he wasn't fucking around. Sun Tzu described it as psychological warfare.

From now on, guns wouldn't be enough. Ruffneck was literally going to decapitate muthafuckas.

Fourth Of July Murder

"Fucking dope-dealing niggers," a fat, white uniformed officer said to another white officer as he roped off the crime scene. "It's nine at night, and instead of being with my kids shooting off fireworks and eating barbecue, I'm out here with these porch monkeys"—he glanced at the crowd of black faces behind the tape—"cleaning up nigger scum."

The other white officer said nothing. He was in the heart of the ghetto and possessed enough common sense not to incite a race riot.

The night was aglow with the lights of EMT units, police cruisers, and fire trucks. Another body had been found in a vacant field—this time sitting inside of a Ford Conversion van—with the killer's signature amputation. Bloody Airman sneakers were found dangling from a high-tension wire in the alley between a vacant field and a barbecue restaurant.

"If you ask me," the fat, white officer continued, "let that fucking Sneaker Stalker Slasher go. Let him get rid of the niggers. It'll be like a self-cleaning oven."

Detective J.C. Webb walked up behind. "I suggest you officers get back to doing your job, instead of letting these civilians know that their tax dollars are going to waste on trailer-trash pretending to give a damn about 'protecting and serving.'"

Both white officers jumped to attention.

Webb went on: "If I ever hear derogatory trash coming out of your mouths again, you will both be unemployed and able to spend as much time as you'd like to with your families."

July weather was off the hook. The night's temp was sweltering, but the humidity was suffocating.

Webb stepped away from the van and stood up straight. He removed his fedora and wiped at his brow with a handkerchief. He was completely exhausted.

The detective—and the Feds—had been chasing this maniac for two years straight, without so much as one lead. And here he was, standing in a field with tall grass near another stinking-ass alley, staring at the ninth body of a young boy without feet. So far, he'd had no luck with running down any information on Michael Steel's brother.

"Webb," said another black detective, sporting a low Mohawk. "Our boy is escalating, changing up his MO?"

Webb put back on the hat and continued processing the crime scene. The body sat in a normal position in one of the back chairs of the van.

Webb pointed out the obvious. "Yes, I would think so.

The head of this victim has been severely twisted around."

Mohawk commented: "Yeah, a little more to the left and the vic would look like Linda Blair's character when her head turned around in that movie."

"Do we have an ID yet?" Webb asked as he carefully maneuvered around the pools of dried blood.

"Henry Fish. Witnesses say this van had been sitting in this vacant lot for a whole day, when a local car thief looking to make good, stumbled on the body.

"Said at first he thought an orgy was jumping off inside because of the loud, sexual noises coming from the vehicle. But when he opened the door to have a quick peek, that's when he made the discovery."

J.C. Webb closely examined the floorboards. "Where is he now?"

"Patrol took him down for questioning."

"How do you account for the noises?" Webb asked.

Mohawk pointed. "A porn DVD was left on. Officers turned the thing off before you got here."

"Prints?" Webb asked.

"Not yet. I'm waiting on the M.E. to come collect the body. Then, the van will go down to the garage to be processed for prints. But we probably won't have any, because this guy is good."

"He will slip up," Webb assured, slipping into a latex glove. "It will happen."

"Our boy has eluded us for two years. The only connection we've been able to establish is that all the bodies belong to that two-bit crew over off Warren and Livernois."

"The Kato Boys," Webb said, running his latex-covered hand between the seats. "A bottom-feeding crew who sell crack, but mostly, their chief source of revenue comes from robbery."

"They all wear the Airman sneakers. What type of score does he have to settle with them?" Mohawk asked.

"That would be the million-dollar question," J.C. said as his hand brushed across something that looked like a business card. "None of those boys are talking, either."

Mohawk stood patiently as Webb pulled the object from between the seats. It was a business card that was smudged by blood. "There were only ten in the crew. It's just one more left and he had the nerve to turn down witness protection. At the rate the Stalker's carving them up, I'm afraid that there won't be any around when we finally close this case out."

"Can somebody bring me an evidence bag?" Webb yelled.

Mohawk walked away and returned holding the bag.

"What you got there?" Mohawk asked Webb.

"Don't know yet," Webb replied, dropping the object inside of the bag. He slid the latex glove off with a pop, holding the bag up. "Looks like we have another lead."

On the ride over to a house on the West Side of town, J.C. Webb's mind was all over the case. The business card that he'd found at the scene was free of prints, but the address on the front belonged to a group home for the mentally disabled. He'd phoned ahead to alert the owner of his urgent needs.

J.C. walked up to the front door of a regular-looking, ranch-style home on Beechdaly, just south of the Jeffries Freeway. He tried to keep his personal problems away from the office, but sometimes the worries wouldn't stay put. His son's behavior was becoming increasingly erratic. The boy had fallen short in a few classes in his junior year and was now making them up in summer school. It was the only way for him to stay eligible to play in the upcoming senior season. Something was up with the kid, but he couldn't do anything right now. There was a cold-blooded killer on the loose.

A short woman wearing a close haircut answered the door.

"Evening, detective," she greeted. The lady moved aside to let Webb enter.

The detective removed his hat. "How do you do, Ms. Tucker?"

"No need to be formal, detective. My name is Pat."

The detective walked into the house, taking in the surroundings. Pat led Webb into the living room. The inside was pretty plain, nothing really splendid to look upon. There was a sofa sitting across from two armchairs. She instructed the detective to have a seat in one

"Pat, I'm gonna get right down to it."

"By all means, detective."

Webb went into his pocket and pulled out a clear, see-through evidence bag. He handed it to Pat.

"Is this your business card?"

Pat looked it over. "Yes."

"Do you know anybody named Henry Fish?"

Pat seemed to study the question. "No, detective, can't say that I do."

"Do you have anybody here with the last name Steel?" The detective went into his pocket and pulled a small photo of Michael Steel. "Do you know this boy?"

She shook her head no to both questions.

"Any new clients within the last year?"

"No. But may I ask why?"

Webb stared at the bag that was handed back. "Your card was found at a crime scene. We have reasons to believe that it was dropped by the suspect."

"I wish I could be of more help to you, detective; but the card could've gotten there by anybody."

Webb let out a sigh that sounded like he was deeply wounded. "Listen, we have a maniac running loose in the street, dismembering people. I need you to think really hard about your residents and staff."

Pat studied the question. "You know, we did have a young man in here about a year ago—real violent. Shammus Curry—yeah, that was the young man's name."

"Do you have an address on him?"

"No, detective. The only thing I have is a box with some of his personal belongings. I can get it for you, if you wish."

J.C. Webb nodded his head and Pat disappeared. She returned moments later with a small cardboard box, covered by a lid.

"Detective, he's seriously unstable; didn't do anything but fight with my staff and the other residents while he was here." She handed over the box.

Detective J.C. Webb thanked Pat and was about to walk out.

"Detective, he shouldn't be too hard to find."

"Why is that?"

"He's horribly disfigured."

The Homecoming Of A Gangsta

All the good people at the Battle Creek Prison Facility had given Ruffneck on his release day was a Greyhound bus ticket back to Detroit, and advice to keep his ass out of trouble. Ruffneck had made it through his two years without further incident. Nothing was going to stop his plan of murdering everybody who'd touched his family. And for two whole years, he'd managed to keep his nose clean, just waiting for a day to take payment out of the ass of those involved.

Ruffneck had caught the bus to the crib and was walking down his block. Fly had asked Ruffneck if he needed to be scooped from the station, but Ruffneck had told his homeboy to fall back. As far as he knew, contracts still rested on their heads and he wasn't going to give hitters the opportunity to come up on a two-for-one. The rest of the crew was also in hiding, awaiting word from their leader to surface.

One of the first things he would do, once he got settled, was to go into the wall of Granny's Sinclair's basement and grab the loot from the Cadillac lottery heist. He intended to spend five grand on a nice, clean ride that he could bounce through the streets in, low key. Ruffneck was walking past Brenda Johnston's crib, when she popped her head out of the door and invited him into her home.

Mrs. Johnston went on to explain that Granny Sinclair had entrusted her as beneficiary on her life insurance policy. The old woman had left Brenda with detailed instructions for her final arrangement. Hootie had been a different story. They'd scoured the neighborhood looking for Granny Sinclair's son, William—Hootie's dad—but couldn't find the crackhead anywhere. Hootie didn't have a life insurance policy, so it was up to donations from the folks in the neighborhood in helping with the burial. Both bodies had been interred at the same cemetery: Lincoln Park Memorial. Brenda handed him a long envelope. Before he left, she hugged and kissed him. She let him know that she was just down the street, if he ever needed anything. Ruffneck thanked her and was out.

Once he walked into Granny Sinclair's, Ruffneck couldn't describe the overpowering feeling of standing inside the living room. He moved over toward her recliner. Nostalgia caused him to push the arm so that it would rock back and forth. He sat in the recliner, gazing at the television. He could remember many a night where the old woman would sit in front of the television rocking, eating prunes and watching *Sanford and Son*. Ruffneck stood, but not before getting up too fast to catch a whiff of the scent from her body lotions. He couldn't believe it. After two years, the smell was still trapped inside the chair's fabric, almost like it had been preserved so that he could have scented memories when he'd finally gotten back.

The pain was too much to bear. Ruffneck choked down a big lump of emotion and walked through the rest of the crib. Nothing was missing. The crackhead community had stayed away. Although it'd been two years ago, the Nizzo beating had been a solid example of Ruffneck's hatred for crackheads and common thieves. Nobody had had the balls to fuck with the house in his absence. There were wood splinters lying around on the floor of the front door. Brenda Johnston had replaced it, but hadn't done a great job of vacuuming up the debris.

Yep, Ruffneck thought as he looked down at the wood chips. *Niggas were going to die behind this.* He planned on killing his way to the top. Everybody who'd brought drama to the old lady's front door would be a done deal. He checked on a few other things before walking to the basement. The air inside his room smelled musty. Ruffneck paid it little mind as he laid the envelope on the bed and went to the wall nearest his clothing closet. The paneling slid away easily. Two black metal doors were behind. He could remember Granny Sinclair telling him that they were chutes leading up to the fireplace. Rubber-banded stacks of cash were inside. Ruffneck walked over to the bed carrying the loot and flopped down. He was completely exhausted. The bus ride had zonked his strength.

He had a feeling that what existed inside the envelope would call for him to cowboy-the-fuck-up. He sat there staring at it like the thing was some sort of time portal. Before he'd walked away from Brenda, she'd warned him that the envelope's contents weren't going to be an easy thing to swallow. He bit down hard as he inserted one of the old woman's nail files beneath the flap and dragged the blade across the length. The moment of truth rested inside the envelope and Ruffneck could feel his heart pick up pace like it was performing a drum roll.

Aside from the night that both his parents had been murdered, he had no memory of faces and voices. That was all about to change. Finally, he would gaze upon his father's face for the first time since that night. The way Granny Sinclair had been tight-lipped about his old man, the dude had to have been some bad-ass gangsta who'd built a drug empire the size that Ruffneck could only dream of. His hands shook with anticipation as his flesh dampened from anxiety. He felt that same tension in the air—the same tension that would be present in the studio audience, right before Maury Povich opened up the envelope to reveal shocking DNA secrets.

He turned the envelope upside down; years of family secrets rushed onto the comforter. But the first thing that stood out was a small, white envelope. It was marked: *Me First*. Ruffneck breathed deeply and opened. He took out the letter:

Well, gangsta, if you are reading this letter, it means that I done gone home. Now, it's only right that I set you straight about yo' family. You see, yo' daddy and I were pretty good friends. I used to run a whorehouse. Yo' daddy and I met while he was in Detroit on a business trip. He used to mess with one of my best gals; a lady named Claudia Bewick. The night that them bastards had killed yo' folks, you were brought to my front door by a man named Johnny Best. Yo' old man, at one time, was the biggest, baddest drug lord in Pennsylvania. Down in Detroit, yo' dad used to do bidness with a man named Douglass Fairbanks. Something happened betwixt those two that spilled bad blood. Anyway, yo' daddy had a baby with Claudia, a baby boy—yep, gangsta, you have a brother. Claudia didn't wanna come twixt yo' momma and yo' daddy, so she disappeared with the baby. Listen, I ain't much for a long story, so I labeled some pictures so you can tell who's who. Gettin' misty-eyed, gotta go now, but if'n I don't lay eyes on yo' ugly tail again, I love you—always will.

—Granny

Ruffneck sat emotionless on his bed. He didn't know what the fuck to do or say. An envelope bigger than the first he'd opened lay next to his right leg. He picked it up and ripped it opened.

There were a few black-and-white photos. One of them held the image of a healthier, youthful-looking Granny Sinclair. The old lady was jazzy and wearing black-rimmed glasses, hugged up with a man that looked exactly like

Ruffneck. Walker Story, Sr. was the name scribbled into Granny's label underneath. For the first time, Ruffneck gazed upon his father's face. The old man couldn't have been any more than twenty-one, wearing an afro and rocking picture-perfect pointy chops. But there was something else vaguely familiar about his father's face.

Ruffneck held the picture a little closer as a chill raced up his spine. His mouth went dry and his eyes blinked rapidly, almost as if he'd seen a ghost. The shit had to be some type of coincidence. He didn't believe in ghosts—spirits maybe, but not fucking ghosts. He made several attempts to explain away the unexplainable. For his father's face and Hole-in-the-Head's—the demon inside of his dreams—were exactly identical. This was on some old Stephen King shit. He couldn't deal with it right now. So Ruffneck placed the photo back into the envelope and dismissed everything as coincidental.

The other photo he removed was of his father with his arms around a very beautiful lady who sat in a wicker chair. She had soft, brown skin; almond-shaped eyes; long, flowing hair; and the prettiest smile God could've ever created. Granny Sinclair's chicken scratch revealed his mother. Ruffneck's heart skipped as he softly traced over Shirley Story's face. He struggled to remember her, but there was nothing. His anger kindled, igniting the combustible fumes of retribution.

Niggas were going to pay. On his life, bodies would drop.

Everything was all gone. There were nothing but ghosts everywhere he turned. The streets had gobbled up his people without the least bit of compassion. But now, it was time for him to make his fucking presence felt. Before he'd gone to jail, Ruffneck wanted to be the biggest drug czar to have ever ruled inside the game. Now, he wanted blood. He craved the deaths of those responsible for the immense pain that was now rocking his world, dealing out so much heartache and suffering. Ruffneck looked at his mother and didn't understand how a young, beautiful woman could've gone out so violently.

He was about to give his emotions a break and make a few phone calls, when he saw another picture with a rubber band wrapped around it, laying face down. He flipped it over, and attached to the front was a folded yellowish-aging newspaper article. Ruffneck removed the rubber band, unfolded it, and the headlines grabbed him immediately: *HEAD HUNTER FOUND DEAD IN HIS MANSION.*

For the next five minutes, Ruffneck was captured by the story about the rise and untimely demise of a kingpin. How his father rose to be one of the most feared rulers inside the Pennsylvania underworld. His old man had gotten on by literally decapitating the competition. Walker Story, Sr. had cut off the heads of anybody who opposed his regime, leaving behind a bloody trail of headless bodies to erect—what the article reported as— the mightiest drug cartel in the country. At a bloody and turbulent time, when drug boys were pulling off some of the sickest shit in the country to establish an identity, Walker Story, Sr. had been the sickest.

His old man had been a legendary beast who feasted on brand-name niggas to earn his stripes. Ruffneck didn't know if he was nauseated, or proud that he'd come from the nuts of a madman. All the questions he'd had about his temper were now answered—and answered to his satisfaction. This also opened up the question about Hole-in-the-Head and why the nigga kept offering Ruffneck the blade in the dreams. Ruffneck still wasn't gonna believe that shit about ghosts. The entire thing was merely a coincidence. He simply looked at it as his old dude was trying to pass on the torch, or machete. Ruffneck would receive it, and in the name of unholy terror, he would rain down upon all who'd caused so much devastation in his life. Ruffneck agreed with his dad's tactics. Cutting off a nigga's head was sick, but would send a powerful message to the bastards who'd touched his granny and cousin. He couldn't have thought up a better method of revenge. This shit was personal and bullets just wouldn't bring the type of satisfaction he was looking for.

He went into his pocket and retrieved the antidepressant tablets. He wouldn't be needing them anymore. They'd been used to suppress his anxiety and channel his anger. Ruffneck tossed them, because the fucking dog was now off the leash. The pills had somewhat kept the dark feeling from penetrating his heart. But all hands were on deck now, and he welcomed any help that his old friend, darkness, could bring to the party.

He was about to put everything back inside, when he noticed one more black-and-white. Granny had scribbled the names underneath three of the four people on the picture. The guy without a name underneath—he'd come back to him. Ruffneck recognized one of the other men in the photo as being the present-day mayor of the city. He hadn't paid too much attention to the name in Granny Sinclair's letter, but here the mayor was, big as day, standing shoulder to shoulder with his father— muthafuckin' Douglass Fairbanks—The Man of Detroit. All three of the men were wearing old school-thick, cable gold chains. Douglass and the stranger wore Jheri Curls, and his father bust a fresh high-top fade.

The lady in the picture was gorgeous. It was the whore that his old man had had an affair with, producing a baby—his brother. Her name was Claudia Bewick. She stood between his father and Douglass Fairbanks, hold- ing a baby in her arms. Ruffneck didn't exactly know why she had the baby's head covered with a black veil. Nor was he going to waste any time on trying to figure the shit out. The cat without a name underneath his body took center stage. It was something about the dude for whom—for some reason—the old woman had forgotten to supply a name. The nigga was dark-skinned and pos- sessed the cold eyes of a killer. Ruffneck couldn't put it together. So he left it alone.

Brenda Johnston had been right. The shit was too much for him to mentally process in one sitting. No wonder the old woman had gone to great lengths to keep the brutal secrets from him for such a long time. The truth would've been too gangsta for a young mind to handle. Now that he was twenty, and somewhat familiar with how the world operated, Ruffneck took all the information and processed it. He made it his power. He would harness that power until he was ready to turn it loose on those who'd killed his family.

Ruffneck couldn't get over the fact that Granny Sinclair had been a madam. His father had been a butcher who'd cheated on his beautiful wife with a whore and produced a bastard son—who could still be running around in the city. Douglass Fairbanks, the mayor of the city, back in the day, had been heavy in the dope game and rumored to still have a hand inside the underbelly. But, it was the nigga with no name who'd raised his suspicions way over the severe level of Homeland Security's Advisory System. It wasn't sitting too well in Ruffneck's stomach about his father's old allegiances.

Before he shoved the picture back into the envelope, Ruffneck glanced over the faces once more. Something wasn't right about that picture. The nigga with no name needed one, and Ruffneck knew who to ask. He put all his sordid history back into the envelopes, but kept out the last picture. Even though he needed answers, Ruffneck needed weapons like yesterday, and a bulletproof. Somebody had some explaining to do.

The next day, Ruffneck woke at the split of dawn. He had shit to do. Before he'd gone to bed last night, he'd made a couple phone calls. The first one he'd made was to the brother of his old cellmate. Because Ruffneck had looked out for the nigga's brother in the joint, the cat was gonna make a deal with Ruffneck on an old school Cutlass Supreme. The ride was in superb condition. Black paint—nothing fancy—V-8, dual exhaust, high-performance rear-end—all the toys. The cat named Chino shaved a grand off the whip and Ruffneck punched out, but not before leaving behind four gee's. After taking care of his business at the DMV, Ruffneck bounced over to see Hootie's nigga, one-legged Jeff. Jeff offered his condolences and got down to business. With the purchase of two Glocks, Jeff threw in a bulletproof for free.

Walmart was the next stop. Ruffneck left with a fresh new look. From now on, he would wear the color of mourning, death. He figured himself to be no longer a part of life, but the bearer of pain and devastation. He would be the Grim Reaper to his enemy. The perky clothes of big brand-name designers were for those who were getting their cheese—those who were happy with life. His new look would describe his negative feelings for the compassion of his fellow man, and spell out doom to the enemy. He would wear Dickies.

Black Dickies.

The brand had long since been the trademark of the

blue-collar world, the standard of excellence in working gear across the country. He was about to descend, waist-deep, into the murkiness of a work world that would solely be driven by the numbers of the dead and dying. Ruffneck would punch the clock belonging to the dark arts. Somehow he knew that his new reign of terror would eclipse the Sneaker Stalker Slasher.

It was almost one in the afternoon when Ruffneck stopped by Lincoln Memorial Cemetery with flowers. The heat was blistering, but he managed to sit at both graves and talk for hours. Granny Sinclair and Hootie were buried right next to each other. He laughed and cried, but promised that somebody would pay; even if it meant his life, somebody was gonna have to fucking pay.

Through tears, Ruffneck finally made it back to the crib and parked. He lugged all of his purchases inside and fixed himself a couple of turkey burgers. In the joint, he'd become conscious of the foods that he put into his body. He found out that lean meats were good conductors of focus and concentration. Ruffneck finished up the snack and went down for a nap. In eight hours, he would go and see a man about some answers.

Like Father, Like Son

Ruffneck found himself whipping the Cutlass through the dark streets at eleven at night. Strip clubs weren't normally his thing, but a regular spot for the nigga he was meeting. The rendezvous went against his better judgment, but it was the only time that the man was willing to meet him. Ruffneck was quite certain that the sticker was still on his head, and those looking to collect, wouldn't pass up an opportunity at plugging his ass inside a public place.

The Show Stoppah topless bar was a magnet for every goon with the sweepstakes-claim at being hood rich. He would be vulnerable and in the open. He wasn't crazy about the move, but it was the only card he had to play.

Ruffneck was halfway there when his homeboy fell across his mind. He hadn't seen Menace in a quick minute. One of the last times he'd seen the nigga was—he couldn't get through the thought without almost throwing up in his mouth. He still didn't know how to approach it. His first impulse had been to run up on them both and get to dumping. Blind loyalty had saved Menace's ass. They'd been through too many wars together for Ruffneck to snuff out his dude without first hearing him out. Maybe there was a logical explanation for his walk on the homo-side of the world. Menace had spent a year in the youth home once. He could've been turned out there, or maybe he had a gay uncle who'd raped him. Ruffneck wasn't sure.

But he had better set his mind clear of the shit, because The Show Stoppah was two blocks up on the left-hand side. The place was jumping as usual. Ruffneck drove right past the packed parking lot. If he had to bone-out with heat on his ass, the one thing he didn't want was to wait for his ride. He took a park on a side street, not too far from one of the club's emergency exits.

As he walked, Ruffneck blended in with the crowd. To those that didn't know him, his black Dickies outfit told the simple story of a guy working a regular 9-to-5, a Mr. Nobody who wished to rub elbows with the elite of the game, and dreamt of the amenities that came with being hood-rich and powerful.

Traffic seemed to pick up the closer Ruffneck drew to the front entrance, until the crowd bottlenecked into a line waiting to be wanded down before they could enter. Ruffneck wasn't sweating the small stuff. He stood calmly, strapped, horizontal shoulder holsters holding two Glocks set on top of the bulletproof. Fly had come through. The nigga had phoned ahead and alerted one of his people that Ruffneck was coming; an enormous bouncer named Bodick escorted him past security and through the door.

Ruffneck hadn't had any pussy in a while, but even the herd of scattered ass on full display inside the bar wasn't going to be much of a deterrent to a man hell-bent on serving up true destruction.

The music pumped and the colorful spotlights swept across the stage as some girl named Honey Treat was just getting warmed up. She was brown-skinned with thick thighs and a huge ass. Cats swarmed her, standing around the stage, dancing along with the music and throwing dollars into the air. The bills rained down on her sexy back, as she was on all fours working it. Her perfect bare breasts swayed with every movement as she arched her back and sensuously grinded her wet kitten into the floor.

Ruffneck kept it moving, past the stage and through the crowd of fake-ass niggas pretending to look hard. The big bouncer led him to the VIP section, where a couple dudes were getting broke off with lap dances.

The section over by the corner was where he spotted his man. This couldn't have worked out any better. Big Truck Turner was posted up near an emergency exit. Ruffneck could get in the wind, if shit got sticky. The fancy hanging lamp over Turner's table provided enough light to reveal a red tablecloth and drinks. The big man stood from the table and extended his hand.

"Ruffneck, good to have you back, young brother."

Ruffneck glanced at Truck's posse who were sitting around jaw-jacking with each other. Turner got the hint and cleared his throat. The gesture sent all of them packing.

"What it do, Truck?" Ruffneck asked, moving away from the opening inside of the flimsy wrought-iron gate that surrounded the section. He allowed everybody an exit before continuing. "It's good to see some things stay the same."

Truck laughed and lit up a cigar. He gestured for Ruffneck to take a seat.

"Yeah, I'm so busy helping young brothers, sometimes I have to get out and get my chill on." He removed the cigar and looked at it. "Now, what can I do for you, young buck?"

Ruffneck took a seat, scanning the club before he took out the black-and-white photo. He handed it to Truck and pointed at the picture of the cat bearing no name.

"You ever see this nigga before?"

Truck looked at the photo. He recognized Douglass Fairbanks right off. The other nigga, he definitely knew. He removed the cigar and sighed.

"Ruffneck, young brother, the cats that you're getting ready to tangle with are responsible for supplying ninety percent of this city's drug trade. They call themselves The Family. People like Billy the Kid and other lower-level kingpins are front men. They keep The Family shrouded in mystery. Nobody knows about the brass, like Bruno, Jax Avery, and Mayor Fairbanks." He pointed at Fairbanks. "They run the fucking city's underworld, dude. It's fucked up about your grandma and cousin, man, but you don't want this fight, son. These fools know everything—every movement. They probably got us staked out right now."

Ruffneck lost himself in the crowd. Another topless dancer was on stage making her ass clap. Men stood around throwing dollars and drinking.

Ruffneck pressed. "No disrespect, Truck, but I lost my fucking family behind these clowns; somebody has to pay, fam."

Truck understood the young man's resolve. He had to admit that if it had been his people, he would be doing the same thing right now.

"All right," Truck said, blowing smoke from his nose. "The nigga you seek is Jax Avery. Most don't know this, but he's the man over Mayor Douglass Fairbanks. Avery is a full load, man—bodyguards around the clock. You gonna wanna get at Bruno and a few others that sit on the board before you can draw out Avery. Plus, word on the street is that Bruno was the one who killed your people, but Avery probably gave the order. Billy the Kid was making mad loot for them."

Ruffneck looked back out at the crowd to watch his back.

"I didn't give a shit about that kid Lil Shorty. I heard he forced your cousin into his little stickup scheme." Truck sat back and took a drag on the cigar. "I don't envy you, son. You're about to take on an organization that will kill everybody in your family if they have to. Your best bet is to start with Bruno. But first, you gonna want to deal with his Frankenstein-looking bodyguard. He does the torturing. That's the nigga you really want to see. Guy goes by the name Ghoul, and once you see 'im, you'll fucking understand. Kill him and Bruno will come to see you himself."

"What type of man is Bruno?" Ruffneck wanted to know.

"He's a commercial real estate investor—office on the other side of town. And just like me, his business is a front for his drug operations."

"You kidding, right?

"Don't let his field of endeavor fool you. Bruno serves as the street watchdog—like some type of area manager for The Family. He's over all the big guns on the street. Billy the Kid was one of them. Bruno might sell real estate, but he's deadly. Watch out, son."

Ruffneck stood from the table and was about to thank Truck.

"No need for thanks, young buck. You ain't heard shit from me, remember dat."

The man named Ghoul was walking through the alley on his way to his house. It was just minutes after midnight and he was dead tired from torturing some fool in an abandoned warehouse ten minutes away. Ghoul had to admit to himself that his boss, Bruno, was in love with the sound of his own voice. Ghoul was growing tired of the arrogant, college-educated prick's two-hour-long dissertations before they sent sumbitches to the life hereafter. All Ghoul wanted to do was torture and maim, much like his idol, the Sneaker Stalker Slasher, was doing. He admired the killer for having the heart to go out into the community and violently share his bloody passion for death and destruction. The Ghoul was jealous of his hero. He was ghoulish in his own right and could get just as creative as the Slasher, but his debt to Bruno had left him a slave.

Bruno had come along on a hot summer night and saved the big man from certain death. The Ghoul was grateful. He'd been in a small town of Kentucky, just outside of Ohio, in the country-side with a noose around his neck. A white supremacist group stood around a gigantic burning cross to witness the big nigger's hanging. His only crime had been being in the wrong white town at the wrong time. But luckily, Bruno and his entire entourage had been cruising through the backwoods—lost—in a procession of expensive cars on their way down to Myrtle Beach, when they'd come across the lynching. Bruno had recognized what was going on and pulled over. Everybody jumped out with automatic weapons and sprayed the sheets bloody. The Ghoul had been in Bruno's debt ever since.

The Ghoul was three houses from his back door when he encountered a figure, no bigger than average height, with a hood pulled over his head, standing alone in the middle of the alley. The Ghoul stopped in his tracks, two houses separating him from the stranger wearing the hoodie. The height difference was unbelievable. Ghoul stood at a freakish seven feet even, with the stranger coming up somewhere around his nuts.

The nerve of the fool, Ghoul thought. And for a moment, he thought that he was staring into the darkened face of his idol. One look down dispelled the wish, because the Slasher was only killing niggas wearing the Airman sneaks. Ghoul had on plain work boots.

"Nigga, better get to kickin' rocks, if he don't wanna get dead," Ghoul warned.

The figure stood his ground, placing his right hand inside his hoodie. "I want names and addresses from you, fam—"

"Nigga pretty disrespectful—I'm the Ghoul."

The stranger still didn't budge.

"What nigga want from Ghoul?"

The hood stood with his right hand inside his pouch. "Your peeps, Bruno. I need his body on my trigger— asap, cuz."

"Then if it's a body nigga wants, how about yours?" The Ghoul broke running, closing the distance on the hoodie. He hadn't been allowed five feet when the stranger pulled a pistol and blew out Ghoul's right knee. The monster screamed as he fell to one knee.

Ghoul was clutching, trying to hold in muscles, ligaments and bones, breathing heavy. "What this about?"

Ghoul didn't see a second hoodie stepping up from behind with a baseball bat hung over his shoulders. This one was much larger than the first, but still a dwarf in comparison.

The Ghoul could hear somebody yell: "Batter up."

Clunk!!

Then everything went black for the Ghoul.

The voices floating above the Ghoul were dull at first, but gradually sharpened. The big man's head throbbed like he'd fallen and hit the ground. His knee was on fire. He slowly opened his eyes to find that he was face-to-face with the ground. His head was still reeling and he couldn't find his bearings. He could remember the creep wearing the hood, but that's when it all faded for him. It was as far as he could remember. Maybe he'd fallen, hit his head and blacked out in the chase. There was light around, but just enough to fragment the shadows.

The big man steadied his head to get up. That's when he found out he couldn't move. Maybe he was paralyzed. Alarmed, the Ghoul kicked and bucked wildly.

No dice!

"Save it, fam," a voice said from above. "You ain't gotta chance."

Ghoul struggled and strained in an effort to get to his feet.

"Tell me what I want to know and I promise that your death is swift and painless."

The statement pushed the Ghoul into another wild

burst of energy. He didn't know if his head had cleared from his latest shot of adrenaline, but for the first time, he was able to see his predicament. He was on his knees and tied in a way where he couldn't move a muscle, with his neck stretched across a cinder block.

"Nigga get loose—"

"It ain't gonna be no getting loose for you, partna"— the Ghoul didn't recognize this voice. "Now tell the man what he wants to know."

"That big fool does look like Frankenstein"—this was a different voice.

"You can save yourself from a painful death, if you just give me addresses," the first voice spoke again.

"I ain't given nigga shit. You gonna have to kill me before I give nigga shit," Ghoul informed.

"Okay. Have it your way, playboy." Ruffneck pulled off the hood and stooped down toward the Ghoul's face. "You know the one that you and your boss Bruno killed with the acid?"

Ghoul burst with sick laughter. "Yeah. Nigga remember that one. Boss was real pleased with the way we sent that one outta here." He paused for a moment. "Save yo' breath. Nigga ain't got no bitch in him." He let his disrespect for Hootie ring out inside of his tormented laughter.

Ruffneck got to his feet, using the blade of a Kukri Machete with the PVC handle to steady himself. Car headlights flooded the perimeter in which he stood. His

Cutlass and a stolen GMC cargo van were facing each other, leaving plenty of space to accommodate the scene, providing the only light inside of the old, abandoned warehouse. Ruffneck looked outside of the lit area in which he stood. Nothing but blackness stared back at him. Fly, Poison, and Menace stood on the borderline of light and darkness, casting the look of shadowy figures.

The three had no idea that Ruffneck would drag out the Ghoul's murder in such fashion. Back in the alley, Fly and Menace had pleaded with him to put a bullet between the big man's eyes. But Ruffneck had insisted on doing shit his way.

They'd followed his orders and ended up in the warehouse with the Ghoul's neck stretched across a cinder block. They hadn't understood what Ruffneck had in store until he'd gone in a gym bag and pulled out a big-ass machete.

Fly casually strolled over to Ruffneck; a look of concern on his face. He went to say something but thought against it once he saw evil and pain plastered across Ruffneck's grill. Poison stood off in the background with an automatic rifle slung around her shoulder by the strap. Menace stood, trying to see how this thing was going to play out.

Ruffneck stood poised over the Ghoul with the handle in both hands. He measured the cut and raised the blade toward the rafters.

"You put your fucking hands on the wrong people,

muthafucka," Ruffneck said as he continued to measure.

"Nigga, fuck your cousin. Nigga, better watch his back because the Ghoul works for people that's gonna make the rest of you niggas disappear."

"Do me a favor, my dude," Ruffneck asked. "When you get to hell, make sure you save me a seat."

Haunting laughter burst from the Ghoul, almost eerily reminiscent of the trapped alien before he'd detonated a bomb that had wiped out half the jungle at the end of the movie *Predator*.

Ruffneck dropped every ounce of hate into the chop, cutting short the ghoulish laughter with the one thing on his mind: like father, like son.

Burning Down The House

"Neck," Fly said as he drove Ruffneck's Cutlass down East 8 Mile Road, headed toward Bruno's office. "Man, I think you need to think this thing through—ol' boy's office; is you serious?"

"Yup. I UPS'd the head of his goon to his office in a box with my calling card inside. They fucking ignored me, G—like I wasn't shit. The nigga didn't even report the shit to the police, homeboy." Ruffneck sat on the side of his dog, running one last ammo check on his weapons.

Fly nervously exhaled. "I wouldn't go that far in saying that they overlooked you. Those ain't the kind of niggas to forget shit like that. It's only been a week since you"—Fly swallowed uneasily—"took the Ghoul's head, man. Trust me, you are on their niggas-to-pay-back list—probably at the top. I think you should rethink this, man."

"It's been thought about—like when they took my grandma…and left my cousin laying in an alley with a mutafuckin' funnel sticking out his crack."

Fly was still tripping off Ruffneck. In all of his years on the streets, he had never witnessed anything so sick and twisted. His boy had come home from prison a monster. And not in the usual street sense of the word; but a tormented, fiendish beast not able to form compassion or mercy. Ever since that night, Fly had burning questions that he wanted answers to, but after witnessing Ruffneck's machete game he'd come to the conclusion that his neck was also made of flesh and bone.

"'Neck, I think this is a bad idea, my nigga," Fly repeated.

"Nigga, I can't wait on them any longer. If that head-and-the box didn't bring his ass to see us, then we'll go to him."

Even though it was late evening and most of rush-hour traffic had died, the sun was still a ball of fire inside the sky, which caused Fly to shade his eyes several times from the glare.

Ruffneck turned on his boy with the same monstrous intensity in his eyes that was present the night he beheaded the Ghoul.

"Homeboy, get your nerve up, fam. It's collar-snatching time, nephew. Now if this is the type of shit that shakes you up, maybe your ass might need to go holla at McDonald's for an application.

"If I remember correctly, before I did that stretch, your ass was talking about some big money game. Nigga, if you ain't a gangsta, then take your ass to church. These fools took away from me more than you can ever lose. I'm riding for mine and I'm not gonna stop until I see all their caskets drop—it's just that simple."

Fly didn't say shit else for the rest of the trip. He reasoned that Ruffneck was too far gone in the head to be reached. This wasn't Cadillac's fat ass that they were going up against. These were the type of niggas that killed for sport. Three people had been murdered behind Billy the Kid's death. Ruffneck was insane for taunting them after taking out the bodyguard, and Fly knew it.

Fly reluctantly pulled into the parking lot of a huge, fancy building with massive marble-style columns. The name "Max" had been professionally chiseled in stone on the marquee over the entrance. He illegally parallel-parked the ride against a curb that separated the front door, and pulled an AK-47 from the backseat. Ruffneck had instructed him to stay behind the wheel and keep the engine running.

With no fear whatsoever, Ruffneck hopped out of the car and headed inside. The directory in the lobby put Bruno's office on the second floor in suite 202. He had scouted out the place earlier and found that the building had both an elevator and public stairway. Ruffneck wasn't really worried about too much jumping off. Bruno was a successful businessman and needed to appear a certain way to society. Ruffneck knew a man like that wasn't gonna jeopardize his image by having a shootout with a convicted felon in public. He casually strolled up the stairs, down the hallway of the second floor, through the double doors of suite 202, and right up to the front desk like he was a potential client.

The elderly white woman tried to explain to Ruffneck that Bruno was in a business meeting with some associates. But the way he disregarded her as he walked right on by, made the woman look as useless as a ten-year-old elementary school hall-monitor with a whistle trying to stop an adult offender.

"Sir, you can't go back there," the lady shouted at Ruffneck's back as he started opening office doors. "I'm going to call the police." She'd picked up the phone when Bruno appeared.

"Geraldine," Bruno said to the elderly lady. "Please, I'll take care of the gentleman." He amusingly looked at Ruffneck and gestured with his hand. "This way, please."

He led Ruffneck down another hallway and past the curious looks from employees who'd come out of their offices to witness the disturbance.

Bruno's corner office was huge and spacious. It looked to be exquisitely decorated by period pieces. Ruffneck could give a fuck about his taste in high-priced shit. He was here for one reason and one reason only: Bruno's ass.

Bruno walked around his mahogany desk, unbuttoned the top button on his expensive suit jacket, and gestured in the direction of one of the two armchairs parked in front, before taking his own seat.

"Mr. Story, please."

"Stop bullshittin', Bruno," Ruffneck spat, "I'll stand. You know why I'm here."

Bruno never removed the I'm-a-sadistic-madman-in-an-expensive-suit-running-a-million-dollar-company look from his face. He reached inside a cigar humidor made from mahogany and pure ivory. "Would you like a Cuban, Mr. Story? I can assure you that they are Havana's very best."

"The only thing that I'm interested in smoking"—Ruffneck removed a business card from a cardholder on Bruno's desk—"is you, Mr. Strong."

Bruno lit up his Cuban and began to puff. "My, I would have to say that I admire your courage. We have all our available staff exhausting efforts in locating you and here you show up in my office." He puffed the cigar. "I have to say that you are going to make for a worthy adversary, Mr. Story. Mr. Story, you are a remarkable piece of work."

"And, Mr. Strong, you are a slimy piece of shit. I can kill you right now if I wanted," Ruffneck said, running his hands over the pistol areas of his Dickies shirt.

Bruno blew smoke up in Ruffneck's direction not even fazed. "But you won't. See, Mr. Story, I can assure you that men like you and I are turned on by the hunt. That's the way nature intended. We are no more than wild savages with common sense. You didn't come here today intending to do bodily harm, just like I wouldn't harm you, right now. But our paths will cross. And I can assure you, Mr. Story, it won't be enjoyable for you. But I must say: be a good sport and indulge me on your visit."

"I just wanted to see how you lived, because I damn sure

as fuck gonna see how die. You touched an old woman who was defenseless, and tortured my cousin who'd been forced to go along in the death of Billy the Kid."

"Such language, Mr. Story. I detect your close relations to your cousin, Mr. Clarence Sinclair. Both of you have the same passion for expletives—I'm sorry to use such a big word, Mr. Story, but expletives means—"

"That you're a high-class"—Ruffneck looked around at the accomplishments hanging in expensive frames from the wall—"educated piece of shit."

Bruno sat back inside his chair and toyed with his cigar. "Yes indeed, Mr. Story. You are going be a fine adversary. Well, if your business here is concluded, then let me show you the door."

"You don't have to show me shit. I found my way in and I'll find it out." Never taking his eyes off his enemy, Ruffneck backed up to the door.

"Sending my associate's head in a box, Mr. Story—it showed me a lot about the type of opponent that you're going to be. Ghoul was quite a physical specimen. I don't know how you did it, but you definitely have the attention of me and the rest of my associates. And for the record, Mr. Story: the old woman was dead long before we had the pleasure."

Ruffneck held up Bruno's business card. "You will die a violent death, Mr. Strong. And that I can *assure* you." He walked out.

Ruffneck was determined to make shit impossible for Bruno. He'd had a secret meeting with Truck and the two had managed to strike an agreement. Truck didn't have all the answers to Ruffneck's problem, but over the last two weeks, he'd been able to supply Ruffneck with three major spots where The Family kept large amounts of cash. The houses acted as storage facilities. It was the last stop before dirty money would be washed clean by many of The Family's lucrative front businesses. In return for the information, Truck would be paid 30 percent of whatever money Ruffneck and crew were able to jack when they laid down the robbery game. Ruffneck was no fool; he knew that he had no shot at successfully robbing all three joints. Just robbing one would be like trying to knock-over Fort Knox. But he had a plan.

He took time to set up the lick, watching the comings and goings of one the houses which sat in the heart of Rosedale Park Historic District. It was a settlement in which building started in 1916 by the Rosedale Park Land Development Company and finished in 1955, offering a variety of styles in homes to choose from. The company favored the area because of its close proximity to Grand River, which gave residents a direct link to downtown Detroit.

Ruffneck's reason for picking this spot was that it offered up unlimited possibilities in escape routes, since the area was bounded by the major streets of Fenkell, Outer Drive, Grand River, and the Southfield Freeway. He needed to send The Family into complete chaos, flushing out the bigger guns from their hiding spots. His plan was diabolically clever, but dangerous. He would rob one of the houses and completely burn down the other two. This would surely lead to Bruno pulling his hair out and causing him to do something outside of his usually calm demeanor. Ruffneck had already left Bruno with the task of selecting a new bodyguard to replace the one he'd beheaded; and just last week, blew out the brains of one of Bruno's street lieutenants in front of the White Castle on Warren. Killing Domino had earned Ruffneck a new respect on the streets and added three more cats to his steadily growing family.

It took three weeks to get the plan perfected. Poison and Menace would join him in moving on the crib in Rosedale Park. Fly and the new cats on the team would each take up position outside the other money spots, and on Ruffneck's command, would fire bomb the houses.

Wearing masks, Ruffneck, Menace, and Poison crept through the shadows of an unusually cold September night. The house was quiet and dark, but niggas were inside posted. Ruffneck knew this from his many nights of surveillance. It didn't matter where they were positioned inside the crib, because when Menace tossed a couple Molotov cocktails in through the back windows of the English Tudor, the punks inside could be heard screaming and scrambling to get out. Ruffneck and Poison held down the front with AK-47s and let them loose as soon as they heard the first fool throw open the door. The sound that the assault rifles made was very distinctive, almost like hearing the working blade of a helicopter. The last three ran out of the burning house, each carrying large duffel bags. They fell to the AKs' awesome power. Menace and Poison grabbed the two bags off the dead bodies and all three jetted to the corner.

A stolen Chrysler minivan pulled up on the corner so fast that it slammed on the brakes and screeched to a halt. The cargo door slid open. All three hopped in the ride and got in the wind. Inside, Ruffneck whipped out his cell and made the call to Fly and a nigga named Sambo, to blow the other houses.

Number 1

Him had one more bad man to play Nasty Feet with on Him's list: Number 1. Then Him could track down the brother from nasty, evil funky man that had been produced from bouncing up and down on Him's mommy. Him was looking forward to playing Nasty Feet with Him's brother. Him had to play Nasty Feet with brother, because Him's brother was evil, just like brother's nasty, funky daddy. Regardless of what the news people were saying about Him being an animal, Him was on a mission from God to clean up all the evil men in the city.

Him was almost there, too. Number 1 was on the dribble ball court—just like Him's hero used to do while wearing the Airman sneakers. 1 was wearing the Airman sneakers, too. Him didn't know why 1 was playing dribble ball so late at night, but it was a perfect time for Him's little game of Nasty Feet. The dribble ball court had some light, but mostly shadows. Him could easily swoop up on the feller and show number 1 the ugly. Him's heart pumped as the "Thriller" song played for Him. Vincent

Price's laughter excited Him. 1 was the last one—with the exception of Him's brother—that needed foot disinfecting. 1 was taking the ball to the rim when Him walked up from behind and surprised the feller. Him was wearing a hoodie, but when 1 turned around, Him had taken off the hood, showing the ugly. 1 dropped the ball and screamed like all the rest that Him had played Nasty Feet with.

"Fuck, the Slasher!" Number 1 yelled. But unlike all the rest, the feller went into the pockets of his sweatpants, and pulled out a can of pepper spray and sprayed Him. Him was real mad now. The spray burned Him's eyes and Him went into the pocket for special tools. Him had them out and was slashing blindly.

"Take that, you muthafucka!" 1 cursed as he continued to spray Him.

But Him managed to grab hold to 1 with his left hand, and with his right. Him shoved the special tool into the feller's chest. 1 was kicking for a bit, but Him pulled upwards on the tool and 1 stopped kicking. Him let 1 drop to the dribble ball court. There no time to waste. Him had to hurry up and play Nasty Feet because a few lights inside of houses next to the court came on. Him was about to cut 1's right foot off when a car rolled up real fast, stopped, and swung open the door. A huge feller got out and yelled for Him to freeze. Him put back on the hood and ran.

Detective Webb jumped out of the car with his weapon drawn.

He screamed at the Slasher to halt, but the man wearing the hood ran in the opposite direction. Detective Webb ran up to the victim, stooped down, and checked for a pulse. The man named Jo-Jo was barely clinging to life. Webb wanted nothing more than to continue the pursuit, but preserving life was first priority. The detective took out his cell and made the 9-1-1 call for help. He ran back to the car and retrieved a towel. Webb was back and on his knees, holding pressure to the wound.

Almost two months ago, the detective had found a crumpled-up piece of paper containing a list of names in the box that he'd gotten from a group home for the mentally disabled. Webb had been too late with all the rest of the victims on the list, but Jo-Jo looked like he was going to be the only surviving victim of the Sneaker Stalker Slasher. Detective J.C. Webb was familiar with the last name on the list…he had to find the boy as soon as possible.

The Power Of The Cheese

"Ruffneck," Menace said, "how in the hell did you know the niggas would come running out of the flaming house with the money?"

Fly chimed in: "Yeah, tell us that shit, 'Neck. How did you know?"

Ruffneck looked around the table at his crew—old family and new. They were posted at Menace's spot. After what had happened the last time Ruffneck was there, he'd been reluctant to make it the rendezvous point after the jobs were done. He sat at the head of the dining room table. Poison, Fly, and Menace sat to the side on his right. Some fat fool called Sambo, a tall skinny nigga named Fat Shady, and some young cat that everybody knew as Tryme, sat on the other. They had made the largest score of a lifetime and were celebrating their asses off by drinking and getting loud with Kush.

"Bruno is the last nigga his employees want to come up short for," Ruffneck explained. "Man, please, the way Bruno is torturing fools now. They knew the last thing that homeboy wanted was for them to come out of a burning house without his fucking loot."

Poison sat at the table with her Chanel shades on. Her lipstick was flawless. She even looked stunning with the ski mask pulled up around her head like a sweatband.

"Ruffneck," Poison said, "we need to get rid of the heat."

Ruffneck shook his head. "Poison, you know where to go, right?"

She nodded her head yes.

Menace still had no idea that Ruffneck knew about his little secret. And it wasn't helping Ruffneck any to cope, with Menace's lover right in the middle of their conversation. The punk even had the nerve to comment a couple of times. Ruffneck kept waiting on Menace to straighten the nigga out about it being a closed section. But Menace didn't do shit. He let the punk run his mouth, and Ruffneck was growing tired of it.

Tryme reminded Ruffneck of Lil Shorty, the only difference being temperaments. Tryme wasn't a hothead and the boy listened. Sambo was muscle, and Fat Shady had the street connects on just about anything. Being the rookies on the squad, the three held their peace.

"'Neck," Fly said. "I wish I could've seen the look on Bruno's face when you ran up in the nigga's office—"

"Fuck that. I wanna see the muthafucka's face when he finds out that he's a half-million dollars light in the pocket," Menace boasted, picking up his Patrón bottle and sipping from the neck.

"Yeah, the guy ought to be pissed off," Menace's bitch spoke up again.

Ruffneck looked at Menace, and then up at the man

named Dex, hovering over the back of Menace's chair. His eyebrows were neater than Poison's and the fool smelled like the fragrance of a woman's lotion. The nigga was light-skinned with curly hair and keen facial features.

"Y'all know they gonna come at us hard behind what we did," Ruffneck explained. "I'm gonna give you niggas your split. Whatever you choose to do with it is on you, but stay the fuck down until we cut off the fucking head of The Family."

Fly cringed and rubbed his neck at Ruffneck's mentioning of severed heads.

"We gonna be up against some pretty big guns, man. The dude Bruno is the only one we know about so far," Fat Shady spoke up. "And what's up with the rumor that the mayor is tied to The Family? If it's true, man, we gonna have to war with the entire Detroit Police Department."

"He's absolutely right. Anybody wanna get the fuck on"—Ruffneck pointed to the front door—"now is your chance, but I have to pull your coattail. You clip and clap a fool for a half-million and he will find you. It's up to you, if you want that nigga to find you alone...or with your family." For some reason, Ruffneck saw no reason to let them in on the whole Jax Avery thing. The last thing he wanted right now was a bunch of questions surrounding the origins of his knowledge. Once again, he saw it as his past and nobody needed to know.

Ruffneck waited for his words to settle in. Nobody went anywhere.

A couple of hours later, they were sitting around in

Menace's basement counting and dividing the loot. Ruffneck had taken Truck's fee off the top and stuck it back
inside one of the duffel bags.

Menace and Dex stood up and dropped a bomb.

"We're taking our split and opening up a unisex boutique for sporting apparel," Dex announced. Ruffneck
stared at Menace like he had better correct and put a chain
on his bitch.

"Are you fucking for real?" Ruffneck went off on Menace.
He was completely disregarding the punk. "Man, we just
blew up two houses and robbed another one—all belonging to niggas who are probably loading up on us now. And
you want to open up a fucking business. Fuck is wrong
with you, Menace?"

Menace said nothing. It pissed off Ruffneck even more.

"Y'all, get the fuck out!" Ruffneck screamed at everybody else. They started moving with the exception of Dex.
He waited until the basement was clear of the crew.
Ruffneck's voice was low and menacing. "Menace, tell
your bitch to leave before I send his head in the other
direction."

Menace looked at Dex and told him to get to stepping.
Dex headed to the stairs but kept on looking back at
Ruffneck like he wanted to try him.

"Get the fuck upstairs!" Menace ordered. He waited
a few moments before he asked Ruffneck, "How long
have you known?"

"It don't matter, fam. What does, is that you are my

fucking family and I don't want to lose you. Man, you know Bruno's soldiers are gonna be all over the place looking for us. It's not wise to open up a business. Hold off until we can get our thing situated. And if you want to get a store, then cool. But not in the middle of a war."

"All right," Menace said, "I'll wait. And Ruffneck, about that—"

Ruffneck stopped him. "What you do is your own fucking business. As long as you are down for this team, I ain't got nothing to say. But don't bring the nigga back in the meetings, cool?"

"Cool." Menace dapped Ruffneck. The two finished counting up the cheese. For some strange reason, Ruffneck knew that Menace was going to ignore him and do the opposite. After the last time they'd divided up loot, his team started blowing money left and right. He wasn't a fucking babysitter. They were all grown. If Fly wanted to give his shit to his baby-momma, it was good by Ruffneck. There was a future beyond this war for Ruffneck and it involved the baby, Princess, and himself.

Return Of The Rebel

Ruffneck had to do something before he lost his edge. Princess and the baby had been like a Hallmark commercial of love, repeating over and over inside his mind until his attention was on the thoughts of a life settled by marriage and family. Suddenly, the war didn't seem so important to him anymore, especially if he'd gotten himself killed. Princess would be all by herself to raise a Story. She'd be in for nothing but a shitload of heartache and pain. All the competitive fire to be bigger than life came with Story men. Ruffneck knew better than most that it took a special breed to raise that kind of stock. He was familiar because he'd given Granny Sinclair all the hell that she could handle in trying to raise him. Quiet as it was kept: he secretly blamed himself for her poor health.

He was distracted all right, because he was walking around in the neighborhood like a bounty wasn't riding his head. Under normal circumstances, the two Glocks and Kevlar vest would've been enough, but an entire army was now out to take his head. He hadn't been in this area in a long time, so he was here to reminisce. Bruno and his boys could've been watching him right now, but Ruffneck didn't give a fuck. He was tired of running and hiding. The last couple of months had seen him hotel-hopping like crazy to shake any tails he might've picked up during the day. He'd scattered his crew and silenced them. Bruno's team was looking for blood, and anybody from his squad would do. Word in the street was out about the half-million dollars they'd muscled from Bruno. Ruffneck knew Jax Avery and the mayor wouldn't be too far off. Almost their entire organization had been kept on the hush because of the mayor's affiliation. Nobody knew about The Family. Detroit had had one scandal in the mayor's office and didn't need another black eye.

It had been almost two months since his team had laid the smackdown on The Family's candy asses. The cold winds of November were creeping into town and slowly pushing out the last week of October. Truthfully, Ruffneck was growing tired of all the death that surrounded his life. And he was responsible for most of it. Within three months, he'd been involved in half a dozen homicides and three firebombed houses. But he had to continue. Cutting the head off the fucking snake would be the only way that he could breathe easily; raise a family. He had to continue. There was no other way. Ruffneck was in too deep to turn back.

He found himself walking by the Body Bag. Ever since the police had discovered Lil Shorty's body, true basketball players had stayed away. So it tripped him out when he saw young Anthony "Ups" Webb taking a couple of practice jumpers on one of the rusted out rims.

"What the fuck are you doing out of school, Ups?" Ruffneck asked, walking onto the court. He looked at his watch. "It's twelve-thirty. What Northwestern have, a half-day or something?"

Ups stopped shooting the ball.

"Don't you got a game tomorrow?" Ruffneck wanted to know.

Ups shot the rock through the netless rim. "Yep. But I'm done with school, Ruffneck." The stress on the kid's face was hard and noticeable. Ruffneck had stared at that face many times inside of his bathroom mirror.

"Man, your pops gonna kick your ass. You better take your little ass to school. Dude, you got a full ride going to North Carolina—home of Air Michael Jeffrey Jordan. You crazy, youngsta. Better get your ass back in school."

Ups went to fetch the basketball, leaving Ruffneck standing alone center court. They were out there, Ruffneck could feel them. And the longer he stayed around this young boy, he was putting his life in harm's way. He took the ball from the young nigga.

"Man, what's your problem?"

Ups looked like he was about to cry.

Ruffneck pressed him. "Speak up."

Ups dropped his head. "Well, it's this fool named Rebel that comes to our games with his crew. He's been hounding me for a few years now to shave points on the games."

Suddenly, Ruffneck perked up. He remembered Rebel's

wannabe badass from school. The stark raving hatred that he had for the yellow nigga was forcing his involvement—plus, he wasn't going to stand by and watch a good kid be bullied.

"And that's why you're out here skipping school?"

"Got that right. He doesn't even go to the school, but he and his crew are there all the time, picking on everybody."

"Why didn't you tell your father?"

Ups gave him a 'man, please' look.

"Yeah—good point." Ruffneck gave the ball back. "What time is the game tomorrow?"

"One in the afternoon."

"I'll be up there. Now, get your ass off this court. It's too dangerous to be here."

Ruffneck was getting ready to step away when an unmarked squad car rolled onto the court. Detective J.C. Webb stepped out of the vehicle, holding on to his fedora.

He looked at his son. "Get in the car, Anthony."

Ups gave dap to Ruffneck and obeyed his old man.

Webb turned his attention on Ruffneck. "I need a minute of your time, Mr. Story."

Ruffneck walked over and leaned against the cruiser. "What's on your mind, detective?"

It only took five minutes to plug Ruffneck in. The detective hadn't told him the entire story, but enough.

"So, you see, Mr. Story, we need to place you in protective custody."

"So I'm next on the killer's list—me, Walker Story, Jr., is next to be without feet. I ain't wearing any Airman sneakers. Why me?"

The detective didn't have too much time for explanation. "All I can say is that your name came up in my investigation. Now, do you want protective custody?"

Ruffneck looked at Webb like the man had shitty toilet paper hanging off his face. "No, thanks. I'm a big boy."

"Okay, Mr. Story, I thought that I'd warn you."

Ruffneck rose from the fender.

J.C. Webb opened the car door. "Oh, yeah. Stay away from my son."

"You got it, detective."

On his walk back to Granny Sinclair's, Ruffneck's mind raced for answers. Like: Why the fuck did the killer want to ice him? It was even more eerie than knowing that he was the son of a man who had risen to power by chopping off heads. Lately, everywhere Ruffneck seemed to step landed him deeper in the shit.

He picked up the cell and called Menace. Somebody had to hear this. Ruffneck was talking on the phone when he walked up to the house. His attention was diverted by Mrs. Johnston's son, Jamaal. The kid was running up the sidewalk toward him at top speed, yelling something. Ruffneck couldn't make out words at first, but they came clearer the closer Jamaal drew.

"Get away from the house!" the boy screamed.

Ruffneck's fight-or-flight response kicked in. He dropped

his phone and ran away from the house, when it exploded into wood and concrete fragments, rocking the area. The force from the blast picked Ruffneck's body up and carried him into the street. Bells were going off inside of his head as he rolled over to look at what was left of the old woman's crib. Everything left standing was on fire. Ruffneck could see debris scattered across yards five houses away.

He wasn't given a chance to recover when a black cargo van rolled up the street; the driver turning the steering wheel hard to the right and quickly careening to a halt. Four huge sonofabitches spilled from the cargo door wielding weapons. Ruffneck was head up getting to his feet and pushing Jamaal to the ground, just before the shooting started. He dragged the kid behind a car by the right ankle.

"Stay the fuck down!" Ruffneck instructed Jamaal over the gunfire.

Ruffneck reached into his Dickies and came out with both Glocks. They had him pinned down good. The automatics would've shredded his ass if he tried to peek out. Ruffneck listened as the bullets riddled the other side of the car that he and Jamaal were hiding behind. He had his back against the car and was about to make an attempt at returning gunfire, when he heard a second vehicle roll up, followed by more automatic gunfire. The sound of this gunfire seemed to override the dudes in the van.

Ruffneck heard somebody yell out in pain that they'd been hit. He heard the sounds of a cargo door slamming shut, and then tire rubber cooking. The gunfire stopped as quickly as it had started. Ruffneck carefully peeked over the hood of the car and saw Menace, Poison, and Tryme standing tall, carrying Russian assault rifles. Ruffneck had been talking to Menace before the blast. Menace explained that when he'd heard the explosion, they came rolling up. Luckily for Ruffneck, his crew had been in the hood when everything had gone down.

He called 9-1-1 for help and passed his Glocks to Menace. They didn't want to be standing around when the police pulled up. The three jumped back inside the car and skirted out.

Jamaal explained to Ruffneck that the men in the van had shown up fifteen minutes before he had walked up. The young boy reported that he couldn't see what the man was carrying when he got out of the van, but he'd taken it around to the back of the house. Minutes later, the man had run back to the front, jumped back into the van, and they took off. Jamaal said that he was scared so he stayed away. But he didn't go too far. Jamaal had chilled at a neighbor's three houses down, hoping that Ruffneck would come so he could warn him. Ruffneck knew that there wasn't a monetary value that could be placed on a life, but he broke Jamaal off with a little sumptin'-sumptin' and sent him home.

It seemed that the man behind the scenes was playing

for keeps, but it was time for Ruffneck to turn the fire up and go for broke. Jax Avery had had one opportunity to get the job done and failed to cash in.

Now, it was Ruffneck's turn to start with Bruno's body and see how far up the shit would go.

The following day, Ups was inside the locker room and going through pre-game mental prep. He stretched and warmed up using different exercises. Today was going to be different for him. He'd lived in terror since his sophomore year. He wasn't afraid today. In the past, he'd been forced to play below his high-profile ability so that Rebel could cover the point spread. The pressure had forced him to miss games and cut classes. He'd suffered behind all of it—poor class performance, failing grades, and a stint in summer school. Ups could've told his old man, but the detective's hard-nosed actions would've only made things worse. And Rebel wasn't the type of nigga that scared easily.

But not today.

Rebel and his goons weren't going to be enough to keep him from dropping high numbers against Southwestern High. Ups was simply going to break a scoring record this game, and he would do it to one of the toughest teams in the PSL. The Southwestern Prospectors were at the top of their game and a force to be reckoned with.

They'd come in Ups' house and punked him in the past because of the natural fear he had for Rebel.

But not today.

After warming up, Ups was sitting on a bench inside the locker room, chilling, leaning against a locker. He had the Monster Beats headphones on his iPod and was listening to DMX with his eyes closed, when they were snatched from his head. Ups was about to go the fuck off when he opened his eyes to see Rebel standing over him with three goons at his back.

Rebel snatched Ups off the bench by the collar and slammed him violently against one of the lockers.

"Where you been at?" Rebel asked through clenched teeth. His face was inches away from Ups'. "Look, it don't fucking matter. I got a lot riding on this game today and you better not disappoint me." Rebel slammed his right fist into Ups' stomach, folding the young boy. "You hear me, bitch?" He relaxed his grip and allowed Ups' limp body to drop to floor, gasping for air.

Ups lay curled on the floor, clutching his stomach and writhing in pain.

Rebel kneeled down close enough to his ear. "You get any bright ideas of going all Michael Jordan out on the court, and I lose my loot, homeboy, after I get through with you, your old man ain't gonna recognize you." Rebel stood erect.

"Man, lemme shank that fool," said a light-skinned cat wearing a long, hairy goatee.

"Yeah, nigga," said a much bigger guy with huge ears, "if a nigga like me lose my cheese"—he removed a pistol from his waistband and racked back the slide—"you will be having a closed casket, playboy."

Rebel went to kick Ups in the back and the boy closed his eyes, bracing for impact. He didn't see Rebel receive a blow to the side of the head that knocked his ass into the lockers. But when Ups opened his eyes, Ruffneck was beating the dog shit out of Rebel. Rebel's niggas were held in check by a bad-ass, light-skinned beauty with what looked to be a Glock. A silencer had been screwed on, making the barrel look longer. She'd relieved the pistol from Rebel's boy and was watching Rebel get his ass twisted.

Ups watched with a smile on his face as Rebel tried to get back to his feet, only to receive a Timberland boot to the mouth. Blood spurted everywhere. Ruffneck didn't stop. He was going hard trying to stomp Rebel into the locker-room floor. To Ups, it looked like the girl was daring Rebel's team to do something. She didn't look like she was bullshitin' either.

After Ruffneck stepped away from Rebel's bloodied, crumpled up body, he walked over to the girl, trying to slow his breathing.

"Poison," Ruffneck said to her, "show these niggas what's gonna happen to them if they ever go near the little homie again."

Without hesitation, Poison lowered the gun and shot

the cat wearing the goatee. He screamed, falling to the floor, clutching his right knee.

Ruffneck helped Ups from the floor. "Go and do your thing, homie. Don't worry about these niggas. I got you. Now go and hang a record on Southwestern."

Ruffneck and Poison escorted Ups upstairs. They stayed for the first half of the game until Ruffneck saw Princess leave her courtside seat, headed for the door. He told Poison to go and finish setting up the plans they had for Bruno. Ruffneck stepped from the bleachers and caught up with Princess. Even though she was dressed down, showing school spirit by rocking Northwestern's colors in the form of a red-and-gray sweatshirt and sweats, Princess was still gorgeous. Her face lit up when she saw Ruffneck.

"What are you doing here?" she asked Ruffneck with a huge smile.

"Just up here to show y'all star player some support." Ruffneck looked into her eyes and smiled brightly. "Where's the baby?"

"Yes, Anthony is going to do quite well in North Carolina," Princess added. "Oh, Little Walker is with my mother. I'm getting ready to go and pick him up now."

The two stood at the driver's door of Princess' car.

"I thought you didn't want to see me?"

Ruffneck smiled. "I've been thinking about you. When I get through with my business, I'll come to you."

A tear of joy slid down Princess's face, and at the

moment, she didn't care who was watching. She kissed Ruffneck on the lips.

"I love you," Princess professed.

"I love you, too," Ruffneck replied. If he'd listened to his first mind, he wouldn't have approached her and walked her to the parking lot. Ruffneck was so into her beautiful face that he didn't see the white man watching them through binoculars from inside of a white Ford cargo van, parked on a side street.

Making A Statement

The man named Bruno had received a call from an investment group two weeks ago. The Bailey Bank Investment Group had expressed firm interest in a newly erected shopping complex on Woodward Avenue, just inside of the Highland Park City limits. Bruno hadn't quite understood why the gentlemen wanted to meet and look at the place after hours. But he'd been in the business for twenty years, and the one thing he'd learned was not to concern himself with the "hows" and "whys." At the end of the day, he was there to get the property sold; and if it meant getting home a little late, then it was his cross to bear. The building was 56,000 square feet, two floors, four anchor stores with length roughly four times greater than its depth. This deal would bring his company $30.2 million.

Bruno stood at the dock of the middle store with the overhead doors raised, waiting, patiently smoking a Cuban cigar. He usually showed property with a few of his bodyguards, but tonight, he'd given them the night off. Bruno had a hot piece of Puerto Rican pussy lined up and didn't want to keep her waiting. He looked out as a thirty-foot U-Haul came into view, whipped around, and started backing up into the dock bay where he was standing. The backup beeping sound that emitted from the truck was nerve-wracking. Bruno figured the driver to have the wrong destination. It wasn't any sweat. He would alert him the moment he stepped from the cab.

As he puffed on the cigar, Bruno waited for the truck to completely back up; its bumper gently touching the dock's rubber stops. He was so focused on waiting for the driver to exit the truck, that he hadn't paid any attention to the back door of the U-Haul. It was slightly cracked. And when he did notice, it was too late. Bruno's cigar fell from his mouth when the door sprang upward. Out jumped Ruffneck, Sambo, and Fly with automatics.

"Hi," Fly said with a grin, and holding an AR15. "We're the Bailey Bank Investment Group."

Sambo clutched an AK-47. He looked around as if taking in the sights. "I think we're going to take this place. I love what you've done with the drapes."

"My, my, my, Mr. Story," Bruno said to Ruffneck. He wasn't even shaken at the sight of the machete in Ruffneck's hand. "I told you that you would make a worthy adversary. Pretending to be an investment group—bravo, you've beaten me at my own game, Mr. Story."

Ruffneck stepped out of the way of the rifles. "And I assured you that I would kill you for touching my family, Mr. Strong."

When he gave the signal, Fly and Sambo opened up on Bruno with a barrage. After the smoke cleared and Bruno lay in a pool of his own blood, Ruffneck didn't have much time. With two swings, he severed Bruno's head from his body and left it lying next to his corpse.

Stupid Doesn't Have A Name

After the explosion, Ruffneck had gotten a room at the Holiday Inn in Farmington. He had been trying to get in contact with Menace since he'd removed Bruno's head three days ago. The shit had made national headlines: *Prominent Local Businessman Found Slain*. The Community was outraged by the amount of senseless blood being shed on its streets and demanded immediate arrests be made. The streets were hot and five-o was locking up every nigga who looked suspect. Without answers or leads, it was convenient for the police to lay the blame for Bruno's headless body at the Slasher's doorstep. The street knew who was behind Bruno's death, but was staying tight-lipped about it. Nobody wanted any part of Ruffneck's machete game. Detroit Police were the only ones who were completely clueless to the war going on between Ruffneck and The Family.

Ruffneck was trying to stay low. But it was hard because he hadn't talked to Menace since Granny Sinclair's house had been blown up. The police had questioned Ruffneck for hours behind the explosion. He wasn't a snitch. The beef was between him and The Family. Ruffneck didn't need the fucking police to fight his battles. Bruno's headless body was testament. Ruffneck had been so busy that he'd forgotten about the warning that Detective Webb had served him. The Sneaker Stalker Slasher was out there, looking for him. He still didn't know why the maniac wanted to kill him, but Ruffneck couldn't worry too much about it. The Family was breathing down his neck and he needed to stay focused. The Slasher wasn't the only madman with the hankering for cutting shit off. Ruffneck had two headless bodies to his credit, and more would roll before it was all said and done.

Menace had him worried. The Family was going after everybody that was affiliated with Ruffneck and his crew. He tried Menace on the cell.

No answer.

He called Fly and got no answer from him, either. Niggas were out spending that loot, Ruffneck thought. After the half-million split, each walked away with seventy thousand. Ruffneck knew that Fly's baby-momma would fuck him crazy until the cheese was all over her body in expensive handbags, designer clothes, and jewels.

Ruffneck tried Menace again. This time the nigga picked up the phone. Ruffneck talked to his boy for a minute and hung up, pissed. Fifteen minutes later, he was pulling up in front of a store in a new strip mall. DEX'S BOUTIQUE was on the huge standing sign in the parking lot of the store. Ruffneck jumped out of the Cutlass and walked inside, watching his back.

Dex looked at Ruffneck and never stopped hanging clothes. The store was getting ready for its grand opening. Menace took Ruffneck back inside the office to talk.

"Are you fucking out of your mind?!" Ruffneck yelled at Menace. "We just fucked up one of their main niggas, and you and your little girlfriend open up a business behind the shit."

Menace sat down at the chair behind his desk. He hung his head. "Man, I've been trying to tell you this for a while."

Ruffneck stood there, almost foaming at the mouth. "What, nigga, spit it out."

"I'm done with the crew, dog. I can't take it anymore. I'm tired of looking over my shoulder, homeboy. The blood, the bodies, they haunt me every time I close my eyes, fam."

"Listen, man, I know this shit is not easy, but you're kidding yourself if you think you can just walk away. The Family knows who you are, man. And once they find out you own this store, they will come for you."

Menace sighed. "Well, fam, that's a chance I gotta take. I'm done—through. Take care of yourself, brah."

Ruffneck backed up to the door. "Naw, you take care of yourself, 'cause when them fools come around here, Dex can't save you."

Menace said shit. He dismissed Ruffneck by lowering his head.

"Okay, if that's the way you want it." Ruffneck turned and walked out.

Dex was finishing the clothing job when Ruffneck walked by and damn-near slapped his ass out of his shoes. Ruffneck wasn't worried with Dex, who was on the floor and holding his mouth, at his back; he was more concerned about who could possibly be waiting for him outside.

Who Shot Cha

Bruno's funeral had received a swarm of media coverage. The service was held at Infinite Baptist, a supermega church that covered almost half a city block on Linwood Avenue. News teams were posted everywhere, but respectful with live coverage.

Thousands were in attendance, showing up to pay their last respects to a man that the community was calling a hero. Bruno Strong had been a philanthropist in the city, giving back to the areas that were the hardest hit by Detroit's struggling economy. Within ten years, he'd managed to build three charter schools, open up scores of recreational centers, and blindly contributed books, computers, and other supplies to the Detroit Public School system—all his acts of charity brilliantly displayed inside of the beautiful obituary being passed out at every entrance of the sanctuary by ushers adorned in white and black uniforms.

The line for viewing the body snaked up the long center aisleway and out the sanctuary door, stopping almost at the sidewalk in front of the church. Exquisite, colorful floral arrangements surrounded his expensive, solid-gold casket that had been roped off to discourage any touching of the body. It only took thirty minutes for the entire sanctuary to fill up until there was standing room only. Those who weren't mindful enough to leave home at a decent time to receive a program before the supply was all gone, would find themselves trying to follow the order of service without an obituary.

The crowd lining the beautiful maple pews and standing around was composed of a hodge-podge of life. Prominent businessmen, wearing Rolexes and dressed in expensive suits, turned out in record numbers to mourn the loss of a close friend and colleague, while those belonging to the underworld stayed in the shadows, careful not to bring attention to themselves by the many uniformed and plain-clothes officers in attendance.

Tears fell as the painful sound of grief rose to the dome of the church that exhibited colorful hand paintings, depicting Christ's crucifixion and resurrection. Some younger women walked around dressed in tight-ass, form fitting garments. They were on full display with the intent of arousing the libido of high-profile business-types, and balling-ass street hoods.

With the church forcing no real dress code, the cat wearing the hood over his head in line, six people away from viewing the body, went virtually unrecognized. He kept his head down and face out of sight as he slowly stepped with the pace of the line. He felt excitement from deep within his gut; a sense of power as he drew near. He hadn't known Bruno, but silently waited for this day so that he could see the one who'd been responsible for a great deal of pain in the lives of others, stretched out at the altar and on display for all to spit on. He wasn't fooled. Bruno being a philanthropist—they could kiss his ass with that one. Bruno had littered the cemeteries with the bodies of fathers, husbands, brothers, a grandmother—all who were never coming home again.

The cat wearing the hoodie could give a fuck. He moved up and heard a lady scream so loudly that he thought she would die from the high-pitched sound of her own voice. His stomach bubbled with anticipation.

It was his turn to look down on the body. He stepped up and almost burst into laughter. The hood bit down on his tongue to give respect, but he was amused. The last time the hood had seen the asshole, Bruno was trying to talk over his head by using college-boy words. Now, Bruno's ass was silent, stiff, face flat as a board and dressed in an expensive suit with hands crossed over his stomach.

The hood leaned in to get a closer look. "Remember who did this to you. Burn in hell, muthafucka," he whispered.

He turned from the casket, kept his head down, and walked up the steep aisleway. He didn't remove the hood from his head until after he jumped in the car with a light-skinned chick wearing Chanel shades and dark lip gloss.

"There's no turning back now," Ruffneck said to Poison as the two drove off in the Cutlass.

Karma Is Her Name

It was eleven o'clock on a Saturday night.

Truck had closed the pool hall to remodel. They had the place to themselves. He and Ruffneck sat at an empty bar. The two were finishing up the deal they'd struck three weeks ago, involving info on the whereabouts of The Family's money houses. Ruffneck handed Truck a bag containing 30 percent of the take. The old man took the money with a serious look on his face.

"Ruffneck, you're like a son to me. It's out on the wire. The Family has a contract out on you and your whole crew, three hundred thousand dollars on each of you."

Ruffneck looked at the old man suspiciously and rubbed his right hand across the gun part of his hoodie. "You ain't thinking about collecting, are you?"

Truck looked hurt. "Man, I don't get down like that. Just thought I'd tell you."

"Niggas have been trying to collect on my head since I've been out of jail."

"Young Buck, do you realize what you've done? You not only killed, but cut off the head of, one of their top men. I can be killed for sitting here talking to you."

Ruffneck sat up on the barstool. "Truck, you trying to tell me not to come back around?"

Truck measured his words carefully. "Ruffneck, son, The Family won't stop until you and your crew is dead. I don't want no parts of that." He held up his hands in submission. "I've gone as far as I'm prepared to go. I'll catch the rest on CNN."

Ruffneck rose from his seat.

Truck tensed up.

"No need for that, old man. I've known you too long." Ruffneck's cell went off. He picked up and listened. "Stay the fuck where you are; I'll be right there!" he yelled into the phone.

Minutes later, he was walking up to the crowd behind the yellow crime scene tape in front of Dex's Boutique. Ruffneck just kept saying to himself that Menace was all right. His boy was a street warrior who'd been proven invincible.

The lights from police vehicles enhanced the streetlights, brilliantly lighting up the entire parking lot. Ruffneck scouted around the huge crowd until he found familiar faces. Fly, Poison, Tryme, Sambo, and Fat Shady walked over to him.

Fly wore a grim look. "Don't look good, man," he said to Ruffneck. "Menace's car is around back."

"That shit doesn't mean anything. Do it, Ruffneck?" Fat Shady wanted to know.

Ruffneck silently stood. For the first time in his life, he

didn't have the words. He kept looking at the door of the boutique like Menace would walk out and let everybody in on the prank. But when the medical examiner's wagon pulled into the parking lot, his greatest fears were starting to take the shape of reality. They rolled in a couple of gurneys. Fifteen minutes later, the M.E. rolled out two bodies.

Ruffneck's feet had started toward the tape before he realized it. Menace didn't have any next of kin and Ruffneck had to find out if one of the bodies belonged to his boy. He ducked under the tape before the officers could see him and bolted toward the bodies. He went to the larger body bag and quickly zipped it down. It wasn't a pretty sight. Menace had been shot multiple times in the face. Ruffneck lost it. Deep sobs wailed up from the pit of his soul.

He blamed himself.

Uniformed officers rushed to restrain him, but a large man wearing a fedora, light jacket and slacks stepped up.

"Officers, back away. He's all right," Detective J.C. Webb ordered.

Webb walked toward Ruffneck and the officers slowly backed off.

"Mr. Story, this one of yours?"—he pointed at the black bag containing Menace's body.

Ruffneck looked as if to say something. He stared at the detective for a moment before walking away, underneath the yellow tape and through the thick crowd. His crew was hot on his heels, but he waved them off. Ruffneck needed some time to himself to think. Poison was pretty persistent. She walked along the sidewalk at his back until Ruffneck stopped her and explained his position.

"Are you sure?" she asked.

Reluctantly, Poison obeyed, stepping backward until she faded into the shadows provided by the huge trees.

The pain Ruffneck was feeling was too much to bear. He'd turned on a faucet of blood and there was no way of shutting it off. A part of him wished he'd stayed in jail. Menace would still be alive. As he walked, Ruffneck admitted that The Family's wallet was too deep and its army too huge for him to continue the fight. He couldn't possibly keep it up. The muscle wasn't there. Yeah, he'd killed Bruno, but now Menace was gone behind it. Truck had been right to distance himself. Ruffneck couldn't blame the old man. The Family wasn't going to stop sending killers after him, until everybody he knew had been dealt with.

Ruffneck walked the dark streets, completely unable to come up with a solution. He'd never run from any man, but this shit was way over his head. Thoughts of taking his family and fleeing town were center stage when he stumbled up on a playground. Not a lot of light surrounded it, but enough for Ruffneck to see past the shadows to the jungle gyms, sliding boards, and swings. He walked across the grass to have a seat at one of the many picnic tables.

Just as he sat down, Ruffneck's cell rang and Princess's name popped up on the caller ID. He tried to compose himself so that she wouldn't hear any stress in his voice. But the voice on the other end didn't sound anything like his baby-momma. It raised the hair on his neck.

"Little Walker Story, Jr.," the deep-voiced male caller spoke. "I've been waiting for this moment."

The voice was familiar. Ruffneck had heard it many times before, but mostly on television trying to explain away the city's horrible economic conditions. Ruffneck said nothing. He knew that his number was up. The Family had played its last card and the bitch just so happened to be Ruffneck's black queen.

"Damn, I knew you would show up one day, little Story. All I had to do was sit back and wait for the headless bodies to start popping up around town. And you didn't disappoint. You're so much like your old man."

"Tell me where?" Ruffneck asked.

"Oooh—just like your old man: direct and to the point—"

"Cut the bullshit, Mayor Fairbanks! Where?"

"Have your ass at the Michigan Central Station at seven to-morrow morning."

Ruffneck picked his head up just in time to see somebody walking in his direction wearing a hoodie, a big sonofabitch, too.

"Little Walker Story, Jr., don't fuck with me. Come alone—and no tricks. I would hate to feed pieces of your bastard baby to my pit bulls. You'll have to follow the dogs around with a pooper scooper for at least a week to scoop up enough shit to collect a body for a proper burial."

Ruffneck didn't respond to Mayor Fairbanks. He kept on looking at the fool in the hoodie walking toward him. The nigga never broke stride while reaching inside of the hoodie pocket for something.

"I'll be at the old train station tomorrow," he responded to Fairbanks.

Ruffneck dropped the phone and managed to retrieve his pistol. He hadn't had enough time to aim it when the hood bull-rushed him, knocking him from the picnic table; the gun flying off somewhere into the darkness. He smacked the ground so hard that his breathe left. As he desperately struggled for oxygen, Ruffneck thought he heard the figure say something about "showing the ugly." The figure stood, pulling off the hoodie, and Ruffneck could feel his body go cold at the sight of the attacker's mug. The Elephant Man crossed his mind. It wasn't the look of the grotesquely disfigured man with the elongated forehead that frightened Ruffneck, but the extremely sharp instruments he was waving around.

"You're the son of nasty, dirty man," the attacker said in a low, ghoulish voice. "Nasty Feet—we play Nasty Feet."

Ruffneck was tripping because this big muthafucka sounded like a kid. Ruffneck was lying on his back, and trying to figure out which direction the gun had traveled. He cursed himself for not strapping on the other Glock before he'd left the crib. It didn't take a detective to figure out his attacker to be the notorious Sneaker Stalker Slasher.

Ruffneck's only defense against the weapon-wielding maniac was his feet. Every time the attacker would lunge, Ruffneck kicked with everything he had. He had to get to that gun. Ruffneck had seen enough news coverage on this lunatic to know the outcome if he'd lost this battle. He could possibly wind up a mutilated corpse with his feet dangling from a high-tension wire.

Ruffneck kicked one more time when he noticed the pistol laying by the leg of a table a few feet away. The black Glock lay still, looking like a dark impression in the grass under semi-lighting. He risked opening himself up to be sliced to pieces if he turned his back on the Slasher.

But today, the Slasher had picked the wrong nigga to fuck with. Ruffneck's family depended on him being in one piece. They had no chance for survival if he didn't make the deadline. He wasn't about to let them down. So with that thought, he turned on his side to go for the gun.

It was just the opening the attacker needed. He dove on Ruffneck and tried to plunge the instruments deep into his neck. Ruffneck flipped over on his back and met the attacker's hand. The two struggled over the weapon in the killer's right hand. The strength of this man was nothing like Ruffneck had ever witnessed, and he seemed to be losing out to the might of the Slasher. The point of the blade was touching the flesh on Ruffneck's throat when gunfire crackled in the distance. The Slasher's body jerked forward. He stopped struggling and his eyes popped wide open with shock. Ruffneck gave it a second and threw the dead weight to the side. He rose from the ground, clutching at his throat and trying to catch his breath.

"I thought you would need my help," J.C. Webb said. He held his gun out in front. The detective carefully leaned in and checked the attacker for a pulse.

Nothing.

"I hate to say I told you so, son." Even though it was too late for the attacker, Webb called for back up and an EMT unit. He helped Ruffneck off the ground. "I told you that you were on his list. You okay?"

Ruffneck walked over to a table and copped a squat. "Can you tell me why the lunatic was after me?"

Webb went on to explain that he'd found Claudia Bewick's diary in the box among the Slasher's personal effects. The Slasher had been born Shammus Bewick. Claudia had changed the boy's name to Shammus Curry at birth to protect him from the wrath of her ex-fiancé, the current Mayor of Detroit, Douglass Fairbanks. The detective told of the secret affair between Ruffneck's old man and Claudia that produced Shammus, Ruffneck's big brother. After the baby was born, Claudia had dropped off the grid and was never seen again, but not before filling Shammus's head with so much hatred for Walker Story, Sr.

The sirens from police and paramedic units wailed in the distance.

"Detective, what triggered all the violence—I mean, why start cutting off niggas' feet?"

"Claudia Bewick had a younger son by a drug dealer named Billy Steel. Michael Steel was an academic freshman phenom at Northwestern High. He was walking home one day and some crew called the Kato Boys robbed and killed him for his Airman sneakers. Shamus was basically seeking revenge on all who'd filled his life with hurt and pain, including you, Mr. Story. He wanted to kill you for the sins of your father."

Ruffneck said nothing.

"Son, you know I have to take you in for a statement."

Ruffneck didn't have time for that shit. He would be meeting Douglass Fairbanks in a little over eight hours.

"I can't, detective. I really have some place to be," Ruffneck informed.

Webb looked at the urgency in Ruffneck's eye.

"Okay, we can do this another time."

Ruffneck rose from the bench as police and EMT's arrived on the scene. He hadn't gotten too far when the detective called out to him.

"Mr. Story, I can't say that I agree with the way you helped out my son, Ups. But thank you. And if you need me, don't hesitate to call."

The Final Battle

Within an hour, Ruffneck had assembled the troops in a dump of an apartment that Fat Shady called home. It took him thirty minutes to explain the last hour of his life to his crew. Fly had been the saltiest. He went off at first, going on about how Ruffneck had held secrets from his family. But he was really hurt that his homeboy had withheld Princess and the baby from the rest. Poison showed no emotion whatsoever behind her dark shades and powerful lip gloss. Ruffneck let Fly vent until he was back in the state of mind to hear his plan.

They all sat around in the front room of the apartment. Weapons were laid out in abundance. A war was brewing, slowly simmering with the serving time being just five short hours away. Ruffneck laid out the game plan. He warned that it would be a dangerous mission, which could possibly end in some of them not making it out alive. Ruffneck was a true leader in every since of the word. He thanked his troops for their loyalty. He also let them know that he would be okay if anybody wanted to back out.

This was his personal war, and he was going to go out swinging with or without. Nobody backed out. Instead, they pledged to get Ruffneck's family back, or die the fuck trying. And for the next three hours, Ruffneck laid out detailed instruction for the final battle.

The building of the Michigan Central Train Station was completed in 1913 and sat around Corktown District near the Ambassador Bridge. It'd been a thriving epicenter for the city of Detroit and the whole Midwest. Roosevelt Park served as the grand entryway to the station. At the time of construction, it hailed as the tallest rail station in the world. In its day, the magnificent landmark was an impressive 500,000 square feet with walls of marble, Doric columns, and skylights—all to give the mighty structure that trademark beauty, craved by people around the country who visited to snap photos.

But it was all ancient history. The station had closed its doors in 1988 and since then, had become a decaying eyesore; an imposing and often menacing structure rising out of Detroit's soil to act as makeshift lodging for crime and homelessness. Since the emergence of Hollywood movie studios in Detroit, the building had become famous, showing up in scores of movies and a staple for rap videos. Despite its many colorful usages, niggas would die here today.

Right at seven, Ruffneck entered the building through a set of large doors, which immediately opened up into an enormous concourse. Early morning rays filtered through the many holes inside the rotting roof, dousing the place with natural light. Pigeons fluttered from rusted beams. Five graffiti-littered, colossal brick-faced columns sat off to the right, almost like they were staring down and watching as he walked over the debris-covered floor. Ruffneck didn't have to travel too far to find Fairbanks. The mayor stepped from behind one of the massive columns.

The boldness of this man, Ruffneck thought. This fool was the fucking mayor of Detroit and here he was trying to get all gangsta with it. Ruffneck had to give up mad props, though. Douglass wasn't just a mayor trying to play gangsta. Instead, it was the other way around: he was a gangsta who'd used the dark art to catapult himself to the apex of the political world. Douglass was dressed in bad boy black—light leather jacket, jeans, and boots.

"Little Walker Story, Jr.," the mayor said, his voice carrying through the surrounding corridors. "Seeing you is refreshing. Brings back all the good times. Your father and I—"

"Get to it, muthafucka," Ruffneck spit. "Where is my family?"

Douglass motioned toward the columns to his left. Two huge goons brought Princess out by the shoulders. She was blindfolded and holding the baby.

Douglass motioned for them to remove the blindfold.

"Walker, I'm sorry. They grabbed me and the baby when I—" One of the men shook her silent.

"Homeboy?" Ruffneck said to the man who violently shook Princess. "Nigga, I'm gonna fucking kill you." Ruffneck went to make steps toward her.

"Stop," Douglass ordered, "I wouldn't try it." He walked over and stood in front of his armed soldiers. Douglass slightly turned his head to look at the firepower. "Your father and I were real tight once. I would've done anything for him."

Ruffneck stood with his hands down by his side, looking at Princess and his baby. He couldn't do a damn thing without risking getting them all killed. He counted five men so far, plus Fairbanks. But the station was huge and he knew more lurked. He hadn't seen Jax Avery, but he was near, Ruffneck could feel him.

"I can't believe how stupid I was back then. Never trust your best friend with your woman," Douglass carried on. "The muthafucka was smiling in my fucking face and fucking my woman behind my back—had a baby with her, too."

Ruffneck let the nigga run his mouth. Douglass's prattle, along with Granny Sinclair's letter—together with Claudia Bewick's diary—were painting a brutal picture of betrayal and jealousy.

"I told them all to kill every last one in your family. But they slipped up and you got away. But"—Douglass removed a Sig from his waistband—"that's a mistake I'm about to erase today."

He shot Ruffneck in the right shoulder.

Princess screamed and startled the baby. The child let out a piercing cry.

Ruffneck fell to his knees holding on to his shoulder and wincing in pain. Douglass became bolder. He slowly walked over to Ruffneck and pointed the pistol at his head.

"You killed my father over some pussy?" Ruffneck asked as he struggled to keep pressure on his wound.

"It was the principle, I believe. Once the butler got you out of the house, they smuggled you to Detroit. Stephanie Sinclair kept you well-hidden. I stopped checking, because I knew one day you would grow into your father. The man was a complete beast, cutting off heads. There will never be another like him. I had to get him before he got me, though. It was just a matter of time before my head was added to the ones in his trophy case."

"Get on with it," another voice said from three columns down. "This walk through history is more than I can stomach. Kill him and let's get the fuck on."

This had to be Jax Avery. Ruffneck recognized the bitch by the picture which the old lady had purposefully forgotten to assign a name to his face.

"Why don't you really tell me why you hoes killed my father?" Ruffneck asked the taller man walking toward them.

"I'm Jax Avery," he said, stopping next to Fairbanks.

"Your old man was blocking my action in Pittsburgh; told me that Detroit niggas weren't welcome in his state. I go where the fuck I want. He was in the way and I wanted that market out there. So now you know. I took out your old man and his bitch for that reason, and that reason only"—he shook his head at Fairbanks—"not some personal shit."

Douglass spoke up. "Before we send you and your family on your merry little way, somebody would like to say something to you."

Some white man came walking out one of the many corridors. He was carrying an AR-15. He walked up to Ruffneck and without hesitation he slammed him in the forehead with the butt of the gun. Ruffneck hit the floor, seeing different shades of light.

Princess screamed and begged for them to leave Ruffneck alone. The baby's crying was loud and carried through the tunnels.

"That man you shot in the face when we came to kill your family was my brother, asshole," the white man yelled. "I was the one responsible for killing your old man. And guess what: Jax told me that I can kill your girl and child to avenge my brother. You lose. Just like good old times, hunh? You watched me kill your parents; now you get to watch me murder your girl and kid." The white man spit on Ruffneck. "We didn't know you had a woman. I was following you. This particular day, I was going to kill you. Instead, you lead me right to your lady. And she led me to your baby. I kidnapped her ass and threw her and the brat inside my cargo van. And here we are."

Ruffneck lay on the ground in extreme pain, but he couldn't give up. His family needed him, so he fought like hell to stay conscious.

"Get to your knees, Little Walker Story, Jr. It's time for this chapter to end," Douglass Fairbanks demanded.

The mayor pointed his weapon once more as Ruffneck struggled to his knees.

Even with blurry vision, Ruffneck saw Fly and Tryme, their guns held low, sneaking up behind the goons that were holding Princess. He saw something else, too: his speeding Cutlass without a driver, barreling down on the set of doors at the far end. The noise that the car made bursting through steel, glass and concrete sounded like an explosion. Douglass dropped his attention and Ruffneck capitalized. From his knees, Ruffneck swung and hit the mayor in the nuts. He snatched the pistol and shot the white man right between the eyes.

Poison, Sambo, and Fat Shady poured in through the hole behind the car, bringing the heat. They sprayed the place with AK-47s.

The car sped through and just missed clipping Ruffneck and Douglass. The Cutlass smacked one of the massive columns and folded the front end. Everybody scattered, but not the two holding Princess and the baby. They didn't have a chance. Fly and Tryme shot both in the head. Fly lead Princess and the baby to safety.

Jax Avery ran off, leaving Douglass and Ruffneck to struggle over the pistol. The two men fought over possession until the struggle produced a 'pop', and Douglass stiffened up and fell to the floor, dead. Ruffneck turned his head and saw Jax Avery running down the long corridor to the right and took off after him. This shit had to end today if he was going to live a quality life without having to look over his shoulder.

Jax Avery saw Ruffneck coming and offered a defensive shot with his weapon. Ruffneck ducked and returned fire with the Sig. His adrenaline was surging through his body, rendering the gunshot wound in his shoulder a non-factor. Ruffneck popped off a couple more times. Jax avoided them and continued down a dark corridor.

Ruffneck ran full speed giving chase. This was the fool who'd been responsible for his hurt and pain. The nigga had taken away all hopes of a happy childhood and replaced them with nightmares of death and dying. He was not getting away. Ruffneck dropped to one knee, aimed, and fired. The round caught Jax Avery high in the left shoulder. He stumbled forward, but maintained his balance.

Jax disappeared down another hallway. Ruffneck was careful in following around the corners. He hugged the wall and peeked around. Jax was gone. Ruffneck slowly trotted on, looking in each room and down every corridor.

Nothing!

Jax Avery had given him the slip. Up ahead, there was

a window. Ruffneck carefully ran to it, just in time to see Jax Avery jump from the ledge of the first floor. He smacked the ground and rolled over like he'd broken his right leg from the impact. Ruffneck took aim again and popped until the Sig was completely empty. He didn't hit shit. Ruffneck had the unpleasant view of watching Jax Avery limp off down the street.

Ruffneck had to pull himself away from the window. There was a dead mayor down on the ground level. He didn't want to be there when five-o arrived. He ran back the way he'd come. When he reached the concourse, the dust was clear and bodies decorated the floor. All the mayor's henchmen lay crumpled up in the debris.

Ruffneck did a quick check on his people. All were accounted for. Fat Shady had taken a round in the leg, Sambo was shot in the foot, and Fly had been grazed. Poison was tight—not a hair out of place. Ruffneck collected his people. They supported one another, while running through the doors that led out to Roosevelt Park. A minivan was waiting. They jumped in and burned rubber. The Cutlass would be reported stolen once Ruffneck reached Poison's crib. Jax Avery had gotten away and could be anywhere by now.

Ruffneck knew beyond the shadow of a doubt that the nigga would be at him again. He and his family would never be safe with Jax Avery on the loose. Ruffneck had to finish the job. Find the sonofabitch and cut the head off of the fucking snake. The souls of his father, mother, grandmother, Hootie, and Menace would never rest as long as Jax Avery was alive. Ruffneck was determined to catch the muthafucka, even if it would take him to the flames of hell to accomplish it.

About the Author

Tecori Sheldon (aka Thomas Slater) is a native of Detroit, MI. He is the author (writing as Thomas Slater) of *Show Stoppah* and *No More Time-Outs*. His next novel is *Take One for the Team*. Tecori Sheldon hopes to create a lasting footprint by stepping off into the cement of literary greatness. Please visit the author at www.hypnoticliterature.com or facebook.com/thomasslater.

IF YOU ENJOYED "WHEN TRUTH IS GANGSTA,"
PLEASE BE SURE TO CHECK OUT

SHOW STOPPAH

BY THOMAS SLATER
AVAILABLE FROM STREBOR BOOKS

"This fucking food is disgusting, girl," Isis commented, pointing to her plate with her fork. "Beggars can't be choosers, but damn, is this slop supposed to be lasagna?"

Isis' body was thin, wiry, with vanilla-colored skin impressively stretched over ridges of lean muscle tissue. She was of average height but nicely portioned, with shoulder-length hair.

Kimpa cracked a sheepish grin. Kimpa Peoples was the closest thing to physical perfection that one could reach. Some said she favored the platinum, Grammy Award-winning pop-superstar Rihanna. She possessed all the voluptuous assets men desired, including high cheekbones, a slender face accented by long, flowing black hair and a magnificent swell in the bosom department. But her best features included: long, flawless legs, adorable bedroom eyes, and a tiny waistline.

"The food at this shelter ain't supposed to taste great," Kimpa said, picking up a cold, hard biscuit and banging it against the table, creating splintering breadcrumbs. "This is a shelter. The folks in here afraid that if they start serving that five-star gourmet shit, us po' folk ain't gonna take the initiative to go out in the world and gain our independence. I'd give anything right now for my bubble bath, aromatherapy, lobster, and champagne ritual."

"That sounds delicious, but expensive," Isis said.

Kimpa stared at her food. "It's a habit I picked up on Stan Larkin's dime."

"That your first trick, right? The lawyer guy?"

"He put me up at the Ritz-Carlton and I ordered room service until I puked. I'd chill out in a bubble bath, surrounded by scented candles, eating lobster and drinking champagne."

"Spoiled heifer," Isis said, teasing.

The two women laughed a little, easing the stress and tension in the air of the tiny, cramped enclosure passing for a cafeteria. The Woman's First Shelter transcended racial boundaries to help, heal, and provide support for women who'd been physically and mentally abused.

Kimpa and Isis sat at a table for two, eating in the presence of other women from different ethnic backgrounds, all bound tightly together by the universal bonds of heartache, pain, and suffering. "Pain doesn't recognize color," was the Woman's First motto, proudly displayed and beautifully painted in bright colors, across one of the walls of the corridor leading into the cafeteria.

"Kimpa, can you believe that broad over there?" Isis whispered, nodding her head at a dark-skinned woman wearing a weave pulled back into one long ponytail, sitting at a table in the corner by herself.

Kimpa turned her head. "Who you talking about?"

"Let everybody in here know we're gossiping, why don't you!" Isis chuckled. She discreetly nodded in the woman's direction again. "The sistah with the bad weave sitting in the corner."

"Yeah, ain't that rough? Her boyfriend was having threesomes with her and their ten-year-old daughter before he disappeared with the child. He left the sistah with nothing but tons of guilt and bad memories," Kimpa said, sipping on a glass of fruit punch.

"I hope the law catches up with his ass, cuts his nuts off, and makes him wear them around his neck." Isis frowned at the contents on her plate. "A reminder that a sickness like his can only be cured by castration."

"Amen to that, girl. Gimme some," Kimpa said, dapping Isis.

Isis thoroughly examined the cafeteria, taking in all the casualties who'd managed to break free from the painful grip of misogynist-masters and who'd been lucky enough not to have been numbered amongst those women who'd fallen to the bloody feet of a much more sinister circumstance.

"This shit's terrible, Kimpa."

"What, these hard biscuits?"

"Get serious. I'm talking about all these women who've been sent here because of ungrateful-ass, selfish muthafuckin' men. Well, with the exception of the Latina lesbian broad over there, Resa. Kimp, how long have we been shacked up at this shelter?"

"About six months."

"Six months too long. I mean, all we ever do is sit around in a group, cackling about how badly we were treated. It's the same routine every single fuckin' day. And I'm about fed up to my nipples with it. Nothing's getting resolved; the bastards that we complain about are still walking around out there in the street. The way some of these women have been mistreated, those bastards should've been locked away."

"I agree with you one hundred percent. They say it's a man's world."

Isis rolled her eyes at her plate before covering it with a napkin. "We're here eating garbage. Them niggas out there who are responsible for us ending up in here, what do you think they dining on?" She pushed her plate away. "It sure ain't generic lasagna."

"What can we do about it?" Kimpa asked. "We're two

women among many who've been used up and thrown away like trash, left in places like this to die of humiliation."

"Granted, some of these sistahs in this place can spin some tales, but nobody's stories in here compare to yours and mine. Not that I'm trying to compare heartache and pain, but we've been through the storm. That's why I believe meeting you at this shelter was fate. Do you see the cynical looks on these heifers' faces when we recount the hell we've walked through? They look at us like we should be writing screenplays or some shit."

"Isis, sis, no disrespect, but sometimes I even find our stories hard to believe. And I lived the nightmare. Had my baby took…" Kimpa's voice flat-lined into soft sobs.

Isis handed her some napkins. "See, sis, that's what I'm talking about right there," Isis said, tenderly caressing Kimpa's free hand. "We got to start snatching collars to let these men know we can get grimy, too. That bastard of yours got away with taking your baby. Shit, at least you know where your baby is. I don't have a clue where in the land-down-under that yellow nigga of mine got off to with my child. But I'll tell you one thing; there are a whole lot of women in this country who need to hear our stories, girl."

An older lady, one of the servers, walked into the cafeteria dressed in a white apron, hairnet, and black-framed bifocals, carrying a portable radio. "They've been taking donations on the radio all day to buy shoes for needy children!" the lady yelled out to another coworker behind the serving counter. "Before I come in here, I took out my credit card and pledged two hundred dollars. Yes, I did."

"Well, Brenda, sit that radio on the empty table right there, turn the damn thing on, and get to work!" the coworker screamed back. Brenda switched on the radio.

"Hey, Detroit, it's five o'clock and you're on the dial with 95.5 FM radio, with everybody's favorite morning eye-opening shock-jock, Mindspeak the Truth," the very distinctive, electrifying voice boomed from the speaker of the portable stereo system. "It's rush hour and Mindspeak will be with you for your evening commute. Yours truly has been pulling double duty, baby, since six this morning; my normal work hours. But our Shoes for Kids Campaign telethon is underway and we'll be jumping off all day long, and since this is a worthy cause, I'll personally be on the dial as long as it takes to champion this cause. We're trying to put shoes on shorties, man, so we need you to go into your wallets and make a monetary contribution, or you can purchase a pair of shoes and send them to 1000 Fourth Street, Suite 120, Detroit, MI 48233."

"I hate his undercover, woman-bashing ass," Isis said with enough sauce in her voice to earn a few glares.

"I don't know what you're talking about, but people are staring," Kimpa said.

"I'm five past giving a damn. How can you women listen to this chauvinist dog? And in a shelter for abused women, for Christ's sake," Isis ranted.

"Mindspeak has done some good things for the city," proclaimed a white woman with dirty blonde hair.

"I don't give a damn," Isis retorted. "Have ya'll ever listened to the man's topics? They're inflammatory. He always goes out of his way to make the man look like the victim."

"Sometimes they are," added an inky-black lady with an ugly scar on the left side of her mug.

"It's clear that group discussions aren't helping you, Barbara," Isis scolded. "Sweetie, you still think it was your fault that your boyfriend went off the deep end and tried to carve his initials in your face with a Rambo blade."

"That was pretty cold, Isis," Kimpa scolded her.

"Barbara, I'm sorry; didn't mean that crack. It's the pressure; that's all," Isis apologized.

Mindspeak spoke again from the radio. "Today's topic is women who kill their abusive lovers. If found guilty in a court of law, should their actions warrant them life in prison?" Mindspeak paused. "This should be a touchy topic. Men, I need to hear from you. Sistas, I'm gonna hear from the brothers the first half of the hour, but don't get 'em in a bunch because the second half belong to you. Hit me up on the hitter; call me at 222-SPEAK."

"You see what I mean?" Isis said, the fire in her eyes present for all to see.

"Look at how the switchboard is lighting up," Mindspeak boasted. "Caller, are you there? State your name."

"Yeah, Mindspeak, baby boy, this is Lil' Mike and yo' show is da bomb, big b-a-b-y. I want to congratulate you on the success of yo' show going national and thangs," the caller said in a deep voice. "But to answer yo' little question and thangs, hell yeah, them broads should receive life for killin' kangs. They were put on this earth to serve our purpose, made from our ribs, but somehow they got it twisted that they can talk back and not get smacked up."

"Very interesting perspective, caller, but we're going to take another. Hi, caller, what's your name?"

"This is Robert Macky at the Chrysler plant on the North side. And yeah, give them rats life. Likes I tells 'em on the job, playboy, equality is equality. You want to work like a man, be prepared to suffer a man's pain. They should be at home barefoots, pregnant, and cookin' a $#!*%@!"—the censor kicked in—"dinner anyway."

"You hear them, ladies. Though their way of thinking might be straight from the Stone Age, they make a serious point," Mindspeak said. "What's good for the goose is always good for the gander. Listen, family, tomorrow's the last day before I go on vacation. I'm gonna leave out of here with a banging show. Tune in here tomorrow for the big celebration."

Isis went off. "That's the kind of fucked-up thinking that's put a lot of us in this shelter today. Fuckin' Mindspit." Isis was trying to be respectful of the older women serving the food, but she couldn't help herself. Her temper was boiling, nostrils flaring like the hood of a dangerous cobra.

"You mean Mindspeak," Kimpa said.

"Yeah, whatever. His show is national, right?" Isis whispered.

"What are you getting at?"

"Just answer the question."

"Yeah. Why?"

"I just found the answer to our problem."

With a worried expression on her grill, Kimpa was afraid to ask, "What you thinking about doing?"

"What better platform to assist us in getting our stories out to all the battered women to inspire unity? To stand up and protect themselves from what happened to us?"

"Isis, where are you going with this?"

"It's collar-snatching time. We gonna hijack Mindbender's show. It's the perfect way to strike a blow for the female cause. Show all these macho assholes that women are far from inferior. What a great way to emasculate the so-called masters of control, by putting Mindblender's misogynist ass in his place."

"Isis, what the hell are you talking about?" Kimpa asked in a voice, dripping concern.

"Getting a few pistols, laying in waiting for old Mindscratcher to roll up in the parking lot tomorrow morning, taking 'im hostage and forcing our way into the building. It's perfect! And while we hold the guns on Mindsucka, we can use the chump's national radio show to tell our stories, girl."

"What you're asking me to do is insane. Have you even factored the police into this little show-stopping equation of yours? And guns? I don't like guns."

ensely aware that Kimpa was worried. Hell,

tle apprehensive. She'd been so juiced

up with adrenaline and rebellion, Isis hadn't factored in that they'd actually be running afoul of the law. The one thing that her ordeal had taught her was to grab the bull by the balls and squeeze tight.

"Listen, Kimpa, I can't promise you anything but a chance to take the power back from the sonofabitch who took your baby, and to take back your self-respect. A woman without it might as well be dead. You with me?"

Kimpa didn't even have to think hard. "Yeah. We sistahs for life. Let's do it."

"Okay, girl," Isis said, squeezing Kimpa's hands. "Mindsnitch is ours tomorrow morning, right before he goes on air. We'll be tuning in, alright. I promise you, he won't be celebrating after tomorrow's show."

"Do I have to carry a gun? I don't like guns. They give me the willies." I grinned nervously. "Do you ever cry?" I wasn't trying to sound dainty, but I'd lost somebody whom I'd loved dearly to guns and I didn't want to go there.

"Yes, you have to go in there strapped. And no, I don't cry; I ran out of tears a long fuckin' time ago. All I got left is revenge," she responded.